Heidi Swain lives in Norfolk with her husband, two allegedly grown-up children and a mischievous black cat called Storm. She is passionate about gardening, the countryside and collects vintage paraphernalia. *Coming Home to Cuckoo Cottage* is her fourth novel.

You can follow Heidi on twitter @Heidi_Swain or visit her blog: http://www.heidiswain.blogspot.co.uk/

Heidi Swain

Coming Home to Cuckoo Cottage

**SIMON &
SCHUSTER**

London · New York · Sydney · Toronto · New Delhi

A CBS COMPANY

First published in Great Britain by Simon & Schuster UK Ltd, 2017
A CBS COMPANY

1 3 5 7 9 10 8 6 4 2

Simon & Schuster UK Ltd
1st Floor
222 Gray's Inn Road
London WC1X 8HB

www.simonandschuster.co.uk
www.simonandschuster.com.au
www.simonandschuster.co.in

Simon & Schuster Australia, Sydney
Simon & Schuster India, New Delhi

A CIP catalogue record for this book
is available from the British Library

Paperback ISBN: 978-1-4711-4728-9
eBook ISBN: 978-1-4711-4730-2

Typeset in Bembo by M Rules
Printed and bound by CPI Group (UK) Ltd, Croydon, CR0 4YY

To Clare Hey
With love & thanks

Chapter 1

For what must have been the hundredth time that morning, I went back to the bedroom mirror, scrutinised my dark ponytail and wrinkled my nose at my reflection. I smoothed down the cherry-patterned skirt of my fifties-inspired dress and glanced nervously at the clock. All I needed were two tiny minutes in which to change into something a little less controversial, but it was too late. If I didn't leave right now I wouldn't make it at all. Wincing slightly, I thrust my feet into my narrow red patent heels, grabbed my bag and headed for the stairs.

'I thought you said you were going to a funeral,' frowned my housemate Helen as we collided on the landing. 'I know my brain's a bit scrambled when I'm on nights at the hospital,' she added, shaking her head, 'but I'm sure you said it was a funeral.'

'I am,' I said, 'it is. If you'd known Gwen, you'd understand,' I called over my shoulder as I rushed down the stairs.

'So I take it you haven't got time to drink this, then?' she shouted after me, holding aloft a steaming mug.

'No,' I said, flinging open the front door. 'Sorry. I'll catch up with you tomorrow, though. Sleep tight!'

Ordinarily I would have been excited by the thought of such a long trip on the bus. My heart would have been fluttering away in my chest like a trapped butterfly, thrilled by the prospect of one hundred and twenty uninterrupted minutes of luxurious people-watching, but all it could manage that morning, even as I jogged to the station, was a dull thud. Its lack of effort was a fitting reminder that this trip was all about the destination, not the journey.

My pretty but uncompromising shoes were pinching by the time I arrived at the designated bay at the bus stop and I could feel sweat prickling the back of my neck. It was going to be another unseasonal scorcher of a day, unnervingly hot for the beginning of April, and far too hot for a full skirt and net petticoats.

'Return to Wynbridge, please,' I panted as I jumped aboard the bus with just seconds to spare and clattered the money I had already carefully counted out into the tray.

'You going somewhere nice?' smiled the driver as he leant over in his seat and looked me up and down. 'Bit early in the day for a party, isn't it?' he added, as the machine spat out my ticket.

'Funeral,' I mumbled, not quite managing to return his smile.

'Oh,' he said doubtfully, 'right.'

I carefully folded and stowed away my guarantee to get home and headed for a window seat at the back. I wasn't surprised by his or Helen's reaction to my outfit, but it did go some way to chivvying my heart rate along a bit.

What if the rest of the mourners had forgotten that Gran's best friend Gwen had long held the desire that her funeral should be marked by a riot of colour and laughter rather than dull reminiscing? What if they had all decided to opt for sober, sombre black? Well, if they had, they certainly wouldn't forget my vibrant retro ensemble in a hurry. If it did turn out to be just me rocking the colour, I would no doubt be the talk of the town by the end of the day.

Gwen and my Grandmother Flora had been friends since childhood, a friendship that had spanned almost eight decades. To my utter dismay they had died within six months of each other, but even though they were no longer with me I could still sense their presence, along with their collective aura of discontent.

They had never stopped nagging me to make the most of my twenties, and when thirty was suddenly closer than my teens, they had really cranked things up a notch. Apparently the small life I had built for myself was nowhere near ambitious or exciting enough for the pensioners who in their youth had travelled the world, partied hard and left the globe littered with a string of keen suitors. As far as they were concerned, I needed to set my sights higher and take a few more risks.

Between the two of them Gwen had been the long-term party girl and had never 'settled down' in the conventional sense, but Gran had. She had married, moved away from Wynbridge and had a daughter, my mother. My arrival shortly after mum's seventeenth birthday caused quite a scandal apparently, but it was nothing compared to the gossip that started when she decided to leave me in Gran and Grandad's care and take off to Los Angeles in pursuit of a life more thrilling than the one on offer in Lincolnshire.

Her departure from our lives had been both painful and shocking and subsequently my life had been marred by an inability to truly trust anyone who entered it. However, my grandparents, although devastated to have lost contact with their only child, somehow still managed to see the good in folk and did their utmost to ensure that I enjoyed a happy and stimulating childhood, and our annual visits to stay with Gwen at Cuckoo Cottage in the Fens were the absolute highlight of my summer holidays.

The trips stopped for a while after Grandad died and then completely some years later when Gran had a stroke. However, Gwen took it upon herself to travel to see us then, bringing with her a huge, dust-encrusted carpet bag and her temperamental terrier Tiny, who was eventually replaced with the equally unpredictable Minnie. It was inconceivable to even think that these two women, whom I loved so much and who had been so instrumental in my upbringing, were now both lost to me forever.

Despite the heat, I shuddered as I thought how I had failed to achieve any of the things I had promised Gran I would get to work on. I had solemnly sworn, just days before she died, that I would start developing a proper career and pushing my ambitions further and yet here I was, six months on, and nothing had changed. Truth be told, I was too afraid to even try.

Having lived with the consequences of my mother's pursuit of her own hedonistic dreams, I hadn't dared to even think up, let alone live out, my own. But now of course, I realised with a jolt, I was completely on my own and could please myself. If only I were that brave and if only I knew what it was that I actually wanted to do with my life ...

'This is your stop, love!' shouted the driver over the noise of the idling engine. 'Are you not getting off?'

'Yes,' I said, jumping to my feet and scrabbling to pick up my bag. 'Sorry, I didn't realise.'

'I hope it goes all right,' he said kindly as I drew level with him. 'At least you've got a nice day for it.'

'That's true,' I said as the door opened and a wave of warm air rushed in to meet me. 'She would have appreciated that.'

I stepped down on to the pavement and blinked in the

bright sunshine, trying to get my bearings. Time was pressing on and if I didn't locate a taxi to take me to the church soon I'd be late.

'Lottie!'

I spun round and spotted a man rushing towards me from the other side of the market square. It took a second for my brain to believe it, but it was definitely Chris Dempster. More at home in jeans and a checked shirt and working on the fruit and vegetable stall that had been in his family for generations, he was now sporting a bright blue suit and struggling to carry the biggest bunch of balloons I'd ever seen. The spectacle was wholly unexpected, but thoroughly appreciated. At least one person had remembered, but then, given that he was such a close friend of Gwen's, I shouldn't have anticipated any different.

'You made it!' he cried. 'My goodness, look at you. It must be what,' he faltered, 'well, I can't quite recall, but it's been a while. You haven't got any taller though, have you, love?' he teased, regaining his composure. 'Are you all right?'

I swallowed hard and nodded, knowing there was no need to remind him that the last time I had seen him was at the funeral of his eldest son Shaun, who had died in a tragic motorbike accident. I willed myself not to cry and felt relieved that he had spotted me before I went in search of a taxi.

'Come on,' he puffed, taking my arm with his free hand. 'I meant to say when I last spoke to you on the phone that we'd give you a lift. I hope you can squeeze in with this lot and that frock.'

The journey to the church, wedged in the back of Chris's car with the balloons while his wife Marie sat with him in the front, was both bizarre and stiflingly hot, but as least I was going to be on time.

'Don't open the windows!' Chris bawled at Marie when she complained of the soaring temperature and faulty air conditioning. 'We'll lose the bloody lot!'

We all began to laugh and I couldn't help feeling grateful for Gwen's quirky sense of humour.

'Was this all Gwen's idea?' I asked, nodding at the bulging bunch around me.

'Of course,' confirmed Marie.

'She's certainly gone out of her way to keep everyone smiling, hasn't she?' I said, biting my lip and blinking hard.

'Oh yes,' said Chris, winking at me in the rear-view mirror. 'I've been running around like a headless chicken these last few days making sure everything's just as she wanted it. Mind you, it was a shock to discover she'd left such detailed instructions.'

'Are you sure you don't want to say anything?' asked Marie, twisting round to look at me. 'During the service, I mean. It's going to be very ad hoc so no one would mind if you got up and said a few words. After all, you're the closest to real family she had.'

'Oh no,' I said, shaking my head. 'Thank you, but no. I just couldn't face it.'

Chris had already broached the subject when we talked on the telephone. I'd said no straight away and I wasn't about to change my mind.

'I still can't believe she's gone,' tutted Marie.

'Me neither,' I whispered, wishing I'd forced myself to pay her a visit after I lost Gran, rather than putting it off on the assumption that I could come in the summer.

'But at least she hadn't been ill,' rallied Chris. 'The coroner confirmed there had been nothing untoward. You know how she would have hated to be a burden.'

'Yes,' I agreed, thinking of Gwen's stubborn streak. 'She would have loathed that.'

It had been late on a Sunday evening when Chris found my number next to Gwen's telephone in the hall and called to tell me what had happened. He explained how he had popped in during the afternoon, just as he always did on a Sunday, and found her in the deckchair under the cherry tree in her little garden. He said she just looked asleep and the Jackie Collins novel resting on her lap suggested there had been no pain or trauma; she had simply taken advantage of sitting out in the early spring sunshine and serenely slipped away.

'Right,' said Chris, pulling hard on the handbrake as we arrived at the church and dragging me back to the present. 'Let's get this show on the road, shall we?'

'Show' turned out to be a pretty accurate description. I was deposited in the church doorway and instructed to give a balloon to as many people as I could convince to take one.

'But mind you don't get blown away,' Chris teased as he handed me the muddled strings. 'One gust of wind and a little thing like you, you'll be up, up and away!'

I appreciated his unfailing sense of humour and was moved to discover that no one actually needed convincing. The line of mourners that stretched from the church to the road were more than happy to walk down the aisle with helium-filled balloons bobbing about above their heads and it was a tribute to just how greatly Gwen was loved that not one person was wearing black.

The service was an upbeat and surprising mix of poetry and anecdotes, interspersed with a variety of music ranging from Sinatra to Queen and everything in between, and for the most part it was a jolly affair. Afterwards, in the church-yard which was awash with primroses, we stood in silence as the tiny coffin was lowered into the ground. There were tears in abundance, but then the atmosphere shifted as everyone released their balloons and watched them float away.

'Right!' shouted Chris at the top of his voice, making us all jump. 'Time to get to the pub!'

The Mermaid, Gwen's much-beloved watering hole, was packed to the rafters and, even though it had been a while since I had last visited, no one had forgotten who I was. That, of course, was how it worked in Wynbridge, and having been adopted long ago as Gwen's surrogate granddaughter, I was considered a token local despite the fact that I hadn't frequented the town or the pub for some time.

'What can I get you, love?' asked the burly barman. 'Lottie, isn't it?'

'Yes,' I smiled, scrambling inelegantly up on to a bar stool and inwardly cursing that they were always far too high for someone of five foot two, even if she was wearing heels. 'That's right, and you're . . .' I faltered, wracking my brains, 'John.'

'Almost,' he beamed, 'Jim, and the wife's . . .'

'Evelyn,' I cut in, 'of course.'

She wasn't the sort of woman anyone would forget in a hurry.

'It's lovely to see you again,' he said, 'even under the circumstances.'

'Likewise,' I agreed. 'I'll just have some lemonade please, with lots of ice and lemon.'

'One glass of lemonade coming up.'

It was cooler inside the pub and everyone was grateful for the gentle breeze which drifted through the open front door and out into the little garden at the back.

'You all sorted?' asked Chris, when he spotted me sitting waiting for my drink.

'Yes, thanks,' I nodded. 'Jim's just getting me some lemonade.'

'Lemonade,' he laughed as he loosened his tie and unbuttoned his shirt collar. 'I had you down as a cocktail kind of girl.'

'Don't be fooled by the outfit,' I laughed back. 'I need something that's going to quench my thirst, not knock me off my feet. I can't believe how hot it is again today.'

'Me neither,' he smiled, looking at the pint glass in his hand. 'I probably shouldn't be drinking this really. I had planned to set up the stall this afternoon.'

'You'll have to delegate,' I suggested. 'Can't you get Steve to take the reins for today?'

'Chance would be a fine thing,' he chuckled at the mention of his lad. 'He's still globetrotting with his girlfriend Ruby.'

'Of course he is,' I said, gratefully accepting the glass Jim proffered and taking a long refreshing sip. 'Gwen had mentioned that they were abroad a few months ago, but I'd forgotten.'

'They're in New Zealand at the moment,' Chris said proudly.

'How exciting,' I said, thinking that my plans for my own future, when I finally got round to making them, wouldn't be anywhere near as ambitious. 'Although if today is anything to go by I'm not sure I could cope with the heat!'

'Me neither,' he agreed. 'Give me a sharp frost and my market stall any day.'

'And what's happened to Gwen's stall?' I asked, the thought only just occurring. 'I hope it's still running?'

Gwen had run a stall on the market for years, selling all sorts of bits and pieces to raise funds for various local charities. Every day, come rain or shine, she turned out to peddle her wares and I hated the thought that now she was gone the stall would disappear too.

'Oh, don't worry about that,' said Marie, who had wandered up to join us. 'It's still going strong. Some of the WI ladies have taken it on and from what I've heard it won't be closing down. There's already a rota in the pipeline and a string of volunteers who are determined to keep it going.'

'Well, that's good,' I said, draining my glass. 'I'm relieved to hear it.'

Gwen had always worked hard, long hours and was a committed trader. It would have been a shame if her efforts fizzled out and were forgotten.

'Fancy another?' asked Chris, nodding at my glass.

I glanced at my watch, just to check I had enough time before I had to head back to the bus. The thought of returning to my meanly proportioned single room suddenly weighed heavy on my heart. I'd far rather stay where I was amongst these friendly folk, talking about Gwen and sitting out in the colourful daffodil-packed garden that I could see through the door over Chris's shoulder.

'Go on, then,' I smiled, 'you've twisted my arm, but I can't be long.'

I had just taken charge of my second glass when Evelyn took her place behind the bar and pulled sharply on the big brass bell.

'Can I have your attention please?' she called out and everyone filed in from the garden to raise their glasses to Gwen and share a moment's quiet contemplation.

It was both cheering and moving to see so many people, so gaily attired, and I couldn't help wondering how many other people in the room, or the town come to that, could have elicited such a turnout.

'While everyone is gathered!' shouted a man in his sixties, wearing a garish suit not dissimilar to Chris's, as the level of chatter began to pick up again. 'Could I just ask if there is a Miss Charlotte Foster amongst us?'

My throat went dry and I could feel my cheeks blazing.

'Miss Foster?' he called again.

'She's here,' said Chris, grabbing my arm and thrusting my hand above my head, 'this is Lottie Foster!'

Chapter 2

'I'm sorry to have dragged you away, Miss Foster,' said the man who had helped me down from the lofty bar stool and introduced himself as David Miller from Miller, Moffat and Matthews, the Wynbridge solicitors who were, he explained, dealing with Gwen's affairs. 'But this is the only opportunity I thought I might have to talk to you in person. As I understand it, you don't live locally.'

'No,' I said, looking around his decidedly beige and beamed little office. 'I don't.'

I had absolutely no idea why he had singled me out and I shifted self-consciously in my seat, my petticoats rustling as I discreetly tried to clear my throat. Sitting bolt upright opposite a man who was staring at me over the top of his glasses made me feel like I was back in the headmaster's office, although on this occasion I had no inkling as to why. I coughed again.

'Can I offer you something to drink?' he asked.

'Could I have a glass of water, please?' I swallowed. 'If it's no trouble.'

'Of course.'

I felt rather foolish minding my P's and Q's but somehow it seemed as necessary as being on my best behaviour. I couldn't shake off the feeling that Mr Miller was weighing me up and felt duty-bound to make a good impression.

'Thank you,' I smiled politely, as he handed me a glass.

'I hope you don't mind my asking,' he said, once again taking the seat behind his desk and fixing me with another intense stare, 'but I can't help wondering if you already know what it is that I am going to tell you?'

'Afraid not,' I shrugged, hoping it wasn't going to be anything bad.

My only knowledge and experience of solicitors had been greatly embellished by the late-night dramas I occasionally watched on TV, and in the vast majority of those there was rarely good news to share during situations such as the one I now found myself in.

'Gwen hadn't spoken to you at any point about what would happen after her funeral?' he probed.

'No,' I said, feeling further confused. 'The only time she ever talked to me about her funeral was years ago, and that was to insist that no one should wear black.'

'She hadn't spoken to you recently about making a will?'

'No,' I said again. I was beginning to feel increasingly unsettled by his dogged interrogation. 'I didn't even know she had one.'

'Well, in that case,' he announced, 'I must warn you that what I am about to say may come as something of a shock.'

'Oh dear,' I squeaked, trying to gulp away the lump in my throat.

I really didn't think my overwrought emotions could cope with another blow. I'd already had far more than my fair share during the last few months.

'I have been instructed by my dear friend Gwen,' Mr Miller continued, seemingly unaware of my rising panic, 'to explain to you that she has left you something rather special.'

'Oh,' I said again, but this time in a totally different tone as my shoulders dropped somewhere back to where they should be.

For a terrible moment, I had thought that he was going to tell me she had passed on some terrifying debt or dreadful secret, but 'something rather special' suggested that this wasn't going to be one of those bad news kind of shocks at all.

'Well,' I said, trying to lighten the mood now that I felt more relieved than neurotic. 'I hope it isn't anything too big. I'll never be able to manhandle her sideboard home on the bus!'

Mr Miller surveyed me over the top of his glasses again.

'Sorry,' I apologised, clumsily lifting my drink and

slopping at least half the contents over my skirt. 'I sometimes say silly things when I'm nervous.'

'It's all right,' he said, laying his glasses on the desk and rubbing his eyes. 'I do understand, but I'm still surprised Gwen never said anything to you. She was so thrilled when she came up with the idea, and given that she was such a rotten secret keeper, I was sure she'd spill the beans.'

My nerves sprang back up again as I wondered what on earth it was that she could have planned that would have gotten her so excited. I hoped she hadn't arranged for me to go and 'find myself' in some far-flung corner of the earth because I really wasn't up for anything like that. That was far more her idea of fun than mine.

'Like I said before,' I insisted, 'she never said a word and it's never crossed my mind that she would want to leave me anything. I can't imagine for one second that she actually had anything to give.'

Aware that I was babbling, I snapped my mouth shut, mentally tried to pull myself together and tucked a stray strand of hair behind my ear. My mind flitted back to Gwen's pretty but cluttered little home and its eclectic contents and I wondered if perhaps it really was the old sideboard that she was so keen for me to have.

'Look, I'm ever so sorry, Mr Miller,' I said, suddenly mindful of the time as my memory struck upon the distinctive chime of the grandfather clock in the sitting room. 'But do you think we could carry on talking about this over the telephone, only I have a bus to catch and, to tell you the truth, I can't afford to waste the ticket. Would it be possible to send whatever it is Gwen wanted me to have through the post?'

'Hardly, Miss Foster,' smiled Mr Miller, looking mildly amused.

'But please,' I put in, 'I really do need to go and could you possibly,' I added, thinking it would make me feel better and stop me stressing quite so much, 'call me Lottie, everyone does.'

'All right,' he said, 'Lottie, but we really do need to talk this through today.'

'But . . .'

'I will happily make sure you have the means to get home.'

'Well, I . . .'

'Miss Foster,' he said firmly, pulling my attention back to the business in hand as opposed to my waiting bus, 'it has fallen to me to explain to you that Gwen has left you Cuckoo Cottage.'

'She's what?' I gasped, my hand flying up to my chest.

My lungs felt as though every last drop of air had been squeezed out of them and I struggled to catch my breath.

'She has asked me to arrange for you to inherit the cottage, its entire contents and the barns and land that go with it.'

That couldn't possibly be right. My ears must have

been making it up. Surely he or I, or both of us, had misunderstood.

'I think you've made a mistake,' I began.

'I can assure you there is no mistake.'

'Are you absolutely sure?' I spluttered.

'One hundred per cent,' he confirmed. 'Everything is all arranged.'

'But,' I stammered, my eyes the size of saucers and my cheeks feeling far hotter than they had been in the pub when he first called out my name, 'but why?'

'Why, what?'

'Why would she want to leave everything to me?'

Shakily I put the glass of water back down on the desk before I ended up wearing the little that was left. I simply couldn't believe it.

'Well,' he said, shuffling through the pile of papers in front of him, 'the gist of it is that she loved you very much, considered you her family, her very own granddaughter and she rather hoped that the gift of Cuckoo Cottage would give you the opportunity to actually make something of your life.'

I looked at him accusingly.

'Her words, not mine,' he quickly added, thrusting a sheet of paper under my nose.

I swiftly scanned the page, the lines of Gwen's spidery handwriting swimming before my eyes as Mr Miller carried on saying words I neither heard nor absorbed.

'Oh, and the final thing,' he was adding when I eventually tuned back in. 'There is just one more stipulation.'

Clearly I'd missed something, but I was too shocked to ask him to go over it all again.

'Gwen was adamant that you have to live in the cottage for at least a year from the day you move in.'

'A year?'

'And not a day less,' said Mr Miller firmly. 'Gwen told me that you would feel overwhelmed by such a dramatic change in your circumstances and would most likely not want to take it up at all.'

I couldn't deny that she had perfectly summed up my immediate feelings.

'She was most insistent that you should live in the cottage long enough to get used to the idea. She wanted you to give the place a chance, but if you decide you want to sell up after that . . .'

'It's all right,' I said, cutting him off and knowing now was the time to dig deep and be brave. 'I've always loved Cuckoo Cottage and if it really is mine I couldn't bear to part with it, not ever.'

'Well, that is a relief,' Mr Miller sighed, 'because to tell you the truth I was actually more concerned that you wouldn't want to move in at all.'

'You wouldn't have worried about that if you could see

where I was currently living,' I shot back, biting my lip as the words tumbled out unchecked.

Forcefully I pushed the thought of my current living arrangements away and skipped back to the long lazy days of summer holidays spent with Gran, Grandad and Gwen. I remembered picking strawberries and raspberries, watching the swallows dart in and out of the barns, riding Gwen's old pushbike through the fields and revelling in the fact that it never rained, not once in all the time I stayed there.

Cuckoo Cottage was simply perfect and now, if what Mr Miller was telling me was true, it was mine. All the time I had been grappling to find myself a future and Gwen had just handed me one on a plate, and yes, just as she had predicted, I was rather terrified by the thought of such upheaval but I wasn't going to deny myself the opportunity to give it a go. But was there something specific she wanted me to do with the place? I wondered. Had she some other plan, besides me just living there, in mind for my future?

'Obviously,' Mr Miller continued, 'there are things we need to go through in order to settle matters, transfer of ownership and so on, but it's all very straightforward. Both I and Gwen's accountant Miss Smith, have detailed instructions. Gwen was extremely organised,' he added with a frown.

'Well, that makes a change,' I sighed, amazed that Gwen even knew an accountant and a solicitor, let alone employed them to work for her.

'It does rather, doesn't it?' he agreed with a smile.

'Do you think she knew what was going to happen?' I gasped, horrified by the thought. 'Do you think perhaps she hadn't been well after all?'

Surely if she had been worried or unwell she would have told me. I hated the idea that she felt she couldn't say anything because she knew I was still grieving for Gran. I reached for my handkerchief as I felt yet more tears stinging my eyes. It was a miracle my body could produce any more. I must have been in a permanent state of near dehydration for the last six months.

'No,' said Mr Miller reassuringly, 'absolutely not. I'm quite sure she wasn't ill.'

I nodded, but couldn't say anything.

'However, when she came to see me she was very keen to have everything in place,' he continued. 'She insisted everything should be properly prepared for this eventuality, whenever it should come. I got the impression that having lost her dear friend Flora, your grandmother, Lottie, she thought it was high time she properly put her own affairs in order.'

'I see,' I said huskily, trying to stem the flow of tears and save the little that was left of my kohl liner.

'I take it you are happy for me to deal with the legalities of the situation as Gwen wished,' Mr Miller asked.

'Yes,' I nodded, 'of course. I wouldn't know where to start.'

'She also left instructions asking Chris and Marie

Dempster to look after the cottage until it is officially yours, but I think it would be a good idea for you to at least have a look at the place before you actually move in.'

'Oh no,' I said firmly, putting my handkerchief away again. 'I don't need to do that.'

'Are you sure?'

'Absolutely,' I said, feeling surer by the second, 'my mind's made up. I know every inch of that cottage by heart. Let's go through what we can today and when I come back to Wynbridge it will be to collect the keys to Cuckoo Cottage and my future.'

Chapter 3

'I can't believe this,' said Helen, shaking her head in disbelief as I sat on the end of her bed the next day and explained what had happened. 'You leave the house a pauper and come back a princess.'

'Hardly,' I said, rolling my eyes and inwardly wincing at her strange analogy.

I hadn't known Helen for all that long, having only moved into the house a few months ago, but I knew she sometimes had a very strange way of putting things. I hadn't particularly wanted to share my news with her at all, but shock could do funny things to a normally private person and it had all tumbled out before I could stop myself.

'But this is the sort of thing you read about in books,' she said, pointing to the pile of pastel-packaged romance paperbacks stacked next to her bed. 'A proper rags-to-riches story.'

I decided not to further feed her fantasy by rushing to

the kitchen, grabbing the broom and twirling around like Cinderella.

'No one gets this lucky IRL.'

'IRL?'

'In real life,' she expanded.

At that particular moment, still tired out from the funeral, the unbearable sense of loss and all the information I was trying to assimilate, I wasn't actually feeling all that 'lucky'.

'Believe me,' I said harshly, 'I'd far rather have Gwen in my life than her house.'

'Of course,' said Helen, her face flushing crimson as she realised her faux pas. 'Sorry, I didn't mean . . .'

'Oh, I know,' I sighed. 'And I didn't mean to snap, it's just going to take me a while to get my head around all of this.'

'I can imagine,' she sighed, a faraway look in her eye. 'But just so I can start advertising for a new housemate, when do you think you'll actually be going?'

Mr Miller and I had been in almost daily contact since Gwen's funeral, but our frequent conversations didn't seem to have any impact on hurrying proceedings along. During the first couple of weeks, as the details of the gargantuan bequest gradually sank in and I began to think seriously about packing up my few belongings and working my notice, I had expected every phone call to be the one telling me it was time to collect the keys, but I soon realised it wasn't going to happen like that. According to Gwen's solicitor, even though the legacy was incredibly straightforward, I wouldn't be going anywhere fast.

'These things always take time,' he reassured me. 'It doesn't mean that anything is wrong, it's just how the system works.'

'OK,' I said, 'I see,' but I didn't really.

'Look,' he added, no doubt picking up on my lack of understanding. 'Why don't you come back to Wynbridge and have a look around the place? Surely if you could be planning any remedial work that might need doing or considering how you want to redecorate, it might help the time pass more quickly.'

'Redecorate?' I gasped, not then picking up on his suggestion that the cottage might need more than a quick spring clean. 'Update! I won't be changing anything.'

Clearly, and in spite of what I had worn to Gwen's funeral, her solicitor had no inkling of my passion for all things authentically vintage, or as plain-speaking Gwen would have put it, 'old'.

'Sorry, Lottie,' he said, sounding genuinely surprised. 'I just assumed you would want to change things a bit.'

'I've always loved Cuckoo Cottage exactly as it is,' I said firmly, 'so thank you for the suggestion, but no, as I explained before, I'd really rather wait, if it's all the same to you.'

Every day I was feeling more and more grateful for the wonderful gift Gwen had bestowed upon me, but the last thing I wanted to do was cross the threshold before I'd signed on the dotted line and had the keys in my pocket. I guess a part of me was still holding back just in case something went wrong.

Even though I knew everything was legal and above board, I was finding it hard to believe that I really could be this 'lucky'. As Helen had so keenly pointed out, it was exactly the kind of thing that happened in the pages of a book, not in real life.

'As you wish,' he sighed, 'and besides, I'm certain things won't take too much longer.'

'Yes, well,' I reminded him wryly, 'you said that last week.'

It was the beginning of August, just over four months after Gwen's funeral, and when the sunshine was only occasionally capable of rivalling what we had enjoyed in April, that moving day finally dawned. Heading back to Wynbridge on the bus again, this time I was more suitably attired and wearing footwear that was fit for purpose.

I had somehow managed to cram my eclectic mix of clothes, along with everything else I wanted to keep, into two old suitcases which had belonged to Gran and Grandad, and a gargantuan camouflage rucksack which I had picked up from the army surplus store in town. Admittedly I didn't have a lot in the way of material possessions but, I reminded myself stoically, this was a fresh start and Cuckoo Cottage was already packed full of wonderful things.

I hadn't found it at all difficult parting company with my tiny bedroom, or Helen who had hardly bothered with me once she knew I was moving on, but saying goodbye to my bosses, Eric and John, was harder. I had joined the pair in their bespoke business when I ditched my waitressing job looking for a change of scene where I could indulge my passion for renovating and recycling and they had become my only real tie to the town.

We had worked together for the best part of four years, remodelling and restyling all manner of campers and caravans, and I had enjoyed every minute. The pair had furnished me with all the skills I needed to complete a total interior renovation and refit and sometimes I even got to help the owners with the decorative finishing touches, which I absolutely loved.

Had I not been moving, this would certainly have been an aspect of the business I would have wanted to develop and I imagined, had Gwen not given me the opportunity to renovate my life, I would have happily worked alongside my two kind and generous employees forever.

'We really are sorry to see you go,' said Eric as he and his twin, John, helped me unload my luggage from the back of their van at the bus station.

'Although we're pleased about the cottage and everything, of course,' John quickly added.

'Yes,' said Eric, 'delighted for you in that sense, but we're really going to miss your side of the business, Lottie. Your creative input has been second to none and the customers love your clever styling.'

'Oh, I'm sure you'll find someone else who can match cushions and curtains as well as I can,' I told them with a dismissive wave of my hand. 'It's hardly rocket science after all.'

John and Eric shook their heads in perfect unison.

'But they won't have your artistic flair,' said John, 'or your finesse.'

'You have such a good eye,' added Eric.

'Well, thank you,' I blushed, feeling awkward about accepting the compliment.

'Is that what you're going to do at your new place?' quizzed John.

'Perhaps you could set up your own business doing something similar,' suggested Eric. 'Although I'm not sure I should be encouraging you to become the competition.'

I hadn't actually worked out what I was going to do once I was settled, but I would certainly have the space to set up a similar business if I wanted to.

'I might,' I said, biting my lip as I considered the potential of the three empty barns.

Perhaps that was what Gwen had in mind for me when she

drew up her will. She had always been keen to encourage me to take the plunge and go it alone and now, thanks to her, I had the perfect space to establish my own business, should I want to. My heart gave an excited little flutter at the prospect of offering a complete renovation package, and adding the possibility of sourcing, supplying and fitting the decorative touches into the mix made it thump all the harder.

'Well good luck,' said Eric, giving me a swift hug as his brother lugged my bags on to the bus.

'Yes, good luck,' echoed John, rejoining him to wave me off.

The bus station was as chaotic as ever and as I lost sight of them in the crowds I couldn't help thinking that, with Gran and Grandad gone and all connections now severed, it didn't feel like I was actually leaving anything behind. In fact, it felt more like I was going home.

The miles flashed quickly by, my eyes eating up the East Anglian summer landscape and towers of fluffy, soft billowing clouds. I could see that in spite of the recent dreary weather some of the fields were ripe for harvesting and my thoughts wandered back to happy afternoons spent eating warm raspberries and tart gooseberries plucked straight from the rows and bushes Gwen had tended for years. Assuming they were still there, they were all mine now. I dozed for a while and then, true to form, just as the coach drew to a halt and the doors opened revealing the bustling market square, the clouds parted and the sun began to beat down.

'You sure you can manage that lot?' asked the driver, making no attempt to leave his station behind the wheel and give me a hand.

'Yep,' I puffed, hauling the second suitcase out of the luggage rack and in the process almost pulling my arms out of their sockets. 'I'm good.'

I staggered down on to the pavement and stood for a minute to catch my breath and take in the scene before me. On the day of Gwen's funeral I hadn't had a chance to look about the place properly, but now it was my turf I was keen to re-familiarise myself with the territory.

The town was busy, but comfortably so, and there were definitely more shops than I remembered from my expeditions when I was younger. I made a mental note to check out The Cherry Tree Café as soon as I was settled, and I could see some sort of second-hand store a little further along. The market was pleasingly heaving, but I could still easily pick out the top of Chris's head as he bobbed about among his customers, no doubt generously overfilling waiting shopping bags full of fresh local produce.

Turning my back on the lively scene, I clumsily weaved my way along the path to the solicitor's and lugged the heavy cases up the steps, cursing my lack of height and upper body strength. As I pushed open the door with my rucksack and reversed inside, my ears were subjected to a barrage of insults and an argument which, unbelievably, seemed to be coming from mild-mannered Mr Miller's office. Granted, he wasn't the one doing the shouting, but it was still something of a surprise.

'You haven't heard the last of this!' shouted a man's voice menacingly. 'This is a bloody joke, an outrage.'

'It really isn't, you know,' was the only response I heard to the heated allegation.

I tried to get out of the man's way as he stormed through the lobby, taking a childish swipe at a stack of papers on the secretary's desk in the process, but I wasn't quick enough and before I knew it he had sent both me and my cases flying into the door frame.

'Hey,' I retaliated, levering myself upright with the help of the weighty pack on my back and drawing myself up to my full, but still diminutive, height. 'Why don't you watch where you're going?'

'And why don't you get out of the way?' he yelled, barging through and slamming the door behind him.

'Well now, that's a fine welcome to Wynbridge,' said Mr Miller, rushing forward to help me manoeuvre the suitcases so they weren't blocking the doorway. 'Are you all right, my dear?'

'I'm fine,' I told him, feeling determined not to let the man's unexpected outburst spoil the much anticipated moment.

'I bet you had no idea the place could be so lively, did you?'

'No,' I said, 'I didn't.'

'Well, never mind him. Come on through and we'll get things sorted. You can leave those there,' he added, pointing to the cases as he swept up the now muddled pile of papers from the floor. 'And could you boil the kettle please, Iris?' he asked the poor secretary who looked more than a little alarmed by what had just happened. 'I'm absolutely parched.'

I didn't get the chance to ask what all the fuss had been about because it was immediately obvious that Mr Miller was keen to get my own business all wrapped up. The second I had wriggled the pack from my back and taken the seat he offered, he was equipping me with the relevant paperwork and a pen. We read through the sheets together and then I signed on a plethora of dotted lines.

'Is that it, then?' I asked huskily as I watched the ink dry.

'It is,' he smiled. 'You are now the owner of Cuckoo Cottage, and I hope you will be very happy living there, Lottie.'

'Oh, I'm sure I will,' I sniffed, not really believing that the legalities had happened without so much as a single bell or whistle, let alone a fanfare.

I reached up my sleeve for a tissue.

'Are you all right?' asked Mr Miller kindly. 'I'm afraid I do this kind of thing day in, day out, so I take it all a bit for granted really.'

'I'm fine,' I nodded, whilst noisily blowing my nose. 'This is just mixed emotions, I suppose. I mean, I'm delighted to have the cottage and everything, but I'd far rather Gwen was still there.'

He was just about to answer when the secretary knocked and came in with the tea tray. I was grateful for her timely interruption because what would have been the point in getting all maudlin about the situation? I may have lost Gran and Gwen but crying more tears and risking further dehydration wouldn't bring them back, and besides, I had the distinct feeling there would be plenty more opportunities for a good howl when I arrived at the cottage.

Mr Miller thanked his secretary for the tea and by the time she closed the door I had regained my composure.

'I thought we could go to the bank tomorrow,' he suggested, passing me a cup. 'If that suits you, of course.'

'Yes,' I agreed. 'That will be fine.'

On the day of the funeral, when he had first told me of Gwen's extraordinary generosity, I had been in such a state of shock that I had tuned out and missed some of the finer details of what he had been saying. Subsequently, during the weeks that followed, we had gone through it all again and I was amazed to discover that Gwen had also left enough financial provision for me to settle in and not have to rush into making any hasty decisions about how I was going to earn my keep.

'That way,' he continued, 'I thought you would have the rest of the day to unload your lorry and at least make a start unpacking, although how you'll fit another houseful of furniture into that tiny cottage is quite beyond me,' he added, scratching his head. 'Perhaps you could store everything in the barns for now. What time are you expecting them to arrive?'

'Sorry,' I frowned. 'What time am I expecting who to arrive?'

'The removals people with the lorry,' he said patiently.

'There is no lorry,' I told him, helping myself to another lump of sugar.

'Van then,' he said.

'No van either,' I shrugged.

'So where are all your things, Lottie?' he asked.

'In this,' I said, patting the packed rucksack, 'and in the cases out there,' I added with a nod to the door.

'You mean to tell me that you've actually managed to pack all your worldly goods into three bags.'

'I have,' I confirmed. 'But they're rather big bags.'

He didn't say anything, just blinked and stared.

'Is that all right?'

'Well yes,' he swallowed, fiddling with his teaspoon. 'Of course, just a bit of a shock, that's all.'

'Well, I have a houseful of things now, don't I?' I smiled. 'Up until now I've preferred to travel light.'

Mr Miller looked at me and smiled and then he began to laugh.

'Do you know,' he said, shaking his head, 'I think Cuckoo Cottage might have just bagged itself another very unique owner.'

I felt myself blushing, not sure whether he was paying me a compliment or teasing me, but a quick glance at his face confirmed that he was actually in earnest.

'And I'll tell you something else,' he went on.

'What's that, Mr Miller?'

'I think it's high time you started calling me David.'

'Well thank you, David,' I smiled, 'for everything.'

We finished our tea and I was just thinking it was time I called a taxi when we heard more shouting in the lobby.

'Has she been?' hollered a familiar voice. 'Don't tell me I've bloomin' well missed her!'

Without any further preamble the office door was flung back on its hinges and there stood Chris, red-faced and panting.

'As you can see,' scolded Iris, over his shoulder. 'You haven't missed her at all.' Forcibly she pushed her way into the office. 'Apologies for the second intrusion of the morning, Mr Miller, only Mr Dempster here was another one reluctant to wait.' With a curt nod she disappeared back through the door, leaving Chris shaking his head.

'Have you had a bit of bother this morning, David?'

My solicitor, professional as ever, said nothing.

'Come on,' encouraged Chris. 'Who is it this time? Someone looking to make a few quid out of some unsuspecting soul, I'll bet!'

'Well now,' I said when Chris couldn't elicit a response, 'do I sense intrigue? And there was me thinking I was moving to a sleepy little backwater.'

'Oh no,' boomed Chris. 'There's never a dull moment in Wynbridge, Lottie. If it's excitement you're after, you've certainly moved to the right place.'

'Oh yes,' said David, finally finding his voice and rolling his eyes. 'Our little town is a veritable hotbed of espionage and exhilaration, but I've already nipped this particular little upset in the bud.'

I couldn't help but laugh.

'Well, I'm relieved to hear it,' nodded Chris, not picking up on the irony in David's tone.

'Well,' I said, 'as enthralled as I am, you'll have to fill me in another time.' I stood up and reached for my rucksack. 'I've got far more exciting things to enjoy today than local tittle-tattle, so if you don't mind . . .'

'And I haven't even said a proper hello!' shouted Chris, pulling me into a suffocating hug. 'I came over especially to say welcome to Wynbridge, Lottie, and I've gone and got sidetracked already.'

'Its fine,' I gasped, taking a lungful of air when he finally released me. 'Actually I was going to come and find you and Marie to say thank you for keeping an eye on the cottage for all this time.'

'Not a problem, my lovely,' he sniffed, looking a little teary.

He certainly was a big softy.

'Well, I really appreciate it,' I told him, 'and I'm sure Gwen does too. I bet she would hate knowing the place has been empty for all these months.'

'You can say that again,' agreed Chris. 'I can't tell you how much I've missed hearing her radio blaring out, and not dropping in on a Sunday for my cup of tea has taken some getting used to, I can tell you.'

'Well, now you'll have to stop and have tea with me,' I smiled.

'I will,' he beamed, 'but let's get you settled in first!'

'Yes,' I said, taking a deep breath. 'Point me in the direction of where I can find a taxi and I'll be off.'

'Oh no,' said Chris, taking my rucksack and throwing it over his shoulder as if it weighed nothing. 'That's what I'm here for. I've come to give you a lift.'

'You don't have to do that, Chris.'

'I know I don't, but I want to.'

'But what about your stall,' I reminded him. 'You can't just abandon it.'

'Marie's there and she's happy to manage on her own for

a bit,' he insisted. 'Now come on, or the better part of the day will be gone.'

'Keys!' called David as Chris headed for the door. 'You won't get far without keys, Lottie.'

He handed over the small bunch and warmly shook my hand.

'I really do hope you will be very happy at Cuckoo Cottage, my dear. I have a feeling exciting times are on your horizon now.'

'Thank you, David,' I said, blinking hard. 'I think you could be right.'

'I'll see you tomorrow at the bank,' he called after me as I rushed to catch up with Chris, who was already through the door with my suitcases in tow. 'Enjoy your new home!'

Chapter 4

It wasn't a particularly long journey by vehicle from the centre of Wynbridge to Cuckoo Cottage, but Chris seemed determined from the outset not to waste a single second of it. No sooner was my luggage loaded and the engine ticking over than he set about filling in the blanks David had left, deciphering my needs and wants, checking out my marital status and, in fact, organising my entire life.

The bustling market square was barely out of sight before he launched off, diving straight to the heart of the matter and a concern which had begun to play on my mind.

'So, Lottie,' he began as we headed off into the Fen, 'I suppose you realise the fate of Cuckoo Cottage has been the talk of the town these last few months?'

'I guessed it would be,' I nodded, as he confirmed my fears and made me question whether 'enjoying my new home' was going to be as easy as David had just breezily suggested.

My early years had been subjected to the unwanted focus of a lot of attention when Mum left for the US and I had absolutely no desire to repeat the excruciating experience. All I wanted was to settle in without any scrutiny or fuss, but I'd had an inkling that was never really going to happen.

'The whole town has been on tenterhooks waiting to find out what's in store for the place,' Chris stated as he drove along, completely unaware of my desire to slip in under the radar. 'And the fact that it's been left empty for so long has only added to everyone's curiosity.'

'Of course it has,' I sighed. 'But what business is it of anyone's what Gwen decided to do with it?'

Chris looked over at me and shook his head.

'By God, you've got a lot to learn, girl,' he said with a wry smile. 'Just because something isn't anyone's business,' he patiently explained, 'it doesn't mean that they won't be able to resist sticking their noses in!'

'Oh, I know,' I said, giving up the defensive pretence and thinking back to the cruel chinwagging I had been subjected to as a child. 'I'm not really under any illusions about how nosy folk are.'

'Well, that's a relief,' he sniffed.

'Especially around here,' I added. 'Gwen was always moaning about the town gossip.'

'Especially when she was left out of it,' chuckled Chris.

'Especially then,' I relented with a smile, 'but nonetheless, I'm still surprised anyone would be all that concerned about the future of her old place. It's hardly a grand country seat, is it?'

'Perhaps not,' agreed Chris, 'but the land and outbuildings cover a sizeable plot and would carry a pretty price tag on their own, should they ever come up for sale.'

'Oh,' I said, my mind skipping back to the angry man in David's office. Was he perhaps someone who had been interested in the future of my new home? 'I see, well, I can tell you right now, that won't be happening in my lifetime.'

'I'm very glad to hear it,' Chris smiled. 'That's the spirit.'

'And I'm guessing word has got round that it's me who's moving in?'

'Of course,' he confirmed. 'You can't keep anything a secret around here.'

'And I dare say that's only fuelled the gossip,' I sighed. 'I bet there were a few locals hoping Cuckoo Cottage was going to come up for sale, weren't there, and now they're all mightily disappointed? Have they been suggesting I've had some long-distance influence over Gwen's decision to leave it all to me?'

I guessed by the way Chris gripped the steering wheel a little tighter that my suggestion wasn't all that wide of the mark.

'Oh, great,' I huffed.

'Let's just say Gwen's will was a shock to some,' he said eventually.

'Tell me about it,' I sighed. 'For a start, I couldn't believe she'd actually made one.'

'And if you hear any rumours,' he carried on, 'just ignore them, OK? The people who really count remember you from way back and they know you were like family to Gwen, even if you hadn't been able to visit for a while.'

'OK,' I swallowed, wondering if folk had actually been totting up the time I had been absent from the town.

'And if you come across any name-calling . . .'

'Name-calling?'

'Yes,' he said shiftily. 'Someone in the pub once referred to you as the "cuckoo" in the cottage nest and it kind of stuck.'

'Oh how nice,' I groaned, 'and original too.'

'But don't you worry,' Chris insisted. 'It'll all stop once there's something new for them to gossip about.'

How long would that be? I wondered.

'Why didn't David tell me any of this?' I said sharply. 'He could have warned me what to expect, then I would have been better prepared.'

'I dare say he just wanted to protect you,' said Chris softly, 'and he no doubt thought it would have all blown over by now.'

I looked out of the window at the unusually flat landscape

to try and settle my nerves. The weather was every bit as perfect as I'd remembered, and I hoped the halo of memories I'd wreathed my new home in didn't make it impossible for the little place to live up to. It was obvious I was going to have a tough enough time settling in without adding disappointment to the mix.

'So,' said Chris, turning slightly pink as he made an awkward attempt to steer the conversation in a different direction. 'Is it just you, then?'

'Is it just me what?'

'Moving into the cottage. Are you on your own or have you got some fella hidden away somewhere?'

I laughed out loud at the thought.

'No,' I said. 'It's just me.'

'I thought so,' he said smugly. 'I told Marie after Gwen's funeral that you were on your own.'

'And how had you worked that out?'

'Well, it stands to reason, doesn't it?' he went on, as if I should know. 'If you had a young man in your life, he would have come with you to the funeral. Any fella worth his salt would want to make sure his young lady was supported during an occasion like that, wouldn't he?'

'Is that so?' I smiled.

Chris was obviously as big a romantic as he was soft-hearted. Marie was a very lucky woman to have someone so considerate to journey through her life with.

'Of course,' he shrugged. 'Well, that's what I thought. Mind you,' he added, 'Marie had other ideas.'

'Did she now,' I asked, amazed that the minutiae of every part of my life had been picked apart in such exacting detail. 'What did Marie think?'

'She said that just because you were on your own at the funeral didn't mean you were single at all. It could just as well mean that you're one of these strong, independent types who can cope with whatever life throws at you . . . or something like that.' He frowned, scratching his head.

I couldn't help but laugh again. I wasn't at all sure I was the tower of strength Marie had me down as. Perhaps Beyoncé had been belting out 'Single Ladies' in the background when she and Chris had their discussion.

'Well,' I said with a dramatic sigh, 'you can tell Marie that I am currently single and most definitely in need of a big strong man to look out for me.'

I knew it wasn't fair to tease him, but I simply couldn't resist.

'Is that right?' he said, his eyebrows shooting up to his hairline.

'Oh yes,' I said, properly getting into my stride as he readily snatched up the bait. 'Preferably someone who can undo pesky pickle jars and reach the highest shelves in the supermarket.'

'Right,' said Chris again, now sucking thoughtfully on his lower lip and frowning in concentration.

Surely he was going to twig that I was joking in a minute. I took another look out of the window, gulped in the warm air and ran my hot palms down my jeans as I realised we were practically there.

'So,' he said, sitting up straighter and puffing out his chest to indicate that he was now a man on a mission. 'We need to find you a fella then, don't we?'

'No, of course not,' I laughed, 'absolutely not.'

'Someone local, looking for love,' he carried on regardless, looking back to the bumpy road with misty eyes.

'No honestly, Chris,' I said, shaking my head and beginning to feel guilty for winding him up. 'I was only kidding.'

'Someone with a bit of height,' he mused, 'and preferably someone who can change a plug . . .'

'Chris,' I said again, thinking his unwavering reaction was a harsh comeuppance for a bit of light-hearted mischief-making. 'I really was joking. I'm perfectly happy on my own, thanks, and more to the point, what makes you think I can't change my own plugs?'

I couldn't, of course. I could cook a mean curry, I could dig for England, I could rip out and replace the interior of any caravan or camper you threw at me, but the intricacies of how to handle electricity had passed me by.

'I know from experience,' he continued seriously and ignoring my question, 'that there's many a true word spoken in jest.'

I felt my heart skip a beat as I realised he had Cuckoo Cottage pigeonholed as a 'spinsters only' abode, and that he was personally going to see to it that I would be married off before the end of the year.

'And besides,' he admitted, giving me a sideways glance, 'I've already been giving the situation a bit of thought and I reckon I know just the chap for you.'

I opened my mouth to protest, but the words were snatched away as I glanced briefly back to the road.

'Here, look out!' I shouted as a truck came hurtling towards us along the narrow track.

Chris was completely oblivious that the two vehicles had somehow squeezed passed one another with less than an inch to spare, but I had my eyes screwed tightly shut and my body braced for the moment of impact.

'Here we are then,' he said, sharply drawing to a halt and sounding completely unconcerned by the near-death experience. 'Home sweet home.'

I took a deep breath, waited for my thumping heart to calm a little and then tentatively opened my eyes. My heart leapt again, but all thoughts of the near miss were dismissed as I slowly took in every last detail of what was laid out before me. I really needn't have been worried about Cuckoo Cottage not living up to my rose-tinted memories because it looked simply perfect in every possible way.

I could see that the fruit bushes and garden which

surrounded the cottage were a little overgrown and some of the pale blue paint on the windows and door frame was beginning to peel in places but, in essence, my new home was every bit as idyllic as I remembered.

Built at an angle on a generous plot, the front of the house faced the vegetable patch and currently empty greenhouse, while the back overlooked a pretty traditional cottage garden and the never-ending horizon over the fields beyond. The drive swept between the house and the vegetable plot and ran across a little yard to the group of barns which were nestled around the back.

To my mind they resembled a ramshackle, nondescript little group, but I could see the potential in them for what I had in mind, and the decision to start thinking seriously about setting up my own business felt a tantalising step closer.

'Well,' said Chris, when I hadn't said anything for what had probably been far longer than I realised. 'What do you think? Is everything all right?'

'It's perfect,' I croaked, still barely able to take it all in. 'Absolutely perfect.'

'Well, thank goodness,' he said, letting out a long breath. 'You had me worried for a second or two there. Thought I'd brought you to the wrong place,' he joked. 'Hop out and open the gate then and we'll get your things unloaded.'

I couldn't remember ever seeing the gate closed before and

it took some manoeuvring to get it open, but eventually I dragged it back and Chris drove through.

'A drop more oil should free that up a treat,' he said. 'I've been working on it but it's not quite there yet, but then you might not want to keep it shut,' he shrugged.

'I haven't thought about it,' I said, biting my lip as I realised there were lots of things I hadn't even begun to allow myself to consider.

So desperate not to get carried away with imagining what my life at Cuckoo Cottage could be in case it never happened, there were now no doubt hundreds of decisions to make, but there was no rush.

'You might find it's a pain to keep opening and closing it when you want to get in and out,' Chris went on. 'You do drive, don't you, Lottie?' he frowned. 'You'll have a hell of a time stuck out here in the middle of nowhere if you don't.'

'Well, I do have a licence,' I swallowed, 'but I'd rather manage without a car if I can. I'm quite happy to go everywhere by bike.'

I wasn't about to explain why I was terrified of driving, to Chris of all people, and that the only reason I had a licence was because on my seventeenth birthday Gran and Grandad had presented me with a package of lessons and forced me to use them. I'd hated the experience, right from the very first time I got behind the wheel, but I stuck it out and had passed my test on the second attempt. I'd barely driven since and now had my hopes firmly pinned on a bicycle as a practical and healthy option.

'I'll keep my eyes peeled for a little runabout,' offered Chris, completely unaware of the impact his kind words were having on my already erratic heart rate. 'You really won't be able to get by without one and there's bound to be someone around here who can help you out.'

I pushed the unsavoury thought away as I helped unload my bags and together we walked up the brick path to the front door. It was lined with abundantly flowering old fashioned Mrs Sinkins pinks, and the sweet scent that rushed up to meet us as we brushed by was a beautiful assault on the senses. Gwen always used to cut them by the handful, I remembered, along with the sweet peas she grew in regimented rows alongside her peas and beans.

'No sweet peas this year,' said Chris, the smell tugging his thoughts along the same track as mine, 'but plenty of these pinks to fill up the house with.'

I nodded and pulled the small bunch of keys David had given me out of my jeans pocket. My hands were trembling and my knees had turned to jelly.

'You should use these really,' said Chris. 'Seems only right, doesn't it?'

I shook my head in disbelief as he handed me the very bunch Gwen had always used, complete with the hula girl key ring. Laughing, I held it up and we watched the plastic beauty spin around, her hips gyrating suggestively and her breasts only just covered by a garland of red orchids.

'Honestly,' I giggled. 'Where did she get this thing?'

'No idea,' Chris smiled, 'but she did tell me once that it reminded her of the time she spent travelling with your gran.'

'Oh good grief!' I tutted, trying not to imagine the pair of them sporting grass skirts and sipping umbrella-embellished cocktails. 'I dread to think. Are you not coming in?'

'No,' he said, taking a step back down the path. 'I don't think I will. I reckon this should be a private moment, don't you, unless you want me to come in, of course?'

'No, you're right,' I agreed. 'I would like to go in alone, but thank you for the lift and thank you and Marie for keeping an eye on the place.'

'No problem at all, it's the least we could do,' he said dismissively. 'You can remember how to open the door, can't you? Shoulder on the top, foot on the bottom.'

'Yes,' I said. 'I remember.'

'Well, I'll see you soon,' he smiled kindly, 'and don't worry; I'm pretty busy on the market at this time of year but we'll soon have you set up. I'll start looking around for four wheels straightaway and a fella, of course.'

I knew he wasn't joking about either.

*

I watched him drive away and then stood for a few seconds as the sound of the engine receded and the merry chatter of birdsong grew louder. There was nothing else. No traffic noise, no shouting, just the sound of birds going about their business and I wondered for the first time how I was going to adapt to the peace and tranquillity at bedtime.

No point worrying about that if I was still on the doorstep though, was there? With a deep breath I turned the key in the lock and shoved the door as instructed. It swung in and for the first time I crossed the threshold and stepped inside what was now my very own home.

I knew how everything inside was going to look, but the feel of the place was a total surprise. I'd been expecting it to be musty and in need of a good airing but judging by the smell of freshly baked bread, pinks from the garden and line-dried laundry, Marie and Chris had been doing an awful lot more than just picking post up off the doormat.

I lifted my bags into the hall and quietly closed the door. The coat rack and telephone stand were the first things I noticed. Gwen's scruffy gardening mackintosh was hanging on its allotted hook and on the notepad next to the phone sat her last rapidly written shopping list. It was all I could do to stop myself from calling out to see if she was going to answer. So much of her was still lingering, even in just the hallway, that it was impossible not to believe that she was pottering about somewhere.

I took a deep breath and walked into the kitchen, filled the kettle and turned it on. Then I flicked on the radio and flung open the windows. The hot summer air rushed in and I felt my shoulders begin to relax. Had I not taken the plunge and made a start, I really think I could have been stuck in the hall forever, not knowing what to do first.

Inwardly cursing for not asking Chris if we could stop and stock up on a few essentials, I opened the fridge and discovered milk, butter and enough supplies to feed an army for a month, and it was the same in the cupboards. I made a mental note to find a way of properly repaying the Dempsters' overwhelming kindness, then ventured up the narrow stairs.

Both bedrooms had fresh linen and the bathroom was sparkling. I couldn't help wondering what Gwen would have made of seeing the place so spick and span. Her housekeeping was slapdash at the best of times, but she had been a busy lady with far more pressing priorities than ironed sheets.

Lightly I ran my hands over the collection of old-fashioned glass perfume bottles on the dressing table and it dawned on me that I was going to have to decide which room I was going to sleep in. When I had visited with Gran and Grandad I had slept in the sitting room downstairs and then, when Gran and I came alone, I had shared the smaller room with her.

However, Gwen's own bedroom had always been my favourite, with its tiny fireplace and shelved alcove and its enviable view of the fields. I looked at the metal bedframe and soft floral-sprigged eiderdown and knew that if I didn't start as I meant to go on I'd never make the change from visitor to proprietor. From that moment on, and hopefully with Gwen's blessing, this was going to be my room.

Back in the kitchen as I made tea my stomach growled and I remembered the beautiful quiche and salad waiting in the fridge. Eating in the garden seemed like a good idea and it wasn't until I was happily ensconced in Gwen's deck-chair under the cherry tree that I remembered that this was the exact spot that Chris had found her that fateful Sunday afternoon.

Rather than making a predictable dash back to the sanctuary of the cottage I was surprised to discover that I had absolutely no desire to move at all. In a funny kind of way I felt as though Gwen was right there with me, waiting to pass on the mantle and see me safely settled. It was a comforting thought, and I hoped that in the months and years to come I would do her legacy justice, and begin living the life both she and Gran had always hoped I'd have.

'I promise I'll do my best,' I said out loud. 'Thank you, Gwen.'

A slight breeze lifted the branches of the cherry tree and everything felt calm and peaceful. I was here. I was finally home.

*

I spent the rest of the afternoon unpacking my trio of bags, (which took less than an hour), dozing in Gwen's chair in the shade and exploring the garden. The pretty plot was in definite need of attention but it wasn't too much of a jungle. Chris had been keeping on top of the grass so it was just the borders that needed bringing back to their former glory, a task I was very much looking forward to undertaking. It had been too long since I had used the skills passed on by my green-fingered grandad and I knew from previous experience that the process would be as much a soothing balm to my spirit as a shot in the arm for the plants.

Along with Gwen's ancient lawnmower, I had spotted the old bike I could remember riding stored in the greenhouse, and resolved that the next day I would give myself plenty of time to cycle back to town for my meeting at the bank with David. I was quite certain that I could manage without a car, despite what Chris had said. I was pretty fit and it really wasn't all that far. Everything would be fine, as long as it didn't rain, of course.

Too tired to check over the empty barns, I closed the gate with some less than gentle persuasion and went back inside the cottage. I was too worn out to even be bothered with a bath and was just about to throw myself on to the bed when my foot caught something that was poking out from under the frame.

It was an old Clark's shoebox, (Gwen might have been

a little on the eccentric side, but she knew the benefit of comfortable footwear) and it was crammed full of old photographs. I tipped it out on the eiderdown, the familiar tears springing back up as I began to sort through the dozens of images. There were lots of me when I was very small, mostly playing outside in the garden or stuffing myself full of raspberries, my face looking more like an extra from a zombie apocalypse film than an angelic child of six, but it was the more recent ones that really caught my attention. I flicked on the bedside lamp and studied them more closely.

I was in my mid to late teens on a few of them, enjoying the annual church visit to the seaside in the company of Chris's boys, Shaun and Steve. Chris hadn't said anything but I wondered if he and Marie had known what had happened between me and their eldest boy during that last fateful summer we were together. Sadly I set the image aside and picked up another of me looking far from happy, but my expression had nothing to do with the tempestuous hormones running amok through my veins.

Bent double, I was attempting to attach a lead to the collar of Gwen's scrappy terrier, but Gwen, standing next to me, was smiling broadly. I turned it over and my suspicions were confirmed: it was Tiny, Minnie's predecessor. What on earth had happened to that little tyrant Minnie? I wondered.

I was ashamed to admit I hadn't given her fate a second thought. I stacked the photographs back in the box and made a mental note to ask David about her whereabouts and then turned off the light. I was just beginning to think it was so quiet I would never be able to sleep when I suddenly dropped off and didn't hear another thing until the telephone woke me the next morning.

Chapter 5

I woke in something of a daze, completely confused as to where I was and what I was doing there. I could hear the shrill telephone ringing out, but when I went to grab it, it wasn't there. I shot up in bed and the room finally swam into focus as I threw back the covers and raced down the stairs. The answerphone cut in just as I reached the bottom step and I was pulled up short as Gwen's voice filled the hallway, requesting that whoever was on the end of the line should leave a message, and if she thought it worth her while, she would return the call later.

'Hello, Lottie, this is David. I'm just ringing . . .'

I quickly snatched up the phone.

'David, I'm here,' I puffed. 'Sorry, I wasn't near the phone.'

A quick glance at the clock told me I'd had a good eight hours' sleep, but the way my head was spinning it felt like a lot less.

'Are you all right?' he said, his tone concerned. 'You sound out of breath.'

'I'm fine,' I said. 'A bit shocked to hear Gwen's voice, but otherwise I'm absolutely fine.'

'Yes,' he mused, 'funny, isn't it? You might think you've covered all bases, but then something unexpected comes along and hits you like a bolt out of the blue.'

I got the distinct impression that he was speaking from experience, but I didn't feel I knew him well enough to ask directly.

'Yes,' I said instead. 'I think I'm destined for quite a few thunderbolts during the next couple of months.'

'But you're sure you're OK?'

'Yes,' I said, 'I'm fine, although,' I added, knowing that I couldn't not mention it, 'I rather wish you'd warned me that the town gossips have been out in force.'

'Ah,' he sighed, 'I was afraid Chris might have let something slip. I am sorry, Lottie. I was hoping I wouldn't have to burden you with it. Given what Gwen said about your potential reluctance to make such a big change, I didn't think it would help to have you worrying about silly tittle-tattle on top of everything else.'

'Well never mind,' I relented, my annoyance softening now I knew he had my best interests at heart. 'I know all about it now so if anyone says anything it won't be such a shock.'

'Oh, I'm sure it won't come to that.'

'And the cottage is simply beautiful,' I said, keen to move the conversation on. 'I had no idea that Chris and Marie had been working so hard.'

'I take it he didn't mention all their hard work then?'

'No, of course not,' I said. 'If anything, he was keen to play their contribution down, but you only have to look around the place, and in the fridge, to know they've taken their caretaking duties very seriously.'

'I can well believe it,' said David and I could tell he was smiling. 'And how did you enjoy the quiche?'

'How did you know about that?'

'I was the one who recommended it,' he said proudly. 'Jemma, who owns The Cherry Tree Café here in town, is the queen of quiches as far as I'm concerned. In fact, all her baking is second to none. If it wasn't for her I'd be a mere shadow of the man I am today.'

Yes, there was definitely a sad story beginning to come into hazy focus around David Miller.

'I think I need to pay that café a little visit after our meeting at the bank,' I said, thinking back to the pretty façade I had spotted the day before. 'I assume our meeting is still going ahead. You haven't phoned to cancel, have you?'

'Oh no,' said David. 'The meeting is still on. I just wanted to make sure you were all right and ask if you would like me to drive out and pick you up. Chris seemed to think you might need a lift. In fact, he was asking around in The Mermaid last night, trying to find out if anyone had a little car they were looking to sell.'

My stomach rolled miserably at the thought.

'Oh dear,' I groaned. 'I really should have put my foot down about that, shouldn't I?'

'I take it you don't want a car then?' David guessed.

'No,' I told him, 'absolutely not.' I was about to add that I didn't need a 'fella' either, but I didn't know if Chris had announced that to the pub as well, so quickly stopped myself. 'And thank you for asking, but I don't need a lift today either. I'm going to cycle to town. I'm looking forward to it.'

'Well, as long as you're sure,' said David doubtfully. 'It's really quite a trek on two wheels, you know.'

'Honestly,' I said. 'I do appreciate the offer, but I can manage.'

'All right,' he said, 'but if you change your mind, just give me a call.'

As I stood at the kitchen counter eating toast and honey and looking out at the garden, I realised I had forgotten to ask about Minnie. David enlightening me all about Chris's super-speedy car hunt had taken me by surprise and I had to acknowledge that even though I was now living in splendid isolation, there were going to be certain aspects of my life that were destined to be more visible than ever before.

Another quick glance at the clock confirmed that I had

some time to fill before my meeting in town and so without further ado I pushed my concerns about living in a goldfish bowl aside and rushed upstairs to dress, my mind full of the exciting possibilities the empty barns might have to offer.

Knowing full well I wouldn't want to wrangle with it before I set off for town, I decided to wrestle the gate open before I became too engrossed in exploring the barns. Thinking back over the distance, I had to concede that cycling to Wynbridge was perhaps going to be a bit more of a challenge than I first thought, especially in the high summer heat which I could already feel building up.

Yet again it took a fair amount of cajoling and some less than friendly persuading to yank the gate open and I had just tempted it as far as I could when I heard the sound of a vehicle approaching. Given the shocking state of the road surface and the narrow nature of the lane, it sounded to me as if it was being driven far too fast and then, sure enough, the very same truck which had squeezed snugly by Chris's van roared by, its horn blaring and a man's hand waving briefly out of the open window.

'Idiot,' I muttered.

I was as much annoyed that the blast from the horn had made me jump as I was by the speed at which the truck was travelling, and made a mental note to see Chris later and ask if he knew who was likely to be behind the wheel.

'Hello!'

So outraged by the speeding truck, I hadn't noticed another vehicle approaching and spun round to discover an ancient yellow minivan parked on the verge.

'Hi there!' called the driver, as she climbed out of the car and rushed towards me with her hand outstretched. 'You must be Lottie.'

'Yes,' I said, with a nod. 'Hello.'

The fact that she already knew my name confirmed exactly what Chris had been saying about everyone express-ing an interest in the future occupant of the cottage, but at least she hadn't called me 'cuckoo'. I stepped up to shake her hand, but the woman, who was around my own age with short, dark hair, pulled me into a hug instead.

'Welcome,' she said warmly. 'Welcome to Wynbridge. How are you settling in?'

'Oh,' I flushed, surprised by her demonstrative introduc-tion. 'Very well, thank you.'

'I'm Maggie,' she said, taking a step back and leaving a slight trace of spicy incense in her wake. 'Although everyone calls me Mags, and this is my son, Edward.'

'Although everyone calls me Ed,' he called, from his seat in the van.

'Hello,' I said, bobbing down to wave through the window.

'I'm sorry we can't stop and chat properly,' said Mags, 'but I have to get to work.'

'And I have to feed Jack,' said the curly-haired boy, who was probably ten or eleven, as he pointed to a large cardboard box on his lap.

'That's his latest addition to the menagerie,' Mags tutted, rolling her eyes. 'Yet another mouth to feed.'

'Puppy?' I asked.

'Jackdaw,' said Ed. 'With a broken wing. Mum has said I can keep him.'

'Mum most certainly has not,' said Mags. 'I swear my son's got Durrell blood,' she laughed, shaking her head, the sun glinting off her pretty crystal earrings.

I didn't quite know what to say. I don't think I could have been more surprised had the boy announced he had a baby dragon on his lap.

'Well, thank you for stopping to say hello,' I smiled. 'Do you live far away?'

'Just up near the crossroads,' she said, pointing along the road. 'We're almost your nearest neighbours.'

'Well, that's good to know,' I said. 'I haven't visited here for a while so I've kind of lost track as to who lives along here now.'

'We're just next door to George,' she explained. 'So you aren't completely on your own. Anyway,' she said, pointing back to the car, 'sorry I can't stay longer, but I'm a bit behind this morning. What with having to wrangle Jack into submission on top of everything else.'

I walked with her to the minivan and laughed as the box on Ed's lap began to rock and energetically sway as she turned over the engine.

'Can I come and have a look at your field?' he asked when he spotted me watching his newest pet's antics.

'Ed!' scolded Mags.

'Please,' he added by way of apology. 'Gwen always let me. I used to come all the time.'

'Well, in that case, come whenever you like,' I told him. 'As long as your mum doesn't mind, of course.'

'Thank you,' said Mags, gratefully. 'He's really missed having this place to explore.'

'Well, you're both welcome any time,' I said.

I was surprised to find myself so keen to invite them. Ordinarily I was more guarded when meeting someone for the first time, but there was such warmth and comfort emanating from this woman and her interesting son that I knew I could do far worse than having them as neighbours.

'Pop in whenever you like,' I added.

With a toot on the horn, Mags released the handbrake and I watched her drive away at a far more sedate pace than the rogue truck I'd seen earlier.

With the lane empty again, I walked down to the yard and stood for a minute watching the pairs of swallows speedily darting in and out from under the eaves of the smallest barn and wondered what it was exactly that Ed wanted to look at in the field.

When I used to visit, I would spend hours drawing pictures of the hedgerows and collecting leaves and the odd discarded eggshell to take back to the cottage for Gwen to display on the fireplace. I rather liked the idea that Ed would want to do the same sort of thing, and if the box on his lap was any sort of indicator, then I was sure that he would.

Mindful of the time, I slid back the bolt of the barn door which was closest to the field and heaved it open. I knew there were arched windows at the end, but they had always been boarded up. My heart began to pick up the pace again as I imagined the shutters coming down and the space filled with light. This would be the ideal spot to create an office area for the administrative end of my potential new business venture, should I decide to go ahead.

As predicted, the space was empty and currently cloaked in gloomy darkness with nothing more than a few cobwebs for decoration and a furtive, frantic scrabbling from somewhere towards the far end that made me yelp, take a step back and quickly close and bolt the door again. I might have enjoyed collecting nature's spoils as a youngster, but I'd never been a fan of rodents. I knew that permanent country living was going to put me in close proximity to any number of furry friends, but so long as they agreed to keep their distance and stayed out of the cottage, we'd get along just fine.

The second barn, which was bigger than the first, was also empty but this one didn't have any windows and I wondered how easy it would be to have a couple put in along the back wall. Letting in the light would no doubt transform the space and the panoramic view across the fields that ran behind would be spectacular.

My eyes roamed the lofty interior, imagining it set up as the perfect place to showcase my completed renovation and makeover projects. I made a rough estimate of the square footage and calculated I was going to need quite a few conversions to make any kind of impact. For the first time since John and Eric had suggested the idea, I felt a tiny, but definite, twinge of doubt.

The thought of setting up my own business had been thrilling in theory and seemed like the perfect way to utilise the wonderful space Gwen had given me, but when actually faced with it, I wondered if I had it in me to see it through. I was used to working away in the background, but this venture would mean putting myself firmly at the forefront of things and I wasn't at all sure I had the confidence for that. My initial exuberance felt a little thwarted as I slammed the door shut and moved on to the last barn.

Gwen had always called this one 'the big shed', which it was when compared to the size of the other two, but calling it a 'shed' was something of a misnomer because it really was too grand for such a mundane title. It had the same boarded-up arched windows as the smallest barn but also boasted a practical and well-stocked workshop area at the back and sliding wooden doors which opened along runners, currently hindered by a build-up of weeds and stones.

After a minute of clearing and struggling I managed to wrench them apart, just far enough to squeeze through, and there, to my utter amazement, sat what turned out to be just the shot in the arm I needed.

'And you're absolutely sure they belonged to Gwen,' I asked David on the telephone for what must have been the fiftieth time.

'Quite sure,' he patiently confirmed again. 'She spent quite a lot of time looking for them online and when she found one she was interested in Chris would take her to look it over. Then, if it was as good as the advert suggested, she would snap it up and he would tow it back to the cottage, usually on a Sunday afternoon. They actually went as far as Birmingham one weekend as I recall.'

'Online?' I choked. 'Birmingham? We are talking about the same Gwen, aren't we?'

'Yes,' laughed David. 'I know it sounds a bit off the wall even for her . . .'

'A *bit* off the wall!' I spluttered.

'But the girls in the Cherry Tree used to help her with the computer side of things, and to be honest, I'd always assumed you had played some part in the venture yourself, Lottie, because she told me, quite specifically, that she was buying them with you in mind.'

'No,' I said, my head in a daze. 'I had absolutely no idea about them. No idea at all.'

'I can't believe she never told you,' he said confusedly, 'but then I probably should have guessed she hadn't when you didn't mention them at the will reading.'

'Believe me,' I said, biting my lip and wondering what exactly Gwen had envisaged for them, and for me for that matter, 'I'm just as surprised as you are, but thank you for explaining everything. I'd better go and get on.'

'Yes, you'll need to set off soon.'

'Don't worry, I'll be there,' I said, glancing out at the sun which was still ruthlessly beating down from a cloudless sky. 'I might have to find somewhere to cool off for a minute by the time I arrive, but I'll make it.'

'And you really are sure you don't want me to come and get you?'

'Yes,' I said, giving his offer an undeserved eye roll, 'thanks, but I'll be fine. I'll see you later.'

I rushed back down to the barn and squeezed through the gap in the door, my heart racing wildly, but this time more from excitement than shock. One tiny Bailey and three pretty little Cheltenham caravans, one in each corner of the barn, sat looking at me, all as cute and gently curved as each other and, from what I could see, all in good condition, on the outside at least. Taking a closer look, I soon worked out that the little quartet hailed from around the mid- to late-sixties and I wondered if Gwen had been thinking along the same lines as John and Eric when she began collecting them.

This, I couldn't help thinking as I ran a hand over the bodywork of the one closest and peered through the window, was just what I needed to launch my idea on an incredibly grand scale. I knew from trawling internet sites and trade magazines for myself that these were all highly sought-after vans, hugely in demand and incredibly en vogue. Gwen had certainly known her onions when she parted with her cash and passed on a truly golden opportunity for me to start 'thinking big', as she and Gran had so often encouraged.

I knew without a shadow of a doubt that I would be able to utilise my skills on these pretty vintage projects and turn them into something even more highly sought after than they already were. With a last lingering look I reluctantly closed and bolted the door, thinking that I needed to pick up a padlock in town, and rushed back to the greenhouse to collect the bike.

It was in no fit state to ride, of course. It was covered in dust and cobwebs and the tyres were flat and a little on the perished side. Determined not to give in and call David, I dragged the rust-riddled contraption outside, undid the pump which was strapped to the frame and began to inflate the tyres as if my life depended on it. Ten minutes later they were considerably firmer, but for how long?

Struggling to catch my breath, I set the pump aside and ran back to the house. If I really got my skates on I'd have time for a quick shower, and if the wind was behind me I might even make it as far as Wynbridge before nightfall, assuming the tyres didn't give up before I did of course.

Chapter 6

Clunky, that's how Grandad would have described the pipework and plumbing at Cuckoo Cottage, I thought, as I listened to the strange rattles and bangs as the shower sprang into life. Evidently it was going to need working on or possibly even replacing. I was already developing quite a mental list of things that needed my attention, what with oil for the gate and padlocks, and now the shower. I really needed to harness my grandmother's passion for lists and start writing things down.

Deciding my desire to freshen up was worth the risk, I stripped off, ducked under the stream of lukewarm water and squirted some of Gwen's apple-scented shampoo into the palm of my hand. I had just worked my hair into a satisfying lather when the water switched from the wrong side of hot to arctic and began to spurt out under immense pressure. Shocked and in pain, I screamed out, leapt to the other end of the bath and made a grab for the towel, which infuriatingly slipped off the windowsill on to the floor and out of reach.

I was just about to lunge for it again when I heard shouting and heavy footfall crashing up the stairs. I cowered in the corner of the tub as the door was flung open and in barged a man so tall he had to stoop under the door frame, and when he straightened back up he entirely filled the tiny space.

I looked at the man and the man looked at all of me. More screaming then ensued as he bent down, threw me the towel, reached over the top of the shower curtain, turned the shower off and disappeared again. I leapt out of the bath, slammed the door shut and leant on it in lieu of the fact that there was no lock.

'What the hell?' I sobbed out loud.

The shampoo was making a speedy bid to reach my eyes and I rubbed it away as best I could with the edge of the towel. A quick glance in the mirror confirmed that, thanks to the remains of my mascara from the day before, I looked like Alice Cooper on a very bad day, not that it really mattered when there was a stranger marauding about and I was trapped naked, phoneless and shivering.

With one ear listening out for noises from below, I took a deep breath, made a mad dash for the bedroom, swapped the towel for my dressing gown and raced down the stairs with the intention of locking the house door. Typically I'd remembered to lock it when I was examining the barns, but alone, naked and in a rush I'd left it ajar for anyone in the world to breeze in, and apparently they had.

'It's all right,' said a deep voice from the cupboard under the stairs just as I reached the bottom step. 'I've sorted it.'

Like a rabbit caught in the headlights, I stopped in my tracks, not knowing whether to run back up or leg it out of the door and scream for help, but who would hear me here in the middle of nowhere? My phone was almost within reach if I made a lunge for it, but I knew attempting a 999 call would have been a complete waste of the final few seconds of my as yet uneventful life.

'I'd been on at Gwen to get that shower sorted for months,' the voice carried on. 'It keeps cutting out and in the process trips out all the electric. Has anyone shown you how this fuse box works? It's pretty ancient. You might want to think about having it replaced.'

The voice was now accompanied by the tall, broad body that carried it about and, had I not been scared witless, I might have noticed what a wonderful specimen of a body that was. I might even have taken on board the thick dark hair and full sensuous lips, but as it was, I was still trapped at the bottom of the stairs and such detailed observation passed me by.

Gwen had never mentioned she had a handsome handyman tucked away for such emergencies, not that I'd noticed he was handsome, of course, but what other explanation could there possibly be? I couldn't really believe he was an opportunistic madman, who just happened to be passing, and by some amazing coincidence knew the intricacies of Gwen's dodgy plumbing and electrics. I allowed myself to unclench a little, but I wasn't ready to let my guard down too far just yet. After all, I was still completely naked beneath my dressing gown.

'Sorry,' he smiled, shaking his head as he took in my shocked and apple-shampoo-enhanced expression. 'I should really introduce myself, shouldn't I? You're probably thinking I'm some deranged passer-by.'

I swallowed, but didn't say anything. Given that he had just burst into my bathroom and seen me completely naked, he was infuriatingly ill at ease.

'I'm Will,' he smiled. 'I'm one of the vets in Wynbridge, and you must be Charlotte.'

'Lottie,' I croaked. 'Everyone calls me Lottie.'

'Actually,' he said, holding out his hand, probably on the misguided assumption that I was going to shake it, 'I'm William, but everyone calls me Will.'

'Is that supposed to be funny?' I swallowed, tightening the belt on my dressing gown and thinking back to my earlier introduction to Mags and Ed who had almost, word for word, said exactly the same thing.

'No,' he shrugged, 'maybe. I'm just trying to pretend the last few minutes didn't happen and as a result using banal humour to try and make it at least a little less excruciating for both of us.'

'Oh,' I said.

Obviously I didn't want him falling at my feet or anything, but surely I didn't look that unappealing without my clothes on. Not that I wanted him to acknowledge that I looked all right either. Oh God.

'No, no,' he said when he realised how his comment had been interpreted. 'I didn't mean that seeing you in the shower was excruciating, it was far from it,' he shook his head again, this time in despair. 'And I don't mean that the way it sounds either.'

Seeing his cool exterior finally begin to crumble, I calmed down a little more. Perhaps he was just a regular guy after all.

'Oh God,' he huffed, running his hands through his hair, 'and now I just sound like a total pervert.'

Pervert or not, I decided to take the risk.

'It's all right,' I said, climbing down the final step. 'I think I know what you're getting at.'

'Right,' he said, nodding enthusiastically. 'Good. So anyway, I'm Will and you are Lottie.'

'Yes,' I said, trying to draw my gaze away from his beautifully tanned forearms. 'I think we've established that.'

'Yes,' he said. 'Of course, OK. Right, well you probably need to get on, and I know I do, so if you could just help me carry the stuff in and tell me where you want her.'

'What stuff?' I called after him as he strode off into the yard. 'Want who?'

I was disappointed to discover that it was his truck that I had seen speeding up and down the lane, and now it was parked across the gateway.

'Sorry,' I told him as he marched back over and plonked what looked remarkably like a dog bed into my arms. 'But I don't actually know what you're talking about.'

'Minnie,' he called back over his shoulder. 'Like I said, I'm a vet. That's how I know Gwen. I'm Minnie's vet. I would have dropped her round last night, but I had an awkward calving to attend and didn't get back until after midnight.'

'Minnie?' I squeaked.

'Yes,' he said, reappearing this time with the diminutive pooch in his arms. 'I take it you two have met.'

'Well, yes,' I stammered. 'A long time ago, but what about her?'

'Well, she's all yours now, isn't she?'

'You have got to be kidding me.'

'I most definitely am not,' he said, trying to hand the scruffy bundle over. 'And by the way, your dressing gown's slipping.'

'Never mind my dressing gown,' I said, taking a hasty step back into the house and slamming the door. 'I'm not taking her!' I called through the kitchen window, my arms still full of Minnie's bed.

'You bloody well are!' Will shouted back. He sounded

furious and not at all like the gallant hero who had just rescued me from certain electrocution. 'David must have told you what Gwen wanted, and this is me passing her on. There's no way on earth I'm taking her back again.'

'Well, I'm not taking her at all!'

It went very quiet for a few seconds and the next thing I knew he was churning up the gravel, roaring out of the yard and away up the road.

'Ha,' I said aloud. 'That told him.'

There was no way I was taking on a dog like Minnie, or any dog for that matter. I stared at my soapy hair and mascara-streaked reflection in the hall mirror and thought back over the many conversations I'd had with David during the last few months. He'd never said anything about me taking responsibility for Minnie, had he?

I deposited the bed on the kitchen table and had just put my foot on the first step of the stairs when I heard howling outside the back door and it sounded unnervingly familiar.

'Fancy that lift after all?' asked David when I phoned him a few seconds after I had rushed back to the window and spotted Minnie tied to the gatepost in the driveway.

I couldn't believe Will had just dumped her there, and he called himself a vet. As soon as I finished talking to David I was going to make enquiries and find out how I could report him for animal cruelty.

'No,' I snapped. 'Thank you and this isn't a social call either. I've got Minnie here,' I launched off.

'Oh good,' David cut in, his tone decidedly soft-hearted. 'I bet she's relieved to finally be home. Will has been so kind keeping her for all this time and I know it can't have been easy for him. She's been pining for Gwen and Cuckoo Cottage, the poor little thing, and Will is such a busy chap. He really has gone above and beyond what any of us could have asked of him.'

Poor little thing! If he could have heard the racket she was making he wouldn't have thought she was a poor little anything, and what was all this about Will? He certainly didn't come across as some gifted dog whisperer to me.

'So let me get this straight,' I sighed. 'This Eric Bana lookalike is the real deal?'

'Sorry,' said David, 'who?'

'Oh, never mind,' I groaned. 'Are you really telling me that Minnie has to come and live with me now?'

'Well, of course she does,' said David, sounding shocked. 'It was one of the stipulations in Gwen's will.'

'But I don't remember ever reading anything about Minnie,' I said, wracking my brains. 'I don't remember her ever coming up at all.'

'I did tell you all about it on the day of Gwen's funeral,' David said. 'Don't you remember?'

There were a lot of things I hadn't remembered from that

initial meeting; most of it we'd since talked over, but the fate of Minnie had never come up for discussion.

'No,' I said truthfully. 'I don't.'

'Well, to be honest, nothing ever got written down,' David went on vaguely, 'but Gwen was most adamant that Minnie should carry on living in Cuckoo Cottage should anything happen to her.'

I couldn't help wishing she might have been a little more forthcoming about the unexpected collection of caravans as well.

'Right,' I sighed. 'I'm sure she was. But does that mean,' I said, a glimmer of hope suddenly appearing on the horizon, 'that if it isn't officially written down then I have grounds to . . .'

'Oh, you wouldn't,' David cut in, sounding horrified, 'surely not.'

Right on cue Minnie let out another sorrowful howl.

'No,' I sighed, 'of course I wouldn't, but I'm afraid this does mean I'm going to have to cancel our meeting for today. I can't possibly deal with her and get to you within the next half an hour.'

'Don't worry,' said David. 'I'll get on to the bank and we'll reschedule. I'll ring you later with a new time.'

'All right,' I agreed, then added begrudgingly, 'Thank you, David.'

'Take your time settling her in, won't you?' he said kindly.

'It's bound to be strange for the poor little thing, being there without Gwen?'

'Believe me,' I said. 'I understand exactly how she feels.'

Having taken to heart what David had said about Minnie being back at Cuckoo Cottage without Gwen, I knew I had no choice but to let her in. It was all right for us humans, we could talk things through and come to some sort of understanding, but dogs and cats and the like didn't have that capability, despite what some of the cranks in the Sunday papers said. Minnie and Gwen had been inseparable, and now the poor little thing was all on her own in the world. She was probably expecting her beloved mistress to appear at any moment and scoop her up in her arms. How could I not feel sorry for her?

'Come on, then,' I said, as I tentatively crossed the drive and untied her lead. 'Be nice,' I begged, expecting to feel her sharp little teeth nipping at my ankles any second. 'Let's see if we can figure out where to put your bed, shall we?'

No sooner had I unhooked her lead than she was off. First she raced into the kitchen, then she was away up the stairs, diving in and out of the rooms and up and over the beds. I followed on close behind, waiting to see what she would do when she finally realised that Gwen wasn't there. I hoped she wasn't going to take her disappointment out on me. Given everything I'd been through in the last few months, I didn't think I could cope with the wrath of Minnie on top of everything else.

When she had eventually exhausted exploring every nook and cranny she jumped back up on to Gwen's bed – my bed now – and began to circle and whimper. Not sure what I could do to comfort her, I sat down and waited. To my surprise the little dog stretched out and wriggled towards me on her belly, still sounding utterly forlorn. Tentatively I rested my hand on the eiderdown and she nuzzled underneath it, her pink tongue hanging out as she began to pant.

'She isn't here, Minnie,' I whispered, stroking her rough little head and realising how thin she felt. 'It's just you and me now.'

I looked up and spotted my reflection in the dressing-table mirror. No wonder the poor little thing was so afraid. The shampoo was rapidly drying my hair into manic stiff peaks and spikes and I knew that if I didn't wash it out soon, I wouldn't be able to do a thing with it.

'Minnie,' I said, pointing at my head, 'I need to deal with this. Are you going to be all right here?'

Not prepared to let me out of her sight just yet, she trotted into the bathroom behind me and watched on as I struggled to rinse my hair in the lukewarm water from the tap over the sink.

'What a mess,' I tutted, reaching for the conditioner. 'We

really will have to get this shower situation sorted, won't we?'

It quickly became obvious that the only danger Minnie posed to my health was that of a roving trip hazard. It didn't matter where I went or what I did, she was under my feet, almost brushing my ankles, and I lost count of the number of times she ran into me because I put the brakes on before she did. I pottered about the house for a bit then went back outside to put the bike back in the greenhouse. The tyres were still inflated, which was something.

'Come on, Minnie!' I called, when I was ready to go back inside, but she didn't come.

I looked about the garden and across the field, but I couldn't see her.

'Where have you gone, you silly dog?' I shouted, feeling slightly panicked.

Surely I couldn't have lost her already? A bark from the direction of the yard reached my ears and I locked the door to the cottage feeling rather pleased that she was leading me back in the direction of those four intriguing vans.

'Oh no,' I chastised when I finally found the naughty little thing trying to dig under the door of the smallest barn. 'You can forget that right now. If you think I'm letting you in there so you can go rat catching you've got another thing coming.'

Looking a little nonplussed, she fell back into step and together we squeezed back through the doors of the big shed.

To my delight the caravans were all unlocked and I quickly set about admiring and exploring their deliciously authentic interiors. The Cheltenhams were by far my favourite with their real wood veneer and cute curves. One of them even had two union flags criss-crossed above the big front window. According to the paperwork on the table inside the Bailey, two of the Cheltenhams were from the Waterbuck range and the other, which was just a few inches bigger, was a Sable.

They all bore their original features, which were wonderful in themselves, but with some pretty floral fabrics and careful reupholstering and accessorising I knew they could be even prettier. In my mind's eye I could imagine each one having a slightly different theme and colour scheme, but I have to admit I didn't like the thought of parting with any of them one little bit.

Even the less curvaceous Bailey was charming and I decided that after my meeting at the bank I would take a trip to the Cherry Tree and ask if the women there could shed any light on what had been Gwen's real motive for buying these travelling beauties from the past, and if they didn't know, then perhaps Chris would.

'What do you think, then?' I asked Minnie, who had been as keen as I had to hop in and out of the vans. 'Do you like them?'

She cocked her head to one side and then flew out of the barn at breakneck speed, heading straight up the drive towards the little yellow minivan that I hadn't heard arrive. I watched on, open-mouthed, knowing that no matter how fast I ran I wouldn't be able to catch her. My heart was in my mouth as Mags bent to scoop her up and relief washed over me as Minnie began to squirm in delight. Either the little dog had undergone a personality transplant recently or she had been so starved of affection under Will's roof she was willing to love anyone who didn't take flight when she made a beeline for them.

'Hello Minnie!' Mags laughed. 'Hello! How excited are you to be home?'

Clearly they were good pals and, as I pulled the big shed door shut, I wondered why Gwen had never thought to mention this lovely neighbour and her nature-loving son to me before.

'Oh, she's excited all right,' I smiled, when I reached them. 'I'm the one who's still in shock.'

'Did you not know you were getting her today?' asked Ed as he climbed out of the van and carefully set the box, which, I assumed, still contained Jack, on the seat.

'I didn't know I was getting her at all,' I confessed.

'But you do want her, don't you?' he frowned. 'Because if you don't . . .'

'Yes,' I said, before he suggested adding Minnie to the collection Mags had already hinted he had. 'I want her.'

'So how's your day been?' Mags asked. 'Apart from the unexpected delivery, of course,' she added, putting Minnie back on the path, where she immediately began to skitter around Ed's feet like an over-exuberant puppy.

'Interesting,' I admitted, thinking of the discovery of the caravans and the impromptu liaison in the shower, 'very interesting. Have you got time to stay for a cup of tea?'

'Not really . . .' she began.

'Oh, go on, Mum,' said Ed, tugging at her sleeve. 'Then I can go and check out the field.'

'Well, all right then,' she relented, ruffling her son's hair. 'But you have to put Jack in the shade first and then take Minnie with you so Lottie and I can have a proper chat.'

'Deal!' he shouted, punching the air in triumph.

Chapter 7

I had literally just put the key in the lock when the phone in the hall began to ring.

'Do you mind if get that?' I asked Mags as I gave the door its customary shove. 'I know it's rude, but I'm expecting a call from my solicitor.'

'No,' she insisted. 'You go ahead. I'll put the kettle on, shall I?'

'That would be great,' I agreed, snatching up the phone. 'Thanks.'

She went through to the kitchen and I turned my attention to the telephone.

'Charlotte?'

My heart sank as I realised it wasn't my solicitor at all, but my local, bathroom-busting, pet-abandoning vet.

'William,' I bit back.

'Touché.'

'What can I do for you?' I snapped.

'I was just wondering how Minnie's settling in,' he asked equably.

'You are kidding?'

'Of course I'm not,' he said. 'That poor little dog has been through a lot these last few months.'

'Not least the latest trauma,' I cut in, 'of being tied up by someone she thought she could trust and then being abandoned with no one other than a complete stranger to rescue her.'

'I think that's a bit strong,' he said defensively. 'You're hardly a complete stranger.'

'Still not the most professional way for a so-called animal lover and vet, to boot, to behave though, is it?' I hissed, hoping Mags couldn't hear my snarky side of the conversation.

'Well, you didn't exactly give me much choice, did you?'

'Don't turn this around and put the blame on me,' I laughed sarcastically. 'You were the one who dumped her.'

'And you're the one who should have been paying attention to what David was telling you Gwen had wanted for her rather than jumping up and down because you were going to get your hands on Cuckoo Cottage!'

I slammed the receiver down and snatched my hand away in shock. How dare he say that? How dare he presume how I felt about Gwen's legacy? At least now I knew one of the people Chris had been referring to when he said that not everyone had been impressed by Gwen's decision to leave her home to me. I was surprised her alleged friend had even remembered to call me Charlotte rather than 'cuckoo'.

'Are you all right?' asked Mags, her head appearing around the door frame just as the kettle came to the boil. 'Shall I fill the pot?'

'Yes,' I said, letting out a slow breath. 'Sorry. Not the call I was expecting. Yes, please go ahead.'

I was just about to say I was now coming to help when the phone rang again. I stood, rooted to the spot and loath to answer it, but I couldn't bear the thought of listening to Gwen's answerphone message again, so I reluctantly picked it up.

'I'm sorry,' said Will, even before the receiver touched my ear. 'I really shouldn't have said that. I didn't mean a word of it and it isn't what I think at all.'

'Don't worry about it,' I shrugged, even though he couldn't see me.

'But I am worried,' he tried again.

'Well, don't be,' I snapped. 'Chris warned me to expect this kind of attitude from certain people.'

'But not me,' he insisted. 'Like I said, I don't feel that way at all. I really am sorry. I shouldn't have let my temper get the better of me.'

'No,' I said. 'You shouldn't.'

'It's just been really hard having Minnie with me,' he went on.

'I can imagine.'

'No,' he said, 'you can't. It isn't just because it's her. It would have been tough with any dog.'

'What do you mean?'

Clearly there was some meaning behind his admission, but I wasn't a mind reader.

'I'm sorry but I can't explain,' he sighed, 'and besides, it isn't really relevant. I just wanted to make sure she was OK. I'm truly sorry for what I said to you just now and I hope you believe that I really do care about Minnie.'

'But you have to admit you've got a funny way of showing it,' I said, still unwilling to forgive and forget what he had done. 'Tying her up like that and driving off is pretty low, don't you think?'

'How was I supposed to know you hadn't realised you were responsible for her?' he shot back, sounding nettled again.

'I would have thought my reaction would have been a bit of a giveaway.'

'Well, it hardly matters now, does it? I had her in the truck, I had an emergency to attend, she'd got a whiff of where she was and I couldn't have taken her away again. That would have been too cruel.'

'More cruel than panicking her by tying her to the gate-post, you mean?'

'Oh God,' he shouted. 'Charlotte!'

'Lottie,' I reminded him.

'This is ridiculous,' he huffed. 'Just tell me, is Minnie all right?'

'Yes,' I said, thinking how happily she had trotted after Ed when he set off to reacquaint himself with the field. 'She's fine.'

'Well that's something,' he sighed.

'So you needn't worry about her any more and actually, while we're on the subject, you can take her off your books.'

'What do you mean?'

'I think it would be best all round if I found a new vet for her,' I said. 'Give her a completely fresh start now she's living with me.'

'Oh right,' said Will, 'and you're sure about that, are you?'

'Absolutely,' I said firmly.

I was going to go out of my way to make sure my path and Will's had absolutely no reason to cross from now on.

'Well, I wish you the very best of luck with that one,' he chuckled and with that he hung up.

'What do you know about a local vet called Will?' I asked Mags once we were settled with tea and biscuits under the cherry tree.

'Not much,' she said, trying to hide her smile behind her teacup. 'His background's a bit of a mystery, to be honest, but he's incredibly dishy.'

'Well,' I said, reaching for another bourbon biscuit, 'that so-called dish saw me naked this morning.'

'What?' she spluttered, sitting up in her seat and rattling her cup against her saucer. 'You aren't serious?'

'Unfortunately,' I said, biting my lip and still not really wanting to believe it, 'I am.'

I relayed the details of shower-gate and the subsequent argument which surrounded the transferral of Minnie from Will's care to mine while Mags listened, sometimes gasping, sometimes frowning, but always with laughter on her lips.

'So anyway,' I said when I had reached the point where our call had just ended, 'I'm going to find Minnie a new vet and then I won't have to see him ever again.'

'Good luck with that,' laughed Mags, swilling the pot and pouring us both another cup.

That was exactly what Will had said.

'What do you mean?' I frowned.

'You won't find another practice to take her round here,' she said. Her words were more a statement of fact than supposition. 'She's on the banned list.'

'Vets don't have banned lists.' I laughed nervously. 'Do they?'

'Not as a rule,' she tutted. 'But this is Minnie we're talking about, remember?'

She had a point.

'Well,' I said, 'whatever. I'll just have to draft in someone from further afield to take her should she fall ill or need a jab or something, because the less I see of that man the better.'

Mags shook her head.

'Are you talking about Will?' asked Ed as he sidled up to the plate of biscuits having just finished checking on Jack.

Minnie, panting hard at his side, came and threw herself down at my feet. She'd clearly had a good workout tearing around the field and I hoped this would bode well at bedtime. The last thing I needed was a sleepless night ahead of my sizzling cycle ride to Wynbridge, assuming David had managed to bag us another appointment with the bank, of course.

'We sure are,' said his mother as she passed him a biscuit. 'Not for Jack,' she said firmly before releasing it to Ed's grubby hand.

'But you'll always be seeing him,' he said, nibbling at the corner and spraying the grass with crumbs. 'Even if Minnie never gets sick.'

'How come?'

'Because,' said Mags, with a smile which suggested she was rather enjoying this little drama, 'he's your nearest neighbour!'

'What?'

'He lives in the big barn conversion between you and us.'

'Oh no,' I groaned. 'Please tell me you're kidding.'

'Nope,' she said with another laugh. 'He's the one you're going to have to call on if you run out of sugar or your lights go bang again.'

'No way,' I said, shaking my head. 'I'd rather move to the other end of the earth than have to darken his door.'

'No you wouldn't,' said Ed.

'No,' I relented, thinking that was perhaps a little over the top. 'I don't suppose I would.'

'It's perfect here,' he said with a contented sigh which reminded me very much of myself when I was his age. 'Why would you ever want to live anywhere else?'

'And anyway,' said Mags, gathering together the cups and plates, 'you just got off on the wrong foot. You'll love him when you get to know him.'

I looked at her doubtfully.

'You will,' she said.

'Will's the best,' said Ed, backing up his mother's words as he surreptitiously pulled another custard cream apart and starting licking at the filling.

'He really is a lovely man, Lottie,' Mags insisted. 'He looks after our neighbour George and is always on hand to help out in an emergency, even though he's always snowed under with work.'

'He helped fix Martha my duck,' chipped in Ed. 'And he's helping out with Jack.'

'Well, I'll take your word for it,' I said. 'But for now I'm just going to stay out of his way, so the pair of you can put down your pompoms.'

'Give it a few days and you'll be wondering how you ever felt like this,' smiled Mags, determined to carry on with her cheerleading.

'A few days won't alter the fact that he's seen me naked,' I reminded her in a low tone.

'He's what?' giggled Ed.

'Never you mind,' said Mags. 'Come on, we need to get home. It's been a long day,' she yawned, 'a really long day.'

Suddenly I realised we hadn't talked about her, or her work or anything. I still didn't really know anything about her or Ed at all.

'I'm sorry, Mags,' I said, 'I've rather monopolised the conversation, haven't I? I haven't even asked you about how your day has gone or anything.'

'There'll be plenty of time for all that,' she laughed, 'besides, what you had to say has been far more entertaining and I only really called in to pass on an invitation.'

'An invitation?'

Ed ran to the car and fished out a pretty card with my name on it.

'It's to a party this weekend at Skylark Farm,' he said as he handed it over.

'It's their Lammas party,' added Mags, 'to celebrate the start of the harvest season with a few close friends and neighbours. Their parties are always fun.'

'Oh,' I said, turning the card over in my hand. 'It's very kind of them to ask me, but I can't make it, I'm afraid.'

'Why not?' The pair chorused.

'Well, for a start, I have no car,' I began. 'So I can't get there.'

'I can take you,' said Mags quickly. 'I'm taking George and I have to drive right by your door.'

My stomach rolled at the thought of attending my first social gathering just days after I had moved into Cuckoo Cottage. I had been hoping to settle in before I ventured out.

'There won't be more than a dozen of us there,' said Mags, picking up on my hesitation. 'And the sooner you get it over with, the better.'

'What do you mean?'

'Your first public showing,' she smiled wryly, knowing exactly what was on my mind. 'And if you do come there'll be plenty of opportunity to get to know more about us and make up for hogging the chat today,' she teased.

'Oh do come,' implored Ed. 'I'll look after you.'

'I don't know,' I said, my resolve weakening with every plea.

'Please,' they wheedled together.

'Oh all right,' I yielded. 'But you have to promise to be my chaperone all night, Ed.'

'All right,' he said, going slightly pink about the ears. 'It's a deal.'

Later that evening, when David called to give me the revised time for our appointment at the bank, talk naturally turned to how Minnie was coping and then it shifted to Will.

'I kind of got the impression that he found having Minnie living with him difficult for some reason,' I said, 'and not just because of who she is. Am I right?'

David was evasive.

'That's not really for me to say,' he answered. 'You'd best ask Will next time you see him.'

'Oh, I won't be seeing him any time soon,' I said with certainty. 'I'm going to find another vet for Minnie.'

'Well, you can try,' said David, his tone echoing Mags. 'But I wouldn't do that if I were you. It wouldn't do to go falling out with your nearest neighbour. You never know when you might need him.'

'I'm pretty sure I can manage living out here on my own,' I said defensively.

'But even so,' he said cautiously.

'All right,' I sighed. 'I'll leave things with Minnie as they are for now.'

'Excellent,' he agreed. 'And you probably wouldn't find another vet in the vicinity to take her anyway. See you tomorrow. Are you sure you don't want me to pick you up? It's getting on for ten miles, you know.'

'I'm pretty sure I can cycle ten tiny miles.'

'But in this heat,' he went on.

'Really, David,' I said. 'I'm sure I can manage. I'll set off in plenty of time, unless of course another little surprise pops up and I have to cancel.'

'I think you've had all the surprises you're due,' commented David.

'I hope you're right,' I said back.

Chapter 8

Up with the proverbial lark the next morning, and wheeling the bicycle back out of the greenhouse, I tried to ignore Minnie, who was looking at me accusingly and refusing all offers to tempt her back inside to eat her breakfast.

'I really won't be all that long,' I promised her. 'You'll hardly notice I'm gone.'

She barked back a curt little response and I glanced apprehensively towards the empty lane. I was really going to have to watch this whole 'in conversation with' thing I was developing. I knew society in general viewed Crazy Cat Ladies with a certain degree of affection, but I wasn't sure what the Wynbridge locals would make of the 'cuckoo' talking to her recently repatriated terrier.

Fortunately the lane was free of spectators and I went back inside to change, feeling grateful that David had secured an early appointment at the bank. At least I would be able to get the first half of the journey under my belt before the heat of the day really hit home. I slipped on the coolest, cotton frock I could find, pulled my hair into a sleek, neat ponytail and set my mind to dreaming up the most innovative way to bribe Minnie back into the cottage.

Needless to say, my efforts failed and I set off, in a somewhat wobbly fashion, with Minnie proudly perched in the basket along with my bag and keys. I hadn't realised before that dogs could pull off smug, but looking at her perky expression she'd totally nailed it.

'You didn't win,' I told her as I swerved around a particularly deep pothole. 'I just changed my mind, that's all.'

Her yappy response suggested she didn't believe a word, but I wasn't going to get drawn into an argument. I needed to keep my eyes on the road. It was already getting hot, but not unbearably so, and we hadn't gone all that much further when I began to relax and look about me, taking in the wider landscape beyond the edges of the narrow road and high verges which were packed with wild flowers.

'Now, Minnie,' I whispered when we had gone on a little further, 'what do you suppose that could be?'

I could clearly make out some movement in the verge ahead, a definite rustling in the long grass that was in no way the result of the light breeze that had so far stopped me from overheating. I had almost reached the spot when out hopped the biggest hare I had ever seen.

The next few seconds became a confused blur. I looked at the ginormous hare, which seemed to be growing with every revolution of the pedals, and the hare looked at me, its wild, amber eyes wide with surprise. Clearly it was shocked to find another silent traveller on the otherwise deserted road. At that precise moment Minnie began to yap excitedly and wag her tail and a distant, but fast-approaching, roar of an engine met my ears.

The hare darted with lightning speed back into the verge, and I steered the bike as close as I possibly could to the side of the road, while simultaneously making a grab for Minnie's lead should she mistake my slowing down for stopping and attempt to jump out of the basket.

A black truck, which I instantly recognised as Will's, flashed by with little more than inches to spare, its horn blaring and the rush of air and disturbed dust it left in its wake almost enough to knock us clean into the ditch. I yanked on the bike's brakes, my bare legs brushing against the nettle-filled verge and stinging even before I'd had a chance to swear.

I jumped off the bike, pulling Minnie into my arms, and danced about in the road, partly in pain, but mostly in anger. Will had disappeared out of sight; the only evidence that he was somewhere ahead was the thick cloud of dust he left in his wake. I didn't care what Mags, Ed and David had said in his defence; this guy was really going out of his way to piss me off.

'Are you all right?'

So preoccupied with swearing at the vehicle which was little more than a speck in the distance, I hadn't noticed the one which had crept up behind us.

'Did you just see what that idiot did?' I raged, rushing round to the driver's window, keen to secure myself an ally.

'He didn't exactly leave you much room, did he?' said the driver. 'Here,' he added, quickly turning off the engine and jumping out. 'Let me give you a hand. I'm Matt, by the way, and I reckon you must be Lottie, the girl who's just moved into lovely Gwen's old place. Am I right?'

'Yes,' I croaked, momentarily thrown by the sparkling azure eyes, deep tan, sun-bleached hair and Sherlockesque powers of deduction. 'That's me. I'm Lottie Foster.'

'Well, I'm pleased to meet you,' he grinned, dazzling me with his almost too perfect smile. 'Although of course the circumstances could be better, for you at least.'

I have to admit I'd almost forgotten about the pain in my legs, Will's irresponsible driving and how relieved I was that another passer-by had called me by my real name rather than my derogatory nickname.

'I take it you knew Gwen then?' I asked, jiggling Minnie, who was more than a little agitated, in my arms.

'Yes,' he said. 'Yes, I did. I'm so sorry for your loss,' he added kindly.

'Thank you,' I nodded.

I couldn't help thinking how wily Gwen had been to surround herself with such handsome, young friends. It was a comfort to know she was still mischievous even though she had been drawing her pension for decades. Minxy, Gran had always called her.

'She'd asked me if I'd do some work for her at the cottage this summer,' Matt went on, 'but I'm afraid I never got round to it before she . . .'

'Oh?' I cut in, to save him having to say the words.

'Sorry,' he said, shaking his head when he realised I had no idea what sort of 'work' he was referring to. 'I'm a builder.'

'Oh right,' I said. 'I see.'

'But I can turn my hand to anything really,' he added.

Yes, I thought, surreptitiously looking him up and down, I could well imagine that he could.

'When you've had a chance to settle in I'll pop round and let you know what she had in mind, if you like.'

'Thank you.' I smiled, 'I'd appreciate that. I've already come up with one or two things myself,' I added, thinking of the dodgy shower, but definitely not of the embarrassing details of my first dousing.

'Well, your plans might be different to what Gwen had in mind, but if I give you my number . . .'

Whatever he planned to say or do next was quickly for-gotten as Minnie tried to lunge towards him, clearly intent on taking a chunk out of his hand, arm or anything else she could reach. When I held firm, she settled back down, but I could feel a deep-throated growl resonating through her fiery little body.

'She hasn't changed then,' laughed Matt, who had taken a hasty step back.

'No,' I sighed, thinking how this was more like the old Minnie I had known, but definitely not loved. 'I'm sorry about that. She's fine with some people,' I said, thinking of Mags and Ed. 'But I'm obviously still going to have to keep an eye on her.'

I plonked her down on the road, keeping tight hold of her lead, and gave my tingling calves a cursory rub. They were bright red and covered in so many spots there were barely any gaps. Having noticed the state of them, they began to throb all the harder and I winced from the pain.

'Here,' said Matt. 'Let me take a look.'

'I'd forgotten just how much nettle stings hurt,' I said, hoping he didn't think I was a complete wimp. 'I don't think I've had a brush with them since I was about ten years old. Horrid plants.'

'Actually,' he said, bending down to get a closer look, but keeping well out of Minnie's reach, 'they're really good for you. They're a great source of fibre, although I'd recommend cooking them before you eat them, of course.'

'Now you come to mention it, I think I've seen something on the telly about a nettle-eating competition . . .' the words died in my throat as Matt lightly ran his hand over my leg and the tingling intensified tenfold and shot through my entire body.

'I think I might have something in the van that could help with the pain,' he said, straightening back up. 'Unless you fancy trawling the verge for some dock leaves, of course?'

I wasn't sure if he was joking or not.

'Anything you can offer will be most gratefully received,' I blushed, trying not to simper or succumb to the sudden weakness in my knees.

I made a point of smoothing down my dress and running a hand over my hair while Matt was out of sight, and tried to ignore the withering look from Minnie who was clearly less than enthralled by my efforts to impress.

I certainly wasn't trying to bag myself a date, because I was happy settling in to my new life without a 'fella', as Chris put it, but I wasn't going to scupper my chances of making at least a half-decent impression on the first good-looking guy who came along. Second, if you counted Will, which of course I didn't. And besides, he might have been a stranger to me but he had obviously been close to Gwen if she had trusted him enough to have him lined up to work on her beloved cottage. Handsome and handy around the house was looking like a perfect combo in my mind.

'Here you go,' said Matt, reappearing from the van with a brand new tube of calamine cream. 'That's the best I can offer, I'm afraid. It won't completely take the pain away, but it should dull it a bit.'

'Thank you,' I said, while attempting to juggle Minnie's lead and open the tube. 'Do you always travel with a first-aid kit?'

'Of course,' he grinned. 'A chap should always be prepared!'

'You sound like a boy scout,' I teased.

'More of an opportunist really,' he winked. 'You never know when you might come across a pretty damsel in distress.'

I wasn't sure I would have assigned myself that particular title, but I was grateful for the cream and sympathy nonetheless.

'So,' I asked, passing back the tube, 'tell me how you know my name.'

'You'd better keep hold of that,' he said kindly. 'You'll probably need a top-up in a little while.'

'Thank you,' I said, reaching down to put it in the bike basket. 'You're probably right, but you didn't answer my question. How is it that you know who I am?'

'Well, for a start,' he said, shaking his head, 'I can't imagine there's anyone in the world that would be crazy enough to take on Minnie, unless they absolutely had to.'

'Ah yes,' I nodded. 'I see.'

'And secondly, rumour spreads like wildfire through these

parts,' he smiled broadly. 'Especially amongst us single guys when there's a pretty new girl in the neighbourhood.'

'Oh right,' I said, blushing again, but hating myself for reacting to such a cheesy line.

I couldn't help thinking that if he and the other local bachelors carried on talking like that they were destined to be single for a long time, irrespective of whether they had Chris trying to play the part of Cilla Black and find them a date.

'Well,' I said, feeling thankful that he wasn't one of the suspicious locals looking to run me out of town, 'thank you for your help. Will obviously wasn't going to stop.'

So much for him being the good guy Mags, Ed and David had suggested he was.

'No,' said Matt. 'He can be an arrogant sod sometimes. Shame he's your nearest neighbour really.'

'Yes,' I agreed. 'That thought has already crossed my mind on more than one occasion.'

Matt picked up the bike and gave it a quick check over as I scooped up the still growling Minnie again and plonked her in the basket facing the opposite direction.

'Don't mind the state of the bike,' I said, mindful of its appalling condition. 'This is just a stopgap until I order a new one.'

'You'd be better off with a car really,' he said, applying some pressure to the rear tyre with the heel of his hand.

I was beginning to think that everyone who had suggested

as much was probably right, but how on earth would I squeeze by the demon driver on four wheels if I could barely manage it on two?

'I would offer to give you a lift,' he added, taking another cautious step back, 'but I think she'd savage me before we even reached the next bend in the road!'

'Unfortunately I think you're right,' I said, giving Minnie a light tap on the nose. 'I'm sorry about her, but please don't worry about the lift. I'm actually enjoying the ride, or I was until our local unfriendly vet ran me off the road.'

'Do have a think about getting yourself a little car, won't you?' Matt said seriously. 'You really can't live out in the sticks with just a bike to rattle around on. It won't be summer forever, you know.'

'I know,' I said, my stomach rolling again at the thought of climbing behind the wheel.

'I'll ask about the town if you like,' he offered helpfully. 'There's bound to be someone selling something.'

'Thanks,' I called after him. 'Great.'

As a result of Will's dangerous driving and Matt's subsequent rescue, I had to pedal hard and fast to make it to town on time and my lungs were burning so much I didn't need to worry about my poor disfigured calves any more. Thanks to the build-up of lactic acid, I could barely feel them.

'I was beginning to get worried,' said David, who had

clearly been clock-watching while waiting for me to arrive. 'Oh, and you have Minnie with you, how lovely.'

'Not through choice,' I quickly explained as I struggled to catch my breath. 'She refused to be left behind.'

'Is that what held you up?' he asked, looking accusingly at Minnie and then at his watch. 'Or was the journey a bit more of a stretch than you thought it would be in this heat?'

'It was neither actually,' I said defensively, even though it was far further than I had estimated with the sun beating down. 'Minnie was as good as gold, once she got her own way, and I was well ahead of schedule until Will drove by at his apparently trademark lunatic speed and put us down a ditch.'

'He what?' gasped David. 'He actually ran you off the road?'

He sounded justifiably outraged.

'As good as,' I backtracked, thinking I needed to temper my temper. 'Look at the state of my legs.'

They were even redder now and as I looked at them the throbbing and burning began to intensify again.

'That's terrible,' said David, shaking his head. 'Look at the colour of them.'

'I know,' I winced, trying not to give in to the temptation to have a good scratch.

'Well, we can't possibly go to the bank before we've found you something to put on them,' he insisted, making for the door. 'Let me ask Iris what she would suggest.'

'It's all right,' I said quickly. 'A chap in a van stopped to help and as luck would have it he had a first-aid kit with some calamine cream in it. He insisted I kept the tube, so if you give me a second I'll just grab it and slap some more on before we go.'

'Well now, that was a stroke of luck,' said David thoughtfully. 'I don't think I've ever owned a first-aid kit that came with calamine.'

'Me neither,' I agreed, 'but I'm awfully grateful that this one did.'

'Perhaps it was fate,' smiled David. 'You must have been meant to meet him, Lottie.'

What was it with the men in this town? First Chris and now David had taken up the role of Cupid. Perhaps I should have made up a boyfriend and told them I'd left my heart behind in Lincolnshire?

'Who knows,' I said with what I hoped was a dismissive shrug. 'Anyway, I'm more annoyed with Will than interested in the contents of this chap's first-aid kit.'

'As am I,' said David, picking up the thread. 'I'm certain he must have had a reason for driving like that, but I'm going to have serious words with him about it nonetheless.'

'Thank you,' I said, rubbing my itchy calves together and biting my lip. 'I'd appreciate that. I would be doing it myself if I was still talking to him.'

'You haven't really fallen out with him, have you?' frowned David.

I thought back to the shower scene, the Minnie incident and now this latest painful run-in.

'Let's just say he isn't exactly top of my Christmas card list,' I said pointedly.

Chapter 9

After our meeting at the bank, which was cut rather short thanks to Minnie, who howled pitifully if I was out of sight for more than five seconds together, David offered to treat me to tea and cake at The Cherry Tree Café, so we could talk through the final few details of Gwen's legacy.

Thankfully there wasn't all that much to discuss and I tried my best to stay focused on what David was saying rather than becoming distracted by the nudges, nods and blatant stares coming from a few of the other customers who had no doubt worked out who I was.

When we finally finished, and with Minnie still happily ensconced with a bowl of water in the shade under our little table in the café's front garden, it was time to properly meet the team who I had already heard so much about. I felt pretty certain they were going to be a friendly bunch and thankfully my thoughts were soon confirmed.

'Angela guessed who you were when she spotted Minnie,' gushed a pretty woman with a riot of red unruly curls and freckles to match.

'Yes,' I agreed, glancing at the other tables. 'She is a bit of a giveaway, isn't she?'

'Just a bit,' she laughed. 'So how are you settling in to life at Cuckoo Cottage?'

'I haven't really started yet,' I admitted, wondering if this was the baking queen David had been singing the praises of. 'But I am enjoying the peace and quiet.'

'Oh, I bet there's plenty of that,' said the woman, rolling her eyes. 'Penny to a pound you've got no mobile signal, and I know for a fact that Gwen had no internet connection set up.'

'But you can always come and use ours until you get yourself sorted,' said another member of the café staff who came to help clear away our empty plates. 'I'm Jemma, by the way,' she added.

'Oh, and I'm Lizzie,' laughed the redhead, her curls bouncing. 'I probably should have told you that.'

'Don't worry about it,' I reassured her. 'It seems to me that pretty much everyone around here remembers who I am, so it stands to reason that you'd think I already know your name.'

'Very true,' she smiled. 'But don't worry about that lot,' she added quietly, nodding in the direction of the tables closest. 'They'll move on to gossiping about someone else soon enough.'

I nodded back, hoping she was right.

'Well,' she said, 'I'd better get back to work. I've got a crafting session to prepare for this afternoon.'

'That's what Lizzie does,' Jemma explained. 'She runs all sorts of crafting courses and sewing sessions here at the café. If you're interested in that sort of thing, Lottie, you'll have to have a look at the schedule and see if you fancy signing up.'

'I'd love to come along,' I said, thinking that the best thing I could do to curb the name-calling and speculation would be to brazen it out and immerse myself in what the town had to offer, even if I would have to force myself to do it. 'I tried to teach myself how to crochet last winter,' I admitted, 'but I couldn't get the hang of it at all. I can knit well enough, thanks to my gran, but the fine art of self-taught crochet has eluded me completely for some reason.'

'In that case, I reckon the weekly knit and natter afternoon would be perfect for you,' called Lizzie over her shoulder. 'We do all sorts of things at that. Bet we could get you on track in a jiffy. We aren't running at the moment but we'll be starting again in the autumn.'

'I'll keep it in mind,' I nodded. 'It would be handy to have another reason for popping to town to eat more of this delectable cake.'

Not that you could really categorise the journey from Cuckoo Cottage to Wynbridge town centre by bike as 'popping' to town, of course.

'You really do need to think seriously about this car business,' frowned David. 'It's all very well cycling in when the sun's shining, but on a wet Wednesday in winter you won't be so keen.'

I could understand the reasoning behind his suggestion, and Chris and Matt's, but deep down I was still resistant to the idea, even though they didn't know why.

'I think I'll just see how things go for now,' I said, keen to take baby steps into my new life, rather than diving in off the high board. 'I'll get settled in for a few weeks and then see how I feel.'

My head began to thump as I realised the question of my mobility wasn't going to go away and I braced myself for David's nagging to commence, but it didn't happen. To my surprise, he fell silent and when I looked up I could see that he had forgotten all about me and was watching the lady who had served us when we first arrived, and who Lizzie had identified as Angela.

As if aware of David's gaze, Angela turned to look at him and smiled. When I looked back at David I saw a slight blush lighting up his usually pale complexion and I couldn't help thinking that perhaps there was a little romance blossoming here. However, I hastily nipped the thought in the bud, remembering how annoyed I had been by Chris's insistence just a couple of days before that he was going to try and 'find me a fella'.

'Feel free to use our Wi-Fi code if you need to catch up with emails or anything, won't you, Lottie?' said Jemma as she rushed by with another packed tray. 'The signal's great here.'

'Actually,' I said, suddenly remembering what David had said about Jemma helping Gwen access the internet, 'you wouldn't happen to have a minute, would you, just a few seconds for a quick chat?'

She made a hasty scan of the tables, most of which were filling with customers hoping to tuck into an early lunch, and nodded.

'Give me ten minutes to get these orders through,' she said with a wink, 'and I'll come back.'

'Thanks,' I smiled. 'I'd really appreciate it.'

'And do you think I could have our bill please?' asked David. 'If it's all right with you, Lottie, I really do need to get back to the office.'

'Of course,' I said, 'and please let me pay for this. It's the very least I can do, considering how much you've done for me during the last few months. I'm sure you've helped with far more than you were obligated to as Gwen's solicitor.'

'Well, perhaps I have,' he admitted with a smile, 'but don't forget I was her friend as well.'

He wouldn't let me pay of course and having given Angela another wistful glance he settled our bill and went back to work.

'He's a lovely man, isn't he?' said Angela, who arrived with another cup of delicious coffee courtesy of Jemma.

'From what I've seen and experienced he's an absolute gem,' I agreed, 'and I hope you don't mind me saying,' I rushed on, completely ignoring my former conviction to keep my observations to myself, 'but from what I could tell, he seems to think you're a lovely lady.'

'Oh, I don't know about that,' said Angela, colouring deeply and looking mortified, 'but we are good friends.'

I looked at her and raised my eyebrows.

'And nothing more,' she said with a smile. 'You naughty girl!'

'See,' said Jemma, sidling up and playfully plucking at Angela's sleeve. 'Lottie's only been here five minutes and she's already spotted how David feels about you.'

'Two naughty girls,' tutted Angela, shaking her head. 'What vivid imaginations you have.'

When she had gone back inside I picked up my coffee and took a long sip.

'I shouldn't have said anything,' I said. 'I hate it when people try and play matchmaker in my life, so I should know better really.'

'Oh, don't worry about it,' shrugged Jemma. 'Lizzie and I have been trying to push those two together for months. She's no doubt getting used to our attempts to interfere by now.'

In spite of what I had just said I was still intrigued.

'So I'm guessing she and David are in a position to . . .' I stumbled for the right word.

'Date?' suggested Jemma, raising her eyebrows.

'Exactly.'

'Yes,' she nodded, 'they are. Both widowed. David more recently than Angela, but they're both free agents. They just need a bit of encouragement, that's all. We'll keep working on them,' she said determinedly. 'Don't you worry about that.'

I was relieved that I hadn't really put my foot in it or opened up a brand new can of worms, but I didn't think I'd mention the situation again. After all, I still didn't really know anyone involved well enough to justify sticking my nose quite so far in.

'So,' said Jemma, 'was there something in particular you wanted to talk to me about?'

'Yes,' I said, thinking back to the treasure tucked away in the barn, 'there is actually. You said yourself that Gwen had no internet access at the cottage, didn't you?'

'Yes, that's right.'

'But she used to come here to use your computer, didn't she?'

'She did,' Jemma confirmed. 'In fact she was very proficient. Had she got access sorted at home, I'm certain there would have been no stopping her.'

'I can well believe that,' I agreed. 'I can't imagine that a woman like Gwen would let something as trivial as modern technology hold her back from making the most of every opportunity life offered her.'

'Quite,' beamed Jemma, 'and I'm guessing,' she added, eyeing me sharply, 'that you want to talk to me about what she dedicated her time as a silver surfer doing, don't you?'

'Yes,' I confirmed. 'I do. David said you helped her find the four pretty little caravans that are now safely tucked away in the barn, but what I'm trying to figure out is what she thought I would want to do with them when I moved here.'

'Well, given the passion she said you had for your job, I'm sure she thought you would be able to guess.' Jemma winked.

'I'm sure she did,' I conceded, knowing that Gwen was most likely encouraging me to set up my own business just as John and Eric had done. 'And I'm thrilled by the idea of renovating and restyling them, just like the projects I worked on in Lincoln, but I think there's more to it than that. Gwen was very particular in the vans she sourced and I can't shrug off the feeling that she probably didn't want me to sell them on.'

'Well, I'm sorry to disappoint you, my lovely,' Jemma frowned, 'but I don't know about that. Given the way she talked about how much you loved your job, I just assumed that she was buying the vans for you to sell on once they'd been through your expert hands.'

I felt the colour rise in my cheeks. I'd never been good at accepting compliments.

'I really am sure there's more to it than that,' I sighed. 'Three of the vans are almost exactly the same, right down to the builder, but the fourth,' I mused, thinking of the little Bailey, 'that's a bit different.'

I was trying to look for a link that might give me a clue as to what Gwen had been thinking.

'Now if you're talking about the Bailey,' said Jemma, her tone quiet and conspiratorial, 'we did talk about what you might be able to do with that particular one.'

'Oh really?' I said, leaning further forward in my seat.

'Um,' she said, looking a little flushed. 'I've got this crazy idea, you see . . .'

Unfortunately I didn't get to hear what her idea, crazy or otherwise was, because at that exact moment the café gate opened and Minnie began to growl. I'd pretty much forgotten that she was even under the table because she had been so quiet and well behaved, but clearly she hadn't forgotten that she didn't like Matt, who was now sauntering towards us carrying a toolbox and cordless drill.

'Finally,' said Jemma, throwing up her hands and jumping up. 'I'd almost given up on you.'

'Sorry,' he said sheepishly, 'I had an emergency call-out.'

'Well, if you'd been much longer, this would have turned into a full-blown emergency as well!'

'Sorry,' he said again. 'I should have called.'

'Lottie,' said Jemma, determinedly turning her back on the dazzling consolation smile Matt was trying to placate her with, 'would you mind if we carried on chatting about this another day?'

'No, of course not,' I said, desperately struggling to keep Minnie under the table.

'But in the meantime, please don't do anything with that van!' she called over her shoulder as she rushed back to the kitchen, obviously expecting Matt to follow on behind.

'Hello again,' he said, turning back to me.

'Hello,' I said, conscious of the gaze of the two women at the table closest.

'How are the legs?'

'Not too bad, all things considered, and mostly thanks to you.' I smiled. I could see Jemma striding back down the path and looking from one of us to the other, an inquisitive frown forming. 'It's a long story,' I told her before she had a chance to say anything and hoping she wasn't going to expect me to tell it with such a rapt audience.

'Well, you can tell me all about it at as you fix this leak,' she said pointedly to Matt. 'Or would you rather I went and called a plumber?'

'OK, OK,' he said, dutifully making to follow on as she disappeared again. 'Here, Lottie,' he said, rushing back, 'this is what I tried to give you before.'

He handed me a slip of paper with a mobile number on – his, I presumed.

'Give me a call when you want me to come and talk you through those jobs Gwen was planning to have done, or just give me a call,' he shrugged, throwing a cheeky grin over his shoulder, 'whatever.'

With Matt finally inside the café and out of sight, I stowed his number safely away in my dress pocket, ignored the muttering which had escalated next to me and let Minnie out from under the table. She looked absolutely outraged to have been denied her quarry and I wondered what she really would have done had she popped out and found Matt within range of her sharp little teeth.

'Come on, you,' I said. 'Let's go and see if we can find Chris and Marie on the market.'

I took one last look at the café, hoping that Matt wasn't embellishing the details of how we'd met and adding his own 'damsel in distress' subplot. I didn't care if the ladies were appalled by Will's ridiculous driving, but I didn't want any of them jumping to the wrong conclusion about Matt and me, especially Jemma. Having witnessed for myself her dogged determination to throw David and her friend Angela together, I certainly didn't want to find myself the unwilling target of yet another Wynbridge matchmaker.

'Well, well, well, if it isn't Miss Foster.'

So preoccupied with worrying about what was being

said in the café, I hadn't noticed I was on a collision course. Jumping to the side of the path and pulling Minnie along with me, I stared up at the thickset, burly, unshaven face of a man I didn't recognise.

'Sorry,' I blushed. 'I didn't see you . . .'

'Not to worry,' he said, fixing me with a long stare. 'I dare say you don't remember me, do you?'

'No,' I said, 'sorry.'

'Well, I remember you,' he said, clearly enjoying the moment. 'You used to come on the seaside trip with your nan and grandad every summer, didn't you? It's funny how you've not been seen around here for ages then suddenly pop up once you've inherited Cuckoo Cottage.'

I felt myself go hot and thought how deluded David had been to suggest my arrival would fail to raise a comment.

'So how is our little bird settling into her nest then?'

Unnerved as I was, I felt my hackles rising as fast as Minnie's had when Matt was in close proximity.

'Got any plans for the place yet?'

'Not that it's anyone's business, but no,' I said primly, 'not yet. However, life at Cuckoo Cottage is every bit as lovely as it always was, thanks.'

'We all thought you might be keen to sell on rather than move in.'

I glanced around, wondering if by 'all' he meant practically every resident in town.

Heidi Swain

'I'm not going anywhere,' I said, daring to look him in the eye and wishing I had been blessed with a few more inches to help me stand my ground.

'Well,' he shrugged, 'if you do find it all a bit too much to cope with I'm sure you won't have any problems getting rid.'

'Look,' I swallowed, backing towards the gate and reaching for my bike, 'I hate to disappoint you, but I have no intention of going anywhere.'

'Well, we'll see,' he laughed after me. 'I give you six months, seven tops.'

That was funny I thought, because Gwen had given me twelve.

Given what I could remember of it from former visits, Wynbridge market looked as if it had recently enjoyed a very healthy growth spurt and it was the perfect spot in which to put some distance between myself and the less than friendly local who was taking bets on how long I would last living in the sticks.

Not only were there more stalls, including a great hardware stall where I found a padlock for the big shed, but there was also a really nice vibe and camaraderie about the place. The stallholders called out happily to one another and I could see there were quite a few more shops opened up as well. Next time I cycled in I really needed to find a way to leave Minnie behind at the cottage so I could have a proper look around.

Unusually there was no sight or sound of Chris, but I soon spotted Marie.

'Hello, Lottie,' she waved, beckoning me over. 'How are you? How are you settling in? You're looking a bit peaky, my love,' she added, taking a step closer. 'Are you all right?'

I had no intention of mentioning the little spat I had just had at the café, even though it had upset me far more than it probably should have, given that I had been forewarned.

'I'm fine,' I told her, with a brave smile, 'and I'm settling in beautifully,' I added, 'thanks to you.'

She waved a hand and shook her head, but I wasn't going to let her get away with that.

'No,' I said firmly. 'I really mean it, Marie. I've stayed at Cuckoo Cottage often enough in the past to know what Gwen's attitude towards housekeeping and polishing the family silver was. The place is absolutely sparkling.'

'Well, I was hoping you wouldn't mind,' she said cautiously, 'because I did give it a thorough going-over. Given everything you've been through in the last few months, I thought you could do without having to do a proper deep clean on top of everything else, and besides,' she added, 'it's easier to do a really good job when no one's at home. You don't mind, do you?'

'Of course not,' I told her, keen to dismiss her fears and express how genuinely grateful I was.

'Only I got part of the way through and Chris said I should have asked you before I even started,' she shook her head. 'I felt awful after that, but I could hardly stop, could I? I had to finish and then I just crossed my fingers and hoped you wouldn't notice.'

I had to laugh out loud when she said that.

'How could I possibly not notice, Marie? The place is spotless, but no, I don't mind at all that you didn't ask.'

'Well, that's a relief,' she sighed, puffing out her cheeks. 'I'm delighted I haven't upset you because, believe me, even just the thought of telling Chris that he'd been right was too much to contemplate!'

'Where is he today?' I laughed.

'He's had to pop to the wholesaler's,' she said, 'but he shouldn't be long. Do you want to hang on to see him?'

'No,' I said, 'that's OK. I'll just have a quick look at Gwen's old stall.'

'Oh now that's typical,' said Marie, shaking her head. 'It isn't set up today, but it will be tomorrow.'

'There isn't a problem with keeping it going, is there?'

'No, no,' she reassured me. 'Not at all. There's just been a bit of a hiccup with the rota today. Can you possibly come back tomorrow?'

I thought about having to cycle the journey in the sun two days in a row.

'Oh, I'm forgetting,' said Marie, 'bit of a trek on two

wheels in this heat, isn't it? You need to get yourself sorted with a little car.'

'Oh Marie,' I groaned, 'not you as well! Everyone I've spoken to keeps telling me I need a car. Oh and a man. Apparently my life will only be complete when I've got four wheels in the yard and two feet under my table!'

Marie burst out laughing.

'Sorry, love,' she chuckled. 'Have I hit a bit of a nerve?'

'Yeah,' I sighed, 'just a bit.'

'Well,' she said in a low voice and with a nod towards The Cherry Tree Café where we could see Matt packing up his tools. 'From what I heard a few minutes ago, you're already well on your way to ticking one of those things off your list. What do you have to say about that?'

I was saved from having to say anything by the timely arrival of two other stallholders, who introduced themselves as Harriet and Rachel.

'And of course we already know you're Lottie,' laughed Rachel.

'Of course you do,' I said. 'It's Minnie, isn't it?' I suggested, pointing at the scruffy little bundle who was showing absolutely no interest in any of the three women. 'She's a bit of a giveaway, isn't she?'

'Nope,' said Harriet, 'I hadn't even taken Minnie into account.'

'So how ...'

'Mags works for us,' cut in Rachel. 'She's helping us get our plant nursery ready for its launch and has been full of excitement about her lovely new neighbour.'

'She's over the moon to have a girl living up the road,' Harriet added with a smile. 'I think she was feeling a bit fed up being so outnumbered by the menfolk.'

Given that one of her neighbours was Will, I couldn't say I blamed her, but I didn't say as much. Practically everyone I had spoken to about him so far had him pinned as 'Warrior Will the Great' so there was little to be gained from trying to convince them that he was actually whatever word beginning with 'w' was most derogatory.

'So we'll see you at the party on Saturday,' said Rachel. 'Mags said she was going to give you a lift.'

'Yes,' I said, 'I'll be there.'

'Oh, and Matt will be too,' added Harriet with a wink as she watched him driving away from the café. 'So you won't need to worry about looking for a date.'

Chapter 10

My trip into Wynbridge had given me a lot to think about during the long cycle ride back to Cuckoo Cottage and, relieved as I was to have everything to do with Gwen's legacy settled, there was now a plethora of other problems jostling to step up and take centre stage in my head and I was determined not to let one outspoken bully stop me getting to grips with what was most important or hinder me from focusing my attention on sorting out my future.

I still wasn't any the wiser as to what Gwen really had in mind for me or those four pretty caravans but she was obviously aware of how much I loved my job and had thought I would be chomping at the bit to give them a makeover, which indeed I was, but I was sure there was more to the situation than that. *'Think big, Lottie!'* she and Gran had always said, *'Take your passion to the very limits of what you can achieve.'*

I simply had to find an opportunity to talk to Jemma again as soon as possible and find out what the 'crazy plan' was that she had come up with for the Bailey. Perhaps once I knew the details of that, the rest would simply slip into place. Well, that was what I was hoping would happen, because nothing would please me more than announcing to the world what I was going to do and stop all the chinwagging and speculation once and for all.

Also on my mind was the fast-approaching party at Skylark Farm, which I really wanted to look forward to. However, wondering whether I would face another confrontation from a disgruntled guest, coupled with the knowing looks that had passed between Marie, Harriet and Rachel when Matt stepped out of the Cherry Tree, had somewhat tempered my enthusiasm for the event. Yes, Matt was hot. Yes, he had been an absolute hero stepping in with his calamine and caresses that morning, but I certainly wouldn't be adding fuel to the gossips' fire and calling him to help with any jobs at the cottage now. I would have to resort to flicking through the Yellow Pages and hoping my eyes alighted on some genuine tradesman's advert, rather than one of these rogue traders you hear so much about on mid-morning TV.

My resolve to look for an alternative Mr Fix-It didn't last, of course. One lukewarm bath that evening, which did nothing to soothe my aching muscles or my nettle-scarred calves, sent me scurrying to the understairs cupboard the next morning to check out the fuse box and weigh up whether or not trying to take a shower that day was worth the risk. It wasn't. From what I could make out, the box was one of those old-fashioned contraptions which required much intricate fiddling and attaching of new pieces of wire somewhere deep inside the mysterious workings every time the electricity went off.

Needless to say, it was way beyond my skills, which were limited to flicking a switch, and a quick look through some old calendars Gwen had kept in the sideboard confirmed that the power did indeed have a tendency to cut out on a fairly regular basis, but especially when there was a thunderstorm in the vicinity.

No, this needed sorting out, and as I had been acquainted with just one tradesman since my move, and in spite of those knowing looks between Marie, Harriet and Rachel, he was the one I was going to have to call in the hope that he would be able to engage the services of a competent spark on my behalf, and preferably before I saw sparks myself.

Dark clouds were beginning to gather on the horizon as I reached for Matt's number and I had everything crossed that when he came out to assess the work, his van on the drive would go undetected and the matchmakers of Wynbridge would move on to interfering in some other poor soul's love life.

'What do you think, Minnie?' I asked, bending down and scooping her into my arms. 'Do you think I should I ring him or not?'

She wriggled free and went back to her basket, clearly intent on reminding me that she would tolerate being held and fussed when and if she chose to be. The giving and receiving of affection was still very much practised on her haughty terms and I would just have to accept a cuddle when she deemed I was fit to receive one.

'Sometimes,' I told her, 'I think you should have been born a cat.'

Clearly disgusted by the slur on her performance as a pooch, she turned her back on me and I picked up the phone.

'Matt?'

'Hey, Lottie.'

'How did you know it was me?' I frowned.

Surely I wasn't *that* predictable?

'Gwen's name flashed up when the phone rang,' he explained. 'I'm going to have to replace it with yours now, aren't I?'

'Oh,' I said huskily, biting my lip. 'Yes, I suppose you will.'

I didn't much like the thought of Gwen being nudged off the contact list on Matt's phone and being consigned to nothing more than memory. Sometimes I could be practical about what had happened, but it was still the little things which had the ability to hurt the most and send me reeling. I still wanted her and Gran to live forever of course, and not just in my heart and mind.

'So what can I do for you?' asked Matt, clearly clueless that his perfectly innocuous suggestion had had any impact on me at all. 'Is this a call about the cottage or the "just give me a call" call I was hoping for?'

'Sorry to disappoint you,' I told him, feeling determined to keep things on a professional footing from the off, 'but this is strictly cottage business.'

'That's a shame,' he sighed. 'Not that I don't want the work, of course, but it's a bummer knowing those cheesy pick-up lines really don't work after all.'

I began to laugh at the mention of the conversation we'd had on the road the day before.

'To tell you the truth,' I told him, 'I'm just relieved that you knew they were cheesy.'

'Hey!'

'Sorry,' I said, 'but come on, you have to admit they were bad.'

'When I came out with all that stuff, I was actually trying to pay you a compliment,' he said faux huffily, the smile still very present in his tone. 'I was trying to flatter you, you know. Make you feel as pretty as you looked in your lovely summer dress.'

Suddenly I realised he'd pulled me straight into the flirtatious back and forth I'd been so keen to avoid, but I didn't resist it. If anything, I felt my spirit perk up. Chris and the others would have been delighted, had they been privy to the conversation.

'Lottie?' I heard Matt say. 'Are you still there?'

'Yes,' I said. 'Sorry. I got distracted.'

'Minnie isn't giving you the runaround by any chance, is she?'

'Do you know,' I said, no doubt sounding as amazed as I felt, 'so far, she's been as good as gold.'

I hoped I wasn't talking anything up.

'Apart from when I'm in the vicinity, of course,' Matt reminded me.

'Hmm,' I sighed. 'Yes, I'd forgotten how much she loves you. Perhaps I should be on my guard,' I joked. 'Dogs are supposed to have some kind of sixth sense when it comes to sniffing out unreliable human beings, aren't they?'

'Oh nice,' Matt snorted. 'Thanks for that, and there was me apologising for the cheesy chat-up lines and all you do is throw insults at me.'

'Oh, shut up,' I retaliated, knowing he was joshing. 'You know I'm teasing. I wouldn't have said it if I meant it, would I?'

'I suppose not,' he said equably. 'So when do you want me to come and see you, then?'

I noticed he didn't ask when I wanted him to come and have a look at the work that needed doing.

'Whenever suits,' I shrugged. 'I'm easy.'

Matt didn't say anything.

'Well done for resisting that one,' I applauded.

'It was a stretch,' he groaned. 'I was actually biting my tongue.'

'Seriously, though,' I said, quickly dismissing all thoughts of Matt's soft, pink tongue, 'I'm not planning on going anywhere for the next few days at least, so whenever works best for you.'

I sent up a quick prayer to Thor in the hope that he would keep his storms away from my little cottage and the power lines that supplied it with electricity in the interim.

'Muscles still recovering from the bike ride, by any chance?'

'Not at all,' I said. 'I'm actually more worried about getting run off the road again.'

I wasn't about to tell him that, yes, I was still feeling pretty wrung out by the journey as well as bruised by the words of the burly brute in the café.

'And how's the rash?'

'Not quite so bad as it was,' I said, looking down at my still sore calves. 'Although it did smart a bit when I had a bath, even though the water was barely warm.'

'And what about the demon driver,' he asked. 'Have you seen any more of him?'

'Thankfully, no,' I said. 'I haven't even heard him roaring by.'

'Then I dare say he's got wind of what happened and has decided to drive the long way home.'

'What, already?' I frowned. 'Word really does travel fast around here, doesn't it?'

'David was moaning about him in the pub last night,' Matt explained. 'I was surprised really because they've always been such good mates.'

'Well, I wouldn't want to come between them,' I said quickly.

The last thing I wanted to do was cause a rift between old friends. I'd only just arrived and I certainly didn't want to be known for stirring up trouble on top of everything else everyone had already assumed about me. I wondered if the guy from the café had caught that particular titbit and passed it on to the bookmakers.

'I'm sure you haven't come between them,' Matt said sensibly. 'But you do seem to have forgotten that you weren't the one driving like a lunatic.'

'I suppose you're right,' I said, distractedly chewing my thumbnail and feeling guilty for being the cause of further gossip nonetheless.

'No suppose about it, and anyway, I reckon David's got a soft spot for you, Lottie Foster.'

'Do you?'

'No doubt in my mind,' he said seriously. 'He and Gwen were very close, had been for years. I reckon he's taken you under his wing; sees himself as a bit of a father figure even.'

'Well, I'm sure he'd be a very good dad,' I said wistfully. 'Not that I have any personal experience in what makes one, of course.'

'What about your dad?' Matt asked. 'Wasn't he up to the job?'

'I never knew him,' I said bluntly. 'Or Mum, for that matter. She left when I was little so I grew up with my gran and grandad.'

'I'm sorry,' he said, sounding every bit as awkward as most people did when they discovered that I had been abandoned by the one person in my life that I should have been able to rely on. 'That must have been tough.'

'Not really,' I said honestly. 'My grandparents were wonderful to me, as was Gwen.'

I was rather taken aback that I had mentioned my upbringing to this man I barely knew. Ordinarily it wasn't up for discussion with anyone, but there was something about Matt's easy-going manner and natural friendliness that had encouraged my confidence.

'So you really are on your own, then,' he reminded me. 'Aren't you?'

'Of course not,' I said firmly. 'I have Minnie.'

'Well, just make sure she's off on her holidays or something when I turn up.' He laughed. 'Otherwise I'm not getting out of the van.'

'I'll check my insurance,' I told him cheekily. 'Make sure I've got some sort of public liability cover.'

'You do that,' he laughed. 'See you soon, Lottie Foster.'

Later that day, Minnie and I went back down to the yard to have another look at the caravans. We had just reached the greenhouse when she began to bark excitedly and prance about on all fours.

'What's got into you?' I said, quickly turning around on the assumption that someone had arrived. 'What is it, you silly dog?'

Out of the corner of my eye I spotted a sudden movement behind the greenhouse and out darted a hare. It was slightly smaller than the one I had startled on the road the day before, but with its massively powerful hind legs and elongated ears, it was still quite a size.

I fully expected it would leap away the second it spotted us, but it didn't. It simply sat in the middle of the drive and stared at the pair of us. We were so close I could see its striking amber eyes in minute detail. It was wild and yet tame, feral but calm, and I watched with interest as it stretched out a leg, had a quick clean between its toes and then, in its own time and with absolutely no concern for either Minnie or me, hopped back behind the greenhouse, through the boundary fence and away into the field.

I had always admired the hares from afar when I used to visit as a youngster, but close encounters with two in as many days left me feeling truly blessed. Cuckoo Cottage was certainly a magical place and I was delighted that magic hadn't disappeared when Gwen died. Whatever I ended up doing here, I vowed there and then that I would do everything within my power to ensure that the wildlife and landscape would be well protected.

'Was that a friend of yours?' I asked Minnie, as we watched the hare move across the field. She woofed in response then shot off down to the barns, clearly intent on gaining entry and ambushing anything that moved. 'Don't worry about me,' I called after her. 'I'll catch you up.'

I hadn't been poking about for many minutes when the sound of dogs barking met my ears. I made a grab for Minnie's collar, but she was too quick for me and dashed outside to discover who had entered her domain. I followed cautiously on, hoping I wasn't about to have to referee some horrendous dog fight, but I needn't have worried.

Two golden Labradors and one shockingly submissive Minnie were rolling about the dusty yard, clearly more intent on becoming acquainted than tearing each other apart.

'Don't panic!' shouted a dark-haired young woman wearing patterned short wellies and a warm smile. 'I wouldn't have dreamt of letting them out if I didn't think Minnie was going to be pleased to see them.'

Clearly she was another local who was familiar with the personality of my temperamental little terrier.

'She really has got herself quite a reputation around here, hasn't she?' I said as I watched the happily reunited trio circle around one another with much sniffing and tail-wagging.

'Oh yes,' said the woman. 'I reckon she's every bit as famous and revered as her former mistress.'

'Well, with an ego the size of Minnie's,' I replied, 'I'm sure she's absolutely delighted about that.'

The woman laughed and bent down to fuss her dogs.

'This pair are Bella and Lily,' she said, straightening back up. 'And I'm Amber. I live at Skylark Farm.'

'You're the lady who issued the party invitation Mags dropped round then,' I smiled. 'Thank you so much.'

'You're most welcome,' she beamed.

'So it really goes without saying that you already know who I am,' I said. 'Don't you?'

'Of course,' she cut in. 'You're Lottie Foster. I know that; we all know.'

'Quite,' I said, chewing my bottom lip. 'Apparently, I'm the current new attraction in Wynbridge who has wheedled her way into receiving this beautiful bequest.'

Amber nodded her head.

'Not that I'm suggesting that you've come to have a nose

around or anything,' I panicked. 'That's not want I meant at all.'

'I know that,' she said. 'And I haven't come to add weight to the cuckoo theory either.'

I had been hoping that Chris was mistaken about how far the silly name-calling had spread, but clearly he was spot on.

'Well, that's a relief,' I said. 'I can't begin to tell you how horrible it is to know people are talking about me behind my back.'

'Oh, I can sympathise with you there,' she said again. Her tone was genuine and the frown that accompanied it suggested that she really did know what I was getting at. 'I left the anonymity of London behind a few years ago,' she explained, 'so I know exactly how you feel, but don't worry, you'll soon be old news. Before long someone else will come along and you won't be the new girl any more. There's always gossip of one kind or another,' she reminded me. 'You just have to brazen it out until people get bored.'

'I suppose you're right,' I agreed. 'But I've never felt so scrutinised in all my life. I keep worrying that I won't live up to expectations or I'll do something silly and make the situation worse.'

I tried to say it as if it was a joke, but actually there was a lot of truth behind the admission.

'I promise you'll be fine,' said Amber, coming to give me a nudge before linking arms as if we were lifelong friends rather than recent acquaintances. 'You just have to stop over-thinking everything and worrying about what's being said in town. Now come on,' she said briskly, 'tell me what you were up to before I so rudely interrupted?'

Chapter 11

Arm in arm, Amber and I walked slowly back down the yard so I could lock up the barn. I had no intention of showing her what was inside. I hadn't shown anyone, not even Mags, but she spotted the vans before I had a chance to pull the big door shut.

'Oh wow,' she gasped. 'My goodness. I always wondered what Gwen kept down here, or are these yours, Lottie?'

'Well, they are now,' I explained, following her inside and knowing I couldn't deny their existence, 'but it was Gwen who collected them. They're part of my legacy apparently. I'm still trying to fathom out exactly what it is she wanted me to do with them.'

We hadn't been chatting for many minutes when I realised the dogs had disappeared.

'Doubtless they'll be in the field,' said Amber sensibly. 'I really wouldn't worry.'

'But I do,' I admitted. 'I know Minnie knows this place like the back of her paw, but I can't help worrying about her. It's such a big responsibility, suddenly having her to look after on top of everything else.'

'It's because she's your link to Gwen,' said Amber, aiming an emotional arrow straight to the very heart of the matter.

I could feel hot tears pricking the back of my eyes and I nodded in agreement, afraid that I wouldn't be able to get the words over the lump in my throat. Without saying anything more, Amber stepped quickly forward and gave me a hug. I hadn't realised I had been holding back the tears, but judging by the brief torrent her kind gesture unleashed, I clearly had.

'Come on,' she said, handing me an embroidered cotton handkerchief once the moment had passed. 'Let's go and call the dogs and have a slice or two of the cake I've got tucked away in the truck.'

We locked the barn and, having tracked down the three dogs, leant over the gate and watched them bounding about the field, their tongues lolling and their exuberance gradually waning. In the distance, I could just make out the hare I'd seen earlier hopping along the furthest boundary.

'It's a great field this,' said Amber with a nod towards the few lush acres that I now owned, but hadn't taken all that much interest in as yet. 'Have you got any plans for it?'

'No,' I said, shaking my head and thinking back to

my argument the day before. No doubt the guy who had approached me at the Cherry Tree would know exactly what to do with the land but I was trying to block him out. 'To be honest, I haven't even looked over it yet, but I know Mags's son, Ed, is keen to keep coming and exploring now I've given him permission.'

'He's a fascinating lad,' Amber smiled. 'What he doesn't know about his local patch, which is pretty vast, simply isn't worth knowing.'

'Mags told me she's sure he's got Durrell blood,' I told her, thinking that the boy would probably have more of an idea about how to look after the place than I did.

'That wouldn't surprise me,' said Amber. 'He's already gathered together quite a collection of furred and feathered waifs and strays.'

'Have you got much land at Skylark Farm?' I asked.

'Yes,' she said. 'A fair bit. Most of it is covered in apple orchards, but we've repurposed the two formerly empty meadows to raise free-range pigs. They graze on the wind-falls in the autumn before they go for slaughter.' She said it as if it was the most natural thing in the world and I realised I had a lot to learn about the realities of life in the country. 'Perhaps you could do something similar here,' she suggested, with a nod towards the field.

Somehow I couldn't see myself as a pig farmer.

'Perhaps,' I said, not wanting to dismiss her land and

livestock idea completely. 'But I think I'd better start with a couple of hens or something first.'

'I might be able to help you out there,' she said thoughtfully. 'We have a few point of lay pullets ready to go, if you're really keen. You could have a look at them when you come to the party.'

'Thanks,' I said, unwilling to admit that I had absolutely no idea what she was talking about. 'So, do you own the farm then?'

'No,' she said, 'the place belongs to my partner Jake's Auntie Annie. We live there with her and our daughter Honey.'

'Well, it all sounds lovely,' I said. 'The perfect set-up.'

'It is now,' she said dreamily, 'but if you'd told me a few years ago that my future revolved around living in the country, raising pigs and birthing a beautiful daughter, I never would have believed you.'

'So you didn't always want to live in the Fens then?'

'No,' she laughed. 'I didn't, and believe me, it's not been easy turning around the fortunes of Skylark Farm either, but I wouldn't change a thing. I loved the place from the very first night I arrived.'

She called sharply to the dogs, who obediently came running with Minnie trailing behind and we all strolled back towards the cottage. As we walked, Amber explained about the farm's other diversification projects. There was cider, made from their own apples, on an ever-increasing scale, and an income from letting out a little bungalow she had renovated and which was called Meadowview Cottage.

I couldn't help but admire Amber's ambition and determination to secure the future of Skylark Farm for her daughter and wondered if I could find a really challenging diversification project for Cuckoo Cottage. Something that would utilise both my skills as well as everything the place had to offer, rather than just the barns. That would certainly show everyone who had been so quick to doubt my ability to do anything productive with the place that I was here to stay.

I unlocked the cottage door and set about making tea while Amber gave the dogs some water outside and collected the cake from the truck.

'It's nothing fancy, I'm afraid,' she shrugged as she handed over the tin. 'I can manage a decent Vicky sponge, but I can't compete with the fancy bakes Jemma whips up at The Cherry Tree Café.'

'I was drooling over the cake counter in there yesterday,' I admitted. 'She and Lizzie have got a really thriving business, haven't they?'

'They certainly have,' Amber agreed, 'and do you know, now you've mentioned them, I think I might know what Gwen had in mind for at least one of those vans after all. You slice the cake,' she instructed, 'while I grab Annie's house-warming present and then I'll fill you in.'

Sitting in the shade of Gwen's beloved tree, I thanked Amber for the delectable cake and admired the red spotty jug crammed full of bright summer blooms that were Annie's way of welcoming me to Wynbridge.

'Pretty, aren't they?' said Amber, her head cocked to one side as she followed my gaze.

'Stunning,' I agreed.

'And all grown from seed and for less than a tenner,' she laughed. 'Annie can't work like she used to on the farm when she was younger, so now she's more involved in developing the garden around the house. Cut flowers have been her new project for this year and she's managed to fill the farmhouse and Meadowview since the beginning of May.'

'Well, you certainly all sound like a resourceful bunch,' I said, pouring us both another cup of tea. 'I can't seem to see my way ahead here at all. It's all such a muddle still.'

'But you only moved in a few days ago,' Amber said kindly. 'And you're still grieving. Don't be so tough on yourself. When the right thing comes along, you'll know what it is.'

'I guess you're right,' I sighed, 'but one thing I am certain of is that Gwen had more of a reason for buying those vans than simply giving me the opportunity to make them look pretty.' I leant forward and brushed the cake crumbs from my lap.

'Oh, I almost forgot,' tutted Amber, smacking herself on

the forehead. 'Sorry,' she laughed, 'baby brain, I'm afraid.'

I had assumed Honey was beyond the baby stage and was about to say as much, but spotting the colour flooding Amber's face decided not to. It was obvious that she had just unwittingly let slip something that was supposed to be a secret and it wouldn't have been fair to pursue it.

'You did say you thought you knew what Gwen had planned for one of the vans,' I said instead.

'That's right,' she nodded. 'I can't be certain, but I think it could be something to do with Jemma at the Cherry Tree.'

'Well, yes,' I said, sitting up straighter in my chair, 'that would fit in with what Jemma said yesterday when I was asking her about Gwen using the café's Wi-Fi. Unfortunately she didn't get a chance to explain in any detail, but she did mention she had a "crazy idea" for the Bailey.'

Amber nodded thoughtfully.

'Occasionally we host weddings at the farm,' she explained, weaving her own thread into the story, 'and Jemma and Lizzie do some of the catering and quite often the styling.'

I could imagine how beautiful the weddings would be, given how picture-perfect the café was.

'And at the last one Jemma mentioned some sort of plan to expand the business. I'm sure,' she said, frowning in concentration, 'that she was talking about finding some sort of practical way to go mobile.'

'A mobile Cherry Tree Café,' I smiled. 'How wonderful.'

'I think that could be it,' said Amber, 'but don't quote me on it. I might have completely got the wrong end of the stick, though, because let's face it, none of those vans look anything like Cherry Tree chic, do they?'

'No,' I agreed, 'but they could by the time I've finished with them.'

If Jemma was going to ask me to transform the Bailey into some sort of tearoom on the go at least that would give me something to get stuck into while I was making up my mind about what to do with the Cheltenham vans.

'Really?'

'Absolutely,' I told her. 'That was my job before I moved here, renovating caravans and campers.'

'Oh wow,' said Amber. 'How exciting!'

'It can be,' I went on, 'especially if you get the chance to be involved with all the finishing touches. Some of the interiors I've helped put together have been exquisite.'

I could feel my excitement bubbling up again and something new adding to it and settling comfortingly into place as I thought back to some of the wonderful projects I had been involved in.

'I'm a bit obsessed with all things retro, you see,' I admitted, 'especially anything from the forties and fifties.'

'In that case I can't wait to show you Meadowview Cottage,' said Amber excitedly.

'Really?' I smiled, feeling intrigued.

'Absolutely,' she beamed. 'I'll give you a tour when you come to the party, but I already know you're going to love it. It's beautifully authentic, you see, thanks to Annie's hoarding in the attic. The place was stuffed to the rafters with fabulous things that her family had fortunately hung on to so I could match the interior to the decade the place was built.'

'Which was?'

'The fifties, of course!'

'Oh wow,' I sighed. 'That sounds like a dream renovation project. I can't wait to see it.'

'Well, who would have thought,' laughed Amber, reaching for another slice of cake. 'We're like peas in a pod.'

'You know what,' I agreed, looking at her, then around the garden and back towards the barns, 'I think we probably are.'

It was late afternoon before Amber rounded up the dogs ready to head back to the farm.

'Well, it's been wonderful to meet you,' she said, pulling me in for another hug. 'And I'm delighted we have so much in common.'

'Same here,' I said, giving her a squeeze. 'And I really appreciate the visit. I have to admit I was feeling a bit nervous about just turning up to the party of someone I didn't even know, but now I'm really looking forward to it.'

'Well, that's good,' she said. 'It can be lonely living out in the Fen. I have Jake and Annie and Honey, of course, but even I feel it sometimes. We are very much on our own out here, but I won't begin the "you need to get yourself a car" lecture, because from what I've heard, you're already familiar with that one!'

I didn't bother asking how she knew.

'Oh yes,' I said, 'I'm expecting a fleet of potential little runabouts to land on the drive any day now.'

Amber rolled her eyes and shrugged her shoulders.

'Bless you,' she smiled, 'try not to let everyone's interference get you down,' she added. 'Most of them mean well.'

'Oh, I know,' I said, trying not to think of what the rest meant, 'and I do appreciate it, it's just taking some getting used to.'

'Of course,' she said, loading the dogs into the back of the truck. 'It's bound to.'

I watched enviously as she made a competent three-point turn.

'I'll see you Saturday,' she called, 'and we'll definitely have a look around the bungalow and sort you out with those hens.'

'Great,' I swallowed, wondering what on earth I was letting myself in for on the fowl front. 'See you then.'

Chapter 12

The heart-warming and considerate visit from Amber, who was not only a fellow vintage and upcycling enthusiast, but also an ambitious and driven woman, was perfectly timed to crank my own plans up a notch. Before she came I knew it would have been all too easy for me to satisfy my critics by sitting back and watching the summer unfold, then heading blindly into autumn having achieved nothing more than paying someone to install a new shower and fuse box, but I was determined not to let that be my only achievement now.

During the next couple of days I began to make a list, not the usual washing-up liquid and loaf of bread kind of list, like the one I still had from Gwen on the hall table, but a thrilling and motivated 'things I could do with this place' version. Listening to Amber talk so passionately about the makeover she had given Meadowview, along with everything else that she and Jake had achieved at Skylark Farm, I realised she was an entrepreneur with a heart, who had maximised the potential of what she had to hand, and I hoped very much that I would be able to achieve the same at Cuckoo Cottage. As I scribbled away on my notepad, I couldn't help thinking that Gwen and Gran would have been proud of this creative and determined upsurge and I imagined the pair of them looking over my shoulder and smiling like a pair of pensionable guardian angels.

I was both intrigued and excited by the idea of creating a mobile Cherry Tree Café and resolved to cycle back to Wynbridge, in spite of feeling nervous about facing more scrutiny and hostility. I wanted to find out if Amber was right about Jemma's plan for the Bailey, and if she was, I hoped she would be happy to offer me the project so I could begin straightaway.

For the first time since I arrived at Cuckoo Cottage I could see myself actually achieving something with real clarity and, if Jemma agreed to my suggestions, I could set about repurposing that little van and getting my creative juices flowing again. I was sure that once I was back in the zone other ideas would soon follow and with any luck I would hit upon the idea of how to combine vintage caravans, empty barns and a couple of acres into something wonderfully worthwhile that the locals couldn't possibly object to.

*

'Amber told us you're planning to have a few hens,' called Mags as she pulled on to the drive.

She and Ed had taken to popping in every day, either just after breakfast or before teatime, depending on how long it had taken Ed to get everything together for his day of adventuring. Harriet and Rachel's nursery, Mags had explained, was on land that used to belong to Harriet's father's farm and included 'The Pit' which, once literally a hole in the ground, was now a vast pond teeming with bulrushes, birdlife and all manner of aquatic delights. It was the perfect environment for Ed to indulge his passions and consequently the little yellow minivan was always packed with nets, jars, buckets and boxes and, of course, one belligerent Jackdaw. Today, however, the load in the back looked a little different.

'Oh, did she now?' I said, leaving my notepad on the table in the shade to go and see what it was that Mags was chauffeuring.

'That is right, isn't it?' she asked, climbing out and opening the back doors. 'That's why we've come to give you this.'

'It's my spare,' explained Ed, as he and his mother man-handled a neat little chicken coop on to the drive. 'I thought I could help you set it up.'

'Well, in that case,' I smiled, 'yes. I'm having some hens.'

Minnie skittered unhelpfully around our feet as we lugged the pretty little wooden house about looking for the best spot.

'There's a run that goes with it,' puffed Mags, 'but we

couldn't get it all in in one trip. I really do need to get a bigger van,' she mused.

'Do you think I'll need a run as well?' I grimaced, as we awkwardly manoeuvred the coop towards the side of the greenhouse. 'Can't I just let them run free?'

'Foxes,' said Ed with a shake of his curly head. 'You don't want to lose the hens as soon as you've got them. Let them start off in the run and then think about giving them a wider area to explore when you're here.'

'OK,' I said, grateful for his practical advice and knowledge. 'Right.'

'I'll set the run up if you like,' he said. 'I built it myself so I know how to put it back together really quickly. It's a kind of flat-pack contraption. It would be no bother.'

'As with most things at our place, it's a bit Heath Robinson, but Ed's done a great job,' said Mags proudly. 'As always.'

'Super,' I said. 'Thank you.'

At least I knew who I could turn to should I find myself struggling with the intricacies of amateur hen-keeping; Ed was clearly an expert. Once satisfied that we had found the perfect position, he disappeared into the field with Minnie, and Mags and I sliced up the rest of Amber's delicious cake to have with the bottle of apple juice she had kindly sent for me to sample.

'So have you hit upon your big idea yet?' Mags asked, with a nod to my notepad and pen.

I hadn't expected to make such firm friends so quickly, but both Amber and Mags had been so helpful and kind that I found myself, although usually more guarded, 'letting them in' and had consequently shown both of them the vans now. Just as I had with Amber earlier in the week, I had also explained to Mags that Gwen had acquired them with me in mind, but beyond renovating them I was clueless as to what the 'grand plan' was.

'Not yet,' I sighed.

'You need to get out more,' she said, pouring juice and eyeing me shrewdly. 'Broaden your horizons.'

'What do you mean?' I asked, taking a long sip of the tangy, apple-infused essence.

'Well, it isn't good for you, is it?' she said. 'Being stuck here all day with only that rusty old bike to take you as far as your legs can pedal, you'll never make any progress like that.'

'But I see you and Ed every day,' I reminded her, 'and Amber has called in and Matt's coming to look at what needs doing to the cottage. I've got plenty to keep me occupied.'

'He's the nettle guy, isn't he?'

'Yes,' I said, trying not to meet her eye.

'Another dish,' she said wistfully.

'Another?'

'Will,' she reminded me with a playful smile. 'A pretty girl like you, Lottie, you're going to be fighting them off soon.'

'Except you're forgetting one thing,' I reminded her.

'Oh?'

'I can't stand the sight of Will, no matter how dishy he is, and Matt and I are strictly business, nothing more.'

She looked at me and waggled her eyebrows.

'Besides,' I said firmly, 'like I told Chris, I don't want or need a man right now. I'm far too busy trying to work out what I'm going to do with my own life to have to factor someone else's into it.'

'Which is why you need to get out more,' she said, tracking back to her original point. 'I'm sure if you had a bit of distance from the situation, inspiration would strike.'

'Really?'

'Really,' she confirmed. 'In my experience that's how all the best ideas come about. You have to stop thinking about it, Lottie, get yourself away from here for a bit, even if it is for just a few hours. At the moment it's all too close. Life's all about striking the right balance, isn't it?'

'Well, there's the party at Skylark Farm Saturday night,' I reminded her as Ed hopped over the gate. 'Let's see what comes to mind after that, shall we?'

I was delighted the next day when Matt's van turned up, but my sunny disposition was soon heading for the hills thanks to Minnie's less than hospitable welcome. She certainly wasn't up for playing the gracious hostess if Matt was the only guy on the guest list.

'Where won't you need to look?' I shouted over the noise of her persistent yapping and growling.

'The greenhouse,' he suggested with a straight face. 'You could stick her in there until she cools off.'

I looked at the greenhouse, the searing sun and cloudless sky and back to Matt again.

'You are joking,' I frowned.

'Of course I am,' he laughed. 'Why don't you just tie her up in the shade under the tree? I'm sure I won't be too long.'

I didn't much like the idea of tying Minnie up anywhere. She might be a complete pain in the backside whenever Matt was in the vicinity, but she'd been subjected to enough drama and trauma during the last few months and as her new owner it certainly wasn't my place to inflict even more.

Matt began to drum his fingers on the steering wheel and I knew I had to make a decision.

'I'll put her in the dining room,' I said, quickly scooping her up before she could object. 'I can't imagine there's anything you'll need to look at in there.'

'Has the damp dried out then?'

'What damp?'

'Last winter there was a terrible patch in the corner under the window.'

'Oh,' I said. 'I can't say I've seen any and it smells all right.'

Minnie began to growl again and wriggle in my arms.

'All right,' said Matt. 'Stick her in there and I'll have a look at that another day.'

Having dumped Minnie in the dining room and made us both a drink, I followed Matt about the cottage, my freshly inflated spirit sinking with every head shake and sharp intake of breath.

'Sounds expensive,' I said when I couldn't cope with the suspense of not knowing a second longer.

'What does?' he frowned as he tucked his pen behind his ear and stretched up to rub at a tiny speck of something on the bathroom ceiling.

I opened my mouth to answer, but catching a tantalising glimpse of his tanned, toned stomach and the slender line of fine blonde hair which led my eyes towards the waistband of his low-slung cargo shorts, the words died in my throat. I quickly turned away, thinking that if the work did turn out to be expensive at least the view of watching him hard at it would make up for some of the cost.

'What sounds expensive?' he asked again.

'Hmm,' I said distractedly, as I played out the little fantasy in my head. 'Oh sorry, it's your body language. Your body language sounds expensive.'

'My body language sounds expensive,' he frowned. 'Lottie, what are you talking about?'

'It's a well-known fact, according to my grandad,' I explained, 'that if a builder goes about shaking his head then that's at least another couple of zeros added to the bill, and God forbid he tuts or chews the end of his pencil, that would mean certain bankruptcy.'

'Is that right?' Matt laughed.

'So he reckoned.' I shrugged.

'Well, I shouldn't worry about any of that,' he smiled. 'I'd already quoted Gwen for most of what needs doing and all the figures we discussed were based on "mates' rates".'

'Well, that's good to know,' I said, feeling somewhat relieved. 'Thank you, Matt. Considering I don't know what you quoted her, you could have plucked any old figure out of the air. That's very generous of you.'

'But how can you be sure?' he teased, pinning me with his beautiful sparkling eyes. 'For all you know, I could be about to pluck numbers out of the air right now. You said yourself you didn't know what I'd quoted Gwen so I could just be adding on those zeros your grandad warned you about.'

'I don't think you'd do that,' I said, squeezing around him and back on to the landing.

'But how do you know?' he pursued.

'Instinct,' I told him. 'Womanly intuition.'

Matt raised his eyebrows and bit his lip and I felt my heart start to thump a little harder.

'I might not know the first thing about household DIY,' I said huskily as I led the way back down to the kitchen, 'but

I know Gwen could read people all right and so can I. I'd recognise a conman if one crossed my path.'

'Well, you might want to have a bit of a rethink about that,' Matt said seriously.

'Why?' I said, spinning round to face him.

'Because you're too trusting by half!'

'No, I'm not,' I said defensively.

I was the last person in the world to go around bestowing my trust willy-nilly.

'Yes,' he laughed. 'You are. Lottie, you never, ever admit to a tradesman, no matter how good his reputation, that you don't know the first thing about what he's turned up to fix.'

'But I don't,' I shrugged, completely missing his point and thinking that if Gwen thought Matt was up to the job then I had absolutely no reason to doubt him or question his ever-growing list of jobs. 'I wouldn't know one end of a U-bend from another.'

Matt groaned and ran a hand through his sun-bleached sandy hair.

'You really are a piece of work,' he laughed.

'What?' I pouted.

I didn't appreciate being laughed at.

'Just promise me,' he said, laying a hand lightly on my shoulder and looking deep into my eyes again, 'that if you decide you don't want me to do the work, promise me you won't get anyone in, or have anything done, unless you've run their name and firm by me first.'

'But—'

'But nothing,' he said, squeezing my shoulder. 'I'm not trying to patronise you or be chauvinistic. You said yourself you haven't got a clue, didn't you?'

'Yes,' I croaked. 'I did.'

'So you promise, then?'

'All right,' I nodded. 'I promise.'

'Good,' he said, removing his hand from my hot skin and waving towards the kettle with a cheeky grin. 'Now make us another drink, good woman, and I'll tell you the damage.'

I peered into the depths of my mug, having heard the facts and figures Matt had just run by me and wishing I'd opted for something considerably stronger than coffee. A dram of single malt or a devilishly strong gin and tonic might have softened the blow, but caffeine-loaded coffee didn't seem to be helping at all.

'Don't look so worried,' said Matt consolingly. 'We don't have to tackle everything at once. Why not make the electrics a priority and we'll work through the rest one job at a time?'

'Yes,' I agreed dully. 'I suppose we could do it that way. In fact,' I sighed, 'I think we'll probably have to.'

'I have a cousin who happens to be a brilliant electrician,' he said heartily. 'He'll be able to install the new shower for you, and make sure it's properly earthed, unlike the death box up there at the moment, and he'll put in an up-to-date fuse box so you won't need to worry about thunderstorms any more.'

'That sounds like heaven to me,' I told him. 'It would be a comfort to know I can have a shower in safety.'

And I wasn't just thinking about saving myself the risk of being electrocuted either.

'I guess I'm just a bit shocked about all the other things that need doing,' I admitted. 'I hadn't even noticed half of them until you began pointing them out, and that's even before we've considered the damp you spotted in the dining room last winter.'

I couldn't help wondering how many more little bomb-shells were waiting in the wings to jump out and surprise me when summer faded into autumn. The list Matt had reeled off made Cuckoo Cottage sound more like a Halloween house of horrors than a comfortable country abode, but if Gwen had been all set to push ahead then I was on board and, if anything, I felt relieved there was someone as helpful as Matt poised to make a start. I would never have tackled half of what he said needed doing myself for fear of messing it up. Cuckoo Cottage deserved the very best of attention and unfortunately my renovation and refurbishment skills weren't going to be a lot of use when it came to tackling major jobs like damp and installing new electrics.

'That,' Matt reminded me, 'is the cost of owning somewhere with a bit of age and character, I'm afraid. It's inevitable, and repairs don't come cheap, especially when the person responsible before didn't quite keep on top of what needed doing,' he added gently.

'Um,' I said thoughtfully.

I couldn't take umbrage about that because given everything we had just gone through I knew he was right; Gwen had really let the work pile up.

'I can't imagine for one second that pointing up brickwork was ever high on Gwen's list of priorities, was it?'

'Exactly,' said Matt, 'but at least having asked me to make a start, she had made an effort to get to grips with the situation.'

'That's true,' I conceded.

'And at least you can get going now, Lottie, and literally have your house back in some sort of order before the winter. There's nothing here that can't be salvaged. It's just going to be a bit of a money pit for a while, that's all.'

I could all too easily imagine myself in the role of Tom Hanks. Getting stuck in a collapsed ceiling and living without a staircase was probably all I had to look forward to for a while now. So much for the grand plans I'd been starting to make. The house alone was going to take every penny Gwen had left me to put right.

'Thank goodness Gwen was a bit of a saver,' I muttered without thinking.

'What do you mean?'

'Fortunately she left me a bit of money,' I explained. 'So at least I can get on with some of the jobs straightaway.'

'Did she now?' Matt chuckled. 'Well, well, I never would have had her down as someone with money in the bank.'

'I know,' I agreed. 'I was surprised myself, and after the many charity bequests there wasn't a huge amount leftover, but I can see now I would have been in a right old pickle without it.'

I might not have been panicking about finding a job before, but with all these repairs mounting up I knew I was going to have to start earning an income again soon because there was no way I was going to give the gossips the satisfaction of giving in. Gwen had seen to it that I would be here for at least a year but they didn't know that, and in that time it was up to me to find a way to swim, not sink.

'I hope I haven't spoiled your day,' said Matt, reaching across the table and lightly resting his hand over mine.

'Not at all,' I said stoically as I turned my hand over and grasped his. 'I just need to work a few things out, that's all.'

'Well, order yourself a new shower and I'll get in touch with my cousin and tell him exactly what needs doing.'

'Thank you.'

I knew I was going to have to go back to town to order the

shower online and thought I could conveniently combine the trip with talking to Jemma, so at least that was the glimpse of a silver lining, assuming I didn't have another run-in at the café gate of course. I really did need to start researching some Wi-Fi options for the cottage because I couldn't be dragging out the bike every time I wanted to google something or check my emails.

'I really do appreciate your help, Matt,' I said, wondering how I would have been getting along had he not stopped to help the day Will nearly ran me off the road. Perhaps our local unfriendly vet had unwittingly done me a favour after all.

'No problem,' Matt smiled as I released his hand and he glanced at his watch and stood up. 'I'm sorry, Lottie, but I really need to get going.'

'Of course,' I said, 'and I'd better rescue the dining room from the madness of Minnie.'

'Do you think she's up to spending a few hours here unchaperoned yet?'

'I don't know, why?'

'Because I'd rather like to take you to a party at Skylark Farm Saturday night, if you'd like to come, and I'd like to do it with as little risk to my health as possible.'

'Oh,' I faltered, 'I see. Thank you for the offer, but I'm already going with Mags from down the road. She's giving me a lift along with her son and neighbour.'

'Oh well,' he shrugged, looking disappointed. 'Not to worry. At least I'll see you there.'

'But I will have a word with Minnie,' I promised, thinking it would probably be a good idea to leave her behind on Saturday now I knew Matt was definitely going to be there. 'I'll see if I can convince her that she could do with a girly night in.'

'Great,' he laughed. 'Only don't mention that you're going to be seeing me or she'll never let you out of the house.'

'Good point,' I laughed back.

'I'll see you at the party, then,' he said as he headed towards the door, adding in a theatrical whisper when he reached the dining room. 'Just don't tell the hound.'

I began to giggle and Minnie, sensing espionage, began to woof.

Chapter 13

It was a relief to have the party to look forward to at the end of the week because, with the cottage in far worse repair than I'd initially realised, and the prospect of so much work to be done, I could feel that I was in very real danger of being completely overwhelmed by the magnitude of everything that lay ahead. Just as my nemesis in the café had predicted, it was suddenly and dishearteningly all 'a bit too much to cope with' and I was devastated by my downturn in spirits, especially given how upbeat I had been feeling after Amber's visit.

I thought back to the months I'd been stuck in my horrid house-share in Lincoln, with my breath held, waiting for the blow which would snatch away my hope to strike and just knowing that becoming the proud and lucky owner of Cuckoo Cottage was simply too good to be true.

I had assumed that once the legalities were dealt with

and I was making friends and daring to dream of an exciting future, my fears would be consigned to the past, but I was wrong because they were still right there and I was heading back to that god-awful place in my mind. Only now I had the responsibility of a deteriorating property weighing heavy on my shoulders on top of everything else.

'Is this place *really* in as bad a state as Matt reckons it is?' I asked Minnie, as I tried to decide which outfit to wear to the party. 'Am I going to come home tonight and find you sitting on top of a crumbling pile?'

Funnily enough, the little dog didn't have a competent answer, but she did yap at the mention of Matt's name nonetheless.

'I know,' I said, hoping that she was thinking of my sanity rather than Matt's ankles. 'I know. I need to stop getting things out of all proportion, don't I?'

She yapped again and I thought back to what Mags had said about how a person can stagnate if stuck in the same environment for too long. Perhaps everyone was right. Perhaps four wheels of my own would give me the freedom to lubricate the creative juices and stop me brooding. I recoiled at the thought of climbing behind the wheel, but I knew I wouldn't be able to put it off for much longer, not living here in the flat, and sometimes unforgiving, Fen.

*

'My goodness, don't you look smart!' gasped Mags as I opened the door when she came to pick me up.

I ran my fingers over my sunflower earrings and looked down at my home-made fifties-style marigold-patterned skirt, and then at her jeans and creased T-shirt and realised I'd got completely the wrong clothes on.

I'd agonised over what to wear for hours, even poring through some of Gwen's old books for more clues as to what Lammas was all about. Yellow and orange, early harvest, grains and bread were overriding themes and consequently I'd made a batch of very misshapen rolls as a gift and teamed my outfit to the corresponding colours.

'Shit,' I muttered, thrusting the basket of rolls into Mags's arms. 'Please tell me I've got time to change.'

'What on earth do you want to change for?'

'Well, this is a bit over the top, don't you think?' I said, pointing at myself and then at her. 'You're in jeans for goodness' sake.'

Mags began to laugh.

'Firstly, no, there is no time to change,' she grinned, 'and secondly, Amber invited you because she wants you to be there and she wants our friends to get to know you, the real you.' She added pointedly, 'And to my mind, that outfit is totally you.'

She pulled me over the threshold, reminding me to lock the door and hurry up, then marched back to the van and threw open the back doors.

'Come on!' she called as I fussed over Minnie and my keys. 'Get a wriggle on. Your carriage awaits.'

I'd completely forgotten her little yellow minivan only had two seats and braced myself for a bumpy journey and inelegant arrival.

'Hello there, Lottie,' called her passenger as I approached and was wondering what would be the best way to hang on to my dignity as I climbed in the back. 'I bet you don't remember me, do you?'

'Yes, I do,' I said, rushing over to the window. 'Of course I do. Mags has been telling me all about her lovely neighbour, but I had no idea it was you. I'm so sorry, George,' I admitted, 'but I didn't make the connection until now.'

Gwen had taken Gran, Grandad and I down to see George in his house, which was built just a stone's throw from Hecate's Rest, quite often when I was little. From what I could remember, he had the best vegetable garden in the area.

'Not to worry,' he said. 'It's been a long time. I was going to talk to you at Gwen's funeral, but I never got the chance. I did pop along to the pub, but that solicitor chap had collared you before I did, so that was that. He didn't half set tongues wagging when he took you off like that.'

'Well,' I said, 'I'm glad we've finally been reacquainted.'

'As am I,' he nodded. 'You'll have to let me know if you want a hand sorting out the veg patch,' he added with a nod to the currently weed-strewn plot.

'Oh yes,' I said. 'I know it's a bit late to get going now.'

'Not at all,' he quickly cut in. 'We could have that cleared, manured and dug, then leave it over the winter, that way it'll be in peak condition for a fresh start next year.'

The little patch certainly deserved a fresh start and I have to admit I felt a little bolstered by the idea of making such a long-term commitment.

'Hey!' called Mags. 'This is all very lovely, you two, but time isn't moving any slower.'

'Sorry,' I said, rushing to the back and inelegantly bundling myself inside. 'Where's Ed?'

'He's already at the farm with his dad,' said Mags, passing me the basket of rolls and waiting until I'd found the least uncomfortable position on the cushions she had provided as a concession to comfort. 'They've been there all afternoon helping to set up.'

'Sorry,' I muttered again as she huffed impatiently while I shifted position and thought how much I was looking forward to finally meeting Ed's dad. 'Well come on,' I scolded when I was finally settled. 'Isn't it about time we got on?'

She slammed the door, plunging me into near darkness and then we were off on what was probably the most uncomfortable journey of my life.

Skylark Farm, as far as my jangling bones could tell, was about the same distance as the cottage was from Wynbridge, not that I had any idea in which actual direction we were heading, of course, because I was more focused on hanging on to my basket of rolls as we bounced through the potholes. When Mags finally drew to a halt, turned off the engine and ran around to throw open the back doors, I sat temporarily stunned and a little dizzy as my eyes grew accustomed to the change in light levels again.

'We never thought you were going to get here,' tutted Ed, as he helped me stand up with a fine disregard for the fact that my skirt had ridden halfway up my thighs. 'Practically everyone else is here already.'

I took a deep breath and checked my outfit over to make sure I had arrived in one piece, even if that piece was now slightly crumpled around the edges.

'You look nice,' said Ed, wrinkling his nose. 'Bit posh, but Mum's always telling me "you never get a second chance to make a first impression",' he mimicked.

'Is that right?' I muttered, reaching for the basket of tumbled rolls. 'Well, thank you, Ed, I'll take that as a compliment.'

As Mags helped George out of the passenger seat, I took the opportunity to look at the other cars parked in the yard. The first I saw made my stomach drop to the floor. Will's truck was there, but then, I countered, so was Matt's work van, so I hoped the evening would balance itself out on the man front.

'Come on, then,' said Ed, who was growing impatient. 'Come and say hello to everyone.'

Taking a deep breath, I set off with him, Mags and George, past the beautiful old farmhouse and flower-packed garden, towards the orchards, which I could see were draped in pretty bunting and beginning to sparkle with hundreds of fairy lights in the fading early evening light. There were straw bales arranged in squares to serve as seating and a delicious smell of hog roast filling the air along with laughter and the faint strains of music.

'Lottie!' waved Amber, when she spotted me.

She rushed over, taking my arm and steering me towards the bales where everyone was chatting.

'Thanks, Ed,' I called over my shoulder, but he was already gone.

'He's on car park duty,' said Amber. 'And he's taking his role very seriously.'

'Talking of rolls,' I said, trying to offload the basket of my first ever attempt at bread-making. 'I made you these. They aren't very good, I'm afraid, but I thought as this was a Lammas party.'

'Oh Lottie,' she beamed, squeezing my arm, but not taking the basket. 'That's lovely. You can give those to Annie. She'll be thrilled. Then I'll introduce you to everyone and give you that tour of the bungalow I promised.'

Amber's Auntie Annie was a formidable woman. Barely

taller than me and with paper-thin skin, she could unnervingly look me in the eye with her periwinkle gaze which suggested that she could see much more than just my physical form. She weighed me up for some seconds before taking the basket and I gabbled on about what I had discovered about Lammas and harvests and sunflowers.

'Well, aren't you a breath of fresh air,' she smiled when I eventually ran out of steam. 'I swear most of this lot only turn up for the free cider these days!'

I could tell she was teasing her guests, but I could also see that she was pleased I'd made the effort and I began to relax as Amber poured me a glass of Skylark Scrumpy and introduced me to the rest of her friends.

Harriet, Rachel and Lizzie I already knew of course, but there was also Lizzie's partner Ben, who was in deep conversation with Matt (who looked up and gave me a butterfly-inducing wink as Amber called out names), Jessica and her husband Henry, and finally Simon and Jude, who ran the vintage store in Wynbridge. Thankfully there was no sign of Will.

I was disappointed to learn that Jemma and her husband Tom wouldn't be coming because their babysitter had let them down, but listening to the sound of laughter and the crackling of the fire pit Amber's handsome partner Jake had just lit, I guessed this was not the night for talking business anyway.

'Have I missed the introductions?' asked a chap who wandered up accompanied by Ed, just as Amber slipped off to check her daughter Honey was being entertained from the comfort of her buggy before she was put to bed.

Truth be told, there were no need for introductions, as this guy was a carbon copy of Ed, or perhaps I should say, Ed was a carbon copy of him. Thick curly, dark hair and glasses, this was obviously Ed's father.

'I'm so pleased to meet you at last,' I said, pumping his hand and feeling that through his son I had actually met him already.

'I'm guessing you're Lottie,' he said, smiling Ed's smile.

'Yes,' I said. 'I'm Lottie Foster, your new neighbour.'

'Pleased to meet you, Lottie,' he said, 'and I'm Liam, but I'm not your neighbour.'

I was going to ask what he meant but was cut off by Amber who called to me from the edge of the orchard.

'Sorry,' I said, 'I have to go. Amber's promised to give me a tour.'

'No worries,' Liam smiled. 'We'll catch up again later.'

Amber and I strolled through the orchards; she introduced me to the animals and then unlocked Meadowview. It was every bit as beautiful and authentic as I imagined and I could have easily spent the entire evening ensconced on the sofa admiring her handiwork.

'We've got guests arriving in the morning,' she told me. 'Sunday isn't our usual handover day, but these are honeymooners who are travelling down after their reception tonight.'

'Well, it's the perfect spot to hide away in for a few days,' I said. 'It's truly wonderful, Amber. You've certainly a great eye for detail.'

'Thank you,' she smiled, as she straightened a cushion and ran her hands over the rose-patterned curtains. 'I was lucky Annie had so much treasure in the loft because these days it's getting harder and harder to find bits and pieces like this for sensible money.'

My own experience confirmed that she was right and I knew I was going to have to shop carefully if I was going to add some authentic touches to the vans I had hidden away in the barn. Fortunately, however, her next comment reassured me that I might not have to look too far from home.

'Simon and Jude take trips to French sales now on the lookout for bits and pieces that will suit what their UK customers are looking for,' she explained as she began to lock up. 'Not that that's a hardship, of course.'

Their shop sounded like the perfect local starting point should my fledging business idea ever make it out of the nest.

I could hear the noise of the gathering had increased since Amber had spirited me away and guessed that the delicious

Skylark Scrumpy was playing its part in loosening tongues and adding more warmth to the occasion. I was relieved to find I wasn't the focus of attention as we rejoined the group and felt that, here at least, I was amongst friends rather than a nosy group of tittle-tattlers like those I had seen and heard in town.

'Lottie!' called Jake, handing over the responsibility of the hog roast to Henry. 'So tell me, what do you make of the place?'

'It's wonderful,' I told him. 'You have so much going on here. I think it's amazing.'

'Well, thank you,' he said, looking suitably flattered, which was my intention as I meant every word. 'And from what Amber tells me, you're going to have a lot more going on at Cuckoo Cottage after tonight.'

'Am I?'

'Is she?' asked Matt, who had wandered over to join us, bringing with him another glass of cider for me.

I made a mental note that this was already my second and I hadn't eaten anything yet. This one was definitely for sipping.

'You're going to pick out some hens, aren't you?'

'Oh yes,' I nodded, feeling relieved.

For a horrible moment I had thought Amber had told him about the vans and that he was going to spill the beans to all and sundry. I had no intention of keeping them under wraps forever but until I had the plans for them settled in my mind I didn't want them to be common knowledge.

'I'd forgotten all about that.'

'Come and do it now,' said Jake, pointing back towards the house, 'before it gets too dark.'

'Well, I . . .'

'Ed said you were all set up with the coop and run and I can give you some straw and grain to tide you over,' he added encouragingly.

'Come on,' said Matt. 'I'll help you choose.'

'All right,' I said nervously. 'But you have to help me pick the most robust because I haven't got a clue what to do with them. If they're going to thrive at Cuckoo Cottage they'll need to be pretty self-reliant.'

Together we walked back towards the house and then Jake, pointing me in the right direction, went on a quick detour with Matt in search of a crate or box that he could use to keep the chickens in overnight.

My gaze dropped to my now dusty shoes when I spotted Will standing at the run with Ed, looking at the hens before they were shut up for the night.

'Lottie,' said Will, stepping forward before I had a chance to say anything. 'I almost didn't recognise you . . .'

'Please don't say with my clothes on,' I cut in under my breath.

'That wasn't what I was going to say at all,' he said, sounding surprisingly embarrassed.

'So what were you going to say?'

'Other than that you look lovely, sorry, I suppose,' he said, burying his hands deep in his pockets. 'Because I had no idea I'd run you off the road and into those nettles.'

'Well, you should be sorry,' I scowled. 'I could sue you for the damage you inflicted on my legs.'

His gaze dropped to my skirt and I felt myself bristle under his scrutiny.

'You were driving far too fast down that road,' I swallowed.

'I won't any more,' he announced, his eyes flicking back up to my face. 'I've learned my lesson and, for what it's worth, I really am very sorry, and if it's any consolation, I did manage to save Mr Tibbs' dog, Tess.'

'What do you mean?'

'I was heading to an emergency,' he explained. 'The crazy pooch had managed to get under the wheels of a delivery lorry and had come off worse. Although the driver was pretty shaken up,' he added, biting his lip.

I was pleased he had saved the dog but couldn't help wondering if another emergency explained the speedy driving I'd witnessed on previous occasions. However, I was let off having to ask as Jake and Matt came back empty-handed and shaking their heads.

'Believe it or not, I can't find anything suitable,' said Jake. 'Nothing big enough to keep them comfortably tucked up in overnight anyway.'

Exactly how many chickens was he expecting me to have?

'I think we'll have to do this another day, Lottie. I'm ever so sorry.'

I was just about to say it didn't matter when Ed rushed in to save the day.

'Why don't you just put the ones Lottie wants in the other coop?' he said, pointing across the yard to a little wooden house that didn't have a run. 'Then transfer them to one of the small pet carriers in the shed in the morning for the trip to the cottage. It's only up the road, after all.'

'I really don't want to be any bother,' I insisted. 'Let's just do it another day.'

'No,' said Will. 'Ed's right. If someone can drop them to you early tomorrow that will work a treat.'

'No one will want to turn out early on a Sunday,' I said, 'especially after such a late night.'

'I don't mind,' Jake shrugged. 'I'll be up for the animals anyway so I could bring them.'

'Well, as long as you're really sure,' I said, biting my lip.

'Absolutely,' he said, striding into the hen run with Ed hot on his heels. 'It'll give me a chance to talk to you about my truck.'

His arrival in the hen's domain was met with much

squawking and flapping, so I didn't have a chance to ask what he meant, but the rolling in my tummy suggested it wasn't going to be something I particularly wanted to talk about.

Chapter 14

I had absolutely no idea which birds to pick, but with the impact of two half-pints of Skylark Scrumpy coursing through my teeny-tiny system, watching Ed and Jake trying to gather up the birds was, to my slightly hazy mind, highly amusing. Apparently this was way after the hens' normal bedtime and as a result the little birds were hilariously flappable.

'Why don't you just go for that one?' frowned Matt, pointing to one that was bigger than the others at the furthest end of the run.

He was clearly bored with proceedings, nowhere near as amused as I was and itching to get back to the party.

'Because she wants eggs, you idiot,' puffed Ed, as he quickly clamped another startled hen under his arm and brought her to the fence for me to have a look at.

'I know she wants eggs,' Matt bit back, sounding even

more childish than Ed. 'That's why I'm helping her choose chickens!'

'But that's a cockerel,' said Will quietly, as he pointed to the bird Matt had picked out.

I couldn't help but laugh, even though Matt was frowning up at Will with something like intense loathing.

'Oh dear,' I giggled after another sip of cider. 'You know as much as I do, Matt. Well done us.'

I was trying to make him feel better, but given his obviously unaltered expression, I'd failed, miserably. I cleared my throat and turned my attention back to the job in hand.

'They're smaller than I thought they would be,' I admitted, again probably showing myself up as equally ignorant of all things fowl as Matt was. 'I thought they'd be bigger.'

'These are all young birds,' Ed explained patiently as he stroked the little lavender lady under his arm, 'but they're bantams anyway so they won't actually get all that much bigger than this.'

'Well, I have to have her,' I said, poking my finger through the metal fence and stroking her silky head. 'She's lovely.'

'So just two more to go,' said Will. 'What about that little grey?'

'Two!' I said, taking a step back. 'Don't they lay an egg a day? What am I going to do with over twenty eggs a week?'

'Three is a traditional number of hens,' said Ed, with a

shrug. 'But it's up to you, of course, although you must have more than one.'

'And they do only lay small eggs,' joined in Jake, bringing over the grey Will had pointed out.

Matt, I noticed, had now gone very quiet amid his fellow poultry fanciers.

'All right,' I said, giving the nod to Will's choice. 'I'll have her as well and that little darker one who's making eyes at the cockerel.'

I looked back at Matt and winked and he began to grin. I was relieved to have won him round. I had no desire to fall out with my builder before he'd even made a start on the cottage repairs, assuming of course that I did decide to offer him the work.

With the girls carefully carried across to the other coop for the night we made our way back to the party.

'Shall I get us something to eat?' offered Matt as the others peeled off. 'I don't know about you, but I'm starving.'

'Yes please,' I said, as I spotted Mags and Liam sitting close together next to the fire pit. 'And I'll find us a seat.'

'So have you picked your hens, then?' Mags asked as I plonked myself next to her on the straw bale.

'Yes,' I said, jumping back up again as my still sore calves met the scratchy straw. 'Ouch. Bugger.'

'Here you go,' said Liam, hopping up and laying his jacket across where I had been hoping to sit.

'No, it's OK,' I said.

'Honestly, it's fine,' he said, sitting back down next to his good lady. 'Mags told me what happened. Are you OK now?'

'Thank you,' I said. 'Yes, I'm fine. My calves are still a bit sore, but there's no permanent damage. So,' I chattered on, keen to make up for all the times I had monopolised my conversations with Mags, 'how long have you two been married?'

'Married?' she spluttered, spitting out her mouthful of cider and fanning the flames of the fire pit, which crackled in excitement at her impromptu alcoholic addition to their vigour.

'Yes,' I said, feeling confused by her reaction. 'You are married, aren't you?'

'Er, no,' said Liam, grinning sheepishly. 'Not married.'

'But you are a couple?' I questioned.

To my mind there could be no doubting that they were 'together' in some sense. You only had to look at their body language to see that they were joined at the hip. However, thinking back, Mags had never actually mentioned she had a man about the house.

'Absolutely not,' she croaked, finally regaining her composure.

'We were once,' blushed Liam.

'On my eighteenth birthday,' Mags giggled, 'for about ten minutes.'

'Hey!' protested Liam.

'Oh, all right,' said Mags, rolling her eyes. 'Twenty minutes then.'

'Thank you,' smiled Liam, sounding soothed. 'That's more like it.'

'But I don't understand,' I rushed on, my face feeling flushed more from embarrassment than from the heat of the fire pit. 'I thought you must at least live together. You seem so, so comfortable together.'

'Well, we've been friends since kindergarten,' explained Liam. 'So we have known each other forever.'

'And on my eighteenth birthday,' Mags sighed, 'we decided, thanks to one too many cheap lagers, that it would be a good idea to take our friendship further.'

'And Ed was the result,' put in Liam. 'So you see, we've always been friends, but we've never been more than that since that one night.'

'Oh,' I said, 'right, I see.'

But I didn't really. This pair looked absolutely made for each other, so it made no sense to me at all that they were anything other than a couple. I was about to say as much, but then remembered how I had put my foot in it with Angela in the Cherry Tree. Not to mention how mortified I had been when Chris had insisted he was going to find me a fella the day I arrived in town.

'Here you go,' said Matt, passing me a plate loaded with succulent hog roast and apple sauce. 'Budge up.'

Mags looked at me and shrugged her shoulders.

'And in case you were wondering,' she whispered, 'we wouldn't change a thing.'

Everyone gathered around the fire pit to enjoy the delicious food, which was further enhanced by frequent refills of Skylark Scrumpy, and before I knew it, I had chatted to practically everyone and it was pitch-black. I could just make out the very top of the full moon as it rose, golden and heavy, over the roof of the farmhouse and added its own magical light to the little party playing out beneath it.

'So,' said Jake, as he came round with the cider jug again. 'Everyone keeps telling me you're on the lookout for a vehicle, Lottie.'

'Oh jeez,' I groaned loudly, my confidence much enriched by the alcohol. 'Is there anyone here who hasn't heard this?'

'No,' the group chorused as one and then began to laugh.

I shook my head in disbelief and Ben began to strum quietly on a guitar.

'I am thinking about it,' I told Jake.

It really was the last thing I expected to hear myself admitting, but I was. Everyone had been on at me about it since the moment I arrived, but actually it was Mags's words about getting stuck in a rut and not tapping in to my creativity which had really struck a chord. As much as I hated the idea, it was time to face my fears and spread my wings a bit.

'Right,' he said, 'great. I'm asking, you see, because

Amber and I are planning to get rid of the truck soon and I wondered . . .'

So much for saving the potentially life-changing conversation until he dropped the hens off in the morning.

'What, that enormous thing?' I choked, pointing back towards where everyone had parked. 'You've got to be kidding me?'

'No,' he shrugged. 'What's wrong with the truck?'

'Well, it's mahoosive for a start,' I began.

'What's mahoosive?' frowned Mags, who had only just arrived back after going with Amber to check on Honey and Annie who were now up at the house.

'My truck,' said Jake. 'Apparently.'

'So?'

'Well, we're getting rid of it,' Jake explained again. 'So I thought I'd offer Lottie here first refusal.'

'But I don't need something that size,' I said firmly.

'Of course you don't,' tutted Mags, 'but I do.'

'You do?' questioned Jake.

'Yes,' said Mags, thankfully letting me off the hook. 'I've been thinking about upsizing for ages. There's no way I can get all of Ed's kilter in the minivan, along with the plants I ferry about for Harriet and Rachel now. It just isn't practical any more,' she added sadly.

It was a shame really. I'd grown rather fond of the sight of her little custard yellow van parked on the cottage drive.

'So you'll buy the truck,' said Jake slowly, as if he was puzzling out some great conundrum. 'And Lottie will buy your van.'

'Oh well . . .' I began.

'What a brilliant idea!' agreed Mags, slapping me on the back and inducing a coughing fit. 'That's perfect.'

'I can't buy your van,' I spluttered. 'I'm sure I wouldn't be able to afford it, and besides, I haven't driven a van before, not even a small one.'

'I can take you out in it, if you like,' said Will, butting into the conversation. 'I'm only up the road, so it would be no bother. Just think of it as my way of saying sorry for my own bad driving and helping to get you off two wheels and onto four.'

'What's all this?' asked Matt, sitting back down with yet another packed plate.

'Lottie's going to buy my van,' said Mags.

'And Will's going to drive about with her until she's got used to it,' added Jake.

I opened my mouth to protest, but didn't get the chance.

'You won't find a better teacher,' said George, while everyone agreed and Ben set his guitar aside as it was obvious no one was ready for a singsong when they could be organising my life for a few more minutes. 'He's a soldier, Lottie, used to driving anything and everything,' George carried proudly on. 'And a highly decorated soldier at that.'

'Ex-soldier,' Matt quickly added. 'And you know, I could take you out.'

'He's driven all over the world, in all sorts of terrain,' George continued, despite the fact that Will was waving a hand and remonstrating silently for him to stop. 'You won't find a better man to get you going again than our Will.'

A few cheers went up as he said that, but I got the distinct impression no one was thinking about his driving skills.

'What do you think?' asked Mags.

She sounded ridiculously hopeful and I knew she was pinning her hopes on me saying yes so she could take the truck off Amber and Jake's hands, and of course she had already become such a kind and helpful friend that I pretty much felt indebted.

'Oh, go on then,' I said nervously, my hands shaking at the thought. 'But if I can't do it, I'm giving you the keys straight back.'

'I'm sorry if I've annoyed your boyfriend,' said Will when we found ourselves side by side as we sneaked a little more crackling from the tasty hog roast. 'But I meant what I said about getting you back on the road.'

'Thank you,' I said, wondering just how those confidence-building lessons were going to pan out.

Not very well if I kept reminding myself that he had seen me naked, and certainly not very well if he was going to bark at me like an impatient sergeant major every time I stalled the engine or crunched the gears. I had to admit my interest in him was rather piqued now I knew a little more of his history and I was dying to ask how a former soldier came to be living in a barn conversion in practically the middle of nowhere and working as a Wynbridge vet.

'So were you a vet in the army, then?' I asked.

'I was,' he nodded.

'And have you really driven in terrain all over the world?'

'Yes,' he sighed. 'I have.'

I could tell he didn't want to talk about it and I swallowed hard, thinking of some of the sights he had probably seen, along with some of the horrid things he had probably had to do. I could imagine him kitted out in fatigues, the strong, tall hero brandishing the union flag and offering a safe haven from further harm.

'About your boyfriend,' he said again.

Instantly it felt as if he had put a pin in the romantic little fantasy balloon I had just begun to inflate around him and I reminded myself that right up until a few minutes ago I wasn't actually all too keen on this chap.

'He's not my boyfriend,' I said quickly. 'He's my builder.'

'Your builder?'

'Yes,' I huffed. 'My builder.'

'And what exactly is it that you're having built?'

'Nothing,' I said, tearing into the salty crackling with my

teeth. 'He's going to do some remedial work at the cottage, should I agree to give him the contract, of course.'

I didn't want Will thinking I was a complete pushover.

'What remedial work?' he frowned, sounding suspicious.

'There's loads of stuff,' I said, sucking at my fingers before wiping them on a napkin.

'There can't be,' he said, now sounding bemused.

'Are you saying that in your capacity as an ex-army vet,' I asked, 'or as a builder?'

'But Gwen looked after the place,' he insisted. 'It was her pride and joy.'

'Well, that's as maybe . . .' I began, the words dying in my throat as Matt called my name.

'Are you coming?' he shouted. 'Some of the others are leaving and they want to say goodbye.'

I started to walk away, but Will caught my wrist. I stared up at him and he let go.

'Just be careful,' he warned. 'I know for a fact that Gwen kept on top of jobs that needed doing at the cottage. She might have come across as scatterbrained when it came to some things, but as far as Minnie was concerned, and Cuckoo Cottage, she left nothing to chance.'

Chapter 15

I knew the second I tried to prise my eyes open that it was going to be one of those rare Sundays where I would vow that I would never, ever touch another drop of alcohol again, only this time I thought, given the way my brain was thumping in time with every heartbeat, I probably had a fair crack at seeing the resolution through. I had never been much of a drinker and now I was being reminded why.

I lay crossways on the bed beneath the sheets and buried my head in the pillows to shut out the light whilst trying to remember the finer details (beyond passing round the cider jug) of what had happened and been said at the party. Yet another disagreement with Will, a trio of hens and something about Mags's van, more specifically me buying Mags's van, swam around my head in a sickening whirl.

On the good side, however, I also remembered that, for the most part, I'd had a great time and made lots of new friends who hadn't treated me like the newest novelty in town or the cuckoo in the cottage nest, but it would have been nice if I could have remembered a little more of what I'd talked to them about.

Gingerly I rolled over and contemplated the possibility of sitting up without falling back down when I heard someone coming up the stairs.

'I had a feeling you'd be awake,' Matt grinned around the door frame. 'And I thought you might be in need of this.'

On the tray he carried in front of him was a mug of tea, a pint glass of water and a couple of painkillers. He carefully set it down on the end of the bed and handed me the tablets and water.

'Back in a sec,' he said, disappearing again. 'I'm just buttering you some toast.'

Without thinking, I swallowed the tablets, set down the glass, reached for the tea and sank back against the pillows again. I could feel my legs were bare under the sheet and I was wearing the tiny T-shirt I had taken to sleeping in because the nights were so hot, but I had no idea how I had got into this state of undress. Surely I would have remembered if . . .

'Where's Minnie?' I croaked, amazed that my voice could still function, as Matt reappeared with some hot, but not too buttered, toast.

'In the greenhouse, of course,' he shrugged, passing me

the plate. 'Not really,' he laughed, when he saw my stricken expression. 'I'm only winding you up. You put her in the dining room when we got back last night. Don't you remember?'

'No,' I said, wracking my brains despite the pain. 'I don't.'

'Well, I'm not surprised,' he smirked as I took a tentative bite of the toast. 'You were pretty tipsy.'

I sat and chewed in quiet contemplation, desperate to ask what had happened after I had banished Minnie to the dining room, but not sure I could really cope with the details in my delicate condition.

'I'm just pleased you made it up to bed all right,' Matt sighed. 'And you even managed to get into your PJs,' he added, pointing at my skimpy T-shirt. 'Ten out of ten for effort.'

'You didn't help me into my PJs then?' I asked tentatively.

'Nope,' Matt grinned, clearly enjoying watching me squirm as he realised I had absolutely no recollection as to what had happened. 'You must have managed that all by yourself.'

'So we didn't . . .'

Matt began to laugh and I gently massaged the side of my skull which objected most.

'Absolutely not,' he tutted. 'Lottie Foster, what do you take me for? I would never have taken advantage of you in that state.'

'Of course not,' I said, clearing my throat. 'I didn't mean . . .'

'I know you didn't,' he teased. 'I'm only winding you up.'

I finished the tea and toast and my stomach began to feel slightly more forgiving.

'I don't think I've ever seen anyone get so tiddly on just a couple of pints,' Matt smiled. 'Although in your defence that Skylark Scrumpy is a pretty potent brew. I'm sure the stuff Jake keeps at the farm is stronger than they stock in The Mermaid. I'll have to take you out one night, Lottie, and you can see for yourself.'

'Oh don't,' I groaned. 'I think I'll be sticking to apple juice in the future. I hardly drink at all and now I don't think I'll ever be drinking again!'

'Well, to be fair, cider is apple juice, isn't it?'

'I suppose,' I agreed with a small smile. 'Of sorts.'

'So,' sighed Matt. 'You don't actually remember getting home, then?'

'No,' I whispered, feeling embarrassed as well as ashamed. 'I don't.'

'Well, Harriet and Rachel gave us a lift back here. They waited in their car while I saw you safely inside and then they gave me a lift home. I used the spare set of keys from the dish on the hall table to lock up, and let myself back in this morning,' he explained, holding aloft the bunch David had given me the day I moved in. 'And Harriet and Rachel are waiting again now to run me back to the farm so I can collect my van.' He beamed. 'And here you are, fighting fit and just raring to go.'

'Crikey,' I said, rolling my eyes and feeling relieved that I hadn't made a complete fool of myself as far as falling into bed with him was concerned. 'I don't think I'd go quite that far.'

'Well, you need to get going in a minute,' he said, patting my leg. 'Isn't it about time for you to take delivery of those hens you picked out last night?'

'Oh God,' I said, sinking further back into the pillows. 'I'd forgotten I'd said I'd take them today.'

'Not to worry,' grinned Matt. 'They'll be a welcome distraction. Anyway, I'd better get off. I have to be in town for lunch in a bit and I don't want to keep the girls waiting.'

'Of course not,' I said, my voice still a little husky. 'Thanks, Matt. Thanks for looking after me.'

'And thank you,' he said back. 'I'm really pleased you've decided to let me push ahead with the work. I'll be seeing Simon later so I'll ask him when he can come and install your shower and replace the fuse box.'

I looked at him open-mouthed.

'That is, presuming you haven't changed your mind,' he frowned.

'No,' I squeaked. 'Of course not.'

'Last night,' he said, when it became obvious that I had no idea what I was agreeing I hadn't changed my mind about, 'last night before I left, you said you were happy for me to get cracking with the work on the cottage.'

'Did I?'

'Yes,' he said, looking worried. 'You said if Gwen was happy to employ me then you were too. You said you were going to order a new shower this week and that you wanted me to push on with getting everything underway before the weather turned.'

'Of course,' I said, doing my best to convince him that I could remember.

Truth was, I had absolutely no recollection of saying any such thing, but then, looking at the puddle of clothes on the floor, I couldn't remember getting undressed either. If all I'd promised Matt was a bit of DIY work then perhaps, all things considered, I'd got off rather lightly.

'So I'm OK to go ahead then,' Matt frowned. 'You want me to carry on getting things sorted?'

'Of course,' I smiled. 'You'll just have to bear with me. My brain isn't awake yet.'

'Well, you want to give it a prod,' he said, as he trotted down the stairs. 'Because I reckon you've got about five minutes before Minnie eats her way through the dining-room door.'

An hour later, wearing the biggest pair of sunglasses I could find and with Minnie somewhat mollified, having been bribed with the choicest morsels of meat I could lay my hands on, I heard a vehicle pull up outside the cottage door. It was quickly followed by another and I painted on my best smile and braced myself to bravely face whatever I had let myself in for.

It wasn't until I heard Mags and Ed talking about heading over to Liam's later in the day that I remembered the embarrassing gaffe I had made and wondered if perhaps I could get away with not answering the door at all. However, listening to Ed's excited chatter as he helped Jake begin to unload the truck, I knew I was going to have to just get on with it. I would face my friend stone-cold sober, apologise yet again and, hopefully, move on.

'Morning,' grinned Mags, the second I opened the door. 'And how are we feeling this morning?'

I bent to grab Minnie's collar, thinking it would be better to keep her out of the way until the hens were settled, but she was far too quick for me and darted between my legs and out into the far brighter than usual, to my mind, sunshine.

'Hungover,' I admitted, grateful for the protection the sunglasses afforded, 'and a bit embarrassed, to be honest.'

'Nice glasses,' winked Jake, as he unloaded a straw bale and some bags of feed.

I stuck out my tongue and he laughed, looking ridiculously bright-eyed and bushy-tailed.

'What are you embarrassed about?' frowned Mags as she

handed me the basket I had used to transport my bread rolls to the party.

'Putting my foot in it with you and Liam, of course,' I said, dumping the basket in the hall and slamming the door behind me.

The noise made my head thump again and I thought I'd perhaps better take a couple more painkillers when I offered everyone tea.

'Oh, for goodness' sake,' tutted Mags, linking arms, 'I wouldn't worry about that. People are always doing it, and how were you to know we aren't together? We've never talked about it, have we?'

'Well no,' I shrugged, wondering again that if it was so very obvious to the rest of the world that they were made for each other, then why couldn't they see it. 'I suppose not. I just felt a bit silly, that's all.'

'You wouldn't be saying that if you'd seen the state Henry was in when he left,' Jake chipped in, having only caught the end of our exchange.

'Oh really?'

'Really,' Jake laughed. 'Jessica was furious with him. They're supposed to be heading to her parents' for some big fancy family get-together today, but Henry can't even open his eyes yet. The poor bugger.'

'I blame you and that cider jug,' tutted Mags. 'You were far too generous with it last night.'

'I think you might be right,' mused Jake. 'Jess told Amber on the phone this morning that she had to stop twice on the journey home.'

'Too much information, thanks,' I said, waving my hand. 'Now, come on, Ed. Tell me what I have to do with these chickens.'

The little coop and run was quickly checked over, thanks to Ed's expert attention, and it was soon time to release the hens from their box. They had been patiently waiting in the shade where I could hear them clucking quietly and no doubt wondering what on earth was going on, as was I, to be honest. How had I even ended up with three hens so soon after moving in? Minnie sat close by, overseeing proceedings, but not with any intention of getting in the way. She was calm and poised and seemed to be taking everything in her stride and I resolved to try and follow her lead.

'I thought you were going to be bringing them in pet carriers,' I said to Jake, a sudden flashback of the conversation we'd had the night before popping into my head.

'We were,' he said, 'but then Amber found this box in the barn and we thought it would probably be a bit roomier for them.'

'Right,' I said, my mind still grappling with what else might have been said.

'OK,' he said, pointing at me, 'you go in the run with Ed and I'll pass you the box.'

I wasn't sure what I was supposed to do, but the sooner I got stuck in, the better, I guessed.

'Don't we have to shut them up for a bit?' I asked.

I could remember once seeing something on TV about letting chickens get used to their bearings before setting them free.

'No,' said Ed, 'it isn't like you're keeping them completely free-range. They'll soon work out where things are for themselves, and besides, it would be a bit hot to keep them cooped up today.'

'Of course,' I agreed, deferring to his words of wisdom.

He gently opened the lid on the box and out jumped the little dark hen. With much clucking and feather-shaking she began to explore her new home, but the other two sat tight, huddled together in a corner.

'Come on,' said Ed, reaching inside and indicating that I should do the same.

He gently picked out the little grey and I tentatively put my hands around the lavender. She was as light as a feather and zipped off after her friends the second I set her down. I stood back up, a sudden thud reminding me that I still wasn't out of the woods on the headache front, and admired my latest additions to Cuckoo Cottage. They looked rather pretty strutting about and I liked the sounds they made as they began to scratch and explore.

'Ed has made you a "what-to-do-with-them" sheet,' said

Mags, from her viewpoint outside the run. 'I'll get it out of the van.'

'Thanks, Ed,' I said. 'I think I'm going to need it.'

'You'll be fine,' he said, with the certainty of someone far older than eleven. 'They're really easy.'

'You must tell me how much you want for them,' I said to Jake as I followed Ed out of the run and locked it behind me.

'A cup of tea and a bacon sandwich will probably cover it,' he winked.

'Seriously?'

'Seriously.'

With a plate of more of my wonky rolls filled with the delicious Skylark Farm bacon Jake just happened to have brought with him, and a pot of tea, the three of us sat under the cherry tree while Ed headed off with Minnie to inspect the field.

'So you had a good time last night, then?' Jake asked.

'I had a brilliant time,' I confirmed. 'Thank you so much for inviting me and thank you for the lift there, Mags.'

'And you haven't forgotten about our deal over the mini-van, have you?' she said, eyebrows raised.

'No,' I sighed, looking at the little custard yellow contraption and thinking it was far bigger than I remembered. 'I haven't forgotten.'

I wondered if Will would still be willing to give me driving lessons now we had crossed swords, yet again.

'Excellent,' said Mags, clapping her hands together and reaching for another roll. 'Because we'd like to have everything sorted as soon as possible, wouldn't we, Jake?'

'Ideally by the end of next week if we can manage it,' Jake confirmed.

'The end of next week,' I spluttered, 'but that's just five days away, and we haven't even talked about how much you want for it yet, Mags.'

'Don't worry about that,' she said, shaking her dark head. 'We can come to some arrangement.'

'And I can give you a hand sorting out insurance and everything,' said Jake kindly.

I hadn't even thought about the added cost of insurance on top of everything else. I'd been too worried about the thought of daring to drive.

'Right,' I said, thinking back to the promise I'd just made to myself to take everything in my stride. 'End of the week, then. I suppose I'd better tell Chris to call off the search, hadn't I?'

'If I know how things work around here,' said Jake, 'and I think I can safely say that I do, I dare say he knows by now.'

'Um,' I said thoughtfully. 'You're probably right.'

I wondered if he was still on the hunt for a potential husband and hoped that having found myself four wheels so soon didn't mean that he would pour all his efforts into seeking out two legs.

'Yes,' agreed Mags, 'and if he doesn't, I'm sure Matt will soon fill him in.'

'What do you mean?'

'Well,' she expanded, 'I saw him at the farm collecting his van a minute ago and he couldn't wait to tell me how he'd helped sort you out when you got back here after the party last night.'

'He didn't stay,' I said, my face flushing at the thought of him going around telling everyone a different version of events to the one he had told me. 'He came back this morning,'

Mags held up her hand to stop me.

'Don't panic,' she quickly added. 'I don't think he was trying to suggest that anything had happened, not that it would have been anyone else's business if it had.'

'But it didn't,' I said firmly.

'I'm just mentioning what he said to make you aware that nothing, absolutely nothing, stays private around here, Lottie, OK?'

'OK,' I said, 'thanks.'

'And that some people would be more than willing to put their own spin on things.'

It was a timely reminder that even though everyone at the party had been lovely, there were still those folk in Wynbridge who weren't happy about my arrival at Cuckoo Cottage and that they would no doubt love a dollop of juicy gossip to fire their suspicions about me further.

'Right,' said Jake. 'I'd better get home. Amber's having a lie-in this morning. She's pretty tired at the moment.'

'But she's all right, isn't she?' quizzed Mags, gathering together the empty mugs and plates. 'She isn't coming down with anything?'

'No, I don't think so,' said Jake, turning as red as I had been just moments before. 'She's just been busy, that's all.'

Evidently they had somehow managed to keep the fact that she was having another baby a secret, in spite of the well-established Wynbridge bush telegraph, but if Jake carried on turning cherry red every time someone asked after his other half, they wouldn't for much longer.

Chapter 16

With the hens soon settled and Mags's words ringing in my ears about taking the van off her hands by the end of the week, and also not forgetting the need to order a new shower, of course, I knew another bike ride to Wynbridge was inevitable. I wasn't particularly looking forward to the journey, but on the plus side the trip would at least give me the opportunity to talk to Jemma about the plans she had hinted at for the Bailey.

Since Matt's visit to assess the work, and the party, I hadn't had a chance to pay the caravans much attention at all, but I couldn't wait to turn my focus back to them, especially now with the extra expenditure adding up. My spirits were on the rise again and now more than ever I needed to find a way to make my new life at Cuckoo Cottage pay its way, and I hoped I would be able to do that without having to travel further afield for work. In my heart I still really believed that there was some gold mine of an idea just waiting for me to strike upon and set me off on a new and exciting path. One, I hoped, that Gwen and Gran would have been proud of.

Fortunately for me, the week dawned cloudier and with the lengthy cycle ride ahead I was grateful that the dial had been turned down on the searing summer heat. Just as before, Minnie refused to be left behind and stood, front paws perched on the very edge of the bike basket, like some regal figurehead, rather than my scrappy little companion.

There was no sign of the hare as we slowly made our way along the drove road and it wasn't long before Minnie was panting and turning around in the basket trying to get comfy.

'Don't you dare tell me you're wishing you stayed at home,' I told her crossly as I wiped my brow, wobbling a little as I pedalled one-handed.

If she was thinking of her bed in the cool shady kitchen she didn't dare let on, but I was surprised by how hot it still was, even though the sun was hidden.

'I should think not,' I said, my own temperature rising with the exertion and my ears conscious of a vehicle approaching from behind.

Thankfully it was moving at a snail's pace so I could get away with just pulling over rather than stopping completely. I might have been reasonably fit, but the bike was old and heavy and getting momentum going again would take more effort than I wished to exert at this point in the journey.

'Can I give you a lift?'

It was Will. He slowly pulled alongside and Minnie jumped back up, her tail wagging and her tongue lolling the second she caught sight of her former caretaker.

'Hello, Minnie,' he laughed as I grabbed her collar lest she leap out of the basket and into his cab.

'I'm heading to town,' he said with a nod in the general direction of Wynbridge. 'Let me take you the rest of the way so you can save your legs for the journey home. Assuming that's where you're off to?'

'Yes,' I nodded, thinking what a different response Minnie gave Will when compared to the one she inflicted on Matt. 'Thanks.'

'Let's see if we can make it as far as the market square without falling out again, shall we?' Will smiled as he loaded my bike into the back and opened the passenger door.

'Well, I suppose that rather depends on whether or not you're going to quiz me about the work I'm having done at the cottage, doesn't it?'

'I'm not going to say another word about it,' he said, jumping in and turning over the engine again.

'Good.'

'Other than . . .'

'Oh here we go,' I sighed.

'Other than,' he continued, one hand stroking Minnie's head as she tried to climb on to his lap, 'that I hope two of the things on your list are the shower and that dodgy fuse box.'

'Well, in that case,' I said, lifting Minnie back on to the seat next to me, 'you should be well pleased that Matt has come to my rescue.'

'So you're definitely giving him the work then?'

'Because,' I carried on, ignoring his suspicion of the builder I still couldn't really remember employing, 'both of those things were at the very top of his list. In fact, that's why I'm heading to town today,' I added with a sniff. 'I'm going to order a new shower.'

'Brilliant,' Will smiled. 'Just don't go for anything too powerful. The water pressure isn't great and . . .' he looked across at me and shook his head. 'Sorry,' he said. 'It's none of my business. How are the hens?'

I was pleased he had changed the subject, especially to one that I had quickly become so fond of.

'Enchanting,' I told him. 'They're so funny.'

I didn't mention that they were also extremely pretty as I wasn't sure Will appreciated their aesthetics as much as I did.

'I've had two eggs already,' I said, thinking of the smooth, warm beauties I had discovered when I went to let them out of their coop earlier that morning.

'So you're pleased you've got them?'

'Definitely,' I nodded. 'Even though I was rather railroaded into it, I think we're going to get along just fine.'

'And what about taking on Mags's minivan?' he asked. 'You were rather railroaded into that too, weren't you?'

'Sort of,' I said. 'Although I have to admit I was slowly coming round to the idea of buying a car. I just didn't expect it to happen quite so soon.'

'Sometimes,' he said, carefully negotiating the bridge over the River Wyn, 'I think we all need a bit of a shove in the right direction.'

'Are you speaking from experience, by any chance?'

'You have no idea,' he said, 'but I meant what I said about driving around with you until you get your confidence back.'

'Thank you,' I swallowed. 'I had wondered if you might have changed your mind about that.'

'Not at all,' he said, competently pulling into a parking space. 'And I promise I won't come over all sergeant major if you over-rev the engine a time or two.'

I couldn't help but laugh. That was exactly what I had been worried about.

'Well, thank you,' I said, 'and thanks for the lift. That distance from the cottage alone is enough to make me think that I've made the right choice about the van.'

'I'm sure you have,' he said, hopping out to retrieve my bike.

'And if you need any help with anything,' he said, as I climbed out and took hold of the handlebars, 'anything at all, then please just ask.'

'I will,' I nodded, not quite able to meet his gaze.

Perhaps we really had just got off on the wrong foot. I mean, stark naked wasn't usually how you'd introduce yourself to your new neighbour, was it? There was bound to be some initial awkwardness after an encounter like that, wasn't there?

'I'm sure Gwen would have wanted us to be friends,' he said huskily.

'I'm sure she would,' I agreed.

He was right, of course. Gwen was the best judge of character I had ever known. If there had been anything even remotely remiss about her neighbour she would have sniffed it out in a heartbeat.

'Thanks for the lift,' I said, lifting Minnie back into the basket.

'Any time,' he smiled, stroking Minnie's head. 'See you later, Lottie.'

'Lottie!' called Jemma in greeting, the second I pushed open the café gate and carefully wheeled the bike and Minnie inside. 'I'm so sorry I haven't had a chance to get back to you. We've been run off our feet here.'

'Not to worry,' I said, propping the bike out the way of the other customers and lifting Minnie out of the basket. 'I've been rather busy myself.'

'So I heard,' she laughed. 'Hens now, isn't it?'

'Yep,' I confirmed.

'Quite the countrywoman already, aren't you?' she teased good-naturedly.

'Apparently,' I laughed, wondering if I was ever going to share a single piece of news that everyone didn't already know. 'And I'm almost sorted with a car.'

She nodded but didn't say anything, so I guessed she was already privy to that little titbit as well.

'What can I get you?' she asked. 'I'm still doing breakfasts if you fancy a rasher or two after the ride in?'

'I'm all right, thanks,' I said, thinking I'd had enough pork courtesy of the hog roast and morning-after rolls to last me a week or two, 'and I didn't cycle in, actually.'

Jemma looked at the bike.

'Will gave me a lift.'

'Did he now?' she said, her eyebrows raised in interest. 'You two are finally getting along, then?'

'So just a coffee please and some toast and the Wi-Fi code, if that's OK?' I said, thinking it really wasn't necessary to add any more fuel to her fire. 'I'm looking for a new shower.'

'You can use my laptop if you like,' she offered, disappearing back inside. 'It'll be far easier than trying to work on your phone.'

'Thanks,' I called after her.

'And,' she said, rushing back out and setting it on the table I had sat at with David during my first visit, 'when I've got a sec I'll come and tell you all about what I want you to do with that Bailey.'

My heart leapt when she said that. Clearly it was going to be my project after all, and if Amber's suspicions about Jemma wanting the café to go mobile were correct, it was going to be a hugely exciting one at that.

With the speediest connection in the area it was mere minutes before I had my new (but not too powerful) shower ordered, and with the guarantee of express delivery, it was going to be delivered by the end of the next day at the very latest. I closed my eyes as I finished my coffee, revelling in the thought of showering in safety and not having to worry about the dreaded complexities of the fuse box from hell in the cupboard under the stairs.

'Well, well, well,' boomed a voice, pulling me out of my moment of indulgent contemplation. 'If it isn't Lottie Foster.'

'Hello, Chris,' I said, opening one eye and then the other. 'How are you?'

'Very well,' he beamed. 'And how are you?' He didn't wait for me to answer. 'From what I've been hearing, you've beaten me to the punch on both fronts!'

'Both fronts?' I questioned, wishing he would lower his baritone a little.

'First you bag yourself one of the handiest fellas in the county, and now you're sorted with four wheels as well.'

'Well, the four wheels bit is right enough,' I said loudly enough to hopefully set the record straight with the customers closest who were soaking up every word. 'But the fella in question has only been bagged, as you put it, to carry out some work at the cottage, nothing more,' I added, assuming he was talking about Matt. 'Like I said the day I moved in, I'm very happily single, thank you very much.'

'Yeah right,' he said with a conspiratorial wink, which did nothing to suggest that he was convinced. 'We'll see. But you did tell me you needed someone to manhandle those pesky pickle jars, didn't you?'

'Oh Chris,' chastised Jemma as she handed him an insulated cup. 'Leave the poor girl alone. She's had enough to contend with during the last few months without throwing the complexities of love into the mix. Isn't that right, Lottie?'

'Totally,' I agreed, momentarily grateful for her timely interruption.

'At least give her time to settle in,' she grinned.

'Well, I'll think about it,' said Chris with yet another wink, 'and I haven't forgotten about that promise of a Sunday cuppa, Lottie.'

'You're more than welcome any time,' I told him. 'As long

as you haven't got the local singles ads with you, and besides, I reckon I owe you and Marie rather more than a few cups of tea given how you got the cottage ready for me before I moved in.'

'Well, I don't know about that,' he said, 'but according to David, we do need to have a chat about Gwen's little collection of . . .'

'No need,' I jumped in before he announced to the world that my benefactor had been collecting caravans. 'Jemma's going to fill me in about all that right now.'

'Fair enough,' he chuckled, 'I'll be round for my Sunday cuppa soon, then.'

He handed Jemma the money for his drink and strode back to his stall.

'He really is incorrigible,' she said, shaking her head. 'Why ever did you tell him you're looking for a relationship?'

'I didn't,' I insisted in a low voice. 'I was just joking about it the day I moved in and now he won't let it drop. Anyway,' I reminded her, 'I didn't pedal all this way to talk about my non-existent love life.'

'You didn't pedal here at all,' she reminded me with a nudge. 'The most handsome man around drove you in, remember?'

There was no point contradicting her.

'So,' I said, 'come on. Tell me. What are these "crazy plans" you have for the Bailey I've got sitting back in the barn?'

'Well,' she began, edging her chair a little closer and laying her order pad and pencil on the table. 'I don't even know if it's doable of course, but Lizzie and I have been thinking about the possibility of having the van converted into a sort of mobile, but very chic, Cherry Tree Café.'

'Wow,' I smiled, delighted that Amber had been on the right track and thrilled by the prospect of being the one responsible for the potential conversion.

'And don't worry about dropping Amber in it,' said Jemma, giving me another nudge, 'I bet she's already said something to you about it, hasn't she?'

'Well,' I began. I could feel my face going red so there was no point denying it.

'It's all right,' she said. 'I don't mind. In fact, it was because of the weddings at the farm that we first came up with the idea.'

'Well, I think it all sounds wonderful,' I told her. 'And yes, it's completely doable. I worked on something similar for a guy last year who had a hankering to make crêpes on the go.'

'Excellent,' she gushed, bobbing up and down in her seat. 'So you'll do the work for us and then once it's finished we'll buy it from you, but only if that falls in with your plans, of course?'

'Absolutely,' I told her. 'I'd be honoured to do it and if you're happy to work to an estimate after we've talked through what exactly it is that you want, how you want the space to work in terms of storage and so on, then I'll be able to get going straightaway.'

'And you'll make it look beautiful, won't you?' asked Jemma, her expression serious. 'It has to look the part.'

'Oh, it will,' I told her, spinning her laptop around so she could see the screen. 'What do you think of these?'

A quick online search had pulled up a dozen or so pretty vans and Jemma grabbed her pencil and began making notes and taking down the details of those she liked the best. Personally I favoured anything that included red polka dots and Cath Kidston rose-patterned fabrics, and for the most part Jemma was in complete agreement.

'How are you getting on?' said Lizzie, as she peered over her friend's shoulder.

'Brilliant,' said Jemma, clasping her hands together before pointing at the screen. 'Lottie has agreed to do the conversion work and then sell us the van.'

'That's wonderful,' Lizzie smiled. 'I had a feeling you would. Oh, I rather like that one.'

'Very practical, isn't it?' I agreed. 'A perfect example of how to squeeze in all those tables and chairs you'll no doubt want to travel with you.'

'And I like this big awning,' said Jemma with a nod. 'At least if the weather lets us down we can still serve people in relative comfort if we have an awning the size of that one. It covers the entire van and all of the outdoor seating.'

'But have you told her the catch?' Lizzie asked, bending down so her head was level with Jemma's.

I swallowed, keeping my eyes on the screen.

'It's not really a catch,' said Jemma, clearly keen to smooth the way.

Lizzie sighed and I felt my stomach sink. I'd only just agreed to take the project on and I certainly didn't want to be beset by problems and hold-ups already.

'Has she not told you when we'd like it for?' said Lizzie, looking at me.

'No,' I said, shaking my head. 'But there isn't a rush, is there?'

My heart picked up the pace as I thought of the potential stress of working under the pressure of a tight timeframe on my first solo project.

'Harriet and Rachel are having a party to launch their nursery,' said Jemma, smiling winningly, 'and ideally, we'd like it ready for that if possible.'

'OK,' I said, looking from one of them to the other. 'And when exactly is the launch?'

'It's in six weeks,' said Lizzie.

I have to admit, I was rather glad I was sitting down when she said that.

Chapter 17

I can't say I can remember all that much of the cycle ride back to Cuckoo Cottage later that day. My head was abuzz with the prospect of beginning the exciting conversion project and, even though I was a little daunted to be tackling it on my own, deep down I couldn't wait to get stuck in.

That evening Jemma and Lizzie came out to see me, bringing with them all their plans, clippings and details of what they hoped I would be able to achieve in the tiny space. It was paramount that the caravan should be functional and efficient, but at the same time still look stylish and appealing.

'Ideally we'd like to be able to seat around four to six people inside,' said Jemma, biting her lip as she paced out the space.

'Two next to the door here then,' I suggested, pointing to where I had in mind. 'They'll be able to sit opposite each other with a little fold-down table in between.'

'And perhaps another four or even five here,' added Jemma, looking at the fixed seating area in front of the big window at the other end.

'So that part of the van can stay set up as it is, then,' I nodded. 'All it needs is reupholstering and some oilcloth for the table, but this end will need completely remodelling.'

Jemma nodded in agreement and scribbled something on to her pad.

'Then how about a bigger fridge slotted in here, next to the sink,' said Lizzie, tapping her pen on her teeth as she squinted, no doubt trying to imagine what it would all look like when it was finished.

'And I can adapt all of these cupboards to make them more practical and secure,' I continued. 'I'm fairly certain I'll be able to use almost all of what's in situ already,' I added, thinking it would be a shame to just rip it all out and start again. 'That way it won't take nearly as long to complete and you'll be retaining most of the original character.'

'That sounds perfect,' said Lizzie.

'Obviously we aren't planning to cater for hundreds,' Jemma mused. 'We'll have very definite numbers booked, so there'll be no danger of overstretching ourselves or not having enough space.'

'We're thinking small weddings and tea parties to begin with,' Lizzie continued. 'Everything will be baked, prepared and packed back at the café, and then carefully transported to the venue, and we won't venture too far from Wynbridge to begin with.'

'So basically,' I said, 'when you arrive, it will just be a case of setting everything up and making it look as pretty as The Cherry Tree Café before serving.'

'Exactly,' said the friends together.

'And if it's a complete disaster,' said Jemma, sounding suddenly doubtful, 'at least the kids will have gained a very chic playhouse.'

'I hardly think that's going to happen,' said Lizzie firmly. 'Folk have been asking us about something like this for months, Jem, there's no way it will fail. We can even make use of it at Christmas when we have the market stall set up again.'

'That sounds like a great idea,' I agreed. Gwen had told me all about the lovely stall and its fabulously festive bakes and wares. 'You could serve some hearty soups perhaps and warm rolls and marshmallow-topped hot chocolate with spiced gingerbread men.'

Given the mini heatwave the east of England was currently experiencing, it was all too easy to get caught up fantasising about the chillier days of winter.

'But we'll need extra staff,' countered Jemma.

She was clearly having a wobble and was determined to voice every challenge this new branch of the business could possibly encounter. Given everything I was currently going through, I could sympathise with how she was feeling.

'And you know as well as I do that we have people by the dozen coming in and asking for weekend work,' tutted Lizzie. 'Finding someone to help out in either the café or in here really isn't going to be an issue.'

'True,' said Jemma, sounding somewhat calmer. 'And I do know you're both right. It's just all a bit scary.'

'In that case,' I said, thinking it would be as comforting for me as it would be for her, 'let's take it just one step at a time. How about I start ripping out what you don't want to keep and then you can come back and have another look?'

'Excellent idea,' said Lizzie.

'Because you might want to reposition a couple of things after that.'

'That's true,' said Jemma, stepping up to give me a hug. 'That sounds like a great idea. Thank you, Lottie.'

'I'm sure you'll feel better if we can talk through the changes at every stage,' I said, hugging her back. 'It's like taking baby steps before you start to run, isn't it? Whatever challenges or changes you face in life,' I added wisely, 'if you take them one step at a time, they don't feel anywhere near as daunting.'

'She's right, you know,' nodded Lizzie.

'Of course she is,' smiled Jemma, looking far happier for having been on the receiving end of my drugstore psychology. 'Now, I'd better get home and see if Tom's managed to achieve the impossible and get Ella and Noah to bed on time.'

Thankfully the conversion wasn't going to be anywhere as near as complicated as it could have been. I knew I could meet the tight deadline and could already picture the completed van in my mind's eye, and what with that and an answerphone message from Matt's cousin Simon, telling me that he would be coming out in the morning to make a start on the electrical work, it really felt as if my new life was finally poised to begin and I didn't care a jot for what the gossips said. I was determined to make amazing things happen.

'So what are your plans for these?' asked Jemma as she hopped out of the Bailey and pointed at the other vans. 'I hope they aren't all going to be mobile cafés. I don't think we need that amount of competition, do we, Lizzie?'

'Oh, I shouldn't worry about that,' I told her. 'I've no more mobile teashops planned. In fact, I haven't got anything sorted for these yet,' I added, looking at the three vans. 'But I'm sure inspiration will strike soon.'

I hung around the cottage the next morning wishing that Simon had been as punctual as the delivery guy who had caught me, still dressed in the miniscule shorts and vest top that were masquerading as PJs in the heat, when he turned up to deliver my new shower.

'Bit warm, isn't it?' he grinned when I had to open the door more than an inch to take the box off his hands.

'Yes,' I blushed, taking care not to lose what little dignity

I had left as I struggled to sign his 'confirmation of delivery' gadget. 'It is a bit.'

'Have a nice day,' he waved. 'Don't forget the sunblock.'

Leaving the shower propped against the hall wall, I rushed back upstairs to pull on a slightly bigger vest and longer shorts, with one ear cocked for the sound of an engine, but I needn't have worried. An hour later and there was still no sign of Simon and I was itching to begin work on the Bailey. The mobile number he had left on his message was annoyingly ringing straight to voicemail, so I tried to send him a text, backed it up with a note pinned to the door, and strode purposefully off down to the barns to begin sizing up my debut solo project.

'Hey, Minnie,' I said to my little companion who was, as ever, close at my heels, 'can you hear that?'

I could hear a woodpecker somewhere in the field, making its unerring call, and remembered what Gwen always said about the big birds foretelling or calling up rain when they started to make that noise. I hoped she was right. The lawn was beginning to look particularly parched around the edges and could do with a prolonged soaking. As long as the bossy bird didn't unsettle Thor, I thought with a little shudder, then all would be right with the world.

In the barn, I took my time having a good look through the paperwork Jemma and Lizzie had left and then went through the van with a fine-tooth comb. This transformation was going to be fairly straightforward but I wanted to have a good look at the plumbing and electrics before I got stuck in. Fortunately a former owner had competently updated both and it wasn't long before I was ready to start dismantling the loo cubicle and cupboard which would make way for the new seating area.

It was hot, thirsty work and later that morning I took a trip back up to the cottage to make a drink and collect the post. There was still no word from Simon so, having left him yet another message and refilled mine and Minnie's water bottles, I went back to admire my handiwork and tidy up a bit. The van already felt far bigger, and where I had been wondering how easy it would be to squeeze two customers in next to the door, I could now see there was ample space.

I sat down at the table in the window for another breather and flicked through the pile of post. Most of it was junk mail for Gwen, but there were two unexpected gems hidden amongst the flyers for invisible hearing aids and inducements to install solar panels that simply took my breath away.

I thumbed through the glossy pages of the holiday brochures she had signed up for and it finally dawned on me *exactly* what she had in mind for the caravans and, joy of joys, it would mean I would never have to part with any of them. Exciting possibilities leapt off the pages and I felt my heart pick up the pace in response.

Giddy with anticipation, I ripped into an envelope with a

telling bump in the shape of a free biro and scribbled until the ink began to flow. I then quickly set about making lists and notes, terrified that now inspiration had struck it would disappear just as quickly and I would have no physical record of my light-bulb moment.

When I had finished writing, I rushed outside and hurriedly opened up the other two barns and stood back, keen to see if they had the potential I was hoping for. Yes, it was all there. With my head fit to burst, and tears pricking my eyes, I could imagine the transformation as clearly as if it had already happened. I could see every last detail in all its glory and wished I could tell Gwen that I had worked it out; that what I was looking at was a truly vintage idea in every possible sense.

I had just about got my heart rate back under control when I heard a vehicle pull off the road and into the yard. Typical. All morning I'd been desperate for Simon to show up and now he had all I wanted was to be left alone with my notes, lists and simmering excitement.

'Hey there, Lottie!'

I was delighted to see that it wasn't Simon after all, but Amber.

This time she was wearing full-length floral-patterned wellies and had her pretty daughter, Honey, with her. The little girl was toddling towards me with painstaking slowness and looking about her with keen and interested eyes.

'Hello!' I called back, waving to them both. 'You have no idea how excited I am to see you.'

Amber was the perfect person to share my moment with and sensing intrigue she scooped Honey up into her arms and picked up the pace.

'I'll come up to the cottage,' I called.

'No, don't do that,' Amber insisted. 'I've got something to show you and I want to take another peek at those vans, if you don't mind.'

I walked to meet her and quickly relieved her of the heavy bag she had on her shoulder.

'Lottie,' she smiled, jiggling her daughter about in her arms. 'This is Honey. I know you didn't really get to meet her properly at the party so I thought I'd bring her to say hello today.'

'Hello, Honey,' I smiled. 'Aren't you gorgeous?'

Honey, rosy-cheeked and dark-haired, pulled off her sun hat, shoved her fingers into her mouth and dissolved into giggles.

'Are you sure you should be carrying her?' I asked, trying to convey my concern without sounding too obvious. 'She must weigh more than this bag.'

'I knew you'd guessed,' Amber groaned, rolling her eyes and transferring Honey from her arms to mine. 'I swear I've still got baby brain from when I had her.'

Honey didn't seem at all concerned to find herself in the

arms of a complete stranger. She lightly touched the plastic flamingo-shaped dangly earrings I was wearing and, after examining them closely for a few seconds, shoved her thumb in and nestled into my shoulder. I was besotted.

'I haven't told anyone,' I said to her mum. 'Not mentioned it to a soul.'

'Thank you,' she said, rubbing my arm and tucking a curl behind Honey's little ear. 'I'm almost at the three month mark so we'll be making a proper announcement after that. Unless of course everyone has already worked it out,' she wailed. 'Jake and Annie know, of course, and you, and Jessica and Harriet. Oh dear,' she added, biting her lip. 'I think the cat is probably already out of the bag, don't you?'

I transferred Honey to my other hip and hoisted her up a bit. I had no idea that such tiny tots weighed so much.

'Well,' I smiled, 'like I said, no one's heard anything from me.'

'Thank you, lovely.' Amber smiled kindly. 'I really appreciate your discretion, especially as my own isn't quite up to scratch.'

I had barely taken three steps when I had to stop again to rearrange the weighty load I was carrying.

'She weighs a ton, doesn't she?' said Amber, wrinkling her nose at her sleepy daughter and taking the bag from my other shoulder. 'I thought she might have fallen asleep on the way here, but she's every inch as stubborn as her father.'

'Actually,' I puffed, my knees beginning to complain, 'she is a bit of a weight. Shall we go and sit inside one of the vans?'

I could feel my temperature rising and my heart thumping more quickly again just at the mere mention of them. Now I knew what it was I was going to do, I couldn't bear to be parted from them.

'Sorry,' tutted Amber, 'I almost forgot I've actually come to show you something and you seemed so excited when I arrived. What's going on?'

'You first,' I insisted, talking to her over the top of Honey's hot little head. 'Show me what it is you've found and then I'll spill the beans.'

While Amber rearranged Honey's blanket and some of the caravan cushions and settled her daughter in a cosy little nest, I stuffed the post together into a haphazard pile, carefully ensuring she wouldn't be able to see what I had been looking at when the penny had finally dropped. I wanted it to be a complete surprise.

Minnie, having overseen what Amber was doing, curled herself around Honey's makeshift bed ready to stand duty, while Amber and I looked at one another and grinned, but neither of us still knowing why.

'OK,' she said, sliding around the side of the table and reaching for her bag. 'Now, you'll just have to go with this because I admit it is a bit off the wall, and it might be way off the mark, but having seen them I simply had to show you. What do you make of these?'

She spread out three much-thumbed magazines. Each had neatly folded, colour-coded Post-it notes attached and I couldn't help but grin at my new friend and her exceptional organisational skills.

'You know what,' I sighed. 'I reckon you must be Monica Geller's twin.'

'Never mind my penchant for order,' she tutted. 'Just listen.'

'Sorry,' I whispered.

'When I first moved to Skylark Farm,' she began, 'I had a bit of an obsession with these magazines. Still do, to be honest,' she admitted. 'And Jake used to tease me all the time, until I turned to them for inspiration when we needed to think seriously about diversification projects for Skylark Farm.'

'I take it these helped then,' I interrupted.

'Oh yes,' she smiled, 'they certainly did, and I've never thrown away a single issue, which is a blessing really because if I had I might have missed out on spotting just what I think you could be looking for.'

She flicked open the magazines to the marked pages and spun them around. I stared at the carefully created images in disbelief and then reached for the pile of mail and showed her what had caught my eye just moments before she and Honey had arrived

'Well, I'll be . . .' gasped Amber. Her face was an absolute picture. 'It's like we're one mind.'

'Isn't it?' I laughed.

'How spooky is that? Is this what you were so excited about just now?'

'Yes!' I said, trying not to squeal and jump up and down in my seat in case I disturbed Honey. 'So I'm not completely bonkers, then?'

'Oh yes,' said Amber, happily paraphrasing Lewis Carroll, 'but all the best people are!'

'Stop joshing,' I said, tapping her hand, 'and be serious for a minute. Do you reckon I'm thinking too big here?'

'Absolutely not,' she insisted. 'If you can pull this off, Lottie, and let's face it,' she said, looking around, 'you've certainly got the best possible start here, then the results will be phenomenal.'

We looked at each other and then back to the papers and magazines again.

'A truly bespoke vintage experience,' I said wistfully. 'Somewhere unique, where people can spend their holidays in beautifully refurbished caravans nestled amongst the backdrop of big skies which frame the Fenland landscape.'

'It's perfect,' she sighed, 'and you've literally got everything you need to get started right here.'

'Obviously I haven't thought it all through properly yet,' I went on, 'but I was thinking that perhaps the small barn would make a good office and perhaps a camp shop, stocking all the basics and some local goods, and the middle one might be suitable to convert into a luxurious shower block.'

'And you could have music and entertainment in here,' said Amber, enthusiastically picking up the thread. 'This would be the perfect space to hang out in if the weather wasn't all that great. You could probably even barbecue in here, couldn't you? I can offer you a great price on local free-range pork.' She winked.

I shook my head, thinking how clever she was. She might still be suffering from baby brain, but her business brain didn't miss a trick.

'I'm going to give these three Cheltenham vans a makeover,' I rushed on. 'Make them picture-perfect and then look for another three from a slightly different era. I don't think I'd want more than six. Too many would spoil the ambience and make it too crowded. I want each van to have its own special place in the field with cars parked somewhere else to keep it all as peaceful and unobtrusive as possible.'

We looked at the magazines featuring slick airstreams and shepherd huts and just for a second I felt a small, but very real pang of doubt.

'But what if no one comes,' I swallowed. 'What if people don't like the idea?'

Now I'd got my heart set on it I really didn't want to give

it up, but I had to be sensible. It wasn't going to be cheap to set up and I wasn't exactly rolling in ready cash.

'Lottie,' said Amber seriously, gripping my hand, 'if I had a pound for every booking I've had to turn down this year because the diary for the bungalow is already full, then I'd never have to pick another apple again.'

'But there's a big difference between holidaying in a cottage and glamping in a vintage caravan,' I reminded her.

'I know,' she said with a wink, 'and I hope I don't regret saying this, given that you're going to be the competition, but actually they're a lot more fun, aren't they?'

Chapter 18

Amber and I sat talking through the prospective project and making more detailed plans as to how the site could look and would run until Honey began to stir.

'So when do you think you'll be taking your first bookings?' Amber asked, as she began to repack her bag.

I had known, right from the first time we met, that she was a fast worker, but I was going to have to settle for a more measured pace to get my own dream business up and running. Becoming more business-minded was going to be a steep learning curve for me. A point hammered home when I remembered I still hadn't negotiated a price for the Cherry Tree caravan yet.

'I don't know,' I said, biting my lip. I had no idea how long it was going to take to get enough money together to make even a tiny start. 'There's so much to think about. My funds are pretty tight at the moment and I've still got to talk to Mags about a price for the minivan, of course, and that's even before I've factored in the cost of all the work that needs doing on the cottage.' Perhaps the fee I would negotiate for transforming the Bailey would go some way to covering that.

'What work?'

'Oh, there are lots of things,' I said dismissively, as if I wasn't worried about it at all. 'I won't bore you with the details, but it isn't going to be cheap getting the place back in decent condition.'

Amber looked at me, wearing the same expression of disbelief that Will had thrown me when I said the same to him.

'Are you sure?' she frowned.

'Hey now, don't you start,' I said, with a small smile. 'Will didn't believe me when I told him either.'

'I'm not saying I don't believe you,' said Amber, stooping to pick up her daughter. 'I'm just surprised, that's all.'

'He was surprised, too,' I told her. 'He said he couldn't believe Matt was right about it all actually.'

'Well, he would know,' she said, passing me the still drowsy bundle that was Honey.

'Who?' I frowned, unsure which of the men she meant. 'Are you talking about Matt or Will?'

'Both, I guess,' she shrugged, 'what with Matt being a builder, but I was actually thinking of Will in this instance.'

'How,' I puffed, hoisting Honey a little higher on to my

shoulder, 'could an ex-soldier possibly have any idea about what's wrong with my cottage?'

'Well, he converted the barn practically single-handedly,' said Amber, 'and it was nothing more than a few crumbling walls when he took it on, so I dare say he'd have a pretty good idea.'

'Did he?' I gasped.

I still hadn't seen this magnificent conversion Mags had mentioned for myself, but I knew it was a gargantuan task transforming a few dilapidated walls into a homely abode.

'Yes,' Amber tutted. 'And you needn't sound so surprised. He's done an amazing job on the place. I think it was some sort of therapy after . . .'

'After what?' I pounced.

'Well, I don't know really,' she frowned. 'He had problems when he first moved here, but no one knows much about them, or his life in the army, come to that. He's a very private person, especially when it comes to his past. He never says much about anything.'

'Except for when it comes to airing his opinion about my home,' I said with a smile.

'Look,' she went on, 'I know the pair of you didn't exactly hit it off, what with the nettle fiasco and everything, but if you do have any doubts about what Matt has suggested then you could do far worse than ask Will to have a look round.'

'I'll consider it,' I said, thinking that I hadn't really had any doubts but if I did decide to talk to Will about it, we were, thanks to the lift into town, on friendlier terms now at least.

'Good,' she said. 'And don't forget, Will was very close to Gwen. I'm sure that if there was anything that required *really* urgent attention then he would have sorted it for her the second it came to light.'

I couldn't help thinking that it was Matt that Gwen had turned to about the work and Will hadn't exactly put his foot down about replacing the shower and fuse box, had he? But he had at least alerted her to the seriousness of the problem, I supposed, and I knew for myself that she could be pretty stubborn when she wanted to be, so the fact that it still wasn't sorted wasn't really his fault.

We finished gathering and tidying the papers and magazines together and then walked back to Amber's truck.

The wind had picked up and, even though it was still hot and disgustingly humid, I could see dark clouds gathering on the horizon. I hoped we weren't in for a storm. I hated thunder almost as much as I hated the thought of driving.

'Do you know,' I said as I helped wrestle a now wide-awake Honey back into her car seat and dismissed the sudden change in the weather in the hope that it would blow in the opposite direction, 'even with all the work ahead and money to find, I feel as if a huge weight has been lifted off my shoulders.'

'Lifted off?' Amber questioned. 'Surely you mean you feel as if a weight has descended?'

'No,' I said thoughtfully. 'I feel liberated in a way.'

'Liberated?'

'Yes,' I said, 'liberated, and all thanks to Gwen. She's given me something I can really sink my teeth into here, hasn't she? She's handed me the perfect opportunity to finally get on with the job of living.'

I knew it probably sounded strange to Amber, but I knew what I meant.

'So,' she frowned, much as I expected she would, 'I take it you've never felt like this before then? Don't you feel as if you've been living life to the full?'

'No,' I said, 'I haven't. I know from what you've told me about your career and the farm that you've always been someone who sets their sights on something they want and then makes it happens, but that's not been me. I've just jogged along really,' I shrugged, thinking how safe my job and limited life back in Lincoln had been. 'For the most part, I've just fitted in with whatever happened to come along. I've never actually gone out looking for a big adventure like this. I've never wanted to.'

'Until now,' said Amber, her eyes lighting up.

'Yes,' I agreed, 'until now. From this moment on I'm going to be brave and I'm going to be the one who makes things happen.'

'Well, good for you,' she laughed. 'That's wonderful.'

'It is rather, isn't it?' I laughed back. 'And it's all thanks to dear Gwen, but you won't tell anyone about my idea, will you, Amber?'

'Why ever not?' she frowned, turning to face me again. 'You're going to need all the help you can muster to get this idea up and running.'

'I know that,' I nodded, 'and I won't want to keep it all to myself forever obviously, but just for now, while I'm getting to grips with it all and thinking it through, I'd rather keep it under wraps.'

'Well, as long as you're sure?' she asked doubtfully.

'I know you think I should be shouting about it from the rooftops,' I acknowledged, 'but I promise you, I do have my reasons for keeping quiet.'

'Do you want to tell me what they are?'

'Not today,' I said firmly. I was already dreading what the suspicious locals were going to say about my ambitious project and knew it was paramount I had it all clear in my mind before I attempted to get them onside. 'But I might one day, assuming they haven't all been forgotten in the excitement when things begin to happen, of course.'

'All right,' she agreed, 'that's fair enough, but don't forget, it really is up to you to make this a success.'

'How could I possibly forget that?' I laughed. 'You're going to be reminding me every five minutes, aren't you?'

Amber laughed along with me.

'Of course,' she smiled, 'and I promise I'll keep your secret far better than I have this baby business,' she added, running her hand over her still flat tummy. 'Just so long as you make sure you put me and Jake down for the first mini-break booking, OK?'

'But it's only up the road,' I reminded her.

'That doesn't matter,' she enlightened me. 'When you've got a farm, a fella, an ageing aunt, a daughter, livestock and a business to run, even a trip to the supermarket can be a welcome break.'

'Fair enough,' I smiled, thinking that she, Jemma and Lizzie were all women on a mission. 'I'll put you and Jake down as my very first guests.'

'Brilliant,' she beamed. 'And how are the hens, by the way?'

'Hilarious,' I said, 'I can watch them for hours, and the eggs might be small, but they're packed full of flavour. They've quite transformed my breakfast. First I cook what they've presented me with, then I sit and watch them darting about the run, fixated on anything that flies.'

'Have you named them yet?'

'No,' I said, 'not yet, but give me time.'

'Excellent,' she smiled, climbing behind the wheel and scanning the horizon. 'You might want to shut them up for a bit if this storm hits.'

Right on cue, there was a distant rumble of thunder and Minnie scuttled back towards the cottage with her tail between her legs.

'I'm hoping it's going to roll around us rather than come over,' I said, with a shudder. 'I hate it.'

'Well, you never know,' said Amber. 'We might get away with it, and sometimes it does seem to track the river. Anyway, congratulations, Lottie Foster,' she nodded. 'I think you've got the makings of a very beautiful and successful business here.'

'Well, I hope so,' I said, biting my lip and looking back towards the barns.

My head was full of exciting possibilities and my heart suddenly seemed to be beating to a very different tune. I was already beginning to wish I hadn't felt the need to keep ambition at bay for so long and I knew that Gwen and Gran would have been delighted that I was determined to make up for lost time.

'I know so,' Amber said firmly. 'I'll see you later.'

'Thanks for coming,' I said, taking a step back. 'Bye.'

'Bye,' called a little voice from the back seat.

'Bye, bye, Honey bee,' I called as Amber pulled away, 'I'll see you soon.'

As they disappeared out of sight I could hear the telephone ringing in the cottage and rushed to pick it up before the answerphone cut in, fumbling with the hula girl key ring in my haste. A vehicle drove by and I glanced back at the road to make sure it wasn't Amber coming back for something she had forgotten. But it was Will. Heading towards home, he was still driving slowly and gave me a thumbs up in the process. I waved back then rushed into the house feeling pleased that he was sticking to the speed limit.

'Hello,' I said, snatching up the phone just before Gwen's voice cut in.

'Lottie?'

'Yes,' I frowned.

'It's Simon.'

I was feeling none too impressed about his no-show and having quickly glanced at the answering machine I could see that he hadn't even called and left a message.

'I'm sorry about this morning,' he began.

'I thought you were coming out to see me first thing,' I snapped. I knew I sounded cross, but I hated being messed about.

'I was,' he said, 'but this emergency came up.'

'Right,' I said, trying not to sound peevish. I might have been annoyed but my bad mood wasn't going to make him materialise out of thin air. 'So when are you coming?'

'Won't be today now, I'm afraid,' he said with a sigh. 'There's the mother of all thunderstorms heading in our direction apparently and I won't be doing any electrical work during that obviously.'

Just as he finished speaking, I saw a flash in the distance and Minnie dived under the table. The storm still looked a long way off, but I could tell it had its sights set on making its presence felt.

'But what about my fuse box,' I swallowed. 'Tell me again what I need to do if the power goes off?'

'Nothing,' said Simon seriously. 'And I really mean that. Don't go anywhere near the damn thing.'

'But what about when the storm has gone?' I said. 'What do I have to do to get the power back on, assuming it's knocked out of course?'

'Oh, it'll be knocked out all right,' said Simon, 'but I don't want you going anywhere near that box. That thing's a tragedy waiting to happen. You ring me later and then sit tight until I come out and sort it.'

I didn't know if that was a comforting suggestion or not. Surely the wretched thing was as much of a threat to Simon as it was to me and if he got hurt, or worse, I was sure there would be someone waiting to sue me.

'Well, all right,' I said reluctantly. 'But make sure you keep your phone handy, won't you?' I told him. 'Because I have a feeling I'm going to become your latest emergency very soon.'

'Just batten down the hatches,' said Simon firmly,

making no attempt to allay my fears. 'It's going to be a big one.'

He hung up and immediately the phone rang again. This time it was Amber.

'Are you all right?' I asked. 'Are you home?'

'Yes,' she said. 'We're just back, but I wanted to warn you about this storm. Annie seems to think it will be with us in about half an hour and it's going to hang around. Will you be all right? For some reason the stretch of drove where you are seems to cop it worse than we do when its right overhead and I know you said you don't like it.'

'I'll be fine,' I insisted, but I was feeling less fine with every passing second. 'I've got Minnie to keep me company.'

'I can come and get you both, if you like?'

There was no way I was going to ask a pregnant woman to come and rescue me, even if I did want to seek sanctuary under a blanket with some company.

'No,' I said, trying to sound as if the prospect of the storm was nothing more than a minor inconvenience. 'Thank you for the offer, but we'll stick it out here. I can carry on working on my plans and lists.'

'Well, as long as you're sure.'

Amber eventually rang off and I was sure for about the next two minutes as I went upstairs to get changed out of my work gear, but then I began to panic. What if the fuse box really was as dangerous as Simon had suggested? What if it sparked and ignited something in the cupboard? My mind was free-falling out of all control as I began to pace the hall and watch Minnie cowering under the table, and consequently I made quite possibly the most ridiculous and dangerous decision of my entire life.

Chapter 19

'Come on,' I said, pulling Minnie out from under the table and holding her close.

I could feel her little body trembling, but my mind was made up and I knew that if we didn't get going straightaway we wouldn't make it at all. I pulled on Gwen's old gardening mackintosh, locked the cottage door, ushered three very startled hens into their coop, dumped Minnie in the bike basket and set off at full speed. I kept my eyes fixed on the road ahead, rather than the rampaging cloud that the wind was whipping towards us far quicker than I had initially realised.

I wasn't all that sure how far it was from Cuckoo Cottage to George's place, but if I pedalled like the wind I was sure I could make it. We could spend the afternoon together watching the storm unfold from the safety of his little house and then I would cycle home to survey the damage when it was all over. But of course, as with most of life's big ideas, my fail-safe plan didn't quite work out like that.

The rain began to fall just as what I guessed was Will's barn came into view, but I knew there was no point turning back. I would just have to keep going at the crazy speed I had worked the creaking bike up to and hope we weren't in for too much of a soaking. To begin with, the drops were few and far between. They plopped heavily on the road, with just the occasional smattering managing to hit us, but they in no way prepared us for the onslaught we were about to experience.

'There you go,' I whispered soothingly to Minnie, naively thinking everything was going to be all right. 'I told you we'd be OK.'

I was just about to stroke the top of her head, and tell her what a clever mummy I was, when I was blinded by a bolt of lightning which touched down terrifyingly close in the field on our right. No longer tracking the River Wyn, the storm had leapt towards us in mere seconds and the clap of thunder which accompanied the flash made my eardrums ache. The rain suddenly began to pummel down and I knew I had to run. I dumped the bike in the verge, held Minnie tight, kept my eyes firmly fixed on the horizon and set off, my legs working like pistons and my heart hammering in fear.

More lightning flashed around us, even closer this time, and the menacing rumble that began straight after it rolled on and on. The depth of sound was so intense I could feel it resonating in my chest and through the road beneath my feet. The next flash struck the power lines either side of us and they began to crackle and spark and as I looked up, just for a second, my foot caught in a pothole and I was sent sprawling. I dropped Minnie and landed hard on the unforgiving road, my hands thankfully saving me from hitting my head.

I'd never felt more of a fool in my life. My knees and palms were bloody and my teeth were chattering, but worse than all of the damage I'd done to myself was the sight of poor Minnie who had made no attempt to run off but stood shivering and crying at my side. My stupid decision to leave the cottage had probably inflicted more psychological harm on the poor little scrap than I was ever going to be able to undo and I forced myself to reach out for her, drag myself up and then carry on, feeling every bit as scared, hurt and miserable as I deserved.

It seemed to take forever for Will to hear me hammering on the door, but eventually he appeared, wearing nothing but a navy bath towel slung low round his hips. He looked as shocked to see me as I was to be standing there and when he wrenched open the door I collapsed sobbing and pathetic into his arms.

'Jesus, Lottie,' he gasped as my cold wet body slammed into his. 'What the hell's happened?'

I opened my mouth to explain, but the words just wouldn't come.

'Here,' he said, pulling me inside and closing the door. 'Give me Minnie. Quick.'

My hands were shaking so much as I handed her over I almost dropped her. Will rushed off and came back with her wrapped in a smaller version of the towel he was still wearing. Conscious that my soaked clothes were dripping and steadily soaking the floor, I stayed rooted to the doormat and watched as he sat and began to rub her dry. When he had finished, he snuggled her down among the cushions in a fresh towel and came back to me.

'Come on,' he said. 'We have to get you out of these wet clothes.'

He knelt down and pulled my feet out of the wellies, taking in the state of my knees, and then stood back up and gently slipped the saturated mackintosh from my shoulders. My clothes underneath were just as wet and I couldn't stop shaking, no matter how hard I tried.

'And these,' he said.

I stared at him, but still couldn't find my voice or move.

'I'm serious,' he said firmly. 'You're freezing, Lottie, and probably in shock. Come on, quickly. It's nothing I haven't seen before, remember?'

My fingers finally fumbled to unbutton my blouse, but I just couldn't do it. Will stepped closer again and took over.

I could feel his breath and the warmth from his body as he slipped off my blouse and then reached around my back to undo the zip on my skirt, which fell to the floor.

'Christ,' he said, gazing down at me. 'You're soaked right through.'

I looked down in dismay. My underwear was plastered to me like a second skin and it was completely see-through, but I didn't care. I didn't have the energy to care, and like he'd said, there was nothing on show that he hadn't seen before in even more detail.

'Come with me,' he commanded, taking hold of my wrist when it was obvious that I was still in no fit state to offer an explanation as to what had happened.

I tripped numbly along behind him and into the bathroom.

'I've set it to warm,' he said when he'd eventually finished fiddling with the shower settings. 'And there are plenty of towels. Take your time, but don't lock the door. I don't want to have to break it down if you pass out.'

I nodded.

'All right?' he frowned, determined to make me speak.

'OK,' I whispered, amazed that I still had a voice.

'Put this on when you get out,' he said, laying a bathrobe on the stool next to the shower. 'And then we'll have a look at your knees.'

'And my hands,' I croaked, holding up my scratched, bleeding palms.

Will shook his head in disbelief and tutted.

'Whatever were you doing out there?'

I shook my head and listened to the storm which was still raging right over our heads.

'Well, you've done a thorough job of hurting yourself,' he said. 'I'll get you a drink ready,' he added, 'something to warm you up on the inside.'

'Not tea,' I begged.

Even though I was numb with shock, I still felt, Skylark Scrumpy aside, as though I'd drunk nothing other than tea since I first arrived in Wynbridge.

'Definitely not tea,' he agreed.

I stood under the warm flow of water in Will's walk-in shower, willing myself not to cry and trying not to think about the fact that even though my body felt like it had been hit by a bus, I had been incredibly turned on as he had peeled off my clothes and undressed me. The brush of his warm skin on my frozen flesh had aroused goosebumps that I was sure had nothing to do with the tumble I had taken on the road.

Struggling to dismiss my feelings, I rinsed my hair and reached for the shower gel. It seemed such an intimate thing to do, covering myself with Will's masculine woody scent, but there were no traces of anything even remotely feminine anywhere, which, I was perturbed to realise, I felt rather pleased about.

'You all right in there?' Will called through the door. 'Do you need a hand?'

'No thanks,' I squeaked as visions of him towelling me down made me feel light-headed all over again. 'I'm all right. I'm almost done.'

Gingerly I patted my scraped knees and palms dry, slipped on the bathrobe – Will's bathrobe – and opened the door.

'All right?' he asked, his brow creased in concern.

'I think so,' I croaked.

'And have you warmed up a bit?'

'Yes,' I nodded. 'Yes, thank you, and my knees have stopped shaking, although I can't say the same about my hands.'

'Well, that's a start,' he said, looking at me seriously.

He had swapped his towel for a pair of jogging bottoms and a close-fitting T-shirt, but his feet were still bare. He looked incredibly handsome, as if he'd just stepped off the pages of the latest Boss ad campaign, and I wondered if perhaps I had hit my head on the road after all.

I'd spent so much of our brief relationship feeling annoyed with my unlikely hero that I hadn't allowed myself to really think about just how drop-dead gorgeous he actually was and the fact that he was now being so kind did nothing to calm the muddled feelings playing out in my head.

'Come and sit down,' he said as yet another clap of thunder shook the barn and the rain lashed against the windows.

I sat as instructed and Minnie shuffled along and curled up by my side.

'I'm so sorry, sweetheart,' I whispered, my eyes filling with tears. 'I didn't mean to scare you.'

She licked the back of my hand and closed her eyes again.

Will knelt down in front of me and gently lifted the dressing gown, revealing knees which looked as if they'd tripped straight off the school playground.

'I have to ask,' he said, as he began gently picking out the tiny bits of stone that the shower hadn't managed to dislodge. 'What the hell were you doing? I take it you had a good reason to be passing my door during the mother of all storms?'

I shook my head, feeling thoroughly embarrassed by the whole silly situation.

'Not really.'

'So what were you doing?'

'I was too afraid to stay at the cottage,' I explained, gasping from the pain. 'The electrician called and told me not to go anywhere near that blasted fuse box if the power went off and I got spooked. I panicked and convinced myself it was going to catch fire or something if the storm hit.'

I knew it sounded ridiculous. It *was* ridiculous.

'But I thought you were going to have the box replaced.'

'I am,' I said. 'It was supposed to be done this morning,

but the guy had an emergency and didn't show up. If he'd turned up when he should have done it would have all been done by now. Jesus!' I winced. 'Sorry. Crikey, that stings.'

Will ignored me and carried on. As a highly decorated soldier, I guessed he'd seen far worse than my few cuts and grazes.

'So have you made arrangements for him to come back then?'

'Not yet,' I said, realising I hadn't.

Simon had been quick to say he would come out and reset the fuse box if the power was knocked out, but we hadn't set another date for him to come and carry out the work.

'And who is this guy?' Will frowned, turning his attention from my knees to my grazed palms.

'Some chap called Simon,' I explained. 'He's a cousin of Matt's, apparently.'

I held my breath, waiting for him to say something scathing about my choice of builder again, but he didn't.

'There,' he said instead. 'All done and this is exactly why we need to get you sorted out with Mags's minivan as soon as possible, isn't it?'

'I guess so,' I said, feeling like a child who was being lectured by someone older and wiser.

'No,' said Will. 'You know so, Lottie. You can't risk this sort of thing happening again and please don't look so downhearted about it. When I said I'd accompany you on the road until you get used to driving again, I really meant it.'

'Thank you,' I smiled. 'I would appreciate that. I can drive. I just haven't for a long time.'

I forced down the reason why I was so reluctant and focused on Will's kind words instead.

'Well, give it a few weeks and you'll be wondering how you've managed without a car for so long,' he said, walking over to the kitchen. 'I promise.'

'Anything's got to be better than relying on that rust-ridden bike,' I relented, with another shake of my head.

'Talking of which,' Will frowned, 'what have you done with it?'

'I dumped it on the verge,' I confessed. 'It isn't on the road or anything so it should be fine. I'll pick it up when I walk back to the cottage.'

'You won't be walking anywhere,' said Will. 'Now, drink this while I go and set the machine to dry your clothes. I've given them a quick rinse. I hope that was OK?'

'Yes,' I croaked, 'thanks.' I was surprised by how organised he was.

'I thought I'd better do it quickly in case the power goes off.' He smiled. 'We can't have you going home in my bath-robe, can we?'

'No,' I sighed. 'I guess not.'

Given how soft and comforting it was, I wouldn't have minded if I never took it off again.

'So what is this?' I said, peering into the depths of the glass of amber liquid he handed me.

'Whisky,' he said, as another rumble of thunder ripped through the ground. 'Neat, single malt. It'll warm you from the inside out.'

Personally I couldn't help thinking I already had enough fire in my belly, but I knocked it back in one and began to splutter.

'You don't have to neck it!' Will laughed. 'You'd better just sip the next one.'

Given the way my throat was burning, I didn't much want another one. I was just about to say as much when the room was lit up and then plunged into darkness.

'Damn,' muttered Will. 'That's the power out then. I'm afraid you're going to have to wait for your clothes after all. You aren't in any rush to get home, are you?'

'No,' I said. The last thing I wanted was to be home alone with the fuse box from hell. 'As long as I'm not in your way.'

'Not at all,' he said. 'It's actually nice to have some company, although I think you could have timed your arrival a little better.'

'What do you mean?'

'Well, when I first saw you on the doorstep,' he grinned,

pointing back towards the bathroom, 'just for a split second I thought you were here to get your own back.'

'As if,' I gasped. 'How could you think such a thing?'

Will wiggled his eyebrows suggestively and reached for his phone.

'Bugger,' he muttered, throwing it back down again. 'No signal. Will you be all right if I just nip out?' he asked, reaching for a fleece that was hanging next to the door and pulling on a pair of trainers. 'I'll be back in a bit.'

'Where are you going?'

Funnily enough I didn't feel daunted by the thought of being alone during the storm in Will's place at all.

'Just down the road to check on George,' he said, dashing out into the rain. 'I know he won't thank me for it, but I just want to make sure he's OK. You never know, he might even want to come here and see the storm out with us. Make yourself at home, won't you?'

'OK,' I nodded, biting my lip. 'Thanks Will.'

Chapter 20

Will wasn't gone for long and I wasn't at all surprised that he came back on his own.

'So how did you find him?' I asked, as he kicked off his trainers and disappeared into the bathroom for yet another towel to dry off with.

'Fine,' he said, rubbing his head until his dark hair stood up in all directions. 'Well, apart from being furious that I'd gone down to check that he was all right, of course.'

'Now why doesn't that surprise me?' I smiled.

'And he was pretty cross with you, of course.'

'What on earth made you tell him what I'd done?'

'Sorry,' he said, but he didn't sound sorry at all. 'It just kind of slipped out.'

Given that he had just saved me and Minnie from certain hypothermia, I thought it best not to grumble about his lack of discretion.

'And what about Mags and Ed?' I asked, remembering that they lived in the house next door to George.

'Not at home,' said Will. 'I did go round and check. I should think they're still at the nursery. Have you had anything to eat?'

'Of course not,' I tutted, 'I'm not likely to go helping myself to the contents of your fridge, am I?'

Will shrugged, suggesting he wouldn't have minded if I had.

'To be honest,' I said, stifling a yawn and feeling more relaxed than I ever had when faced with a wall of lightning, 'I haven't budged from this spot. I've been too mesmerised by the light display in front of me.'

'Much better watching it from the safety of the sofa, isn't it?' he teased.

'Definitely.'

Will's barn was immaculate and beautifully finished and I had felt perfectly safe cosseted in the cushions of his massive sofa, even though he had left me all alone in the middle of such a tempestuous storm.

He busied himself in the kitchen and a few minutes later presented Minnie with a dish of what looked like succulent steak cut into tiny pieces and me with a huge slice of chocolate cake.

'Obviously I can't give you anything warm now the power's out, but I thought this might fit the bill. It's Jemma's finest and I don't think the extra sugar will do you any harm, given everything you've been through.'

'Oh wow,' I said, 'thank you. It looks great. She's an amazing baker, isn't she?'

'The best,' Will nodded, through the first mouthful of his own delicious slice. 'Although I have to say she's not so great when it comes to helping me keep the pounds off.'

He had looked fine to me, standing in the doorway all taut and toned in his towel, but I thought it best not to comment.

'I'll have to run this off later,' he said, taking another massive bite.

'Do you run a lot?'

'I try to,' he nodded, 'but I'm probably not as disciplined as I should be.'

'I suppose you had to be pretty disciplined when you were a soldier, didn't you?'

Will nodded, but didn't say anything.

'You weren't very happy when George let slip at the party that you're ex-military, were you?'

'No,' he said, 'I wasn't.'

'I've never really thought about the role of the vet in the armed forces before,' I carried on, not yet picking up that he still didn't want to talk about his life before Wynbridge. 'But I suppose there are plenty of animals that need looking after, aren't there?'

'Yes,' he said, 'there are.'

'Dogs and horses,' I blithely carried on as I took another mouthful of the velvety cake.

'Lottie,' he said, putting down his plate and turning to face me. 'Please don't take this the wrong way, especially as this is the first time we've actually managed to spend some proper time in each other's company without falling out, but do you mind if we drop it?'

'No, of course not,' I blushed. 'I was just trying to make conversation.'

'I know,' he said, 'but I don't talk about it with anyone, so please don't think I'm being awkward. It's just a part of my life that I've moved on from.'

'Of course.'

'Why don't we talk about you instead?' he suggested. 'Tell me about your life before you moved to Cuckoo Cottage.'

I looked across at him and bit my lip.

'Well,' I sighed, suddenly remembering how difficult it was to talk about things that made me uncomfortable now he had served up a dose of my own medicine. 'I suppose I didn't really have one.'

My mind flitted back to my telephone conversation with Matt. How on earth had he managed to get me talking about my childhood and absent parents? Was it because it was a phone call rather than a face-to-face conversation? I couldn't put my finger on it, but it made me feel rotten about not being able to tell Will.

'But you must have had a job?' he tried again. 'Some sort of career?'

'I had a job,' I said unhelpfully, 'a job I loved, but it wasn't a big career like you had.'

'Oh,' he said. 'OK.'

'But that's all about to change,' I announced, thinking back to the vans and the idea of setting up my own glamping site. 'Thanks to Gwen I've got great plans for the future now.'

'Have you?'

'I have,' I sighed then quickly added, 'but I'm not going to tell you what they are, not yet anyway.'

'Crikey,' smirked Will. 'First I don't want to talk and now you don't. Aren't we the life and soul of the party?'

'Well,' I said, biting my lip, 'perhaps you aren't the only one with a past that's tough to talk about.'

'And perhaps we're a lot more alike than I first thought,' he smiled kindly.

'Perhaps we are,' I smiled back.

'Do you miss her?' he asked, pulling me out of the dream state I was falling headlong into. 'Gwen, I mean.'

'Of course,' I said.

I hadn't realised I had been holding my breath.

'So how come you hadn't visited her for so long?'

His tone was far from accusatory, but even so, I could feel the familiar old remorse rearing its ugly head. My colour deepened and my throat tightened as guilt wrapped around my heart and gave it a long, hard squeeze.

'Sorry,' said Will. 'That's absolutely none of my business. I shouldn't have asked.'

'No,' I whispered. 'It's OK.'

'You don't have to tell me anything, Lottie,' he insisted. 'Especially as I haven't told you a thing about me.'

'Honestly,' I began, thinking I could at least talk about this if nothing else, 'it's fine. I couldn't visit for a while because if I wasn't working I was looking after my gran who had suffered a massive stroke, and to be honest, after she died I just couldn't face coming back.'

Will nodded and I got the impression that he understood.

'I thought there were too many memories wrapped up in this place and I had no idea that I'd be living here one day, but Gwen and I used to talk on the phone all the time and I was just beginning to think that I should come and see her when ...'

My words trailed off and Will nodded again. It was the first time I'd suggested to anyone how guilty I felt and I realised I hadn't let much go in the way of emotional baggage yet. That was probably why I was so determined to make something of my life at Cuckoo Cottage. I owed it to Gwen to make her efforts to put everything in place for me worthwhile.

'And she never spoke to you about me?' Will asked.

'Never,' I said, shaking my head.

Now I was finally getting to know him properly I think I was just as surprised about that as he was.

'I can't say that isn't a blow to my overinflated ego,' he smiled, puffing out his chest.

'Oh, I don't think she left you out on purpose,' I said, giving him a nudge. 'My guess is that she was waiting until I came to visit to introduce me to you in person. Perhaps she didn't think describing you on the phone would do you justice.'

Will laughed.

'So tell me,' he said. 'Now you've met me, what do you think?'

'I think,' I said carefully, looking everywhere but at him, 'that if I answered that question you would have an overinflated ego.'

'Excellent,' he beamed, jumping up, crossing to the window and neatly changing the subject. 'I think we've seen the worst of this storm now.'

'By the looks of that sky,' I sighed, standing up and looking at the lightening clouds, 'I think you could be right. Your poor roses have taken a hell of a battering, though.'

Will shook his head as he surveyed the damage.

'Haven't they just?' he tutted. 'And they were so good this year. Sometimes I wonder why I bother to grow them when the weather can decimate them in one afternoon.'

I thought back to my plans for the caravans and hoped that the Fenland thunderstorms weren't going to batter those as well.

'Is this kind of thing a regular occurrence?' I swallowed. 'I'm sure it never even rained when I was here on my holidays.'

'From what I've experienced since I've moved here,' said Will, 'we do get a few storms, but they aren't normally this bad. Quite often they seem to miss us altogether and track the river. I'd say what you've endured today has been pretty unusual.'

I smiled up at him, relieved to know that what I had witnessed was the exception rather than the rule.

'I don't know why you're smiling,' he said, looking down at me. 'You could have been fried out there.'

'I know,' I breathed, feeling that there was a part of me that had been hit by a lightning bolt the moment I crossed the barn threshold.

I tried to look away but found that I couldn't. It was Will who eventually broke the moment and only then because he had spotted something in the garden.

'A hare!' I laughed. 'I don't believe it. Do I keep seeing the same one or are there lots around here?'

'Oh, there's a fair few all right,' he said. 'Far more now the police have finally cracked down on the coursers.'

'I guess a lot of people don't think there's all that much to this landscape, do they?' I mused. 'But they couldn't be more wrong, could they?'

'Do you think so?'

'Absolutely,' I sighed. 'Every evening now when I take Minnie for a little wander I spot something new.'

'And what about Grace?' Will whispered.

'Who?'

'Grace, have you spotted her?'

'Who's Grace?'

'She's the barn owl who lives and hunts in your field.'

'Really?' I asked, wide-eyed. 'No, I had no idea. How wonderful.'

'She and her partner have raised broods in the nest box on the end of the small barn I use as my garage over there,' he said, pointing, 'for the last couple of years.'

'How exciting,' I gushed. 'Gosh, you've kept that quiet, haven't you?'

'Well, I try to,' he said seriously.

'Why?'

'Because not everyone with a so-called interest in ornithology has the most honourable of intentions, I'm afraid.'

'Whatever do you mean?'

'Sabotage,' he said darkly.

'Sabotage,' I frowned back.

'Yes,' he said, 'I work closely with the local barn owl charity and I'm sorry to say it isn't unusual to come across nests that have been raided. Sometimes it's the eggs that are taken, sometimes the chicks.'

'But that's appalling,' I gasped. 'Who in their right mind would do that?'

'You have a lot to learn about wildlife crime,' said Will. 'The stories I could tell would curl your toes, Lottie, and not in a good way.'

'Well, as awful as that sounds, I'm honoured to have Grace flying on my land,' I said, 'and I hope that she and her partner will be there for a long time to come.'

'So do I,' said Will. 'I'm pleased that you feel the same way.'

I was delighted to know that Cuckoo Cottage was a sanctuary and a stronghold for Grace and her family and I hoped that what I was planning to do with the field wouldn't disturb or unsettle her. It was my hope that my ideas would work with the landscape and the wildlife that inhabited it, rather than against it.

'Will?' I said, thinking that I was going to have to tell him what it was I had in mind for the place now.

'Yes?'

He was standing so close I could feel his breath moving the top of my hair.

'Can I tell you something?'

'Of course,' he said, breathing deeply.

'And if I do, do you promise it won't go any further?'

'Of course,' he said, sounding concerned, 'whatever is it?'

I looked up at him and, not realising he had bent down to hear what I had to say, suddenly found my face dangerously close to his.

'What?' he whispered, the trace of a smile playing around his full moist lips.

I had absolutely no idea what it was I'd been going to tell him, the inside of my head had turned to mush and something wriggly had crawled inside my stomach and was doing cartwheels.

I was just about to give in to temptation and lean in when the lights came back on, the washing machine began to spin and the refrigerator kicked into life.

'The power's back on,' I swallowed.

'So it is,' he smiled.

Chapter 21

Convinced that it was the electricity between us that had sparked Will's appliances back into life, I thought it best to keep my distance until my clothes were dry and then hastily dressed in the bathroom. I hung the bathrobe on the hook on the door and tried not to think about what I would have happily allowed to happen had the gods of the electricity company not seen fit to intervene.

I had been completely naked under that robe and every erogenous zone in my body had been yearning for Will to undress me, just as he had when I arrived on his doorstep, soaked through and terrified. Considering I had found him both infuriating and incendiary up until a few days ago, my body was certainly going out of its way to convince me that I'd got him all wrong. Not that I needed a relationship right now, of course, or even a brief encounter for that matter. I was fine on my own and knew it would have been foolish to complicate things.

'You all set then?' Will asked when I eventually left the sanctuary of his bathroom.

'Yes,' I nodded, 'I think so, and I can't thank you enough for everything you've done today, Will. I was an absolute fool to think I could get to George's place before that storm hit.'

'Yes,' he agreed, 'you were.'

I couldn't argue with his response.

'I don't quite know what you would have done if I hadn't been here.'

'Neither do I,' I said, biting my lip as I imagined myself cowering on his doorstep with Minnie in my arms.

'Well, I'm pleased that I was here and that you've felt safe,' he said, then added awkwardly, 'you know, if you'd have called, I would have come and picked you up. I know Gwen always kept my number in that address book of hers on the hall table.'

'I didn't think of that,' I admitted, feeling more ridiculous by the second. 'I was so intent on making it to George's before disaster struck that I completely forgot I'd have to pass you first.'

'Don't you mean, before lightning struck?' he said, reaching for his keys.

'Um,' I shuddered, remembering just how close to catastrophe I had come.

'Well, now you know. Gwen always had my number on

hand in case madam here did herself a mischief,' he added, stroking Minnie's head. 'And I'm never further than a phone call away.'

'Thank you,' I said. 'I'll certainly bear it in mind in the future.'

'Although of course,' he reminded me, 'you'll be able to drive yourself here in perfect safety next time around, won't you?'

'Um,' I said again.

'Now come on, let's go and find that bike and check on your hens.'

The power at Cuckoo Cottage was still down, of course, but Will was familiar with the situation and it didn't take him many seconds of fiddling about with the fuse box before the kettle was boiling and the fridge had gone into overdrive.

'As much as I appreciate it, I wish you hadn't done that,' I said, letting out a long breath as I watched him wash his hands at the sink. 'I did say I was happy to wait for the electrician.'

'I know,' he said, 'but what would have been the point? I'm here and I knew what to do so it made sense for me to just get on with it. Resetting it isn't a job that requires a qualified spark anyway and at least I've saved you a few quid.'

'You're very resourceful, aren't you?' I mused, thinking back to how he had taken charge when Minnie and I had landed in a saturated heap in his arms.

He hadn't been in any way bullying or overbearing, but his decisive actions had meant that the calamity was soon over and I was grateful for that.

'Of course,' he said proudly, assuming that I was referring to his hands-on handyman approach, rather than his ability to manage in a crisis. 'Who do you think converted the barn you've been sitting in all afternoon?'

'Did you *really* do all that yourself?' I asked, gazing up at him in awe.

I know Amber had said that he had taken the barn on when it was in a crumbling state, but having now seen it for myself I couldn't believe that the beautiful work could have possibly been carried out by anyone other than a specialist team of craftsmen, and a huge one at that.

'Pretty much,' he said, sounding slightly more humble, 'and as a result I can turn my hand to most things when I put my mind to them. I enjoy it.'

'Blimey,' I said, feeling truly impressed. 'I really had no idea. So when I made that dig about you being a builder the other day—'

'Yeah, well,' he grinned, 'you were in a bad mood so I thought I'd just let that one go.'

'So where did you learn to do all that stuff?'

'Some things I learnt during my time in the army. Make do and mend comes in handy in a war zone, but the more specialised stuff I studied and perfected as I went along.'

'That's amazing,' I said.

I had no intention of fawning all over him, but the barn was so stunning it was incredible to think that he'd achieved that standard of finish and finesse more or less on his own and I was pleased that he had mentioned the 'A' word so readily and without a hint of the self-consciousness that I had seen before.

Having worked on the caravan and camper conversions, I did have my own specific skills, of course, but I didn't rank them anywhere nearly as high as Will's and they certainly didn't stretch far enough to give me the confidence to carry out the work that Matt had said needed doing on the cottage. There was no way I was going to blunder in and make a hash of any of the repairs on my beloved little home, especially when Gwen had already picked a handyman she knew she could rely on.

'I can't even change a plug,' I admitted to Will. 'My practical household skills are pretty much non-existent.'

'But I thought you had a hands-on kind of job back in Lincoln,' he frowned.

'Oh, I did,' I agreed, 'but I wouldn't have a clue how to tackle that wretched fuse box.'

The rewiring and plumbing in the conversions had always

been the domain of Eric and John, which was a shame considering the work I now needed to fund.

'Well, that's probably no bad thing,' said Will. 'But I could teach you some stuff if you like,' he offered, taking the mug of coffee I passed him. 'Just a few day-to-day basics that will help around the house.'

'Would you?'

'Of course.'

'That would be great,' I said, thinking that I could transfer my new skills to the caravans as well, assuming they were up to scratch, of course. 'I'd really appreciate that.'

'No problem,' he said. 'I really miss the work now the barn's all finished.'

'Well, you can always come and help out here,' I joked. 'I've got a list as long as my arm of things I need to sort out before winter comes.'

'Is that your list or your builder friend's list?' Will frowned.

'Mine,' I fibbed. 'I've spotted lots of jobs that need doing.'

'Well, in that case, count me in,' said Will enthusiastically. 'I've been dying to strap the old tool belt back on for ages.'

Oh dear. I really had let my mouth run away with me this time. Of course, I was delighted that Will was so keen to help out, but according to Matt I'd apparently already promised the work to him. I might not have been able to remember saying the actual words after the party at Skylark Farm, but nonetheless I had felt obliged to accept the generous 'mates' rates' terms he had offered to Gwen and promised to honour for me. Having Will suddenly turn up bedecked in his overalls was bound to lead to trouble.

'But are you sure you'll have time?' I asked, not wanting to put Will off completely, but keen to temper his enthusiasm a little.

'Absolutely,' he said, 'and especially if you don't mind me popping in at the weekends. I can't tell you how often I find myself rattling around with nothing to do when I'm not on call. I'm planning to extend the garden,' he rushed on, 'but I won't be starting that until next spring. We'll get cracking here as soon as we've got you on the road. How does that sound?'

'Perfect,' I said, taking a swig of my coffee and hoping that if Will just came at weekends I would be able to split the work between the two men and stop them crossing drill bits. 'Thank you,' I nodded, 'that couldn't be better.'

It would be tricky not letting on that Will had helped, of course, but if I could convince Matt that I was the one getting stuck in to save myself some money then how could he possibly object?

Having telephoned Simon after Will left to tell him his services weren't required that afternoon, we made arrangements for him to come out the next day and, true to his word, early the next morning he was hammering on the house door armed with a wonderful array of tools and devices all designed to transport Cuckoo Cottage into a new era of electrical safety.

'Morning,' he puffed, as he staggered in. 'You must be Lottie.'

'I am,' I said, taking a step back, 'and I'm guessing you're Simon.'

'What was it that gave me away?' he asked, with a cheeky grin, not dissimilar to his cousin's. 'Was it the van or this lovely new piece of kit?'

He deposited his cargo and held up what I guessed was the shiny new fuse box.

'I take it you survived the storm all right?' he carried on before I had a chance to answer. 'It was quite something, wasn't it?'

'I suppose that's one way of putting it,' I said, hoping I wouldn't have to face anything like it again in the near future.

'So who sorted the fuse box then?' he asked. I had been sparse with the details the day before. 'You didn't fiddle about with it, did you?'

'God, no,' I told him. 'I wouldn't have known where to begin. A neighbour who happened to know what to do dropped by and sorted it, so no harm done.'

Simon shook his head and tutted.

'Fair enough,' he said, 'but I'd far rather you'd let me deal with it. I'm hoping there isn't a fried corpse hidden under the stairs, is there?'

'No,' I said. 'Don't even joke about it.'

My body gave an involuntary little shudder as I realised that Will really had put himself in danger for the sake of the contents of my fridge.

'I guess you were lucky that someone with a bit of know-how happened to pop in, weren't you?' said Simon, eyeing me astutely.

'Yes,' I said. 'I suppose I was.'

I knew he was digging to find out who had muscled in on his electrical turf, but I wasn't going to tell him. There was already enough friction between Matt and Will and I certainly didn't need to be throwing another disgruntled tradesman into the mix.

'Well, at least by the end of the day you won't have to worry about it any more. If it goes off again you'll be able to see exactly where any problems are and then just flick a switch when they're sorted.'

'That sounds like a far more satisfactory situation,' I told him. 'But I hope I won't have to deal with it too often. To tell you the truth, it's the only thing that's really worried me since I moved here. There are plenty of other things that need sorting, of course, but nothing as hazardous as this. There's not been a day go by when I haven't worried about it, or missed having a shower.'

'Well we can't have that, can we?' Simon smiled. 'Why don't you quickly boil the kettle while I get organised and then I'll crack on? By the end of today you'll be able to shower in perfect safety.'

Armed with a mugful of tea, Simon set about turning off the power again and pulling the understairs cupboard to pieces and I gathered together some things to take down to the barns. Minnie had been behaving herself, up to a point, but I could see she was on edge and thought it would be best all round if I took her out of harm's way, just in case temptation got the better of her and she decided to have a go at Simon's ankles.

I packed lunch for the pair of us along with a flask and pulled on my wellies, which still felt damp from my storm chasing the day before.

'You don't need me for anything, do you, Simon?' I called up the stairs as he was crashing about in the bathroom.

'Don't think so,' he said, his head appearing around the door frame. 'Are you off out for a bit then?'

'I'm just going down to the yard,' I told him, 'and I thought I might have a walk around the field. I haven't really got the measure of it yet.'

'Fair enough,' he said. 'I'm going to be here most of the day, is that all right?'

'Absolutely,' I reassured him. 'No problem, but if I lose track of time you will come and find me, won't you?'

'Of course,' he said, 'I'll want to give you the rundown on everything before I go.'

I called sharply to Minnie, who had been stealthily creeping up the stairs, and shut the cottage door behind me so she didn't have the opportunity to skulk back. Having let out my three fluffy girls who, given the egg count, hadn't been at all fazed by the storm, I found walking down to the barns a totally transformed experience.

Rather than seeing what was actually in front of me, I couldn't help imagining how it would all look when the glamping site was up and running. Lengths of pretty bunting featured strongly, as did strings of twinkling clear bulbs. I already knew the big shed was going to be the perfect hideaway should the weather do its worst, and there was enough space in there to ensure that every visitor had their own privacy if they didn't feel like joining in with the parties which I could imagine happening on a weekly basis throughout the summer.

Resting my picnic and folder against the field gate, I climbed over. My feet didn't sink anywhere as deeply as I had expected, given the amount of rain that had fallen, and I hoped that was a good sign. No one would want to camp out in a waterlogged, muddy field. I was aiming to create vintage chic and *Darling Buds of May*-style hospitality, not Glastonbury on a bad year.

Minnie tore off, having no doubt caught the scent of

something worth her attention, and I walked the perimeter, trying to get a feel for the size of the place and how the vans could be arranged. Concrete pads to set them on would be the best option and I imagined each with its own area of decking, pots of pretty flowers and striped awnings for when the sun shone.

There were groups of young trees dotted around and I hoped that with some careful positioning it shouldn't be too difficult to provide the seclusion I was hoping for. I also pictured the space with mown paths leading to and from the yard to each van, interspersed with beds of wild flowers and undisturbed rough patches where Grace and her family could hunt.

I really hoped that what I had in mind wouldn't have a negative impact on the birds and wildlife. Given how passionately Will had talked about the hares and barn owls, I knew he would never forgive me if my business venture threatened the local haven he had played a part in creating. And I would certainly have a hard time forgiving myself.

Minnie barked from the far side of the field and I looked up to the sky, shielding my eyes as I spotted a kestrel hovering overhead. With its wings outstretched and its head perfectly still, it was obviously focused on some delicious morsel and I turned back to the yard lest I should disturb its focus.

Minnie joined me at the gate, dripping wet and with her tongue lolling. She shook herself off and traipsed on behind as I opened up the first barn. There were no scrabbling noises today and I walked to the end and broke off the corner of one of the boards that was covering the window. The view beyond the grubby glass was a perfect panorama of the field, hedge and horizon beyond and I couldn't imagine I would be able to find an office with a more picturesque view anywhere.

After a brief coffee break, and with Minnie curled up in one of the Cheltenhams, I set to work on the Cherry Tree Bailey, thinking that I needed to come up with a professional plan if I was really going to make this venture work. As lovely as it was dreaming up the perfect colour schemes and layouts for the other three vans, I knew there was no point in getting carried away. Common sense demanded that I needed to think things through carefully before I started ordering fabric swatches and melamine crockery, but in truth my heart was set on pushing on with the project and I couldn't quite believe it.

Banished was my desire to live the quiet, dull life I had stuck to for so long. Now I was ready to grasp every opportunity Gwen had bestowed upon me with both hands. Unbidden, my mind flitted back to Will unbuttoning my blouse and I wondered what it would feel like to grasp him with both hands.

Resolutely I picked up my tape measure and notepad and set about checking through the lists of everything I was going to need in order to complete the Cherry Tree conversion.

Will was totally not my type, I reminded myself. He was far too tall for a start and even though we had reached a new level in our relationship it was purely platonic, and what was more, it was going to stay that way.

Chapter 22

'Hey Lottie!'

Startled, I looked up from my hammering to find Simon standing in the barn doorway scratching his head and looking at the vans. I felt furious that I'd lost track of time. When I set to work it had been my intention to have everything all locked up before he was finished but I'd become so engrossed in what I was doing, I hadn't realised the hours had ticked by and now he had had to come and find me.

'Hey,' I called back, pulling off my safety glasses. 'I'll be there in a sec.'

I was relieved to see him walk back out again and, abandoning my tools and calling to Minnie, I quickly followed his lead and pushed the barn door shut. I had no reason to think I couldn't trust him, but I still wasn't ready to share my grand plan with anyone other than Amber and was concerned that if he had the opportunity to look for too long he might start asking questions, or worse still, guess what I had in mind.

'All done up at the cottage,' he said, rubbing his hands together. 'Shower works a treat and the new fuse board is in place.'

'Oh, that's great,' I said, for some reason thinking of the shower in Will's bathroom. 'No more baths for me this summer then.'

'I was actually surprised by how good your water pressure is,' said Simon with a nod back towards the cottage. 'Some places round here can barely manage a trickle sometimes, but yours wasn't all that bad. It wouldn't have been able to cope with a really powerful shower, of course, but all things considered you were lucky there. You made a good choice.'

I made a mental note to thank Will for the heads-up and guessed that was something else I was going to have to think about when it came to setting up the site. As soon as Simon left I would add 'water supply' to my ever-increasing list of queries.

'That's a relief then,' I said.

'You've certainly got a lovely place here, Lottie,' said Simon wistfully. 'I'd give my right arm for a spot like this.'

'I know I'm very lucky,' I agreed. 'But I also know there are a few people round here who would rather it wasn't me who had moved in.'

'What do you mean?' Simon frowned.

'All the gossiping in town,' I told him. 'Chris Dempster told me the day I moved in that there were some who were hoping this place would come up for sale and haven't been too impressed with the fact that Gwen has left it all to me. Bit of a contradiction for a town which prides itself on being so welcoming to outsiders, don't you think?'

'Well, to tell you the truth,' Simon confided, 'if I'd seen a "For Sale" board anywhere near here I would have put in an offer straight away, but as far as any gossip goes, I haven't heard anything.'

'Well, I have,' I said bluntly, thinking that he was being more than a little economical with the truth. 'Only last week some chap told me that I would be putting the place up for sale before the year is out.'

I was annoyed that a few sniffs and dirty looks in my direction and one person's nasty words were still preying on my mind, but they were and I owed it to myself and Gwen to make a success of things, if only to prove the doubters wrong.

'Well, I shouldn't worry about it,' Simon shrugged. 'It's no one else's business who Gwen chose to leave Cuckoo Cottage to and I'm sure you'll be very happy here.'

'I couldn't agree more,' I told him, hoping he wasn't just saying what he thought I wanted to hear.

'So,' he continued with a nod to the barns, 'what are your plans for these? You could rent the space out, I suppose. I'm guessing Gwen was letting someone store their caravans in the big shed, was she? Although I have to say I was surprised to find you bashing the hell out of one of them.'

I didn't explain what I had been doing.

'Yes,' I said, latching on to the storage idea. 'She was keeping them for someone.'

'You'd think the owners would want them on the road by now, though,' he went on. 'Given the weather we've been enjoying.'

'Um,' I said.

'Well, if you are thinking of offering storage on a permanent basis you'll probably want to have electricity installed, for an alarm of some sort, if nothing else.'

'There's power to the big shed already,' I said, my mind rushing back to my plans, 'but nothing in the other two. Would it be hard to set up, do you think?'

Decent electrics and plumbing were going to be paramount if I was going to convert the middle-sized barn into the luxurious ablutions block I had been imagining.

'I wouldn't have thought so,' he said, looking over my shoulder and eyeing the area up, 'especially as you already have a supply of sorts, although I dare say the fuse box for that will need updating as well.'

I hadn't thought of that.

'Let's have a quick look and see,' he suggested.

The last thing I wanted to do was give him a tour, especially with my plans and paperwork scattered about, and I was just about to make some excuse when Matt's truck pulled into the yard.

'Oh sorry, Lottie,' Simon tutted, 'looks like we'll have to have a gander another day.'

'That's fine,' I said, my eyes following Minnie who had already made a beeline for Matt's truck. 'And it looks like I'd better go and rescue your cousin.'

I ran and scooped Minnie up and quickly shut her in the cottage before she had a chance to sink her teeth into any part of my trusty builder, or his tyres.

'Hey, Lottie,' Matt smiled as he climbed out.

'Hey,' I smiled back.

'How are you getting on?' he called to Simon.

'All done.'

'Well, almost done,' I cut in. 'You've still got to show me how it all works and I haven't actually paid you yet.'

'Don't worry about the money,' laughed Simon. 'I know where you live, and besides, you might want to stick it on your tab if you decide to go ahead with the other job.'

'What other job?' frowned Matt.

'Lottie and I were just discussing the possibility of getting some more electricity sorted for the barns,' Simon launched off before I had a chance to say anything.

'Were you?' frowned Matt. 'But why would you bother?'

'Because I might want to use them for something,' I said evasively.

'Like what?' he probed.

'I haven't made up my mind yet,' I told him.

'There's power to the big shed already,' said Simon, clearly not picking up on the fact that I had no desire to elaborate further.

'Just a couple of sockets for the workshop,' I shrugged dismissively. 'And a central light.'

'Gwen's got a load of caravans down there,' said Simon.

I could have kicked him when he said that.

'Has she?' asked Matt, turning his attention back to me.

'A couple,' I said, knowing I couldn't possibly deny it when Simon had seen the evidence for himself.

'So what did you say you had planned for the other barns?'

'I didn't,' I said, twisting Gwen's hula girl key ring around my fingers. 'I said I hadn't decided what I'm going to do with them. I just thought power down there might be useful.'

'Be expensive, though,' he said, rubbing his chin.

'No, it wouldn't, mate,' countered Simon. 'Not really, not when there's power already down there.'

'It might not have been properly installed, though,' said Matt testily. 'You know what Gwen was like when it came to cutting corners.'

I looked up and spotted a glance between the two men. It was over in a second, but I had definitely seen it. For some reason, Matt wanted to put Simon off the job, or me off having the work done. I wasn't sure which, and I didn't much care for his slur on Gwen's caretaking skills either.

'Actually,' said Simon, following his cousin's lead, 'you might have a point there. Perhaps it would be better if you got the house sorted first, Lottie, then think about the barns when everything's shipshape up here?'

'Yes,' I agreed, as keen to change the subject as he was. 'You're probably right.'

'You don't need to go wasting money on stuff down there when the cottage is falling apart,' put in Matt. 'Better to get things up here back on level ground first.'

He was right, of course, but given everyone else's opinion on the place, his suggestion that the cottage was practically derelict was a little over the top.

'Oh Matt,' I laughed. 'Stop being so melodramatic, it's hardly falling apart.'

He didn't say anything else, just stared over my head, sucking his lip and looking like a child who had lost his comforter. I didn't know what had come over him.

'Right,' said Simon as the air between the three of us began to crackle with the same electricity I'd felt when the lightning touched down next to me the day before. 'I'd better get on.'

'I thought you were going to show me this fuse box,' I reminded him.

'You'll be able to suss it out,' he said. 'Everything's labelled up so if something does trip out you can see exactly where the problem is.'

'It really couldn't be simpler,' said Matt, clearing his throat.

'Fair enough,' I said, addressing Simon and ignoring Matt. 'If I'm not sure about anything I'll give you a call.'

'Please do,' he smiled.

'And thank you for putting in the new shower.'

'Is this the model you went for?' asked Matt, pointing at the empty box which was now propped next to the back door ready to go in the recycling bin. 'I thought you'd have gone for something with a bit more power, Lottie.'

So grateful to have gotten off the subject of the barns, I grabbed this new twist in the conversation and ran with it.

'I was going to,' I said without thinking. 'But a neighbour mentioned the water pressure might not be up to it.'

'That wouldn't be the same neighbour who fixed your fuse box yesterday by any chance, would it?' asked Simon with a wink.

I could feel my cheeks blazing, but I had no reason to keep Will's help and advice a secret. He was a neighbour and he was just being neighbourly after all.

'It was,' I said.

'I thought as much,' he grinned when I didn't offer up a name.

I was sure Matt had already worked out who we were

talking about so there was no need to spell it out and aggravate the situation further.

'So are you coming to the pub tonight, Matt?' asked Simon.

'I thought I might pop in,' he nodded. 'That was actually what I drove out to ask you about, Lottie. I was wondering if you fancied a night out in town, or do you still have an aversion to everything alcoholic after the Skylark party?'

'Afraid so.'

'Oh, come on,' he wheedled. 'It can be my way of thanking you for giving me the go-ahead to get on with the work here.'

'Well, I suppose I could avoid the Scrumpy, couldn't I?' I said with a little shudder, thinking back to the hangover from hell and wondering if I could have a catch-up with Jemma as well as enjoy a night on the town.

'Exactly,' laughed Matt, sounding suddenly far cheerier. 'You could stick to something less potent. How do you feel about vodka?'

I shook my head, but didn't say anything. My mind was too preoccupied with the warming impact whisky could have on a girl's insides. If indeed it had been the whisky that had been responsible.

'It's going to be a good night,' Simon joined in. 'Jim's booked three live bands so it'll be packed. Everyone I've spoken to is planning to go.'

If he was right, there was every possibility that Jemma would be there. I decided to let Matt's earlier sulkiness pass.

'All right, then,' I nodded. 'I'd love to come, but there's one condition.'

'What's that?' asked Matt.

'You don't leave me to take on the town gossips alone and you certainly don't let me touch a drop of cider, no matter where it's from or what its alcohol content is.'

The last thing I needed was to be making a show of myself in front of my critics.

'Deal!' laughed Matt, holding out his hand to seal the agreement.

I shook it heartily, but realised with a jolt that even though he was giving me his widest smile, there was absolutely no spark between us whatsoever.

Chapter 23

As predicted, The Mermaid was absolutely heaving. Clearly the prospect of live entertainment, even if it was from three local bands they'd heard a hundred times before, was enough to pull in quite a crowd and there were already small groups of early evening revellers spilling out on to the pavement.

The weather was hot and humid and I was pleased I had opted to wear a light cotton dress and cardigan rather than jeans and reminded myself that sticking to tonic water or lemonade was going to be the best option this evening. Matt didn't know it, of course, but I had business with Jemma to discuss so I needed to keep my head clear and I was also determined to have my ears open for any more gossip.

My date had just put his foot inside the pub door when Will came striding out at speed, ducking low to avoid the door frame. At the same time calling over his shoulder and laughing to someone in the bar, he was completely unaware

296

that he was on a collision course and sent Matt, who hadn't time to step out of the way, flying. A jeer went up from the rowdy crowd and Matt went bright red as he scrambled to grab a chair and regain his balance along with his dignity.

'Mate,' said Will. 'I'm so sorry.'

'You want to watch where you're going,' Matt growled, self-consciously brushing down his shirt and readjusting his collar.

'Oh, it's you,' said Will, the remorseful tone banished in a heartbeat. 'Had I realised, I wouldn't have bothered apologising.'

Matt took a step forward and then thought better of it. Standing at well over six foot and with shoulders the width of the pub door, Will was an impressive sight. I certainly wouldn't have wanted to take him on, not in the confrontational sense anyway. My mind thought back to what was lurking under that unassuming plain grey T-shirt and gave an inner sigh.

I hastily reminded my lusty inner stirrings that Will was my nearest neighbour and now, thanks to my storm-chasing antics and his offers of help, we were fast becoming friends as well and that was all I wanted us to be. It was a shame, of course, that he and Matt seemed determined to cling to this mutual loathing and posturing, but that was nothing to do with me. They were big boys and would just have to get on with things.

Will stepped aside to let Matt pass and he disappeared inside without another word.

'Hello,' I said, feeling it would be rude not to say anything.

'Lottie,' Will beamed. 'Hi. How are your knees?'

Another cheer went up from the crowd.

'Hey mate, I bet that's what you ask all the girls the morning after!' shouted some anonymous jester.

Will rolled his eyes, but didn't shout back.

'Much better, thanks,' I told him, hoping that my face wasn't as flushed as I thought it might be. 'And you'll be pleased to know that the electrics are now all sorted, along with the shower.'

'Brilliant,' he smiled. 'I bet that's a weight off your mind.'

'It is,' I nodded. 'And Simon, the electrician, said I'd picked the best sort of shower given the water pressure, so thank you for your advice on that. You've no doubt saved me some hassle there.'

'You're welcome,' he said and then, bending low so only I could hear him, added, 'but you're always welcome to come and use my shower again should you have any problems.'

There was that heady scent: masculine, spicy and warm. I drank it in. The temptation to lean a little closer and kiss his tanned neck was almost irresistible.

'I might just take you up on that,' I whispered back.

He quickly straightened back up, obviously as shocked that I'd decided to play along as I was.

298

'I mean, if I get a problem,' I stammered, backtracking as if my life depended on it. 'If this new shower doesn't work or something . . .'

'Don't ruin it,' he grinned, recovering far more quickly than I had.

'Lottie,' called Matt from just inside the door. 'Are you coming, or what?'

'Sorry,' I called back. 'Yeah, I'm on my way.'

So entranced was I by Will, I'd completely forgotten I was supposed to be with Matt. That kind of behaviour was completely out of character for me and I couldn't help wondering what Gran and Gwen would have made of my conduct. To be honest, they'd probably think it was more spirited than rude.

'You'd better go in,' winked Will, stepping neatly around me, but still within tantalising reach. 'Don't keep him waiting. His ego's taken enough of a battering already.'

'We're just going to talk about jobs at the cottage,' I said, even though there was no reason in the world why I had to explain.

Will shrugged his shoulders to confirm that he felt it was none of his business either, and I felt a bit of an idiot for having said anything at all.

'Just don't forget, my offer still stands,' he said. 'I can help you out if you want me to, and I'm a good teacher.'

Another cheer went up.

'You lot are like a load of bloody kids,' Will laughed before leaving the half-drunk rowdy bunch to enjoy their innuendos.

Pushing my way through the crowd to reach Matt, who was now sporting an even deeper scowl, I bumped into Chris and Marie.

'Well, well, well,' boomed Chris with a wink. 'Has the cuckoo finally left her nest?'

Marie dug him sharply in the ribs, clearly unimpressed that he had used my nickname even though it was only in jest.

'Just for this evening,' I said, in a voice which I hoped was loud enough to carry to anyone present who doubted my determination. 'But I'll be back there later and if you carry on like that, Mr Dempster, you can go without that Sunday cuppa you keep threatening to call in for.'

'Ignore him, love,' said Marie. 'He's only teasing.'

'I know,' I said with a smile, 'and to tell you the truth, I don't mind. In fact, the name's rather growing on me, although given my size perhaps wren would be more appropriate, although that little bird would never commandeer another's home, would it?'

Marie winked, guessing that I was ready to give back as good as I was likely to get.

'So what have you been up to?' she asked as Chris continued to massage his side. 'Simon's been telling everyone that Gwen's set up some sort of storage facility in one of the barns.'

'Has he now?'

'Yes,' said Chris, sounding confused. 'Are you sure about that, Lottie? Because when I took Gwen to pick up those caravans I didn't think . . .'

'Sorry,' I said, cutting him off and waving at Matt, who was still scowling, 'I have to go. Matt's been waiting for ages.'

I had no desire to get drawn into a conversation about what Gwen may or may not have had in mind for the vans or stand by while Chris announced their presence to everyone who might have missed Simon's earlier proclamation.

'Of course,' said Marie. 'And don't worry, love. I'll try and stop this one unwittingly fanning the flames.'

'Thanks, Marie,' I said gratefully. 'I'll see you later.'

I eased my way through the crowd to Matt and sipped at the glass of ice-packed lemonade he passed me.

'So what did he want?' he demanded, with a nod to the door.

'What, Chris?'

'No,' he snapped. 'Will. Is he still looking to get into your good books after running you off the road?'

'Of course not,' I said, following on behind as he made his way towards the little garden at the back of the pub. 'That's all water under the bridge now. He just wanted to remind me that Minnie's due to have her booster jab soon.'

'Is that right?'

I knew I could just as easily have said I was thanking him for his help with the electrics, but I didn't feel my honesty would add anything to the evening, which had already got off to such a rocky start. Given Matt's lowly opinion of my neighbour, confirming him as my storm-busting hero would only have made things worse.

'Hey, Lottie!'

I spun round to see Jemma waving at me from the other side of the pub and I tapped Matt on the shoulder.

'Sorry,' I shouted in his ear above the noise of the crowd. 'Do you mind if I just go and have a quick word with Jemma?'

'Why not,' he shrugged. 'You seem to be Little Miss Popular this evening. I'll be out here with Simon.'

'Thanks,' I said, squeezing his arm in the hope that a show of affection might alleviate at least some of the guilt I felt for deserting him again so soon. 'I won't be a minute.'

I knew he wasn't impressed that I was off again, but this was too good an opportunity to miss.

'Hey,' I said when I finally reached Jemma. 'I was hoping to see you tonight.'

'Snap,' she said, taking hold of my hand. 'Follow me. It's a bit quieter through here.'

The restaurant was still busy, but the level of chatter was much quieter and we grabbed a couple of chairs next to the thankfully unlit fire and settled down for a quick tête-à-tête. I couldn't help noticing there were a few glances thrown in our direction, but whether that was because we had just walked in or because everyone had spotted the 'cuckoo', I couldn't be sure.

'Look,' said Jemma, discreetly pointing to a table at the other end of the room.

'Finally,' I whispered as I spotted David and Angela with their heads together, deep in conversation.

'This is the third time they've been out,' Jemma confided. 'I've been meaning to tell you, but I haven't had a chance. Once they got the so-called awkward first date over with last week they haven't been out of each other's sight.'

'That's wonderful,' I smiled, feeling secretly pleased that I had been right about their mutual attraction.

'So come on,' said Jemma, her eyes bright with excitement. 'How are you getting on with the conversion?'

I explained that the insides of the Bailey were now prepped and primed ready to be painted before the new upholstery, fridge and fittings were installed. Jemma was thrilled and as keen as ever to come out and have another look before I started the next phase. She had chosen a similar colour palette to the café, and the same cupcake-patterned fabric Lizzie had designed, to tie the two schemes together, and couldn't wait to see it transferred from the mood board to reality.

'And how have you found the work?' she asked. 'Not too

complicated, I hope. As you know, I had been planning to take a look before now, but I just haven't had time for those "baby steps" we talked about. I feel like we're at more of a gallop already!'

'Well, the work has been pretty straightforward,' I told her, 'I haven't stumbled across anything out of the ordinary yet so it's all progressed pretty quickly. In fact, I'm just about ready to have someone check over the electrics. Obviously I'm not qualified to deal with that myself.'

'Of course,' she said. 'That's fine. Perhaps you could ask that cousin of Matt's.'

'I suppose I could,' I said, thinking that if I did then what was really going on in the big shed would be common knowledge soon enough, although given what Chris had just told me, it already was, to a certain extent. 'He's been working at the cottage today actually.'

'Well, that's great,' smiled Jemma, 'so you already know him.'

'Yes,' I hesitated.

'What's wrong?' she frowned. 'Aren't you happy with his work?'

'Oh, the work's fine . . .'

'But?'

'Well, he came down to the barns earlier and spotted the vans and now he's going around telling everyone that Gwen was renting the place out as a storage facility. He also saw me working on your Bailey, so I'm afraid keeping it under wraps for much longer is going to prove difficult. I'm certain no one knows it's connected to you just yet, but it's only a matter of time.'

'Oh never mind,' she said, 'I'm surprised folk haven't got wind of it before, to be honest. Don't worry, it's not a problem.'

'Are you sure?'

'Absolutely, when it comes to tradesmen, better the devil you know, I always think.'

That had certainly been my way of thinking when it came to taking on the builder Gwen had already lined up. Perhaps, given everything else that had happened today, it was time to stop being so secretive about my plans. If the townsfolk heard about the conversion job first they might not be so surprised by the glamping idea. Well, that was the theory. Perhaps this really was the final push I needed to come clean and get the ball rolling?

'OK,' I said, taking a big breath. 'As soon as I'm ready I'll ask Simon to take a look.'

'And I'll come out and see you as soon as I can,' said Jemma. 'Just to check the paint colour and deliver the fabrics.'

'Sounds good to me,' I said, taking another sip of lemonade.

'And of course we need to sort out the cost of everything,' she said, shaking her head. 'We haven't exactly gone about this in the most professional way, have we?'

'No,' I said, 'I guess not.'

'Well, don't worry,' she said. 'We're more than happy to pay the going rate for the whole package, so please don't be thinking that we're expecting you to do it for a song. Lizzie and I know exactly how much time and effort you've been putting in, along with exactly how much these vintage vans are worth.'

'Thanks, Jemma,' I smiled, feeling relieved.

'And we're also desperate to hear what you've really got planned for those Cheltenhams,' she winked.

Yes, this was definitely the time to forge ahead.

Chapter 24

The bar was even more packed as I squeezed my way back through to the garden and I felt a definite buzz in the air, but whether that was in anticipation for the entertainment ahead or my own excitement, I couldn't be sure.

'And where have you been hiding?' asked Simon, when I finally reached him and Matt. 'Not off with that horse whisperer again, I hope.'

'Oh dear,' I said pointedly, having taken on board his disparaging tone, unfocused gaze and slightly lopsided stance. 'Have you been here ever since you left the cottage, Simon?'

I was annoyed that he and Matt had obviously been gossiping about what had happened when we arrived and felt my recently inflated enthusiasm leaching away like the air out of a week-old balloon that has slipped unnoticed behind the sofa after a party.

'Pretty much,' he admitted, holding up an empty glass.

'Um,' I frowned, 'I'm guessing you've been here just about long enough to tell everyone about Gwen's caravans.'

He didn't even have the grace to look guilty and I decided I'd better let it drop before I ended up getting really stuck into him. This was life in a small town, I reminded myself, and I'd just have to accept it.

'So where were you?' Simon asked again. 'Not really off with that squaddie, surely?'

'Squaddie?' I frowned, feeling annoyed on Will's behalf and shocked by Simon's change in personality.

He was borderline aggressive and nothing at all like the amiable guy who had turned up to eradicate my decrepit electrics just a few hours ago.

'I think you'll find Will was a top-ranking highly decorated soldier actually,' I retaliated.

He burst out laughing and even Matt, who had so far ignored Simon's remarks, looked mildly amused.

'Is that right?' he frowned.

'Oh never mind,' I said, determined not to bite back again.

'He's actually not a highly decorated anything,' Matt went on. 'He left the army under one hell of a cloud and came to work here because his aunt took pity on him and gave him a job in the family firm. He hasn't worked for anything he's got, but his sort never do. He's got it easy.'

I thought back to all the years of professional training Will must have undertaken and the beautiful barn and how hard he had worked to convert it, not to mention how many times late at night and early in the morning I had seen and heard him driving by to attend some emergency or other. It didn't sound to me like Will had 'got it easy' at all.

'You don't want to believe everything you hear around here,' said Simon, sounding surprisingly less bullish than his cousin.

'Oh, I don't,' I said, 'which is just as well for you two really.'

'What do you mean?' frowned Matt.

'Well, according to some . . .' I didn't identify Will's suspicions of course, 'you're just out to make a few quid off me, Matt.'

Simon burst out laughing and I realised I didn't want to be anywhere near either of them any more. I certainly wouldn't be asking Simon to look at the Bailey now and I would find someone else to help out with setting up the electrics for the barns. I wasn't even sure I'd be letting Matt do the work on the cottage.

'Don't worry about giving me a lift home,' I announced, plonking my empty glass down on the table. 'I'll get a taxi.'

Determined not to rush back to the sanctuary of the cottage straight away, I ordered a small glass of wine, just to help stave off my annoyance, and rejoined Jemma, who was standing next to the piano with Lizzie. It turned out that Tom and

Ben made up one half of the first band who had been drafted in to entertain the crowds.

After a couple of minutes chatting I felt a light tap on my shoulder and spun round thinking it was Matt coming to apologise.

'Hey you, I didn't know you were going to be here!'

It was Mags.

'Mags!' I gasped, relieved that I wasn't the only Drove-dweller left amid the townies.

'Do you want to come and sit with us?' she asked, pointing to where Liam was sitting at a table near the door. 'It's a bit cooler over there.'

'Yes,' I said, 'thanks. I'll just tell Jemma.'

Sitting knee to knee, Mags and Liam still looked like the perfect couple to me, but I forbore to comment. If David and Angela had finally made their way to one another without any well-meaning, match-making interference (Jemma's aside, of course), then perhaps this pair would some day manage to do the same.

'Are you here on your own?' asked Liam, looking round to see who I might have been with, if anyone.

'I am now,' I explained. 'I came in to town with Matt, but we've had a bit of a disagreement.'

My annoyance might have been more directed at Simon and his silly attitude, but I wasn't prepared to let Matt, and his harsh words about Will, off the hook completely.

'Well, we'll give you a lift home if you like,' Liam offered.

I was grateful that neither he nor Mags expected to be filled in about what had been said. They really were the most straightforward non-interfering of friends.

'I understand you and Will settled down for a spot of storm watching yesterday?' grinned Mags with a mischievous twinkle in her eye.

Perhaps not quite so straightforward and non-interfering after all.

'How did you know about that?'

'George,' she and Liam said in perfect unison.

'Of course,' I nodded.

I might have known word would find a way of getting round.

'But don't worry, you'll have the minivan by the end of the week, Lottie,' said Liam. 'We can't have you out riding that bike in all weathers. It isn't safe.'

My stomach gave a lurch at the thought of driving again, but at least Will had offered to accompany me until I felt confident. Given the way my tummy rolled and my head thumped every time driving was mentioned, I couldn't help thinking he might end up being my passenger for life.

'To be fair, I wouldn't normally have been out in the storm,' I said, knowing what had happened was entirely my own fault and that now the electrics were up to date it certainly wouldn't be happening again, no matter what mode of transport I had parked on the drive.

'Well, that's as maybe,' said Mags, 'but the sooner you're properly and safely mobile, the better.'

The band struck up just as she finished talking and consequently all further discussion was thwarted. There really was no way for me to wriggle out of taking on her little van now and perhaps that was a good thing. Just like my decision to forge ahead with the glamping idea, I needed to make a commitment and stick to it.

The band's repertoire was lively and varied and after a couple more 'small' glasses of wine I had pretty much forgotten I was in a bad mood with Matt. After all, it had really been Simon who started the silly conversation, not my builder.

'I thought you'd gone home,' said a voice behind me when I went back to the bar for another round.

'Not yet,' I said, looking around and finding Matt at my elbow. 'Where's your lovely cousin disappeared to?'

'He's gone outside for a smoke,' he said. 'I'm so sorry, Lottie. I should have warned you he can be a bit of an idiot when he's had a drink.'

'A bit,' I tutted, with a small smile, 'and what about you?' I asked. 'You didn't exactly keep your thoughts to yourself, so what's your excuse?'

Fortunately he took the question in the spirit it had been intended.

'I'm sorry,' he said. 'Will just rubs me up the wrong way, but I shouldn't have let my dislike of him spoil my evening with you. I guess I was just jealous that I didn't have you all to myself.'

In my tipsy state that sounded fair enough. I had managed to talk to practically everyone other than Matt since crossing the threshold and that had kind of been my motive for accepting his offer of a night out. Perhaps he wasn't the only one who should be apologising.

'Anyway,' he went on, 'I can't just leave you standing here while everyone talks about you behind your back.'

'What?' I frowned, looking surreptitiously around.

I hadn't noticed anything beyond a few glances when I'd been with Jemma in the restaurant and thankfully there was no sign of the bully who had tackled me at the Cherry Tree.

'I don't think anyone is talking about me behind my back,' I said, eyeing everyone in a slightly more suspicious light and wondering if I'd let my guard down too quickly.

'That's what makes it all the worse for me to hear,' said Matt, rubbing my arm and making me feel paranoid in the process. 'Come on, as it was me who asked you here, let me take you home, if that's OK, of course?'

'Well, all right,' I relented, manoeuvring glasses and having another furtive look around. 'Let me get these drinks sorted and I'll tell Mags I'm going back with you. Could you just help me carry this tray to Jemma, please?'

'What is it with you and her?' he asked. 'I didn't realise you knew each other so well.'

On the way back to the cottage I tried not to think about what was being said in the pub and as a result, and with the help of the three glasses of red, I let my mouth run away with me and ended up telling Matt all about the work I was doing on the Bailey.

'But I'd rather word didn't spread too quickly,' I said for the umpteenth time, 'even though Jemma's happy for folk to know about it now.'

Just an hour ago I'd been happy for folk to know about it too, but now I knew the gossiping still hadn't died down I wasn't so sure. Perhaps the leap from carrying out one simple conversion to setting up an entire glamping site would be too much for the narrow-minded critics moaning about me over their beers.

Matt didn't say much, but I could tell he was taking it all in.

'So the conversion job is just a sort of doing a favour for a friend situation, I take it?'

'Sort of,' I said, 'but she's going to pay me for the work I've done, obviously, and the van of course.'

'So not really just doing a mate a favour, then?'

'No,' I said, wrinkling my nose. 'When you put it like that, I guess not.'

'You need to be careful who you talk to about this, Lottie, and what you say,' he said seriously.

'Why?' I hiccupped. 'What's the problem?'

'Well, you can't run a business out of those barns, can you?'

'Can't I?' I frowned, feeling panicked.

'No,' he said, shaking his head. 'Of course not. Is that why you were asking Simon about having extra electricity installed?'

'Why can't I?' I asked again. 'Why can't I run a business from the yard?'

'Because of the agricultural restrictions and regulations, of course.'

'The agricultural what?'

'Restrictions,' said Matt again. 'You can't just go around setting up whatever you want in those barns, you know, Lottie.'

'And what about the field?' I squeaked, my former excitement suddenly receiving a hefty nudge as a big dollop of fear descended to take its place.

'The field will be even more strictly regulated.' He frowned. 'Surely David explained all that to you when you took the place on.'

I shook my head, but didn't say anything. I was afraid that if I opened my mouth I'd throw up.

'Are you all right?'

I nodded and stared out of the window.

'You hadn't been making plans, had you?' Matt asked. 'Plans that didn't revolve around farming?'

'No,' I managed to blurt out. 'I've just been mulling over a few things, that's all. I haven't had anything specific in mind.'

If I couldn't use the barns or the field for my business, then what was I going to do with them, and more importantly, how was I going to earn a living from Cuckoo Cottage? If Matt was right, this would mean I was going to have to kiss goodbye to the glamping, grow potatoes or something and rent different premises to carry out conversions, and I already knew my purse strings wouldn't run to that.

'Like I told you before,' he continued sympathetically, 'owning an older property isn't always all it's cracked up to be, especially in the countryside.'

'I had no idea,' I muttered.

'Well, check things out by all means,' he sighed, 'but I think you'll find I'm right.'

How typical was this? Just when I'd settled upon something I could really get excited about, it was being snatched out from under me. Surely Gwen must have known about these restriction thingies, but then she'd never been much of a one for playing by the rules. Perhaps she thought I would just be able to get away with ignoring them.

'Don't look so fed up,' said Matt, leaning across and grasping my hand. 'If I were you I'd get on with doing the work for Jemma, just don't tell anyone that she's paying you for it.'

'So what am I working for?' I grumbled. 'Magic beans?'

'Quiche and cake,' he suggested. 'If anyone asks, she's paying you in quiche and cake!'

He sounded almost amused by his quick wit and obviously had no idea just how truly devastated I was by what he had just told me.

Back at the cottage everything was in total darkness. It had been light when Matt picked me up and I hadn't thought to leave a light burning to guide me to the door. He parked in the yard and came round to help me out.

'Wow,' I whispered, looking up at the night sky and for the first time noticing just how different the stars looked without the added glow of orange street pollution.

'Quite something, isn't it?' said Matt, also looking up.

'I've never seen so many stars,' I gasped, feeling dizzy by the sheer number, coupled with the sudden rush of fresh air. 'One day,' I sighed, trying to blank out how utterly miserable I suddenly was, 'I'm going to learn all the constellations.'

Matt took my hand and led me further towards the field.

'I know a couple,' he said. 'That there,' he pointed, tracing a wobbly course with his finger, 'is the plough.'

'Uh-huh,' I said, following the line and craning my neck as far as I could.

'And that's Orion's belt,' he squinted. 'I think. It's a long time since I looked.'

'We should take a blanket into the field and lay down,' I said, rubbing a sore spot on the back of my neck.

Matt stepped behind me and began to work on the pain with the tips of his fingers, using just the right amount of pressure to elicit a low moan that I was mortified to make.

'That feels better,' I said, taking a step away, 'thanks.'

Before I had time to say another word he pulled me close and kissed me. The firm caress of his lips seemed to go on forever and I don't know why I let it. Whether it was my alcohol-induced impaired judgement, the romance of the stars, or whether I was still feeling guilty for abandoning him in the pub, I couldn't be sure, but it was a tender kiss, sweet and comforting, but in no way passionate or feverish. When we finally broke apart there was a sudden screeching and scrabbling sound close by and I leapt back into his arms.

'Sorry,' I whispered. 'It made me jump.'

'We've probably disturbed the wildlife on its nightly prowl,' he said, wrapping his arms around me again. 'Do you get scared living out here on your own?'

'No,' I said, turning my face away a little. 'Of course not, why would I?'

'I just wondered if you felt vulnerable out here all on your own when things go bump in the night.'

'I can't say I've ever heard anything go bump in the night,'

I said, my isolation and potential vulnerability only just becoming apparent. 'Besides,' I said, brushing off the fledgling feeling of unease, 'I have Minnie.'

'Of course,' said Matt, tucking my hair behind my ear, 'and like I said, it was probably just a mouse of something.'

'More likely to be the barn owl, making a noise like that,' I said.

'There aren't any barn owls round here,' said Matt, brushing my cheek lightly with his lips. 'There haven't been for years.'

'That's not what Will said,' I blundered on, completely forgetting that it was supposed to be a secret, and a secret that he had trusted me to keep.

'Is that so?' frowned Matt. 'Well I never.'

Chapter 25

Thanks to Matt and his devastating declaration, I didn't sleep well that night. Having finally decided what it was that I was going to do with Gwen's magnificent bequest, and indeed the rest of my life, I was shattered to think that my hopes and dreams were dashed before they had even been attempted. I wasn't even going to have the chance to fall at the first hurdle because I wasn't going to make it that far.

Added to that, I was feeling foolish for not picking up on the gossiping locals Matt had told me be about at the pub and I was also on high alert, listening out for noises, no matter how distant or apparently inconsequential, with Minnie restlessly tossing and turning next to me. In the wee small hours, I lay, alternately trying to fathom out why David had never mentioned agricultural restrictions, why I hadn't been turned on by the kiss I should never have allowed to happened and then, when I had finally exhausted both topics, I began playing out all manner of home-alone horror stories in my head.

All it would take was one snip of the phone wire and I would be done for. Out in the Fen no one would hear me scream, would they? The reality of my vulnerable position sounded like the strapline for the latest horror movie to hit the cinema screens and I pulled the bedsheet up a little higher, wishing I had a baseball bat hidden under the bed.

When my head wasn't pounding with fifty ways to die in bed (and none of them through sexual ecstasy), I was admonishing myself for allowing that kiss with Matt to go on for so long. True, he was pretty enough in a cool surfer dude kind of way, and yes, for a moment our intimacy did make me feel less vulnerable in the darkness, which hadn't bothered me at all until he brought it to my attention, but there had been no real spark, no fireworks in my belly and certainly no stirrings further south as there had been when I caught sight of Will in his bath towel. I sighed and rolled over again, hoping Matt hadn't gone home harbouring the assumption that that kiss was the start of something more.

I eventually fell asleep, with Minnie's hot little body pressed close to my side, but mere seconds later, or what felt like mere seconds later, I was woken by hammering on the front door. Terrified that I was about to be murdered in my bed, I hunkered down, but Minnie, who was thrilled with the early morning alarm call, went woofing down the stairs, presumably to let the madman, or woman, in.

'Charlotte!' called a man's voice right beneath the bedroom window.

It was Will. Clearly he was trying to get my attention, but there was something about his tone that suggested he was trying to be quiet at the same time. I tiptoed to the window and peeped out between where the curtains didn't quite meet.

'Lottie!' he called again, catching sight of my curtain-twitching manoeuvre. 'Hurry up and come down.'

I glanced at the bedside clock and opened the window a crack. The air that rushed in to meet me felt damp yet cool and refreshing.

'Whatever's wrong?' I hissed, trying to push Minnie, who had pelted back up the stairs and leapt from the floor straight on to the windowsill, aside. 'It's half past four in the morning.'

'Nothing's wrong,' he said exasperatedly, 'but Grace is flying in your field and I thought you might like to see her.'

'Oh,' I said, quickly ducking back inside then out again. 'I'll get dressed.'

'No time,' he urged. 'Just hurry up.'

I raced down the stairs, tripping over Minnie, in my girly boxers and frilly vest, all thoughts of sleep and my impending gruesome death banished. Now all I could think about was how Shakespearean and romantic it was to be summoned from my bed by a handsome beau beneath my window. Although, I hastily reminded myself, Will was not my beau and Romeo and Juliet did meet a rather tragic end, despite their passionate beginnings.

'Well now, look at you,' Will grinned as I opened the front door. 'I should call round at this time every day, but you'd better take this,' he added, reaching around me and grabbing Gwen's mackintosh, 'and stick your wellies on, it's damp this morning.'

Shrouded in early morning mist, the cobwebs strung between the tall patches of weeds and wild flowers looked like diamond-studded strands across the field. They were strikingly beautiful as they glistened in the increasing light and bobbed about jewel-like in a sea of green. Quietly we slipped through the gate and, keeping close to the barn wall, crept around the back so we had an uninterrupted view across what was now my very own field in the Fens.

And then I saw the owl. She appeared through the mist, flying low, her wings hardly beating as she cut a silent path through the air. Her elegance was everything and I felt tears pricking the backs of my eyes as I watched her circling the field before stopping and hovering over one particular spot which had drawn her undivided attention. Her heart-shaped face was firmly focused on a patch of grass directly beneath her and it didn't move even a millimetre.

'What's she doing?' I asked Will, leaning in close so I didn't disturb our ghostly companion.

'Hunting,' he said, his eyes never leaving the beautiful bird.

Suddenly, but still in complete silence, she dropped momentarily out of sight and then reappeared with what must have been a mouse or a vole gripped in her sharp talons. We watched her fly across the field to the opposite side and land on a post, where she sat and serenely surveyed the landscape.

Will turned to look at me and smiled. There was an element of surprise in his expression and I was surprised myself when I realised that a tear had escaped and was gently running down my cheek. He stepped close and brushed it away with the soft cuff of his jumper.

'Sorry about the early start,' he said huskily.

'I wouldn't have missed it for the world,' I said, smiling up at him.

'She's quite something, isn't she?' he said, looking back to where Grace was still sitting regally on her post.

He sounded besotted and I wondered what it would feel like to hear him say something like that about me.

'Oh yes,' I agreed, 'she's the most beautiful bird I've ever seen.'

'She's the only girl for me,' he added, stepping back and scooping up Minnie, who had been incredibly patient while we watched Grace, into his arms. 'Apart from you, of course, madam,' he laughed, kissing her nose.

My fears from the night before about living alone out in the Fens were now firmly kicked into touch; there was nothing to be afraid of out here, and although I had a vague recollection of dreaming about owls last night, I couldn't quite remember the details; however, when I tried to reach for them I was left with a mild feeling of unease.

'Do you fancy some breakfast?' I asked Will, trying not to feel jealous of the attention Minnie was still getting. Mind you, had he rolled me over and started tickling me like that I probably would have been squirming too. 'It can be my way of saying thank you for looking after us during the storm.'

'All right,' nodded Will, 'thanks. I'd like that. I'd like that very much.'

As we walked back to the cottage the sun began to burn through the mist and I knew that in just a few minutes the magic would evaporate along with the dew. It was really very lucky that Will had the easy life Matt had alluded to and happened to be passing by my door so early.

'So,' I asked, 'what were you doing up at this ungodly hour, Will?'

'Oh I had an—'

'Don't tell me,' I cut in, guessing what he was about to say from conversations I'd had with Mags about his seemingly never-ending early starts and late finishes, 'an emergency?'

'Yep,' he sighed. 'Skylark Farm this morning, but nothing too serious. Nothing that made me break the speed limit,' he quickly added, no doubt noting the look of panic on my face.

'It must have been a bit serious to call you out at this time,' I stated.

Will didn't expand on the details and I knew it wouldn't be appropriate to push him.

'You know,' I said. 'I can't work you out.'

'What do you mean?'

'Well, I thought vets either worked with small animals, pets and the like, or large, farm animals and so on, but you seem to do a bit of everything.'

'There's a certain amount of crossover in the role these days and mine is mostly down to my time in the army,' he explained as easily as if we chatted about his former career all the time. 'You were expected to treat anything and everything in a war zone. I had to operate on a camel once,' he said with a laugh.

'You did not,' I said, giving him a nudge on the assumption that he was teasing.

'Bloody did,' he chuckled. 'It was a hell of a beast; stubborn as a mule and as strong as a bull elephant. It took six of us to manhandle it so I could sedate it.'

I wasn't sure if he was joking or not, but it made a funny story.

Back at the cottage I was desperate to carry on the conversation. I wanted to know all about his experiences as an army vet and soldier. I'd been told he had left the armed forces 'under a cloud', but I just couldn't see it. Despite my best efforts, however, Will expertly steered the chat back to ground he was more comfortable with and for the moment the opportunity to probe deeper was denied me.

'I'm afraid I can only offer you cereal, toast and fruit,' I apologised, as I peered into the depths of the much-depleted fridge.

I was really going to have to do a proper shop soon. There was always the option of ordering online when the Wi-Fi was sorted, of course, but Gwen had always adhered to the 'shop local' ethos, even before it was fashionable, and I rather liked the idea of carrying her principle on and supporting the hard-working Wynbridge growers and producers.

'That sounds good to me,' said Will, sounding satisfied as he washed his hands at the sink. 'Far better for my cholesterol than the belly-buster I had planned back at the barn.'

I closed the fridge and turned to look at him.

'Belly-buster,' I frowned. 'You hardly look the type to indulge anything that would compromise your arteries.'

'All grilled,' he insisted, giving his six-pack an affectionate pat. 'Nothing fried, and besides, if you'd had a slice of Skylark Farm bacon you'd know there was no way you could deny yourself the pleasure of the occasional cooked breakfast.'

'I have sampled it,' I admitted, filling the kettle for the first time that day.

'Well, you know for yourself then,' Will nodded enthusiastically, 'and in that case, I'm surprised you haven't kept stocked up. But it's not just the bacon that's top-notch; the sausages are sublime, especially the pork and apple.'

'Incorporating apples from their own orchards, I suppose?'

'Of course,' said Will, 'and all made using their own custom recipes.'

'They really have got an amazing set-up there, haven't they?'

'Definitely,' Will confirmed, 'and from what people tell me, it's all happened since Amber arrived on the scene.'

'She's quite a gal,' I laughed.

'Yes,' agreed Will. 'She is and she's certainly turned around the fortunes of the farm, that's for sure.'

Will sounded rather in awe of my new friend, but I could hardly blame him. Amber had arrived, seen what needed addressing and, with Jake and Annie's help, made it all happen. For a moment I thought about telling Will about my dreams for the glamping site, but then realised there was no point.

If setting up a business here really was the non-starter Matt had suggested then there was nothing to be gained by getting further excited about it, but perhaps I should give David a ring and run it by him nonetheless, just to be absolutely sure.

Not because I didn't believe what Matt had told me, he had no reason to lie or put me off, but more because Amber had never mentioned any rules and regulations when we talked things through and, of course, David knew Gwen's legacy and everything to do with Cuckoo Cottage like the back of his hand. He would be the person who could tell me for certain whether my dream was dead in the water before the first string of bunting was hung.

'You all right?' asked Will, gently touching my arm. 'You look as if you've got the weight of the world on your shoulders.'

Lost in my thoughts, I jumped as our skin touched.

'I'm thinking about the car,' I lied, fumbling to escape my true thoughts and landing on the second biggest concern on my horizon. 'Mags said she would be coming to drop it off in the next few days.'

'But that's a good thing, surely?'

'Yes and no,' I admitted. 'You know I'm terrified of getting behind the wheel again.'

'Oh, please don't keep worrying about that, Lottie,' smiled Will. 'I'm sure you'll be fine. We'll take a few turns around the yard before venturing out on the open road.'

'I wish I had your confidence,' I admitted, feeling my knees weaken at the mere thought of handling a handbrake.

'Just you wait and see,' he said encouragingly. 'Give it a couple of weeks and you'll think nothing of ditching that bike and popping over to see Amber and Jake whenever you feel like it.'

I did rather like the sound of that.

'Seriously,' he laughed as the first two slices of toast popped out of the toaster, filling the kitchen with the delicious smell of home. 'That little custard-coloured van is just what you need, and it couldn't be more *you* if it tried. You two were made for each other.'

'I'm not sure what you mean by that,' I laughed.

He didn't elaborate.

'And don't be fretting about the paperwork because we can sort all that out on my laptop back at the barn, although you really could do with getting your internet access sorted soon.'

He was right, of course. Had I got it up and running already, I could have googled agricultural restrictions the second Matt mentioned them.

'And I haven't forgotten about your DIY lessons either,' Will carried on. 'I need to teach you how to change a light bulb, don't I?'

'Oh, I'm not sure about dealing with light bulbs,' I smiled, passing him the butter. 'Don't you think you should start me off with something really simple?'

I watched on as he then set about devouring two eggs which the girls had obligingly laid the day before, a bowl of muesli and a handful of raspberries then more toast, and after that, two doorsteps of bread and honey. Somehow he managed to wash it all down with about a gallon of tea and a good half a litre of orange juice. I certainly needed to restock the cupboards now.

'So what did you really think of Grace?' he asked when he finally pushed away the mountain of crockery he had used.

'Well, there are no words, are there?' I said truthfully. 'Or none that I can think of to describe how truly stunning she is.'

Will smiled broadly and I knew I'd said the right thing, but I really meant it. She was incredible.

'We were lucky with the light,' he said. 'Dawn and dusk are her prime hunting times obviously, unless the weather's been rotten. We'll try and spot her at sunset next time. I can't wait for you to see how golden she looks against the backdrop of the setting sun with the gnats and shadows . . .'

He stopped suddenly as Minnie jumped to attention and began to bark and a vehicle came to a halt out on the road. I heard a van door slam and I knew exactly who it was.

'Anyone about?'

Just as I had guessed, it was Matt. My heart sank in my chest. Not only did I not want to have to referee another sparring match between the two men, I also resented the intrusion. It was still ridiculously early, so unless he was trying to catch me in bed I had no idea why he would be calling.

'Hang on!' I shouted back, darting to grab Minnie and rush her into the dining room.

Will looked at me and raised his eyebrows.

'She hates him,' I hissed, 'and I can't risk the lawsuit if she chews his leg off.'

Will began to laugh and I bit my lip, trying not to giggle. I was just about to go and answer the door when Matt strolled in and caught us in the middle of what looked like a private joke about him. Which of course it was.

'I'm not interrupting anything, am I?' he asked, looking suspiciously from one of us to the other.

'Nope,' said Will, pushing back his chair.

Matt nodded and looked me up and down and I realised I was still wearing my boxers and frilly vest. I crossed my arms self-consciously. I hadn't been in the least bit bothered when it was just me and Will, after all he'd seen me naked the first time we met, but Matt's gaze was far too inquisitive for my liking.

'You left this in the van last night,' he said, stepping forward and handing me my cardigan. 'I thought you might be wondering where it had got to.'

To be honest, I hadn't even had a chance to miss it.

'Thanks,' I said, quickly unfolding it and pulling it on. 'I was going to give you a ring later to ask about those roof tiles,' I added.

'What roof tiles?' cut in Will.

'Well, I'll pop back later,' nodded Matt, completely blanking Will. 'I'll leave you two to your cosy breakfast.'

I knew exactly how the situation must have looked, especially given the ungodly hour, and I felt obliged to explain, even if only to stop Matt from gossiping.

'Will just called in to show me—'

'Oh, I'm sure Matt doesn't need to know the details,' said Will, jumping up, 'and besides, I'm off, so don't feel as if you have to leave on my account, Matt.'

In an instant the puzzle pieces slipped into place and I felt my face flush, but not for the reason Matt was no doubt thinking. I hadn't dreamt about Grace, Will's beautiful and best-kept secret, I'd blabbed all about her, and to Matt, one of the few people around here he didn't get on with.

'So what did he want?' asked Matt the second I'd shown Will out of the door.

He was helping himself to the last cup of tea in the pot and I rather resented his casual and slightly proprietorial handling of Gwen's things.

'Sorry?' I blinked.

'Will,' he said, pointing to the door and pulling a silly face. 'What did he want?'

'That's really none of your business,' I snapped.

I knew I probably sounded more annoyed than I intended but I felt unnerved by this sudden shift from 'builder I'd recently met' to 'man getting his feet under the table', and

I tried to ignore the little voice in my head that was keen to remind me that the shift in our relationship was at least fifty per cent down to me and that if I'd wanted to keep everything on a purely professional footing then I should never have gone to the pub with him in the first place and I certainly shouldn't have reciprocated when he kissed me.

'Sorry,' Matt mumbled sulkily as he watched me swoop around the table tidying away the breakfast things. 'I didn't mean to upset you.'

'You haven't,' I said brightly but still feeling no more inclined to share the reason behind Will's early morning appearance. As far as I was concerned I'd already done more than enough damage to his endeavours to keep Grace's presence at Cuckoo Cottage a secret.

'Thank you for bringing my cardigan back,' I said.

I didn't want Matt thinking I was ungrateful as well as miserable.

'You're welcome,' he said, drinking his final mouthful of tea.

I shifted uneasily from one foot to the other.

'And thinking about last night,' I began, 'I want to apologise for the way it ended.'

'What do you mean?'

'The kiss,' I elaborated, feeling my face flush crimson. 'It should never have happened. I blame the wine.'

'And the stars,' Matt added helpfully.

'Exactly,' I sighed, grateful that he understood. 'Ours is a business relationship, nothing more.'

Matt nodded and changed the subject.

'Are you planning on going out today?'

'Nope. The weather's supposed to take a turn for the worse again later, so I'm going nowhere.'

I glanced out of the window at the sunshine and wondered if Grace had tucked herself away somewhere for the day.

'Looks all right to me,' said Matt, following my gaze.

'That's as maybe,' I said, 'but you've lived here long enough to know that makes no difference, haven't you?'

'Yeah, you're right,' he agreed, the cheeky-chappie grin back in place. 'Could be tipping it down in an hour, and with that in mind . . .'

'Yes?'

'I have nothing lined up for today that I can't put off, so how about I get up on your roof and have a look at sorting out those wobbly ridge tiles?'

'Don't you need scaffolding for that?' I frowned. 'Surely that's a job for a roofer?'

'Nothing I can't manage,' he said.

'Well, as long as you're sure,' I said resignedly.

I'd been looking forward to a peaceful day working on the Bailey. The campsite plan might have fallen at the first hurdle, but the date of Harriet and Rachel's grand nursery opening was creeping quickly closer and I couldn't afford to waste a single day if the mobile café was going to be ready in time to provide the tea and cakes Jemma had been planning.

'Absolutely,' said Matt, as if he was doing me a favour, which really, I suppose, he was. 'I'll get my stuff together, but you'll have to keep Minnie inside for the day, I'm afraid.'

'No, it's all right,' I told him. 'I'll take her down to the barns with me.'

'Oh right,' he said, tapping the side of his nose and whispering with a wink, 'mum's the word.'

Matt kept himself busy with jobs at the cottage all day. We had a quick lunch together outside with Minnie tethered to her lead, which she absolutely loathed. I watched her skulking about and knew that if I let her anywhere within range she would quite happily feast on whichever piece of Matt she could reach. Down in the barn I didn't really settle to doing anything productive and spent more time fretting about my dashed dreams than moving the conversion project forward.

I was also mulling over the rivalry between the two men in my life, and resolved that when the time was right I would ask one or the other, or possibly even both, if there was a genuine reason behind their posturing.

'You all finished, then?' I asked at the end of the afternoon as Matt slung the last of his tools back in his van and lashed his ladders to the roof bars.

'For today,' he said, chewing his lip and frowning.

I'd noticed there had definitely been more tutting and head-shaking as he packed away and hoped he hadn't found yet another problem that needed fixing.

'Let me grab my purse,' I said, not daring to come straight out and ask.

'No, you're all right,' he said. 'Let's just settle up when everything's done, but I have to warn you the costs are mounting up a bit now, I'm afraid. You might find you need more than the cash you carry about in your purse, Lottie.'

I didn't like the sound of that at all, but couldn't bring myself to press him for an exact figure.

'Well, all right,' I reluctantly relented, 'but if you could warn me roughly how many zeros I'm looking at next time you come, because I haven't got endless funds to draw on.'

'Of course,' he smiled grimly.

There was that concerned frown again.

'Oh, come on,' I said, rolling my eyes. 'You might as well just say it. I know you've found something else.'

'It's the septic tank,' he blurted out.

'What about it?'

'Well, I haven't lifted the cover, but I reckon there might be a crack.'

'How do you know if you haven't inspected it?'

'You kind of get a nose for these things,' he said discreetly.

'Oh,' I blushed. 'I see, and I suppose that's going to be another expensive job, isn't it, as well as unsavoury?'

'Can be,' he said thoughtfully. 'Leave it with me and I'll see if I can think of anyone who can recommend someone to come out and have a look.'

'Surely you must have an uncle or another cousin tucked away somewhere who can sort it,' I said. 'You seem to have every other trade in the book covered.'

'Not this time,' said Matt, shaking his head and cranking my stress level up a notch, 'but don't worry about it. I might be wrong, after all.'

As I watched him leave I began to wonder just how many more little problems there were still to discover with my seemingly idyllic abode and whether I was actually cut out for this new life in the country business after all. Perhaps Gwen had underestimated her timing when she thought I would only need a year to establish myself; perhaps a decade would have been more fitting.

Chapter 26

True to her word, by the end of the week Mags had taken ownership of the sizeable Skylark Farm truck she needed for ferrying about plant stock and Ed's ever-increasing menagerie, and the little yellow minivan was parked in the yard awaiting my attention.

'Now you have to promise to look after her,' Mags sighed, as she gave her trusty old runabout an affectionate stroke and braced herself to hand over the keys. 'And talk to her nicely every time you take her out.'

Liam stood in the background, chewing his lip and shaking his head.

'Are you really sure you want to give her up?' I asked. 'I'll completely understand if you'd rather keep her.'

'No,' said Liam, stepping in and prising the keys from Mags's grasp. 'Absolutely not, everything's sorted. She's all yours now, Lottie.'

Between us we had worked out what I considered was a ridiculously fair price for the vehicle, based on the promise that if I did ever decide to part with her – it, I mean – I would give Mags first option on taking her/it back.

'Well,' I said, taking the keys with a hand that was less than steady. 'I promise to do my best by her, and yes, I'll talk to her lots.'

Mags looked at me and smiled, thankfully mollified by my Girl Scout-style pledge.

'I'm so pleased it's you,' she said, 'and not just because I'll get to see her every day, but because I think you need her.'

She was definitely right about that. Ever since Will had suggested I would be able to take myself off to wherever I wanted to go without having to worry about the weather, I had been feeling ever so slightly more excited than terrified.

'She's really going to transform your life, Lottie,' Mags said wistfully.

Also potentially true, given the magical powers my friend seemed convinced the little van possessed and I wondered if it were capable of spiriting away such tiresome things as agricultural restrictions and damp patches. The crack in the septic tank had fortunately turned out to be a false alarm, but I had still endured stress-filled hours prior to the announcement worrying that I was going to wake up one morning to a garden filled with . . . well, you get the idea.

Rather than settling deeper into life at Cuckoo Cottage,

I found I was now living on tenterhooks and absolutely dreading Matt finishing one job because it inevitably seemed to lead on to another, bigger one. He still hadn't given me any real indication as to how much it was all going to cost and that only compounded the worry. If he didn't stop soon then I decided I would have to put the brakes on myself.

When I had first met him and discovered his connection to Gwen, I had hoped to feel comforted that he was handling the work because she had chosen him herself. I thought his presence would make me feel safe and looked after, something I hadn't felt in quite some time, but actually I was feeling more fraught than protected and, added to that, the guilt I endured for having let him kiss me after our trip to the pub meant everything was turning into a bit of a nightmare rather than a dream come true.

'Right,' I said bracingly, determined to make the most of this historic moment in my life. 'I think we could all do with some tea, don't you? And I've baked,' I added enticingly. 'It's only a Vicky sponge, but this one is definitely better than the last.'

Mags looked at me and raised her eyebrows.

'It is,' I said defensively. 'If you launched this one at the greenhouse it wouldn't go through the glass, I'm sure of it.'

As well as the slightly weighty Victoria sponge, I had also made sandwiches and scones, and the four of us – Ed having bombed back from the field with Minnie in tow at the mere whisper of cake on the air – sat under the cherry tree sharing news and catching up.

'And did you know David's gone away for a few days?' asked Mags.

'No,' I said, 'I didn't.'

That would explain why he still hadn't called me back. I had rung and left a message with his secretary asking him to get in touch, but I was still waiting to hear from him. I had been thinking it was out of character for him not to return a call and wished she could have just told me he wasn't around at the moment.

'It was a spur-of-the-moment thing,' Mags went on. 'And coincidentally, Angela's taken a few days' holiday from working in the café as well.'

'Well I never,' I began, a small smile spreading as I realised what she was suggesting.

'It's the first time she's taken a proper break since she started working there apparently . . .'

'You aren't gossiping are you, Mags?' said Liam, opening one eye to survey her from beneath the brim of the battered straw hat he was sporting.

'No,' she said, with a wink in my direction. 'I'm just bringing Lottie up to speed with all the news from town as she hasn't been able to get there herself.'

'Until now,' I said, glancing over at the van. 'As of this

afternoon I'll be able to keep up with all the gossip, I mean news, myself.'

'Are you looking forward to driving?' asked Ed as he surreptitiously fed Minnie pieces of crust under the table.

'Sort of,' I said honestly. 'I'm more excited now than I was a couple of weeks ago and I know there are certain things I can't keep putting off, driving being top of the list.'

'No, I suppose not,' he said without a touch of condescension. 'When you get to your age,' he continued, now addressing us all, 'I guess you want to make the most of every minute.'

'Ed!' chorused his parents in dismay.

'What?'

'I'm not even thirty yet,' I told him, but all the while knowing it was a fear I'd been carrying for far too long which was holding me back.

He looked at me and shrugged his shoulders and I guessed to him I was probably just one step away from drawing my pension.

'So this is it, Lottie,' Will announced later that evening. 'Just check she's out of gear and then turn the key in the ignition.'

I hadn't planned to have a lesson that evening but Ed's words had stuck with me and I had phoned Will on the spur of the moment and asked if he could spare a few minutes to chaperone me around the yard. He was delighted by my determination to get going straightaway and now here we sat, side by side, with my knees knocking and my hands unhelpfully shaking.

'Look,' I said, twisting around in my seat and thinking if I didn't explain why I hated driving now I probably never would, 'just be patient with me, OK?'

'Of course,' Will frowned. 'I've already said I will be. Just don't let your nerves get the better of you.'

'I won't,' I swallowed, 'but this is about more than nerves. I do have another reason for not wanting to do this besides my own cowardice.'

'Would you care to tell me what it is?'

I could see he thought I was playing for time and that I was just jittery because I hadn't driven for so long. I couldn't bear it a second longer.

'Because,' I went on, taking a big breath and pushing the words out in a rush, 'when I was growing up I had the biggest crush on Shaun Dempster.'

'Chris and Marie's eldest son?'

'Yes,' I croaked. 'I thought he was the best thing since sliced bread and the last summer I saw him . . .'

'Go on.'

I shook my head.

'The details aren't relevant,' I stammered.

I didn't think it was necessary to tell Will how I had lost my virginity one steamy August night or how my crush had suddenly turned into something more serious for both of us as a result.

'Let's just say that when he was killed up at Hecate's Rest I was heartbroken and I vowed that I would never even learn to drive, let alone own a car of my own.'

'I don't understand . . .'

'Look, no one really knows what happened that night, do they?' I went on. 'No one knows whether another car was involved or not, but I couldn't bear the thought of climbing behind the wheel and getting it wrong. I never wanted the responsibility of being able to snuff out someone's life because I made a mistake.'

'But Lottie, that's . . .'

'Please don't say silly,' I cut in. 'I don't expect you to understand, but I do ask that you respect my reluctance. I'm trying my best to make my peace with what happened now and consequently I'm not letting it hold me back any longer. I want to try, OK?'

'OK,' Will nodded, 'of course. I had no idea.'

'Of course you didn't,' I sniffed. 'No one did, not even Chris and Marie, and I'd like to keep it that way.'

'Absolutely,' he nodded. 'Now come on. Be brave, Lottie. Just take your time and get a feel for her. There's absolutely no rush. Check your mirrors, listen to how the engine sounds and then, when you're ready, put her in gear and release the handbrake.'

I took a deep breath, knowing Will wasn't prepared to let me waste another minute, and imagining Shaun watching over me, I launched off.

I was surprised by how quickly I remembered how everything worked and given the age of the van there were thankfully no distracting dials or switches to have to worry about. Having managed two or three turns around the yard in second gear, I slowly came to a stop back outside the cottage door.

'Well?' asked Will, twisting round in his seat.

'Good,' I said, relief that I hadn't completely forgotten what I was supposed to do with my hands and feet coursing through my already adrenalin-fuelled system. 'Brilliant, actually.'

'I couldn't agree more,' Will said heartily. 'You're a natural.'

'Thanks,' I blushed, giving the steering wheel an affectionate rub and mentally thanking the little vehicle for getting me safely out of the blocks.

'So why don't you lock up the cottage and drive us down the road to see George?'

'What?' My hands leapt off the wheel.

'He's barely further than my place and you can go down to Hecate's Rest to turn around. You won't even have to reverse.'

'Hecate's Rest?'

'Yes,'

'But that was where ...'

'Lay the ghost to rest once and for all, Lottie.'

'I don't think so,' I stammered, 'and what about the ditches running either side of the road? It's barely wide enough for two bikes.'

Will didn't say anything.

'You said you wouldn't rush me,' I reminded him. 'You said I could do this at my own pace, in my own time.'

'Well, there's no time like the present,' he said reasonably. 'And it's just two minutes down the road, just two teeny-tiny minutes and you'll be free from all those fears that have been holding you back for so long.'

'But what if we meet a tractor or something?'

'That's hardly likely at this time of day,' he shrugged. 'But there are plenty of places to pull over.'

Thinking of my resolution to 'grab every minute' and how proud Shaun would be if he could see me, I nervously locked the cottage, handed Minnie to Will through the window and climbed back into the driver's seat.

'I can't believe you made me do that!' I gasped, when I eventually pulled up outside George's cottage.

We hadn't met one tractor during the short ride, but two, and I had held my breath as they both squeezed by, gripping the steering wheel so tightly my knuckles had turned white.

Pulling around the crossroads at Hecate's Rest had felt like a doddle after that and it hadn't been the traumatic experience I had expected at all.

'Lottie,' said Will, 'you do realise you've just driven beautifully for the first time in God knows how long and now you can go wherever you want, whenever you want?'

'I know,' I laughed, grinning like an idiot and leaning over to plant a hasty kiss on his soft lips before I had time to temper my excitement. 'Isn't it brilliant?'

'What's all this then?' said George, suddenly appearing at Will's window before I had time to register what I'd just got carried away and done. 'Have you gone and hot-wired Mags's precious van?'

'Nope,' I beamed. 'She's my precious little van now!'

'Hop in,' said Will, who had turned the brightest shade of red, as he climbed out with Minnie in his arms and helped George into the passenger seat, 'and Lottie will take you for a spin.'

'Lovely,' said George, speedily settling himself in the seat and reaching for the seat belt.

'I don't think so,' I said. 'Where am I going to go?'

'Just drive up as far as the barn,' said Will through the window, 'and turn around in the yard. I'll get the kettle on while you're gone.'

Without another word, he disappeared down the side of the house.

'Come on then,' said George. 'We don't want the tea stewed, do we?'

The journey was almost a complete success – had I not stalled when I tried to pull out of Will's drive when I had turned around, it would have been a total triumph – but all things considered, I was feeling remarkably proud of myself by the time we got back.

'So how did she do?' Will asked the second we were in George's little kitchen.

'Marvellous,' said George. 'She was absolutely brilliant.'

'I did stall once,' I admitted. 'Pulling up the slope on your drive.'

'That's no bad thing,' said Will. 'Now you know how the engine sounds and feels, and how much oomph she needs to get going.'

'Technical term that,' winked George and I couldn't help but laugh. 'So how long are you planning to have this fella here as your wingman?'

'I've told her I'm at her disposal for as long as she needs me,' said Will reassuringly. 'Isn't that right, Lottie?'

'Absolutely,' I agreed, feeling grateful that he was going to respect my secret and not reveal why I feared flying solo, 'and I really appreciate it, but do you know, I think I'll be able to handle the roads around here. However I wouldn't mind a bit of company when I head into town, if that's all right with you?'

'Of course,' he said.

'And if Will can't come with you, you only have to come and get me,' offered George. 'I don't mind the odd trip to town.'

'Thank you, George,' I smiled, taking the mug of tea and thinking what a fool I had been for putting it off for so long. I knew Shaun would be furious that I hadn't driven because of what had happened to him. His life may have been cut horribly short but he had lived it to the full and I felt I owed it to him now, as well as Gwen and Gran, to do the same. 'I thought I might pop to Skylark Farm tomorrow,' I announced before I had time to change my mind. 'It isn't all that far, is it?'

Of course, the only time I'd visited the farm was for the Lammas party and I'd been stowed away in the back of the minivan for that particular journey and consequently my internal satnav was a little hazy.

'Oh here we go,' laughed George. 'There'll be no stopping her now.'

'End of the road, turn left and carry on for about five miles, then left again for another mile,' said Will. 'It couldn't be easier.'

'Right,' I said resolutely, feeling somehow even more excited than the day I moved into the cottage. 'That's settled. Tomorrow I'm making my first solo journey.'

I was bang on schedule on the Cherry Tree caravan now

so I could certainly spare the time. I was going to drive to see Amber and ask her and Jake what they could tell me about agricultural restrictions and regulations before David came back from his mini-break with Angela, assuming they had gone somewhere together of course.

'Excellent,' grinned Will. 'I've got to pop and see them later so I'll tell them to expect you.'

Chapter 27

When Matt arrived at the cottage early the next morning, the van, which I had decided to call 'Birdie' because of her distinctive custard yellow colour, was packed to the gunnels, ready for my first solo expedition. I'd been having a bit of a tidy-up in the workshop area of the big shed while waiting for the first coat of primer on the Bailey to dry and had discovered some bits and pieces I thought Amber might like for Honey. Birdie's surprisingly capacious interior was plenty big enough to take everything in one trip, even the little plastic slide I had managed to take apart, and as soon as the sun had appeared over the horizon I had packed everything up ready to go, including Minnie.

'Morning!' I called to Matt as he swung into the yard.

I unwound the van windows as far as I dared, making sure Minnie could get her nose out but nothing else. Given the fact that Matt had been practically living at the cottage lately, it really was high time she had got used to him turning up by now.

'Hi,' he yawned, hauling himself and his tool bag out of the van. 'You can't leave her in there all day,' he said, with a nod to Minnie who was eyeing him furtively and no doubt trying to weigh up her chances of crawling through the inch and a half of open glass I had allowed her. 'That thing will heat up in no time, even if it is a bit chilly at the moment.'

I was none too impressed with him referring to my new mode of transport as a 'thing'; however, he was right about the weather. For the first time that morning the air had a definite edge to it and had I not known what the date was I might have assumed it was somewhere far nearer autumn than it actually was. However, shored up as I was by the heady prospect of hitting the open road (quiet country lane actually), I let his disparaging comments about my transport pass.

'We're going out,' I told him, 'so she'll be fine just for a minute.'

'Out?' questioned Matt, his eyes as round as Polo mints.

'Yes,' I said, laughing at his reaction, 'out. You'll be all right on your own here for a bit, won't you? I'm not planning to be long.'

'Well, I suppose so,' he said, scratching his sun-bleached head as if I wasn't making any sense.

'And at least you won't have madam here to contend with,' I told him.

Right on cue, Minnie gave a disgruntled woof and I went to reach for the door, but Matt stopped me.

'Are you not waiting for Will, then?'

'Not for this trip,' I shrugged. 'I'm only going as far as Skylark Farm so I should be all right.'

'Well, as long as you're sure,' he said doubtfully, biting his lip as Minnie let out another woof of frustration.

'I thought you'd be happy I could manage without him,' I said, my freshly formed confidence crumbling a little in the face of his concern. 'Especially given the way you two seem to feel about each other. I thought you'd be pleased I didn't need him.'

'No, I am pleased,' he said. 'Of course I am, I'm just a little taken aback, that's all.'

'In what way?'

'Well,' he sighed, 'whenever the topic of driving has come up you've been reluctant to even consider it.'

That was true enough.

'And I always felt you were cajoled into taking the van on, rather than really wanting it.'

Also true.

'If anything, you've looked like a rabbit caught in the headlights when considering the prospect of climbing behind the wheel.'

'That's because I've felt like one,' I said with a laugh.

'But now,' he went on, 'literally within hours of buying Mags's van, you're off and running.'

'It's only up the road,' I said, keen to remind myself as much as him that this really was a fool-proof journey and no big deal.

'But even so,' he said, 'it's a bit of a speedy turnaround, considering you said you were terrified of driving. Or am I getting this a bit out of proportion?'

'I know it's all happened really fast,' I agreed, 'but Will took me out last night, or rather I took Will out,' I murmured, amazed at the thought that I had found the courage to do that, 'and everything just seemed to click into place. It was brilliant, actually.'

I was talking about far more than just doing a few runs up and down the deserted drove road but Matt didn't know that and I wasn't about to tell him.

'I see,' he said.

'No,' I replied, 'you probably don't, but that's not your fault.'

'Tell me then.' He was beginning to sound impatient. 'Explain to me what it is that I'm missing.'

I had absolutely no desire to tell him about my heartbreak over losing Shaun or how I had finally admitted to myself just how devastating and long-lasting the impact of Mum leaving me had been. Her desertion had meant I had ended up living the tiniest, safest life possible.

I could see now that I had spent literally decades jogging sedately along life's path, blinkered to all diversions and digressions for fear of putting a foot wrong and hurting someone in the process, but that was all far too much personal information to share with someone who was fixing up my house and with whom I had shared nothing more intimate than a tipsy kiss.

'Things have been changing for me ever since I moved here,' I said simply.

'What things?'

'Everything,' I said. 'I just want to get on with things here now and start enjoying myself. I want to grasp my new life with both hands and make the most of this wonderful gift that Gwen has generously left me.'

'Even if it is all in a bit of a state,' he reminded me, 'and is going to cost a small fortune to put right?'

'Even then,' I sighed, looking over towards the cottage and imagining the numbers on my bank balance rolling back to zero. 'I'm planning to make a real future for myself here, Matt,' I said determinedly, then quickly added, before he had time to interrupt again, 'in spite of the initial teething problems. Cuckoo Cottage is my life now, and until you mentioned the agricultural restrictions, I thought it was going to be my vocation as well, but the jury is out on that one now.'

'What do you mean by that?'

Matt had been looking more and more confused with every word I said, as well he might, given that he had no idea what I had planned for the caravans still stored in the shed.

I shook my head.

'Never mind for now,' I said. 'But if it does end up happening, I promise you'll be the first to know.'

Second, if you counted Amber, of course, but for the moment I'd forgotten that she and I had stumbled upon the idea in separate but perfectly timed synchronicity.

'But perhaps I could help,' said Matt eagerly. 'If you just tell me what it is that you're planning, then I might be able to find a way of helping you make it work?'

I looked up at him for a second and wondered whether perhaps I should just tell him. After all, he was a local, and a builder to boot. He knew all about the restrictions and probably came across tricky situations like this all the time, and even if he didn't, I dare say he had a cousin or some other relative who did.

'Maybe,' I said, still not entirely convinced it was time to share. 'Thank you. I'll think about it, but if it all comes to nothing,' I added, opening the door and pushing Minnie aside before she had gathered her wits and jumped out, 'you'll have wasted your time trying to help with something destined to fail.'

'But if you do tell me and I can help,' he said reasonably,

'you'd be saved no end of time and worrying. You said you had business plans, didn't you?'

'And you said there would be agricultural restrictions to scupper them,' I reminded him.

'I know,' he said, 'but sometimes there are ways around them, room for manoeuvre, especially if you know the right people.' I was pretty sure that was a suggestion that he might know the right people, but I still wasn't prepared to give anything away. Our relationship was finally back on a professional footing and I was in no hurry to blur the edges of it again.

'Look,' I said, turning over the engine, 'I told Amber I'd be there soon so I'd better go or she'll be sending out a search party, but I promise I'll think about what you've said.'

'All right,' he said, stepping back.

'I won't be long,' I called. 'Perhaps we'll talk again when I get back.'

'OK.'

'And please, try not to discover any more problems while I'm gone.'

'I'll try,' he called back. 'But I'm not making any promises.'

It was a slow, but thankfully uneventful journey to Skylark Farm and I pulled into the gateway feeling suitably proud of myself for having negotiated the twists and turns without incident. I wasn't sure if the townsfolk of Wynbridge would much care for my 'slow and steady' pace, but I would worry about that another day.

'Well, look at you!' laughed Amber as she rushed out of the farmhouse door with Honey nestled, as ever, on her hip. 'How does it feel to finally be driving?'

'Liberating,' I told her, even though my hands were still shaking. 'I feel as if I can go anywhere now.'

'Good,' she smiled.

'As long as I can drive there before the rush hour, of course,' I added with a wry smile.

As the grass was still damp we decided to leave unloading the van until later.

'Morning, Lottie,' beamed Jake as he appeared in the doorway with a slice of toast and a mug of coffee. 'Fancy a spot of breakfast?'

'Yes, please,' I nodded enthusiastically. 'I was too nervous to eat before I left and now I'm starving.'

'I'll make you a bacon sarnie if you like,' he offered. 'Assuming Will hasn't eaten it all, of course.'

'Has he been here already?' I asked, concerned that he'd had another call-out to the farm.

'Just a social call,' said Jake. 'He wanted to talk about you actually, Lottie.'

'Oh?'

'Jake!' said Amber sharply, before turning to me. 'You'll

have to excuse him. He's hardly the soul of discretion, is he?'

'Well, it's hardly a secret,' said Jake, looking puzzled. 'Is it?'

Amber shrugged and stepped out of the way to let the Labradors, Bella and Lily, get to Minnie who was rolling about the floor, clearly delighted to be reunited with her doggy pals again.

'I hope you don't mind me bringing Minnie,' I said. 'Only, Matt's working at the cottage today and she still can't stand the sight of him. She gets upset if I shut her in the dining room, but I haven't had much choice.'

Amber and Jake exchanged looks.

'Do you mind?'

'Not about Minnie being here,' said Jake pointedly. 'But I'm not sure about all this so-called work that Matt keeps discovering needs doing. Perhaps you should pay a bit more heed to Minnie's reaction to your ever-present handyman, Lottie.'

Amber didn't say anything as she strapped Honey into her high chair and kissed the top of her soft little head.

'Is that what Will came to talk to you about?' I frowned. 'I know he doesn't think much of Matt either, but given that you invited him to the Lammas party the other week I'd sort of assumed that you and he were friends.'

'Friendly rather than friends, I'd say,' corrected Amber.

'He's helped us out with a couple of jobs here this year, but that's all. Will was actually wondering about the validity of this connection Matt claims to have had to Gwen.'

'So why hasn't he asked me about it?' I said, feeling a little disgruntled about Will, but also surprisingly relieved that I'd made a point of setting Matt straight after our kiss. 'We've seen each other practically every other day recently and he hasn't said a word.'

'Because you made it very clear that it was none of his business,' said Jake bluntly as the bacon began to sizzle on the Aga.

'But that was ages ago,' I said defensively. 'Before we became friends.'

'Well, I'm guessing he still thinks the subject is off-limits and he doesn't want to fall out with you again, especially given how long it took the pair of you to start being civil to one another.'

'He likes you, Lottie,' said Amber quietly.

She may have only whispered it but those four words made my stomach roll in a way that had nothing to do with the sizzle of the delicious breakfast Jake was cooking.

'Just be careful,' he warned as he began to butter the bread Amber was slicing. 'Don't just rush in and agree to everything Matt suggests you have done. Think it through first, OK?'

'I have been questioning him about things,' I said

defensively, 'but he's always been able to prove he's right. I'm guessing you don't think I can trust him either then, Jake?'

'Let's just say I think you need to think carefully about prioritising how you spend your money,' he said meaningfully, 'even if Matt can allegedly justify what he's doing.'

I was a little hurt that Will felt he still couldn't broach this subject with me, especially given how our relationship had developed since our rocky start, and what about his promise to help me with some of the work on the house?

He might have jumped in the passenger seat of my little van to act as my chaperone, but he hadn't so much as shown me how to change a plug in the cottage. Was he staying out of the way because he didn't want to stand on Matt's toes, and if that was the case, had he made the mistake of thinking there was more between my builder and me than blocked pipes and crumbling plasterwork?

'So what did you really want to talk about?' asked Amber as she passed a plate stacked with the biggest bacon butties I had ever encountered. 'I'm guessing you haven't just braved the lanes to drop off toys for Honey, or am I wrong?'

'No,' I said, taking a delicious bite and groaning in pleasure. 'As pleased as I am to pass the things on, there is something else,' I added as I savoured the crisp saltiness.

'Not a bad breakfast this, is it?' said Jake proudly.

'I've never tasted better,' I confirmed.

'So come on,' encouraged Amber as she fed Honey tiny bits of sandwich from her plate, 'what's on your mind?'

Jake pushed back his chair and put his dishes next to the sink.

'I think I'll leave you girls to it,' he said, kissing Amber's cheek. 'I'm guessing you won't need my input.'

'I might,' I told him, 'but I'm not sure.'

'Well, come and find me if you want me,' he said. 'I'll be in the orchards.'

'Thanks,' I said, 'and thanks for the breakfast.'

'Anytime. I hope you don't mind me mentioning my concerns about Matt?'

'Not at all,' I told him. 'I'm sure you and Will are wrong, at least I hope you are, but it's nice to have people looking out for me nonetheless. I've never really had that luxury before.'

'Well, I hope we're wrong too,' he smiled. 'See you in a bit, Honey bee.'

Honey looked at him and wrinkled her nose before breaking into a toothy grin and waving goodbye with buttery fingers.

'So,' said Amber when Jake was out of earshot. 'What's up? You haven't changed your mind about the glamping site, have you?'

'What makes you say that?'

'Well, I thought you'd be telling everyone about the idea

by now. I know you've been busy getting the Cherry Tree van finished but I assumed you would want to spread the word and see what folk thought. I'm sure the gossiping would stop if everyone knew what you had in mind. I mean, no one's going to complain about having a few more tourists in the town, are they? Just think of the extra income they would generate.'

'Well, I don't know about that,' I said sadly. 'In fact, I think it's lucky I've managed not to say anything if that's how you really think people would have reacted. I would have hated to build their hopes up only to disappoint them again.'

'Whatever do you mean?'

'I do still want it all to happen,' I told her, 'more than anything, but I'm not sure it's going to now.'

'Why ever not?'

'Because of the agricultural restrictions on the land,' I explained, 'and the fact that I probably won't get permission to run a business from the yard.'

'What agricultural restrictions?'

'I have it on very good authority,' I sighed, 'that running any kind of business from Cuckoo Cottage is not going to be possible.'

I hadn't had it officially spelled out for me yet, of course, but Matt had said it in such a way that I had no reason to think he was wrong, and the fact that he had been so surprised that I hadn't realised that there would be rules and regulations about what I could and couldn't do with the place only increased my belief in what he had said. Even though Jake and Will had their doubts about the work he was doing, I was fairly certain he knew what he was talking about and waiting to speak to David was, to my mind, nothing more than a formality.

If possible, Amber looked even more perplexed than I felt.

'Are you absolutely sure about this?' she frowned. 'Have you had it all properly confirmed? What does David have to say about it?'

'Can I take it from your reaction that you don't think there are any regulations, then?'

'Well, I don't know,' she said, wiping the butter from Honey's hands before she spread more through her hair. 'I haven't given it any thought. When we talked about the project, I knew you would have to get planning permission and so forth, but then so did you, surely?'

'Yes,' I said, 'but I didn't think it would be too much of a problem.'

'Well, neither did I,' she said. 'I'm so sorry, Amber.'

My spirit sagged a little further. I had hoped she would tell me outright that I was wrong, that there had been some mistake, but the fact that she did neither only served to confirm that what Matt had said was indeed right. I hoped David would soon come back from wherever he had gone.

'I can't deny I'm devastated,' I croaked, a lump forming in

my throat and my vision blurring. 'I seem to be taking one step forward and three back these days.'

'But you're still pleased about the fact that you're finally driving and with the work you're doing on the Cherry Tree van, aren't you?'

'Oh, absolutely,' I nodded, blowing my nose. 'I couldn't be happier about all that.'

But, truth be told, suddenly everything felt as if it was on the edge of going wrong, and if it carried on going much further downhill I really would have no money left and would be preparing to put the place up for sale even before the year was up.

It was the last thing I wanted to do, of course, especially as Gwen had been so kind and gone to so much trouble over the cottage and collecting the vans, but it was a possibility I could no longer deny. If things didn't start to look up soon, my new life at Cuckoo Cottage was going to be over before it began.

'Let's go and unpack these things,' I said, trying my best to rally. 'The grass must be dry by now.'

Honey absolutely loved the little plastic slide and quickly pulled off her socks as Amber filled the paddling pool with a tiny bit of water for her to splash about in. We stood watching her giggling and playing and I looked at the idyllic Skylark Farm set-up, thinking how I had hoped to create something similar for myself.

'Don't look so worried,' smiled Amber encouragingly, 'I'll ask Jake if he has any thoughts about these regulations. I won't tell him what you're planning, of course.'

'All right,' I nodded, 'thanks.'

'I didn't know you'd installed a pool?'

We turned round to find Harriet and Rachel walking down the drive.

'Invitations to come and swim are in the post,' laughed Amber.

'I should think so too,' smiled Harriet.

'Do you want tea?' asked Amber.

'Thanks, but I'd rather have something cold, if it's no trouble?' requested Harriet.

'Same for you, Rachel?'

'Yes, please.'

Rachel and I stayed outside with Honey while Amber and Harriet went to get some apple juice and glasses from the kitchen.

'So how's the cottage?' asked Rachel as she knelt next to the pool and began splashing, much to Honey's obvious delight.

'Good,' I said, 'it's finally coming together and the mini-van's great.'

'Mags is like a cat with two tails this morning,' Rachel laughed.

'Is she?'

'Oh yes,' said Harriet as she came out carrying the bottles of juice. 'Although she's more pleased that you've taken on her beloved van than she is about getting herself a new truck.'

That sounded like Mags, generous to a fault.

'Well, I've promised to look after her,' I said, looking back at my little Birdie. 'Perhaps I'll pop down and see her later.'

'She'd like that,' said Rachel, 'although she's working late tonight. You wouldn't believe the amount of work involved at the nursery at this time of year.'

'Every time of year,' butted in Harriet, handing round glasses.

'True,' Rachel agreed.

'Did you have any problems setting the nursery up?' I asked.

'What sort of problems?'

'Getting planning permission and dealing with restrictions and things?'

'Well, the initial set-up was simple enough,' confided Harriet, 'and there were no restrictions as such. The land belonged to my dad's farm, you see, but there have been a few hoops to jump through now we're opening to the public, but, by and large, it's all been pretty straightforward really.'

'Why do you ask?' asked Rachel.

'I just wondered how these things work,' I said, draining my glass.

'You aren't thinking of setting up a nursery as well, are you?' Harriet teased.

'Absolutely not,' I smiled bravely while wishing my own plans were going to fall into place as easily as Harriet and Rachel's. 'I can't even keep a cactus alive.'

Chapter 28

Back at the cottage, Matt's van was still parked in the yard but he wasn't anywhere to be found in the house. I had been careful to keep a tight grip on Minnie's collar as I worked my way through the rooms, but I needn't have bothered. Forgetting I had left the front door ajar, I set her down in the kitchen and in a heartbeat she was off, tearing out of the door, with me hot on her heels.

It didn't take a genius to work out where she was heading, just someone with average hearing, and I followed the expletives all the way to the bottom of the ladder that she had chased Matt back up and which was propped up against one of the barns.

'What are you doing down here?' I frowned, annoyed to have caught him looking, what could only be described as, up to no good. 'I thought you said you had jobs to finish in the house? I don't remember asking you to come down to the yard for anything.'

Having just had a conversation with Jake about his and Will's reservations about my builder's credentials, I was none too pleased to find him skulking about somewhere which, although not exactly off-limits, was certainly none of his concern.

'Do you think you could call her off?' Matt requested, with a nod to the bottom of the ladder where Minnie was standing with her front feet on the second rung, her teeth barred and a menacing growl resonating through her tiny chest.

'In a minute,' I said. 'When you've answered my question.'

Matt looked rather taken aback by my response. He gripped the ladder a little tighter and stepped up another rung. To my mind he couldn't have looked guiltier if he tried.

'I'd rather not say, if it's all the same to you,' he muttered.

'I'm sure you wouldn't,' I said, 'but unless you do, you're going to find yourself up there for a very long time.'

'All right, all right,' he caved as Minnie attempted to balance a paw on the next step up. 'Just don't go off on one, OK.'

'All right,' I said, bending to clip on Minnie's lead, but I still didn't pick her up.

'Are you going to take her back up to the house?'

'Not yet. Come on, out with it. You've left the cottage unlocked and I'd like to get back up there at some point today.'

Matt let out a long breath and I braced myself to listen to the excuse he was going to come up with to try and justify what he was up to.

'I had a message from Simon earlier.'

'Right.'

'He said he was worried about you working down here when he hadn't had a chance to check out how the electricity had been installed. He was concerned that it was rigged up illegally or something and that you were in more danger down here than you had been inside the cottage.'

'And what has any of that got to do with you?' I demanded, thinking that drunk and bullish Simon was very different to the sober and considerate version. 'You aren't an electrician.'

'He wanted to come back himself but he's busy today and when I told him you were worried about the work stacking up, he gave me a few pointers to look out for that would give him an idea as to whether his concerns were justified.'

'So why didn't you tell me any of this earlier, and what exactly are you looking for up there?'

'I'm checking the connection and I didn't tell you earlier because, like I said to Simon, I didn't want to stress you out over spending more money if everything turned out to be all right.'

That sounded fair enough. Sort of. He did know I had been worrying about the bills stacking up and therefore having me out of the way before he had a look did make sense, but I still wasn't entirely convinced.

'Oh great,' said Matt, his head dropping as he looked back up the yard.

'Hello, hello,' said a voice behind me. 'What's going on here then?'

Will sounded incredibly amused to have stumbled upon what must have looked like a scene from a farce. Minnie momentarily took her eyes off her prey, wagged her tail in Will's direction, gave a playful little yap and then turned her attention, as well as her teeth, back to Matt.

'I suppose you know the psychology behind this kind of scenario, don't you?' Will said to me playfully. 'Never trust a human your dog hates. That's how it goes, isn't it, Minnie?'

Another yap from Minnie and a head shake from Matt.

'What do you want, Will?' he called down.

'Do you know,' said Will, rocking back on his heels and clearly loving every moment, 'right now I can't remember.'

'Matt's just checking how the barn is hooked up to the electric,' I said, pulling Minnie away.

'But don't the cables run underground?' frowned Will.

I didn't say anything because I didn't know, but I hoped he was wrong, for Matt's sake if nothing else.

'So have you remembered what you want?' I asked.

'Oh yes,' he said with a grin. 'I wanted to ask how you

got on driving to Skylark Farm this morning. I take it you've been?'

'Yes,' I nodded, 'and it was fine. Better than fine actually, brilliant.'

'Well done you,' said Will, giving my shoulder a squeeze and sounding genuinely delighted. 'And I also wanted to let you know that David is going to be back in town from tomorrow. Mags mentioned that you were hoping to see him about something, is that right?'

'Yes,' I said, feeling pleased that I would finally be able to get some answers from the expert. 'That's great. Thanks, Will; although I'm not sure I'm up to driving in to Wynbridge just yet.'

'Well, that's where you're in luck,' he said. 'I have a day off tomorrow and I need to go to town. I thought you could pick me up and we'd go in together. How does that sound?'

'Perfect,' I said quickly before my nerves got the better of me again and I asked him to drive me in. 'Absolutely perfect.'

'I don't suppose there's any chance you could pick that bloody dog up, is there?' Matt called down from his lofty spot at the top of the ladder.

So caught up with what Will had to say, I'd momentarily forgotten that he was still up there.

'I was hoping you'd say that,' Will smiled down at me, completely ignoring Matt's request. 'We could have a spot to eat in the Cherry Tree if you fancy it?'

'That would be lovely,' I said. 'I can't think of anywhere better.'

'You are sure he's up there for the reason he says he is, aren't you, Lottie?' he said quietly.

I swallowed but didn't answer.

'Thanks mate,' said Matt in disgust. 'I can hear you, you know.'

'So?' shouted Will. 'I don't care if you can hear me, and I'm not your mate.'

'It's all right,' I said, laying a hand on Will's arm. 'It's fine. If anyone's got the situation wrong, it's probably Simon. I dare say he's told him to look in the wrong place or something.'

I wanted to believe that was the case, but really I couldn't be sure. Will shook his head and glared up at Matt and I knew that all it would take was one hint of a doubt on my behalf and Will would be knocking Matt off the ladder and throwing him off my land.

'Will,' I said loudly, pulling his attention back to me for fear that he was about to actually do just that. 'I would love to drive you to town tomorrow, but for now would you please just take Minnie back up to the cottage and put her out of harm's way in the dining room for me?'

'Sure,' he said, scooping Minnie up. 'I'll see you tomorrow.'

Without another word he strode off up the yard and into the cottage. I was amused to see that Matt stayed up the ladder until Will came back out of the house empty-handed, climbed into his truck and drove off.

'I wish I knew what it was he's got against me,' he said as he joined me back on solid ground. 'We were both close to Gwen,' he went on, 'so it's not as if he didn't know all this work needed doing, is it?'

'I don't know,' I shrugged.

'I mean,' Matt went on, 'if he was such a good friend and such a hero then surely, given all the work he did on his barn, you'd think he would have offered to do these jobs for her, wouldn't you?'

'Maybe,' I relented.

'Well, you want to watch yourself with him, Lottie,' he said, echoing what others had said about him. 'He's got one hell of a temper on him.'

I didn't say anything, just waited while he folded up the ladder.

'And what did you want to see David about?'

'Just a couple of things I want to clarify.'

'It isn't about the ag regs, is it?'

'Might be,' I shrugged non-committally.

'Well, I hope you won't be disappointed when he charges you a fortune just to confirm what I've already told you for free,' he said, striding ahead. 'I thought you were supposed to be watching the pennies.'

Chapter 29

I felt really nervous about driving into Wynbridge the next morning and not just because I hadn't ventured further than the quiet drove roads behind the wheel before. Unbeknown to Matt, Will and practically everyone else, what David was going to tell me about the rules and regulations, which restricted what I could and couldn't do at Cuckoo Cottage and in the field, would either secure or condemn the future I had been getting so excited about.

I was desperate for Matt to be wrong and I had to admit my feelings towards him were tempered with suspicion now. Having caught him poking around the barns on top of his ladder the day before with, let's face it, a pretty flimsy excuse as justification, I couldn't help but wonder if he had an ulterior motive and had thought it was in his best interests to trot out a convenient lie when Minnie had found him.

I honestly didn't know how I was going to feel if I discovered Matt had betrayed the trust I had put in him. Having been abandoned by the one person I should have been able to rely on without question meant that I had never been able to 'let people in' easily, and I didn't think I could bear it if I had been duped into putting my faith into someone else who was hell-bent on letting me down.

'You all right?' asked Will when I pulled into his drive early the next morning. 'You look a bit peaky, Lottie.'

'I'm all right,' I said, trying to rally. 'Just a little apprehensive about the drive, but I'll be fine once we get going.'

'That's the spirit,' Will smiled, hopping into the passenger seat and glancing into the back. 'No Minnie today?'

'No, not today. I thought I had enough to contend with this morning, and besides, she isn't everyone's cup of tea, is she?' I added, thinking that even if no one else minded her presence, David's secretary Iris certainly would, and I needed my solicitor and all his staff on my side today.

'I suppose not,' agreed Will. 'Does she mind staying home alone?'

I wasn't sure if he was trying to show concern for Minnie's welfare or if he was surreptitiously trying to work out if Matt was still working on the cottage.

'She wasn't particularly impressed, but she'll be fine,' I told him. 'A couple of hours' peace and quiet won't do her any harm; she's had more than enough excitement lately.'

'Lottie, about yesterday—'

'Do you mind if we just get going?' I cut in. 'Because if we don't leave soon all the easy parking spots will be taken.'

The journey wasn't quite as scary as I'd imagined, but negotiating the bridge which straddled the River Wyn and the big roundabout which followed immediately after was a little tricky, but I did it. I even managed to reverse into the parking space without losing a mirror or taking out anyone else's.

'There,' I announced, pulling on the handbrake and turning off the engine. 'We made it.'

'You made it, you mean,' said Will, grinning from ear to ear. 'And to tell you the truth, I'm a little disappointed really.'

'Why?' I gaped, appalled when just a second before I had been feeling so elated.

'Because,' said Will cheekily, 'when I offered to accompany you on your first few trips I thought you'd need far more support than this. I kind of hoped you were going to need me for quite a while, but you're more than capable of doing this on your own and I'm redundant already.'

I didn't know what to say. I wasn't sure if he was teasing or not.

'I really mean it, Lottie,' he said. 'You're good to go.'

'Well, how about I stall at the roundabout on the way

home,' I suggested, trying to make light of what I imagined was the true meaning behind what he was saying.

'Oh, all right then,' he laughed. 'That will certainly prolong my station in the passenger seat and perhaps manipulating a near miss when you pull out of this space might not be a bad idea either.'

'Oh please,' I groaned as I released my seat belt. 'Don't even joke about it.'

'I'm very sorry, Miss Foster,' said David's secretary, Iris, 'but Mr Miller won't be back until after the weekend.'

'But a friend said they'd heard he was back yesterday,' I said, my shoulders dropping in resignation.

'Back in Wynbridge,' she confirmed with a frown, 'but not back to work.'

I bit my lip, disappointment and frustration battling it out in my brain for the upper hand.

'I take it you wanted to see him about something specific?'

'Yes,' I sighed, 'very specific.'

'Then perhaps you'd rather talk to one of the other partners if you don't want to wait,' she suggested. 'Mr Moffat is going to be available later this morning.'

I was shaking my head even before she reached for the old-fashioned appointment book.

'Thank you, but no. This really is a query for Mr Miller. I'll wait until after the weekend.'

'As you wish,' she smiled. 'If you call on Monday I'm sure he'll squeeze you in.'

I left the office downhearted and walked over to The Cherry Tree Café where I had arranged to meet Will to celebrate my prowess behind the wheel and give Jemma and Lizzie an update on the caravan which was fast approaching completion.

'Coffee and a slice of carrot cake please,' I ordered at the counter before taking a seat next to the window.

The café was still quiet and without Minnie to keep an eye on it was nice to have the opportunity to sit inside and soak up the warm and welcoming ambience. If I could convince my little companion to stay at home more often I might even consider signing up for Lizzie's knit and natter session in the autumn.

'Hitting the sugar a bit early, aren't we?' teased Jemma as she appeared at the table with my order.

'I'm celebrating,' I said, quick to justify my sweet tooth. 'I drove to town for the first time this morning and in the absence of fizz, for obvious reasons, I thought coffee and cake would be a satisfactory alternative.'

'Well congratulations,' beamed Jemma. 'You must be feeling on top of the world.'

I wasn't sure if that was right, but I was still feeling pretty pleased with my unexpected achievement. If anyone had told me, even just a couple of months ago, that I was going to be driving before the end of the summer *and* navigating my way around Hecate's Rest, I never would have believed them.

'Have you got time for a quick catch-up?' I asked. 'I drove in with Will and was hoping to bring you up to speed about progress on the caravan before he turns up.'

Jemma's eyebrows had shot up at the mention of my travel companion, but she didn't say anything. Given that Angela and David had finally got their act together, I guessed she was all 'matchmakered' out. At least I hoped she was.

'I only have a minute, I'm afraid,' she said, plonking herself down on the chair opposite. 'I'm a little short-staffed at the moment,' she added with a weary nod towards the kitchen where I could hear someone crashing about.

'I did hear on the grapevine that Angela and David have both coincidentally disappeared at the same time,' I admitted.

I had no desire to gossip but wanted to let Jemma know that I was aware of her current staffing predicament.

'Have you taken on some new staff in her absence?'

'Yes,' she said with a huff, 'but *only* for as long as her absence. Don't get me wrong, I'm absolutely thrilled Angela and David have finally got their act together, but let's just say this new girl isn't going to work out, and leave it at that. Now,' she said, sitting up straighter, 'drink your coffee before it gets cold and tell me how things are going with the caravan café.'

*

I had just finished my second cup of coffee when Will finally arrived. Jemma was delighted with how the project was coming on and even more delighted when I showed her the selection of photographs I had had the foresight to take on my phone. She and Lizzie had been so busy that neither had managed to come out all that often to see for themselves how things were progressing, but when I reassured her that all was well and that the grand reveal would be an even bigger surprise she was thrilled.

Ironically her excitement sent my spirit sagging again as I realised just how disappointed I was going to be if I didn't get the chance to renovate the other three vans and my business idea failed to launch.

'I see you've started without me, then,' said Will, nodding towards the empty coffee cups and crumb-filled plate.

'Well, I was beginning to think you'd stood me up,' I said. 'Where on earth have you been?'

'I had to see a man about a dog,' he said elusively. 'Literally. Now, can I get you another coffee?'

'I'd better not,' I said, 'but thank you. Do you mind if I just have some orange juice instead?'

'A liquid fruit portion to balance out all the refined sugar, eh?' he quipped, pointing at my plate.

'Exactly,' I smiled.

I watched on as he wandered over to the counter to place our order and couldn't help noticing how red Jemma's temporary waitress turned as she took his money and carefully counted out his change. Ordinarily a complete table service was in place, but I got the impression that Angela's time off had been the cause of one or two irregularities in the café's usual smooth running. Evidently, Angela really was indispensable and I wondered what Jemma would do for staff cover when the mobile café finally hit the road.

'So,' said Will, taking the seat opposite me and denying the blushing waitress the benefit of his handsome face, 'did you get sorted at the solicitor? Did you manage to see David?'

'No,' I sighed, 'afraid not. You were right about him being back in town, but unfortunately he won't be back to work until after the weekend.'

'And why do I get the impression that's such a problem? Are you really that desperate to see him? Couldn't you perhaps make an appointment to see someone else in the interim if that's the case?'

'No,' I said, making space on the table for the extra cups and plates as the waitress wobbled over, the crockery rattling on the tray. 'It's no big deal,' I lied. 'It'll keep.'

Will didn't say anything while the girl unloaded his order and then helped her fill it again with my dirty dishes. It was obvious that he had absolutely no idea of the impact he had on the opposite sex and as a result came across as even more desirable.

'Look,' he said, when we were finally alone again, 'at the risk of annoying the hell out of you, Lottie, and sounding like a cracked record to boot—'

'It's all right,' I cut in. 'I know you're still worried about Matt and all this work at the cottage. Jake told me yesterday that you'd mentioned it, and given that we both saw Matt up that ladder up to goodness knows what, I can't say I'm not a little suspicious of his motives myself now.'

'So you really hadn't asked him to look around the yard, then?'

'Absolutely not,' I said, thinking of my precious vans and all the effort I had gone to to keep them under wraps. 'Like you heard him say yesterday, he was checking the electricity supply.'

'Badly,' frowned Will.

'I know he was doing it wrong,' I said defensively, still not really wanting to believe that my builder was potentially more villain than hero, 'but he isn't an electrician. That's Simon's job and Matt was only doing what he thought was right from the sketchy instructions his cousin had given him. He must have got the wrong end of the stick or something.'

'Um . . .'

'And anyway,' I added, thinking that I had probably already said far too much, 'I know that he knows I'm worried about all these bills piling up. I guess he was just trying to check things out when I wasn't there so if Simon's concerns were unfounded I wouldn't have ended up worrying over nothing. You know I never slept a wink all the while I was waiting to find out if there was a crack in the septic tank.'

'Um,' said Will again as he thoughtfully stirred his coffee and shook his head. 'And I did say I was going to help you out as well, didn't I?'

'Yes,' I said, 'you did. Why haven't you been dishing out these DIY lessons you promised? Is it because Matt's always around?'

'Of course it is,' he confirmed. 'I just thought it would be best all round if I stayed out of his way, to be honest. Especially if you two . . .'

'Especially if us two, what?' I pounced.

'Oh, it doesn't matter,' he shrugged, 'but I do stick to what I said before. The only work that I was aware of that needed doing at the cottage was replacing the shower and updating the fuse box. Everything else was fine.'

'Well, perhaps it was stuff you hadn't noticed,' I suggested, trying to justify the catalogue of additional problems Matt had unearthed. 'I don't think you can really tell what's wrong with a place until you've actually lived there.'

Will looked at me doubtfully.

'Well, Matt hasn't lived there,' he reminded me.

'You know what I mean.'

'So are you telling me you'd noticed all these things for yourself, then?' he asked searchingly. 'Since you'd moved in, were these issues you'd picked up on before Matt magically stepped in to repair and improve them?'

I hadn't spotted anything, of course, because I had barely moved in before Will had quite literally thrown me across Matt's path with his out-of-control driving. I wondered if he would be prepared to shoulder some of the blame for what had subsequently happened if I reminded him of that fact.

'Is your coffee all right?' asked Jemma, whose timely appearance saved me from having to answer Will. 'Only I've had a couple of complaints,' she whispered. 'I've got a horrible feeling I'm going to have to let this girl go before the day is out.'

'It's fine,' said Will, gulping another mouthful to prove the point. 'A bit on the strong side perhaps, but otherwise OK.' Jemma looked concerned. 'Honestly, it's fine,' he coughed, 'and besides, I've got a busy afternoon planned so the caffeine buzz will help me through it.'

Having negotiated my way out of the parking space and the town without incident, talk again turned to the goings-on at Cuckoo Cottage.

'I know you're worried about these bills, Lottie,' said Will, 'so are you looking for work to help pay for them?

Have you thought about how you're going to fund your future?'

Had I been able to pin David down earlier, I might have been able to answer that question there and then, but unfortunately, with everything still so up in the air, I didn't feel it was worth sharing the details of what might never happen.

'I've been mulling a couple of options over,' I said evasively. 'But I'm not in dire straits just yet.'

'Well, please don't wait until you are,' said Will seriously. 'And remember, Lottie, you can always call on me if you need to.'

'And you won't say "I told you so"?'

'Of course not,' he frowned. 'I just want you to enjoy living at Cuckoo Cottage every bit as much as Gwen did, and if I can do anything to help you do that, I will.'

'Thank you,' I said huskily, trying to focus on the road rather than the tears that had sprung up at the mention of my benefactor.

Gwen had enjoyed literally decades of contented living at Cuckoo Cottage and when I moved in just a few weeks ago I had envisaged myself doing the same, but now I wasn't so sure. The house was a mess, the business was probably dead in the water before I'd even given it a name and I still had the winter, spring and the beginnings of next summer to get through before I could even consider calling an estate agent.

I gave a little shudder as I imagined a van turning up and

the driver jumping out to hammer a 'For Sale' sign into the verge. I had been so sure that I would never leave Cuckoo Cottage when David told me what Gwen had arranged, and given the beautiful caravans that she had gone out of her way to buy in readiness of my arrival, she had obviously been sure too. How was it possible that my dream-come-true had turned into such a nightmare already?

'Are you all right?'

'Yes,' I said, perhaps a little too brightly. 'I'm sorry, Will. I haven't been the best company today, have I?'

'You're fine,' he said kindly. 'You've got a lot on your mind and you've had this drive into town to contend with. It's hardly surprising you haven't felt like the life and soul.'

I was pleased he understood, but his kindness made my eyes well up even faster. So many people had gone out of their way to counter the gossips and welcome me to Wynbridge: Amber with the party invitation and the hens, and Mags with the van, to name just two, and I couldn't shake off the feeling that I was just making a mess of everything and letting everyone down.

I had waited all my life to trust people and form close bonds and now I finally had I felt like I was falling short and incapable of repaying their kindness. I really needed to buck my ideas up because if I was going to be packing my bags and moving on next year I would want happy times to look back on, not a catalogue of regrets and mistakes.

'Well, I appreciate your understanding,' I told Will as we passed the cottage and carried on towards his barn, 'and I promise that if I do need you, I'll ask.'

'Good,' said Will, sounding genuinely pleased. 'And don't forget you've got Mags just up the road if you need a girly chat, and Amber.'

I was amused to hear that he had assigned my female friends the roles of confidante and saved action man for himself.

I parked up at the barn and helped unload his bags. When we had finished he reached out and pulled me into a friendly hug. It wasn't until I was in his arms, my head nowhere near his shoulder, that I remembered how tall he was. I looked up into his face and laughed.

'What's so funny?' he frowned, loosening his grip a little and looking down at me.

'You're so tall,' I said. 'Thank goodness we aren't a couple.'

'What do you mean?'

'Well, I could never date you, could I?' I said, thinking I could actually get used to dating him very easily if he sat down all the time.

'Why ever not?'

'I don't think my neck could cope with the strain,' I explained.

'I'm sure I could find an old apple box to carry around and stand you on,' he suggested as I began to giggle, 'or I could lift you up like this.'

He picked me up as easily as if I weighed nothing and I could see right into his eyes. I swallowed and licked my lips, sure he was just about to kiss me, when we heard a van drive by and spotted Matt glaring out of the window.

Chapter 30

In line with my renewed determination to make the most of my time living at Cuckoo Cottage, no matter how long that turned out to be for, I telephoned Mags that evening to let her know how I was progressing with driving around in her much beloved minivan.

'I'm pleased you've got on with it so quickly,' she said when I explained that I had driven to Wynbridge as well as Skylark Farm. 'I bet you feel like you can conquer anything now, don't you?' Fortunately she didn't give me time to answer. 'And you have to promise to come and see me and Ed very soon. It feels like ages since we were all together. You can come now, if you like.'

That was typical Mags.

'Thanks for the invitation,' I laughed, 'but I'm all driven out for today. How about we arrange something for the weekend instead?' I suggested.

'Maybe,' she said, her tone unsure. 'Only I might not be about much after I finish work on Saturday.'

'How come?' I asked. 'Have you got a hot date lined up?'

'Sort of,' she said cagily, her answer completely taking me by surprise.

'Oh, come on then,' I insisted, wanting to hear her news. 'Spill the beans. Who's the lucky fella?'

Mags didn't say anything.

'Of course you don't have to tell me—'

'It's Liam,' she said in a rush. 'I'm seeing Liam.'

'You're always seeing Liam,' I reminded her. 'He's Ed's dad for a start.'

'I know that silly,' she tutted.

'So are we talking about seeing him as in actually dating him?' I gasped, my brain suddenly completing the romantic equation.

'Yes,' she said, 'but it's a secret. No one knows, especially Ed.'

'But why ever not?'

I imagined he would have been delighted that his parents were giving a relationship together a go after all this time.

'Because if it all goes belly-up he'll be heartbroken,' Mags explained, 'as will I, to be honest.'

'I knew you and Liam were made for each other,' I said smugly, not really hearing the apprehensive edge in her tone. 'Didn't I say so the very first time I saw you both together?'

'You did,' my friend confirmed, 'and you weren't the first to say as much, which is part of the reason why we've decided to start seeing each other properly, but it's complicated, Lottie.'

'In what way?'

Personally I couldn't see what the problem was.

'Because we decided when I fell pregnant with Ed that we would keep our relationship on a purely platonic footing, just like it had always been before that one crazy night, and consequently since then everything has been fine and now I'm terrified of messing it all up.'

'I'm sure you won't mess anything up,' I told her, as I finally began to see the situation from her point of view, 'and I'm certain Liam wouldn't have asked you out if he thought there was even the slightest danger of anything going wrong. He loves his son every bit as much as you do, Mags.'

'I know that,' she said, 'but it was actually me who asked Liam out.'

'Well, the same still applies,' I said. 'There's no way he would have said yes if he was anything other than one hundred per cent certain that it was the right thing to do.'

'OK,' said Mags, letting out a long breath. 'OK. Thanks, Lottie. I'm sure you're right.'

'So where are you taking him?'

Mags had arranged the perfect romantic evening, but there was just one problem.

'Not that I've been on many dates in the last few years, of course,' Mags confided, 'but whenever I've had an evening out, Ed has gone to stay with Liam.'

'Ah yes,' I said, wrinkling my nose. 'I can see why that's a bit of a conundrum.'

'Exactly,' she said, 'and the last thing we want is for Ed to find out before we're ready to tell him. I know you and half of Wynbridge are convinced everything will work out, Lottie, but we can't risk upsetting our lad if it doesn't.'

'Perhaps you could just tell him that you and Liam want to go out to talk about something, some access arrangement or plans for Christmas?' I suggested.

'Ed would see straight through that, and besides, we always talk about that sort of thing at home when we're all together.'

As far as I could tell, they were already the perfect little family unit, but I didn't say as much.

'All right,' I said instead, wracking my brains and digging deep for inspiration. 'How about Ed comes and spends the night here at Cuckoo Cottage? I've been meaning to ask him for a proper tour of the field and my local patch for ages. I know he can talk for England when it comes to flora and fauna so we wouldn't run out of things to discuss.'

'Maybe,' said Mags thoughtfully.

'And he could bring Jack,' I told her. 'We could put him in one of the barns for the night.'

'No, Jack's fine,' said Mags. 'Will has helped build a proper enclosure for him now he's almost flying again.'

I might have known Will would have helped sort that out.

'Well, have a think about it,' I told her. 'If we make it sound as if this was all my idea then Ed won't think anything of it, and if he's here he certainly won't twig that you and Liam have gone out together.'

'All right,' said Mags, sounding far happier. 'I'll see what Liam says and let you know.'

'I'm so happy for the pair of you,' I told her, thinking of Angela and David as well. 'I think there must be something blowing about on the Wynbridge wind at the moment, wafting romantic inclinations and assignations about the place.'

'Well in that case,' she giggled, 'you want to watch out, Lottie Foster. It could be you next.'

'Ha,' I laughed, 'I don't think so.'

'Oh, I wouldn't be too sure,' she teased. 'From what I heard, you can't keep that chap of yours from your door for two seconds together.'

I was fairly certain she was talking about Matt, but I was only really interested in Will turning up on my doorstep.

Early the next morning I set to work on the Cherry Tree van again. I was determined not to let my enthusiasm for the project be thwarted by either my worries or the heat which built up early in all three of the barns. I might not be able to achieve what I had set my sights on as far as the business was concerned, but I had made a promise to Jemma to have the van ready in time for Harriet and Rachel's launch party and I had no intention of letting her down.

Minnie, unusually lethargic and still in a bit of a sulk about the fact that I had gone to town without her, had opted to stay in the cool kitchen and consequently she wasn't in earshot to let me know when Matt's van pulled into the yard.

'Blimey!' he shouted above the noise of the radio, making me jump almost right out of my skin. 'These are a bit of all right, aren't they?'

I clambered out of the Bailey and turned the volume down to zero.

'I wasn't expecting to see you today,' I said, trying to steer him back towards the door.

'When Simon said Gwen had got some vans in here, he never said they were like this! Crikey, these must be what, fifty years old?'

'Probably,' I shrugged.

'At least, I reckon,' he said, walking further in. 'I thought she was just doing some friends a favour and storing their family tourers,' he whistled under his breath. 'Who did you say these belonged to again?'

'I didn't,' I said, determined not to be drawn into giving out any more information than I had to and thinking that if he really had the same amount of sense as Simon, he would have realised that at this time of year the run-of-the-mill 'family tourers' would have been pitched up on some site somewhere. Perhaps I should have been grateful that he seemed to be somewhat lacking in the common sense department?

'So what was the plan?' he asked, finally coming back over to where I was standing. 'To do this lot up like that one,' he said, pointing at the Bailey, 'and sell them on?'

'Something like that perhaps,' I said, my stomach rolling as I realised his brain was finally catching up. 'I hadn't really thought that far ahead.'

'You're pretty handy with a paintbrush,' he said, admiring my handiwork. 'I'll give you that.'

I was a bit put out that he sounded so surprised. I prided myself on giving everything I converted the very best possible finish, whether that meant skilful application of the brush, bespoke fittings or beautiful soft furnishings and finishing touches.

'What can I do for you, Matt?' I asked bluntly. 'Not that I'm not pleased to see you of course, but I'm a bit behind and I need to get on.'

'That's what happens when you go off on jollies,' he smiled. 'It's always the work that suffers.'

I knew he was referring to seeing me with Will the day before and that he was probably expecting me to explain what he had witnessed, but I was in no mood to pander to his thinly disguised inquisitiveness.

'I'll keep that in mind,' I said, turning towards the cottage.

'And I saw David,' he said.

I spun round to face him again.

'Where?'

'In the pub last night.'

'Oh.'

'And I hope you don't mind, but I took the liberty of asking him about the agricultural restrictions tied to this place and how restrictive they are.'

'And?'

I was furious that he had gone behind my back, but was too keen to hear what David had to say to pick an argument about what he should and shouldn't have done without my say-so.

'Well, he didn't want to talk about it to begin with,' Matt explained. 'He said it wouldn't be appropriate to talk about it with anyone but you.'

'Right.'

'But then I told him that we were . . .'

'We were what?'

'Friends,' he said, wriggling his eyebrows, 'and that I was getting the cottage back in shape for you, and he loosened up a bit.'

'And what did he say?' I could feel the sweat trickling down my back, and if I gripped the paintbrush I was holding any harder it was going to snap in two.

'It wasn't good news, I'm afraid,' he admitted. 'The property including the barns are bound and have to remain as they are, and the field can only be left fallow, as it is or used for agricultural purposes.'

'What, you mean I can plough it up and grow sugar beet in it?'

'Exactly,' he nodded, 'and the barns can store things, of course, but you certainly can't set up or run a business from here, I'm afraid. He said you'd never get permission for change of use.'

'But what about Skylark Farm?' I countered. 'They've made all sorts of changes to what they're doing there.'

'But it was already a working farm,' said Matt reasonably. 'The changes they've made have been pretty insignificant in the grand scheme of things.'

'But the bungalow,' I said, clutching at straws, 'renting out the bungalow?'

'The bungalow was already there. Look,' he said, 'I don't know what you really had in mind for this place, Lottie, but whatever it was must have involved some pretty drastic changes because you haven't exactly got a lot to start with, have you?'

Personally I thought I pretty much had everything I needed and in all honesty what I was planning wouldn't have had that big an impact on either the environment or the look of the place. Beyond the few caravans in the field, nothing

would have looked different at all and I had been going to
try and make everything as eco-friendly as possible.

'So what was the big idea?' he asked.

'It wasn't drastic at all,' I said, stuffing the paintbrush back
into the pot. Suddenly I didn't care if he knew every last
detail of what I had been dreaming up. 'I was going to set
up a glamping site,' I explained. 'Convert these vans, put
them in the field and market the place as a bespoke holiday
experience.'

Matt didn't say anything, but spotting the tears of frustration coursing down my cheeks, he came over to give me
a hug.

'I'm all right,' I said, quickly untangling myself from his
embrace, 'just disappointed, that's all.'

'What will you do with the vans now?'

'No idea,' I sniffed. 'Sell them, probably.'

I couldn't believe that Gwen had gone to all the trouble
of sourcing the vans and getting them here without having
first checked out whether or not I would actually be able
to do something with them. According to the dishearten-
ing news Matt had just shared, I couldn't even refurbish
them, let alone rent them out for romantic reminiscent
mini-breaks.

'Was David absolutely sure?' I asked, just to be certain
there wasn't even an inch of wriggle room.

'He was adamant,' Matt confirmed. 'I even asked him if I

should let him check out the details next week before I said anything to you, but he said there was no need. There was no doubt in his mind.'

'I can't believe it,' I muttered, pulling the heavy door shut.

I didn't want to even think about the vans now, let alone look at them.

'I could help you sell them on, if you like,' Matt offered as he helped me reattach the padlock. 'If you can't face it.'

'Thanks,' I choked, 'and they might not be the only thing coming up for sale before much longer.'

'What do you mean?'

'Nothing,' I said, rushing back towards the house to sob in private. 'I'm sorry, Matt. I'll give you a ring tomorrow, OK?'

Back inside the house I listened to him leave, then flopped down on the sofa to have a good howl. I know I'd had my suspicions recently about all the work he had been coming up with, but this information was straight from the horse's mouth and I knew there would be nothing suspicious about that. If David was certain about these non-negotiable regulations then there was no doubt in my mind that he could have made a mistake.

How was it really possible that, just weeks before, I had arrived with my few bags and high hopes and now everything was falling so spectacularly apart? Of course, I still had the cottage, but knowing my luck, Matt was going to be right and the place really was in a far worse state than

I'd realised when I had so keenly signed on the dotted line. Having lost Gran and then Gwen, I didn't think my life could be any sadder, but now it seemed determined to sink to new depths, even by my standards.

I was just about to crawl up to bed and give in completely when the sound of raised voices met my ears and Minnie ran to the front door and began to growl. I quickly picked her up as the argument got louder and, having dumped her in the kitchen, ran to find out what all the fuss was about.

'You're a liar!' bawled Will, his fists clenched and his expression menacing as he stood over Matt, who was in a heap on the ground, bleeding and groaning.

Evidently I hadn't heard Matt leave at all but Will arriving, and the pair had been winding each other up ever since I shut myself inside the cottage.

'Get up!' shouted Will, trying to pull Matt to his feet. 'Tell Lottie what you've just told me and then we'll know once and for all.'

Matt slumped back down again, the gash on his head trickling blood down his face as he tried to catch his breath.

'Leave him!' I shouted, rushing over to Matt's side and standing between him and Will.

'No,' spat Will. 'Let's hear it again and then I'll move.'

I stood my ground, terrified by the expression in Will's eyes but knowing that if I backed down, Matt was going to be in real trouble.

'I think you'd better go,' I said, as calmly as I could manage.

'Not until I've heard it from your own lips, Lottie Foster.'

'I don't know what you're talking about, Will,' I said truthfully, 'but I think you'd better go before I have to call the police.'

'Call them,' he laughed, 'and then we'll find out once and for all . . .'

Before he had a chance to say another word, Matt leapt up, pushed me to one side and began pummelling into Will, fists flying and the air blue with language I never wish to subject my ears to again. There was only one thing for it, and without stopping to think whether I was going to get hurt, I leapt between the two men, felt a blow to the side of my head and fell to the dusty ground.

Chapter 31

I had absolutely no recollection of what happened after that. My head hit the ground and the lights literally went out for what felt like days, but in reality, I later discovered, it was nowhere near as long.

'Lottie?'

Gingerly I turned my face towards the sound, wishing that the persistent thumping in my head would go away, and slowly opened my eyes.

'Lottie.'

It was Mags.

'Where am I?' I croaked, my voice was barely audible and my throat was tight and dry. I felt as if I hadn't had a drink in weeks.

'You're in hospital,' she said, 'you've had a bump on the head, but you're going to be OK.'

'Where's Minnie?' I croaked again, trying to lift my head

but finding I couldn't. It felt as if someone had strapped a ten-tonne weight to the back of it. 'Where's my girl?'

'She's at my house with Liam and Ed,' said Mags softly, 'and she's fine, as is the cottage and everything else. You just have a nice rest and I'll be back in a bit.'

The next time I opened my eyes it was dark, but I could make out the silhouette of a man sitting next to the bed. I wasn't sure if it was Will or Matt or a figment of my imagination.

'So how are we feeling?' asked a cheery nurse at what I guessed was early the next morning.

'Sore,' I said truthfully.

My whole body ached, I could feel my face was grazed and there was a lump easily the size of a ping-pong ball above my left eye. I dreaded to think what the bruising was like.

'Well, if you will go around trying to break up bar-room brawls.'

'It wasn't a bar-room,' I said, suddenly remembering and wondering which of my two knights in shining armour had been the one to strike the blow.

'Anyone at home?'

'I asked you to wait,' tutted the nurse, as she fussed with my blanket and scowled at the policeman whose ruddy face appeared around the side of the curtain.

'Any chance of having a quick chat, Miss Foster?'

'You can have a chat when this young lady has had some breakfast,' insisted the nurse.

'How about, while she has some breakfast?'

As I slowly worked my way through a beaker of tepid sweet tea and a slice of rubbery, barely buttered toast, PC Williams took me through the finer details of what he had discovered had played out in the yard of Cuckoo Cottage the morning before.

It soon became obvious that he knew little more than I did. Matt and Will were fighting, Matt was coming off worse and I had stepped in before things took an even nastier turn and ended up getting thumped in the process. Neither man could be sure who had delivered the blow which sent me reeling, but as Matt was the worse for wear, the general consensus was that it was probably Will. Did I want to wait and see if I could remember more in a day or two and press charges? No, I certainly did not. It was simply a misunderstanding that wasn't worth the court's time and that was the end of that, or so I thought.

'The nurse says they'll be discharging you later this afternoon,' said Matt, who turned up around lunchtime sporting at least half a dozen stitches, a black eye and was walking with the support of a stick.

'Look at the state of you!' I gasped.

'You're a fine one to talk,' he said, shaking his head. 'Have you looked in a mirror?'

'No,' I said, 'not yet.'

Considering there was a one in two chance that he was the one who had inflicted my injury, I was rather taken aback by his off-the-cuff remark and laid-back attitude and wondered if he knew for certain that it had been Will who had knocked me out.

'Are you all right?' I asked, as he carefully lowered himself into the chair next to my bed.

'I've been better,' he said with a shrug, 'but I'll mend. To be honest, what's going on in my head is causing me more concern than this,' he added, pointing to his face.

'What do you mean?' I frowned, even though it was agony to do so.

'Why didn't you tell me you thought I was stringing you along, Lottie?'

'What?'

'Why didn't you ever say you weren't sure about the work I was doing?' he said accusingly. 'If you'd asked me a few more questions I would have explained what I was doing in more detail and exactly why I was doing it. There was no need to ask that bloody thug to take me to task about it all when a simple conversation between us two would have sorted it.'

I didn't know what to say.

'Have I really been that overbearing?'

'No, of course not,' I squeaked, feeling furious with Will. 'Is that what you and Will were arguing about?'

'Of course.'

'But I never asked him to say anything,' I insisted. 'I didn't know he was going to say a word and I certainly never put him up to take you to task, as you put it.'

Who the hell did Will think he was? I might have been having my doubts and concerns about Matt, but I never would have dreamt of sharing them with Will if I thought for even one second that he would take matters into his own hands and use my worries as an excuse to have a brawl with my builder.

'I just feel such an idiot,' Matt went on, shaking his head and looking thoroughly fed up. 'I've only ever tried to be your friend, Lottie,' he said, making my guilt escalate even higher than my temperature had been. 'I've only ever tried to help you.'

'I know that,' I said, 'and I should have talked to you sooner. I was going to talk to you, had I been given the chance. I've just had so much on my mind.'

'Well, I'm almost done at the cottage for now,' he announced, 'and I don't want a penny for anything I've done. I have a reputation to uphold around here and I don't want anyone saying that I took advantage of the situation.'

'I would never do that,' I said firmly.

'I know you wouldn't,' said Matt, 'but what about Will? You saw for yourself yesterday just what an explosive temper he's got, didn't you? I wouldn't put it past him to tell everyone that you've confided in him and that I've been taking you for a ride. You've discovered for yourself first hand just how quick folk are to jump to conclusions.'

'I'm sure Will wouldn't do that,' I said, 'temper or no temper.'

'Oh really?'

'Yes, really.'

'You do know why he left the army, don't you, Lottie?' Matt asked, suddenly changing track.

'No,' I said, and given his change of tone I probably didn't want to know either.

Having seen the dangerous expression in Will's eyes as he towered over me the day before, I knew that I would never want to pit myself against his temper again. He had been a beast of a man, and not in an attractive, protective way, but in an unhinged, explosive way. He couldn't have been further from the gentle, caring soul who had patched me up after my silly trip out during the thunderstorm if he tried. The transformation was as shocking as the fact that he had gone behind my back and talked to Matt when I hadn't asked him to.

'It was his temper,' said Matt. 'His stupid temper got the better of him, yet again.'

'I'm not sure I want to hear this, Matt,' I said, wondering how he could possibly know when no one else did. 'This is really none of my business.'

'Of course it is,' he said. 'He's your friend, isn't he? I think you need to know what you're letting yourself in for if you decide to keep in contact with him.'

'So how come you know why he left when no one else does?' I asked, unable to stop the question tumbling out.

'That's hardly relevant right now,' he said darkly, 'and I'm sure Will would rather I didn't know at all. After what happened back at the cottage I'm even more convinced he'd far rather no one knew his shameful secret.'

I closed my eyes and listened as Matt explained, in far more detail than I would have liked, how Will had served in Afghanistan and how, having worked closely with the bomb disposal unit and lost a colleague as well as their dogs in a roadside bomb, he'd set out to deliberately gun down an entire civilian family before being bundled back to barracks and then to England, where he was hastily discharged and stripped of every medal he'd ever earned. According to Matt, he'd been lucky to escape a lengthy prison sentence.

I knew Will had been reluctant to take on Minnie after Gwen had died, and I could appreciate that if he had lost a loyal companion in a war zone then that was certainly an understandable reason as to why he wouldn't take on another dog, but as for the rest, surely that couldn't be right? I knew that these things happened and that soldiers the world over, working under extreme pressure, occasionally made mistakes, but not gargantuan ones like this surely, and certainly not Will.

'I know you find it hard to believe,' said Matt. 'I did when I first heard it for myself, but think about it, Lottie. What do you *really* know about him? You've only known him five minutes. How can you possibly think you know someone who you've spent so little time with? Surely what you and I were subjected to yesterday is enough to prove that he's dangerous and not to be trusted?'

'But I've only known you a few weeks as well,' I pointed out.

'But I haven't gone around picking fights and telling tales, have I?'

He had a point. I really didn't know what to say. I needed time to think. By tackling Matt about the work at the cottage behind my back, Will had already proved he thought nothing of betraying a confidence, so perhaps Matt was right. Perhaps I should make a point of staying out of Will's way, for the time being at least, but how difficult was that going to be, especially given the fact that he lived just up the road?

Chapter 32

I needn't have worried about how difficult it was going to be to avoid Will, because as Mags solicitously drove me home from the hospital and then tucked me up in bed, she explained he had decided to take a couple of weeks' holiday to visit an old friend abroad. I can't deny I was relieved that he had gone.

'From what I can gather,' she said, checking the jug of water next to my bed was icy cold, 'he's feeling pretty ashamed about what happened.'

I didn't mention anything that Matt had told me about why Will had been thrown out of the army or how terrifying he had looked during the fight. I didn't want her to think I had picked a side, because I hadn't. It was up to Will if he wanted folk to know about his past and it was also his decision to choose that moment to take a break.

At least his absence would give me time to think things

through without his distracting presence, and as Matt was temporarily out of action as well, I was looking forward to enjoying Cuckoo Cottage in relative peace and isolation for the first time since I had arrived. With every passing day it was looking more and more likely that I would have to sell up, so the opportunity to make some special memories of my own to take with me was most welcome.

'But we don't even know that it was Will who hit me,' I reminded Mags. 'It could just as easily have been Matt, and besides, whoever it was, it was an accident.'

'I don't know why you would think that would make him feel any better about what happened,' Mags tutted.

'Well, Matt seems to have resigned himself to the situation without a fuss.'

'Will isn't making a fuss,' said Mags.

'What is he doing, then?'

Mags sighed and walked over to the window to check on Ed who was cleaning out the chicken coop and keeping an eye on Minnie for me.

'He just thought you'd be pleased to see the back of him for a bit,' she said eventually. 'The pair of you haven't exactly had a smooth ride since you first met and now, just when things were getting better between you, this has happened.'

'But running away won't solve anything,' I said, ignoring the little voice that was suddenly so keen to remind me that if I moved on then that was exactly what *I* would be doing.

'No, it won't,' agreed Mags, 'but it will give you both some distance from one another and hopefully some perspective. He really likes you, Lottie,' she added meaningfully, 'and he doesn't want to lose your friendship.'

I didn't say anything else. I didn't think it would matter how long he disappeared, for I would never really be able to come to terms with the horrific things Matt had told me that he had done. Part of me was desperate to try and make some sense of it by talking it through with Mags, but the greater part was still slightly concussed and not up to such an important conversation.

'You look tired,' she said, turning back to the bed. 'Shall I take Minnie home with me again for tonight and see how you feel about having her back in the morning?'

'No,' I said, closing my eyes, 'but thank you. I don't know what I would have done without you these last few days, Mags. I really appreciate your help, and Ed's, but I'll be all right on my own now.'

'Are you sure?'

'Yes,' I nodded. 'I'm just going to potter about around here for a few days.'

'And do you promise to ring if you need anything?'

'I do.'

The next couple of days, in spite of the occasionally pounding head and multicoloured bruises, were the best I had had since moving to Wynbridge. I managed to reassure Mags that I was fine via frequent but brief phone calls during the evenings and the days were spent slowly pulling together the threads and putting the finishing touches on The Cherry Tree Café caravan.

By the time I had finished I was feeling extremely proud of the results. The electrics and plumbing hadn't needed tweaking at all and consequently this was the first complete refurbishment I had undertaken independently, apart from the online ordering Jemma had taken responsibility for, and it had turned out beautifully.

As I stood back to admire my handiwork and silently thanked Eric and John, my former employees, for equipping me with far more skills than I initially realised I had, I couldn't deny the twinge of sadness in my heart. Were it not for the ridiculous agricultural restrictions, this kind of project would have played a major part in my future and I would have been rather happy about that.

The splendid isolation I was enjoying didn't last long. As soon as Matt was well enough to drive, he arrived back on the scene, keen to finish the work he had started and, to my mind, milk the situation for all it was worth. It seemed we could barely have a conversation without him mentioning either selling my beloved vans before the summer ended and prices took a nosedive, or raking over what Will had accused him of. Truth be told, by the end of the week I was feeling more annoyed by the fact that he wouldn't drop the subject than guilty for what I had said in passing to my neighbour which had been the cause of all the ructions.

'How do you fancy a trip to the pub tonight?' asked Mags at the end of the week. 'I haven't seen you since I tucked you up in bed the day you came home from hospital and I want to say thank you in advance for agreeing to have Ed for the night this weekend.'

'I'm not sure,' I began.

'Don't tell me you aren't up to it, Lottie Foster,' she said bluntly, 'because every time I've driven by your place this week those barns have been open, so I know you haven't been sitting on your backside doing nothing. You're obviously up to something.'

I couldn't help but smile at her clever observation.

'I'll pick you up in half an hour,' she said, then hung up.

It was another warm evening in Wynbridge, but as I sat at a table in the bar of The Mermaid, discreetly trying to cover my fading bruises with my hair, I could feel a slight chill in the air. The place was pretty quiet, even for a week night, but there was an unusually unwelcome atmosphere that I hoped my arrival hadn't caused.

I had already spotted and heard the usual furtive mutterings and glances from the bar and looked among the customers, wondering if anyone present had been responsible for the gossip Matt had mentioned but that I hadn't noticed, during my last visit.

. 'So is Liam looking after Ed tonight?' I asked Mags as she came over to the table with our drinks.

'No,' she said, 'he's spending the evening with George. They're planning when would be the best time to start helping you renovate Gwen's old vegetable patch actually.'

I didn't have the heart to tell her that I probably wouldn't be there to enjoy next year's harvest now.

'I think they're hoping to get it cleared this autumn, then mulch it and leave it to settle over the winter ready to dig over and plant up in the spring, or something like that.'

'That sounds like the right idea,' I said, taking a sip of Diet Coke. 'Just the sort of thing my grandad would have suggested.'

'So have you heard from Will?' Mags asked.

'Sorry?' I frowned, thrown by the sudden change in conversation.

'Has he phoned, sent a postcard?'

'No,' I said, 'of course not. I haven't been expecting him to. Has he been in touch with you, then?'

'Yes,' she said, the colour rising in her cheeks as she carried on. 'He phoned this afternoon. He's the reason I've asked you out tonight, actually.'

'I don't understand,' I said, looking about me and fully expecting him to walk in.

Part of me wished he would. I had missed him more than I thought I would, given what I now knew about him, and when the door swung open I held my breath, but it was just Chris. Perhaps Mags had been right, even though she wasn't privy to all the horrid details; perhaps the time apart had helped me gain some perspective about the situation after all.

'I thought you said you wanted to thank me in advance for entertaining Ed while you and Liam enjoy some private time this weekend?'

'Yes,' she said, studying the menu on the table. 'I do.'

'But?'

'But what?'

'Well there's obviously some other reason why you've dragged me out and I'm guessing now that it has something to do with Will, yes?'

'Yes,' she said again as she carefully put the menu back down. 'There are a couple of things he's asked me to talk to you about, Lottie.'

'So why couldn't you do it back at the cottage?' I asked.

'I just thought a change of scene would do you good.'

'Well, come on then,' I said, ignoring the fact that she had my welfare at heart and just wanting to hear what she had to say. 'What is it?'

This was like trying to get blood out of a stone. She shook her head and I began to panic. Admittedly I hadn't known her for long, but I knew when there was something wrong, and judging by the look in her eyes and the colour of her face this was very definitely one of those occasions.

'Hello, Lottie dear,' cut in Chris before she had the chance to say anything else. 'How are you? I heard you'd been in the wars.'

'Hello, Chris,' I said, looking up at him, 'just a bit of a misunderstanding, that's all.'

'So I see,' he said, eyeing up my bruises. 'I bet you wish you'd let me get on with the matchmaking now, don't you?'

'They weren't fighting over me!' I laughed, keen to dispel any rumours that were being bandied about.

'Oh right,' chuckled Chris. 'You sure about that, are you?'

'Quite sure,' I said firmly. 'It was just crossed wires about some work that I'm having done at the cottage, that's all.'

'And how are you finding life out in the sticks? I'm sorry I haven't found time to call in as often as I'd promised. I hardly know where this summer's gone.'

'That's all right,' I said. 'I know how busy you and Marie are. It's been lovely,' I told him enthusiastically, although not entirely truthfully. 'It's everything I hoped it would be.'

'And much more, from what I'm given to understand,' he added quietly with a frown.

'What do you mean?'

'I think Chris is talking about your new business venture,' said Mags under her breath.

'My new what?' I squeaked.

How on earth did either she or Chris know about that? I knew Amber wouldn't have told anyone and I hoped I hadn't been going about telephoning all and sundry and spreading the word myself since I'd had my bump on the head.

'I have to say it was a bit of a surprise,' said Chris, rubbing his chin and looking around the bar, 'and I dare say you've worked out that it accounts for the less than friendly welcome you've no doubt received here tonight.'

I followed his gaze to the row of bar stools and discovered quite a few people had turned around and tuned into our conversation. I looked back at Mags, who shrugged her shoulders and looked apologetic.

'Do you really know about what I've been planning?' I asked.

'We all know!' called Jim from behind the bar.

'I had no idea *they* knew,' said Mags urgently, grabbing my wrist. 'I never would have suggested coming here tonight if I thought it was going to be a problem. I had no idea it was already common knowledge.'

'What was common knowledge?' I demanded.

'That you're going to turn that field of yours into a massive campsite,' said Jim.

'That you're planning to clear the whole area and have it tarmacked over so you can squeeze in as many touring vans and motorhomes as you can,' chipped in Chris.

'And drive off all the wildlife in the process,' added the man who had tackled me at the Cherry Tree.

'And make the drove road even more hazardous to drive down!'

I sat open-mouthed, too shocked to respond.

'But you'll find you've got a fight on your hands now, Missy,' Evelyn harshly added as she took her place next to Jim behind the bar. 'Folk around here won't stand for it. Even though you're no doubt going to try and convince us the extra visitors will be good for the cash registers and bring more business to town. It's too much!'

'Who has been saying this?' I shouted. 'Who has told you this is what I had planned for my land?'

'Will!' they chorused.

Even Mags mouthed his name.

'Well, I can tell you right now,' I said, blinking back my tears and feeling determined to stand my ground, 'he's wrong.'

'Well, you would say that, wouldn't you?' You were probably hoping to keep the whole thing quiet until you'd got planning permission!'

'I have no intention of applying for planning permission,' I insisted, 'and I would never consider clearing that field or setting up anything as destructive as what you're all suggesting.'

'Yeah, right!'

'And even if I did want to use the place for something

different, I couldn't because of the agricultural restrictions which are tied to it.'

'The what?' said a voice behind me.

'The rules and regulations that are going to stop me doing what I actually want to do and which is absolutely nothing like what has been suggested here tonight!' I said, spinning round and finding myself face to face with David Miller. 'David,' I gasped.

'Lottie,' he said, looking thoroughly confused, 'what are you talking about?'

'The ridiculous regulations which have put a stop to me earning a living from Cuckoo Cottage and its land.'

'But . . .'

'The rules that mean I'm going to have to sell up next year and move on, just as you,' I sobbed, pointing at the aggressive ringleader, 'said I would.'

'Lottie!' said David, shaking his head. 'There are no agricultural restrictions tied to Cuckoo Cottage.'

'What?'

'There are no restrictions,' he repeated. 'I explained that to Matt ages ago. He assured me that he was going to tell you.'

Chapter 33

I didn't catch a wink of sleep that night. Mags had bundled me out of the pub door before the scene turned really nasty and I had refused to talk about any of what had just been said and discovered during the journey home. I wasn't going to be discussing the situation with anyone until I had got things a little clearer in my own head.

Not only did it seem I had been betrayed by Will, who for some reason had taken it upon himself to tell everyone that I was planning to turn Cuckoo Cottage into some caravanning and camping Expo, I had also been duped by Matt, who knew full well there were no ag regs but had insisted to the contrary and in the meantime had been tempting me to sell up, move on and forget my freshly formed dreams. The very dreams I was certain Gwen had had in mind for me.

Of course she would have known the glamping site would have been a possibility. There was no way she would have gone to all the bother of finding, buying and storing the Cheltenham vans if there was even a hint of a doubt that I wouldn't be able to make use of them. I should have taken that into account when everything started to go wrong.

Bitterness threatened to engulf me as I thought how for years I had been struggling to trust folk and now, the very moment I had begun to, I had been tricked and made to look a fool, but not by everyone, I forced myself to remember.

As soon as it was light, I dressed and fed Minnie and set out in Birdie to apologise to Mags. My dear friend hadn't deserved my sullen company on the way home the evening before and I wanted to apologise and ask her if she could shed any light on where Will had got his twisted ideas from.

'Well, I'll be . . .' I said under my breath as Will's barn came into view and I spotted his truck parked in the yard.

I swung into the drive, screeched to a halt, jumped out and began hammering on the door. I didn't give his fiery temper a second thought or what Matt had said he'd done to that poor family in Afghanistan. I knew now that Matt was so full of crap that was probably all lies anyway. I hammered harder, desperate to get to the truth.

Eventually Will appeared: half dressed, half asleep and, given his expression, only half surprised to see me.

'Why are you telling everyone I'm out to destroy my land and turn Cuckoo Cottage into some sort of camping cash cow?' I demanded as soon as he unbolted the door.

I pushed my way into the barn and waited to hear what he had to say for himself.

'Hello, Lottie,' he said, closing the door and running his hands through his mad bed hair. 'Do come in.'

Gosh, it was good to see him, with his lovely bare feet and toned, tanned torso. No, no, no, I scolded my heart and stomach which were turning my insides to mush. Focus, Lottie, focus.

'I said—' I began again, louder this time.

'I heard what you said,' said Will sternly.

'So answer me!' I shouted. 'Why?'

'Because,' he sighed, 'Matt said you'd told him that's what you were planning to do. He said that's the reason why you have those vans in the barns and why you've applied for planning permission to build on the field. He told me he's been helping you fill out the applications and that you've asked him to go into business with you.'

'What?' I whispered, my legs turning to jelly.

Will shrugged.

'But that's, that's bullshit,' I stammered.

'So you aren't planning to run a caravan and camping site, then?'

'Not the sort that Matt's been describing,' I said truthfully, 'absolutely not, and I certainly haven't applied for permission to do anything or asked him to go into business with me.' Perish the thought. 'If my idea ever does get off the ground,' which I had to admit was still looking unlikely, 'you'd soon see exactly how small-scale and unobtrusive the whole thing was.'

Will mulled this hopefully reassuring information over for a minute and then shocked me by adding, 'He also said that you were the best sex he'd ever had.' He looked slightly embarrassed as he said it and I dare say I did too. 'And even though that might be true for all I know, I couldn't bear to hear him talk about you like that so I laid him out.'

'Is that why you were fighting?' I gasped.

'Yes,' he said. 'What did you think it was all about?'

'He told me that you knew I was worried about him making work up and finding problems with the cottage that didn't exist.'

'Well, I did know that because you'd told me, but I would never have betrayed your confidence, Lottie. I never would have said anything to him without discussing it with you first.'

Of course he wouldn't, and I bet his reason for leaving his army career behind and settling for a quiet life in the country was nothing like the story Matt had told me either. Will was an honourable man; I should have realised that.

'I can't believe you thought I'd say that to him,' he murmured, sounding disappointed.

'And I can't believe you thought I'd sleep with Matt,' I shot back. 'Or that I'd purposefully set out to destroy the wonderful wildlife on my little patch. Didn't our conversation the day we watched Grace fly in the field mean anything to you? Did you think I was lying or making my reaction up?'

'Of course not,' he said, walking across to the kitchen to fill the kettle. 'I never thought that for a single second, but the day of the argument I couldn't think about anything other than how disrespectful Matt was being. He managed to push all my buttons and I'd just had enough.'

'You can't solve every argument with your fists, you know.'

'I know that,' he said, reaching for two mugs, 'but I did feel better when I saw him hit the deck. I know I shouldn't say that, but I did. In fact, I was feeling on top of the world until you came out and ended up getting hurt for your trouble. How are you, by the way?'

'Fine,' I said, running a hand over my pastel-shaded bruises. 'Will,' I said, taking a deep breath and plunging in before my courage failed me, 'will you tell me why you left the army?'

'Why?'

'Because I want to hear the truth,' I said simply, 'from your own mouth.'

'Has Matt been making out he knows?'

'Yes,' I nodded. 'I'm afraid he has.'

Will quietly made us both coffee and then sat and relayed

the tragic events surrounding his decision to leave the army. He and his colleagues had been ambushed during a routine tour of one of the towns. He was the only soldier to survive the roadside bomb and subsequent exchange of fire and was taken in and hidden by a local family. When it was discovered what the family had done, they were slaughtered without mercy by the local rebels. All were killed except the father who, it was considered, would suffer more if he was left alive with his memories.

'It was the final straw for me,' said Will huskily as I nursed my mug and wiped my eyes. 'I was the reason that man had lost his family and the horror of it almost killed me. I had to get out, Lottie, and I had to help get him out.'

'And did you succeed?'

He looked at me and didn't say anything, but I knew in my heart that the answer was yes. Somehow he managed to secure that man's safety in return for his life and he was going to have to live with what had happened for the rest of his life.

'I know,' said Will, 'that there's no way on this earth that this is the version of events that Matt told you because no one except George knows, and in return for my honesty, Lottie, will you now tell me what Matt told you I had done?'

I shook my head.

'Tell me what he said to you,' he demanded. 'I need to know.'

I knew without a shadow of a doubt that if I told Will

the lies Matt had spun about what he had done, then Matt's life wouldn't be worth living, and as much as I hated him right now I couldn't live with the consequences of what Will might do.

'Tell me why he said I left the army!'

I stood up, knowing it was time to leave. I needed to find Matt myself before he heard what had happened in the pub last night and had time to concoct more lies and half-truths about why he had befriended me and carried out all manner of unnecessary work at the cottage.

Will stood up at the same time and for the first time I felt a flicker of fear. He was so impossibly tall and strong. I was no wimp, but I was certainly no match for him.

'Do you know,' he said slowly, 'do you have any idea how hard it is for me to trust people?'

'Yes,' I said, because I did. 'Of course I do.'

He looked down at me but didn't say anything.

'My mother left me when I was very young,' I said, looking right back up at him, 'and I haven't really trusted anyone aside from my grandparents and Gwen since. I thought I could trust Matt in the beginning,' I went on, tears pricking my eyes. 'I thought I could rely on him to shoulder some of the responsibility for bringing the cottage back to life, but I was wrong. It didn't need bringing back because there was nothing wrong with it, but his actions won't stop me trying to trust again.' The faces of Chris and Amber and Mags swam before my eyes. 'I'm not going to let what he's done destroy my new-found faith in people and you shouldn't either. Look at all the good people. Look at George and Mags and Ed and Amber,' I began.

'And you,' he cut in huskily.

'And me,' I whispered.

Thankfully there was no time for me to duck out of the way. I had barely time to take a breath before Will pulled me to him and covered my mouth with his. His body felt hard and uncompromising against mine, which yielded without hesitation to his touch. He scooped me up in his arms and carried me off and I let him. I gave in and trusted him completely.

'Do you have to go?' said Will, leaning across the crumpled bed and trying to pull me back down next to him.

'Yes,' I gasped, my resolve weakening every time his fingers touched my skin. 'I have things to sort out.'

'With Matt?' he asked, propping himself up on his elbow.

'Yes,' I said, 'with Matt.'

'Then I think I should come with you.'

'No,' I said quickly.

The last thing I wanted to witness was another showdown.

'I can deal with him.'

'Are you sure?'

'Absolutely,' I said, reaching for my clothes which lay in a heap on the floor. 'Don't forget I have a secret weapon.'

Will looked at my bare body and licked his lips.

'Not that,' I laughed, flicking him with my lacy knickers.

'Good,' said Will. 'You do know I haven't been able to stop thinking about you since the day I saw you in that shower, don't you?'

'I'm not sure I feel comfortable about that,' I frowned.

I wasn't prepared to admit that I hadn't been able to stop thinking about him since I had seen him in his bath towel on the day of the storm.

'Well, it's the truth,' he said, lightly running his fingers down my arm. 'So anyway,' he said, 'what's this secret weapon you're planning to terrorise your demon builder with?'

'Minnie, of course.'

I refused Will's offer to use his shower before I went home because I knew if he followed me inside that cubicle I'd never leave. The day was pressing on and I was determined not to waste (not that my tingling body thought for one second that being seduced by Will really was a waste) a single second of it.

However, I now knew that, thanks to Matt, my entire time living at Cuckoo Cottage so far had been built on a foundation of half-truths and fabrications and I was determined to get to the bottom of them all and find out if there really was a way I could start living the life and building the business I had been dreaming of.

'Call me,' said Will, when I was eventually ready to leave. 'Just ring if you have any problems and I'll be there.'

'I will,' I told him, reluctantly untangling myself from his embrace. 'Thank you, Will.'

'And we'll go out tonight so you can tell me what you're really planning for Cuckoo Cottage, yes?'

'Yes,' I agreed. 'From now on we'll talk to each other and cut out the gossiping go-betweens who have been the cause of so many problems.'

'Good plan,' beamed Will, slamming Birdie's door shut. 'I'll pick you up around seven.'

'No,' I said, 'I'll pick you up and together we can set everyone in the town straight.'

I needn't have worried about whether or not I was going to have trouble tracking Matt down because he was already waiting at the cottage when I arrived. The doors of his van were open and his tools were set out ready for the final full day of faux work. I thought for a moment that perhaps I should just hang the situation out until he had replaced every window, wall and door and then let Minnie at him, but one look at his cocky expression was enough to make me realise that that was not going to be an option.

'Are you all right?' he asked, as soon as he caught sight of me in his wing mirror and jumped out.

'Yes,' I said, 'I'm fine, thanks.'

'But you look a mess and your hair's all dishevelled,' he noticed. 'I've been here for ages. I've been worried sick.'

'Well, that's sweet,' I said, making for the door, 'but considering I wasn't expecting you today I had no reason to wait in, did I?'

'Has something happened?' he started again.

I was relieved he hadn't got wind of what had played out in The Mermaid the night before and that I finally had the upper hand.

'No,' I shrugged, 'not really. Come inside,' I said, keen to get him across the threshold before the penny dropped. 'I want to talk to you.'

'But what about Minnie?'

'Believe me,' I tutted, 'she's the least of your worries right now.'

Matt reluctantly followed me inside and I closed the door and scooped Minnie up before she had a chance to make the customary dash for his ankles.

'Are you going to put her in the dining room?'

'No.'

'I'd feel better if you did.'

'Well, I'm not very concerned right now about making you feel better.'

'What's going on, Lottie?'

'You tell me,' I shrugged, my eyes never leaving his increasingly confused face.

'Nothing,' he said, but there was a slight waver in his voice that suggested otherwise.

'I went to the pub last night.'

'Right.'

'And you'll never guess what Will has been saying.'

'Oh God, what?' he sighed, looking slightly relieved. I do believe the poor fool thought he was off the hook. 'I said you couldn't trust him,' he went on. 'He's unhinged.'

'He must be,' I laughed, as Minnie wriggled in my arms and Matt momentarily dropped his gaze to check I still had a tight hold on her. 'Apparently, he's told everyone that I'm planning to rent out the field to the caravan club or something like that.'

'He never has?'

'He has,' I said, 'and that I'm planning to have the entire place tarmacked over.'

'No way.'

'But now I've found out there aren't any agricultural restrictions to stop me, I suppose I could, couldn't I?'

'What?' frowned Matt.

He was trying to look shocked but it didn't wash. I clipped on Minnie's lead and put her on the floor, where she immediately made a lunge for him and he took a speedy step back.

'Don't look so worried,' I laughed. 'I'm not going to let

her go. She's just a bit heavy. I've been feeding her up on rogue tradesmen.'

'Lottie, what's going on?'

'Why did you lie to me about what David said?' I demanded.

I had no desire to drag the conversation on now. I'd never been much of a one for playing games and I just wanted to get to the truth, however unsavoury and unpalatable it turned out to be.

'And why did you think it was a good idea to tell Will such a massive lie about what I had planned when you didn't even know what I had in mind yourself?'

Matt shook his head but no explanation was forthcoming.

'And why did you lie about all the work that needs doing here and your connection to Gwen, and more importantly and shocking than all of that put together, why did you make up such a horrific story to explain why that poor man had to leave the army?'

For a moment my mind was reeling. It was hard to believe that one person alone could sink to such deceptive depths, especially when they had only days before gone out of their way to say that all they had ever wanted to be was my friend and someone who I could rely on to help put things right. I don't think I'd felt this much animosity for one person in a very long time. I was almost tempted to let Minnie go to town on him.

'Well?' I shouted.

Whatever Matt was going to say, if anything, was cut short as someone began hammering on the door and shouting. For a mad moment I thought it was Will, come to sort the situation out with his fists again, but then I realised it was a woman and she sounded absolutely terrified.

I ran to the door, Minnie taking an opportunistic swipe at Matt as we passed, and wrenched it open.

'There's been an accident!' sobbed a woman I didn't recognise. 'You need to call an ambulance.'

Chapter 34

My heart was in my mouth as I dialled 999 then passed the receiver to the woman and set off on foot up the road with Matt hot on my heels. I hadn't had the sense to jump in the car but it wasn't all that many paces from home that I felt bile rising as I caught sight of Ed's bike strewn across the drove in a mangled heap and the pile of clothes that I guessed was Ed in the ditch on the left.

'Oh Jesus,' I gasped, coming to a sudden halt and looking over my shoulder at Matt who was right behind me. 'Will you go to him?' I asked. 'Can you see if he's all right?'

'I can't,' shuddered Matt, shaking his head and taking a step back. 'I daren't.'

Without hesitating, I dumped Minnie, who I had run all the way up the road with, into his arms, and scrambled down the ditch to where Ed was lying in a crumpled heap.

'Ed,' I whispered, edging my way towards him and hoping

for more than anything I'd ever hoped for in my life that he was all right. 'Ed? It's me,' I said a little louder, 'it's me, Lottie.'

A quiet groan met my ears and I let out a sigh of relief. The situation was bad, but not as bad as it could have been.

'Ed,' I said again, as I pushed aside a massive patch of nettles and weeds to get to him.

'My leg,' he groaned, 'I think I've broken my leg.'

I wanted to cry when I heard him speak but one glance told me he was right. No limb could be sitting at an angle like that and not be broken, even if the owner of it was double-jointed. I knew there was nothing I could do. Trying to move him when I didn't know what else was wrong could have been disastrous, so we would just have to sit tight until the ambulance arrived.

'It's all right,' I said, pushing his curls away from his face, 'the ambulance is on its way.'

'My arm hurts as well,' he gasped.

I looked at the sleeve of his left arm. It didn't take a genius to work out that the fabric of his long-sleeved T-shirt should have been the same pale blue as the rest, but it was rapidly turning red and darker by the second.

'I think you've cut it,' I told him. 'I'm going to take a look.'

Carefully I pulled back the fabric. There was a deep gash which was pumping out blood, quite a lot of blood.

'Oh God,' said Matt, who had finally dared to peer into the ditch.

'What?' cried Ed, struggling to look. 'What is it?'

'It's all right,' I said soothingly, laying a hand on Ed's chest to stop him moving while glaring at Matt. 'Matt's just a bit of a wuss, that's all. You've got a cut on your arm, but I'm going to use my shirt to stop it bleeding.'

'OK,' said Ed, biting his lip and turning paler than ever.

'And to hide it so Matt won't pass out,' I added.

'OK,' said Ed again, the shadow of a smile playing around his pale lips.

'You just lay still,' I instructed, 'and we'll have you out of here in no time.'

'The ambulance is on its way,' said the woman who had alerted us as to what had happened, 'and I phoned Will who lives up the road as well. He'll be here any minute.'

'OK,' I said, 'did you hear that, Ed? Your mum's always telling me you're part animal, well, now you're going to get some treatment from the vet.'

Ed nodded, but didn't say anything. The poor boy looked terrified.

It wasn't many seconds before I heard Will's truck flying along the road and this was definitely one occasion when I wouldn't be moaning about his driving.

'What's happened?' he said, jumping straight into the ditch with a first-aid kit which would no doubt do far more good than my old shirt.

'Broken leg,' I told him, 'and a nasty cut on this arm.'

'Has he been moved at all?'

'No,' I said, 'not an inch. I know he's uncomfortable but I'm not qualified to assess him so he's been stuck like this since he landed here, I'm afraid.'

Will nodded and reached into the kit for a thick cotton pad.

'Let's swap your shirt for this pad on the count of three, Lottie,' he said, manoeuvring it into position. 'One, two, three.'

The transition was smooth and the flow of blood nowhere near as fast as it had been when I first applied my shirt.

'I haven't been pressing too hard,' I said quietly. 'I'm not sure if there's anything in it or not.'

'You've done great,' said Will, as we carefully swapped places. 'Really great.'

'Ed,' I said, 'where's your mum?'

'She's with George,' he croaked. 'She's been helping him with his housework.'

'So she isn't likely to drive up here any time soon?'

'No,' he gasped, wincing from the pain, 'but she was worried that she'd upset you last night. She was cross with herself and said that she'd listened to gossip when she should have talked to you instead.'

'She hasn't upset me, Ed,' I told him, looking accusingly at Matt, who was still keeping his distance and had passed Minnie on to the passer-by. 'Not at all.'

'I didn't think she had,' he said, 'and I told her that, but I thought I'd come and see you myself. I wanted to make sure everything really was all right. That's why I was coming up the road.'

'So how did you end up down here?' asked Will.

'There was something on the road,' panted Ed. 'I didn't see it until it was too late and I ran over it and it flipped me off. Is my bike OK?'

'Listen,' I said, deciding not to tell him that his bike was totalled. 'I can hear sirens.'

Thankfully the ambulance came from the Wynbridge direction and not via Hecate's Rest, which would have alerted Mags far sooner. As it was, she and George arrived just as Ed was being carefully lifted into the back of the ambulance by a pair of efficient paramedics who had taken no time at all to make him more comfortable and stable. I grabbed hold of Mags before she had a chance to panic.

'Ed's fallen off his bike,' I said, holding on to her tight and looking right into her eyes. 'He's broken his leg and cut his arm, but he's conscious and he's been talking the whole time.'

'I'll take you to him,' said Will, taking her arm and steering her in the right direction, 'and then I'll take you to the hospital. Will you be all right?' he called to me over his shoulder.

'Yes,' I said. 'Yes, I'll sort things out here then follow on.'

It wasn't until the ambulance went off with Will, Mags

and George following on behind that I realised how much I was shaking.

'I'll drive you back to the cottage,' offered Matt once we had loaded up Ed's mangled bike and the first-aid kit into the back of Mags's truck.

'Are you all right, love?' asked the woman who had stopped to help as she passed Minnie back into my arms.

'Yes,' I said, 'yes, I'm fine. Nothing a hot, sweet tea won't cure.'

I knew I was talking gibberish but I didn't know what else to say. I didn't want a fuss. I just wanted to be left alone.

'Do you mind if I call by later to find out how he's doing?' she asked.

'Not at all,' I said, 'and thank you for your help.'

Matt drove us back to the cottage in Mags's truck in silence. Minnie for once settled on my lap, intuitively aware that this was not the time to take a chunk out of Matt, not that I would have been inclined to stop her.

'Are you happy now?' I spat as he parked on the drive. My temper had been gently simmering during the short journey back, but now it had reached boiling point. 'Are you satisfied?'

'What?'

'Well, this is all your fault, isn't it?'

'Mine!' he gasped, looking horrified. 'How do you work that one out?'

'Well, if you hadn't gone spouting lies and spreading rumours about me, that poor little lad wouldn't have been pedalling down here trying to find out what was wrong between me and his mum, would he?'

I didn't care if what I was saying was right or fair. I had been betrayed, Ed was badly injured and Will had been viciously slandered, and the person responsible was sitting right next to me and I was determined to call him to account for his actions.

'You might not have dumped whatever it was that was lying in the road, but you as good as put that poor boy in the back of that ambulance,' I accused. 'I don't know what your motives have been, Matt, and right now I don't much care, but I do know I never want to see you or your cousin or any of your damn family ever again. Now get off my property before I set my dog on you, and don't you ever come back.'

It wasn't until he was gone and I was in the house that I realised I had nursed Ed and spoken to the ambulance crew wearing nothing more than a blood-splattered lacy bra and the tiniest pair of shorts imaginable. Not that it mattered, I supposed. I may have been scratched, bitten, bruised and bloody but I was in a far better state than poor Ed, and I hoped that Mags could find it in her heart to forgive me for being at least partly responsible for the state her dear son was in.

*

On autopilot I threw my soiled clothes in the washing machine and then jumped in the shower and let the warm water rush over me. I didn't wait to dry my hair but fed Minnie and shut her in the kitchen then went back outside to Birdie. I had absolutely no idea how to get to the hospital, no satnav and no phone signal, but fortunately I did have a huge dose of luck as just at that moment Amber pulled on to the drive.

'Will telephoned from the hospital,' she explained. 'He told me what happened and asked if I would come over to see if you're all right.'

'I'm OK,' I told her. 'A bit shaken up but otherwise all right, although I could do with directions to the hospital. I was just going to try and find my way there.'

'I can do better than directions,' said Amber, leaning across and opening the passenger door. 'Hop in and I'll take you now. This is certainly one occasion when you can get away with not driving yourself.'

'Are you sure?'

'Of course,' she nodded. 'Mags is going to need all of her friends around her right now.'

'Has anyone phoned Liam?' I asked, jumping in the passenger seat and trying to ignore the pain in my legs inflicted by the stinging nettles. It felt unnervingly familiar and reminded me of my first few days at Cuckoo Cottage.

'Jake was trying to get hold of him as I left,' Amber said.

'He'll find him, don't worry. Let's just get there and find out how Ed is.'

En route I explained to Amber what had played out in the pub the evening before and how that was the reason why Ed was on his way to see me when he hit something in the road and ended up in the ditch. Needless to say, I didn't mention what had happened between Will and me in the interim.

'I've never told a soul about what you have planned for Cuckoo Cottage,' she said the second I had finished my explanation of events. 'I haven't told anyone. Not even Jake.'

'It's all right,' I reassured her. 'I didn't think for one second that you had said anything.'

'So how did Matt know?'

'Well he didn't, did he? He just took what little he had seen for himself and decided to fabricate that evidence and make up the rest.'

'But why?'

'I don't know,' I said, biting my lip and looking out at the mysterious landscape. 'I still haven't worked that one out yet, but he also lied about Will and why he had to leave the army. He said some terrible things, which I'm guessing he knew would keep the two of us apart, but I get the feeling this is about far more than just trying to stop me becoming friends with my neighbour,' I mused.

'But you know the truth about why Will left now?' she asked.

446

'Yes,' I said. 'I've spoken to him myself and everything that needs to be out in the open finally is. I've also told Will that I never had any intention of harming the wildlife or jeopardising the field and he's explained to me why he felt the urge to knock Matt out before everything became such a muddle.'

'And what was his reason?' asked Amber as we reached the town and turned down the road marked with a large 'H'.

'If you don't mind, I'd rather not say.'

'Of course,' she said. 'I'm sorry, I shouldn't have asked. It's none of my business.'

'It's not that,' I told her. 'I'd just rather wait and see if there's any more to find out before I say anything. By this time tomorrow I'll probably have even more to add to the terrible tale.'

I had no idea just how true that statement was going to turn out to be.

Amber expertly parked the truck and we rushed off to A and E to find out what we could about where Ed had been moved to.

'He's already heading up to the ward,' said the busy nurse behind the reception desk. 'And I don't know if you'll be able to see him. He already had a couple of people with him.'

'We don't mind waiting,' said Amber. 'We just want to make sure he's all right.'

'He's going to be fine,' said a voice behind us.

'Will,' I gasped, spinning round and throwing myself, without a care for who could see me, into his arms.

'Come outside,' he said to Amber over the top of my head, 'and I'll explain what's happened.'

As suspected, Ed had a broken leg and the gash on his arm, although deep, didn't have anything nasty stuck in it, but did require stitching. Apparently he had been incredibly brave and the team looking after him were extremely sympathetic. Mags, now the initial crisis was over, was a little weepy, which was hardly surprising.

'Do you think you should get back to her?' I said to Will once he had finished bringing us up to speed.

'No, it's all right,' he said, 'Liam arrived just a few minutes before you did. He's with them now.'

'Did Ed tell you why he was out on his bike?'

'Yes,' frowned Will, 'and if it wasn't for that buffoon over there, he'd still be walking about on two feet instead of hobbling about on one.'

'What the hell?' I muttered as I followed his gaze and found he was looking at Matt, who had just pulled into a parking space. 'What's he doing here? You'd think he'd seen enough of this place in the last few days.'

'Shall I go and warn him off?' suggested Amber. 'Let him know he isn't welcome?'

'No,' said Will, levering himself off the back of his truck, 'I will.'

'No,' I said. 'I will. This mess has more to do with me than anyone else. I'll speak to him. You two go and wait inside. I won't be long.'

Ignoring Will's protests that my suggestion wasn't a very good idea, I set off across the car park.

'What are you doing?' I demanded, as soon as I was in earshot.

'You said I couldn't come anywhere near the cottage,' said Matt. 'You can't stop me coming here.'

'But why would you want to?' I seethed. 'Don't you think you've done enough?'

'I want to explain,' he said, his eyes beseeching me to listen, 'and to leave this for Ed.'

He opened the back door of his van and inside was a bike. Not dissimilar to Ed's old one but obviously in perfect condition and, if the tag on the handlebars bore any truth, brand new.

'Where on earth did you find that in such a hurry?' I scowled, not at all moved by the gesture. 'And more to the point, why?'

'I had to do something to make it up to Ed,' he shrugged, 'because you were right, Lottie. He's here because of me.'

'I'm glad you realise that.'

'I never should have gone along with it all in the first place. If I'd stood my ground then none of this would have happened.'

'What do you mean, "if you'd stood your ground"? What are you talking about?'

'Let me buy you a coffee,' he said, 'and I'll explain.'

Having reassured Will and Amber that I was fine, Matt and I went together to the hospital cafeteria.

'I'm so sorry,' he began. 'This whole mess has been my uncle's idea and it goes back months, years actually.'

'Then you'd better start from then, hadn't you?'

'All right,' he said, running his hands through his sandy sun-bleached hair.

I can't say I felt a single ounce of sympathy for him, but he did look absolutely worn out.

'It all started when the barn that Will now lives in came on the market. My uncle was absolutely thrilled. He'd been waiting literally years for the farmer who owned it to part with it.'

'But why?' I asked. 'From what I've heard, it was a crumbling mess.'

'Yes,' said Matt, 'it was, but it was a crumbling mess that came with some land and no agricultural ties and he was looking for somewhere suitable to relocate his plant yard and store his machinery. It would have been perfect for his business.'

'So why didn't he end up buying it, then?'

'Because the farmer wouldn't sell it to him. It didn't matter how much money my uncle offered, the chap knew what he had in mind and absolutely refused to take the bait. He was insistent it would go to someone who wouldn't knock the remains of the barn down but would create something from the little that was left.'

'And consequently not decimate the land in the process.'

'Exactly,' said Matt.

'But I don't understand what this has got to do with me having all these so-called remedial repairs carried out on my cottage.'

Matt sighed and the rest of the colour drained from his tanned face.

'My uncle never got over losing out, and to an incomer, of all people,' he went reluctantly on.

'And what did Will make of that?' I asked, momentarily sidetracked from my beloved Cuckoo Cottage.

'He had no idea that my family had any interest in the place at all and I wasn't really involved until recently.'

I should have realised that. If Will had had even the slightest inkling about Matt or his ruthless uncle, he would have stopped him in his tracks before he started any work on the cottage.

'My uncle knew that Gwen was as stubborn as the farmer,' Matt went on, finally weaving my own home into the fabric of the story, 'and that she had played a part in helping ensure the barn didn't come our way.'

'Oh,' I said, 'I see.'

'So obviously there was no way she was going to sell Cuckoo Cottage to us.'

'Which I'm guessing your uncle wanted, because he knew there were no restrictions tied to it either.'

'Exactly. After the site where the barn was located, the cottage was the next best thing, and as soon as Gwen got wind of the fact that my uncle had his eye on it, she had a watertight will drawn up to ensure it could never come to us. My uncle tried everything to find a legal loophole but David had it all sewn up.'

'Of course,' I realised. 'He must have been the guy who sent me flying when I first arrived in town. So what was the plan when I moved into the cottage?'

'I,' Matt swallowed, looking thoroughly ashamed, 'was assigned the task of bleeding you dry and doing everything I could to make you fall out of love with the place. It was down to me to make you think that selling up was the best and only thing to do and then being conveniently on hand to take the place off you in a speedy cash sale.'

'You bastard,' I said under my breath. 'And all that time you made out you were doing me a favour, that you were my friend and that you thought I was attractive to boot. How could you?'

'I couldn't in the end,' he said, trying to reach for my hand. 'But the whole situation got so out of hand. Don't get me wrong, Lottie, you're an attractive girl, but I only kissed you to see if I could make you fall for me rather than Will. It didn't work of course. Despite the height difference, you two are made for each other and consequently he's been a thorn in my side, right from the start.'

'That's disgusting behaviour, Matt.'

'I know,' he said, hanging his head. 'But I was desperate. At one time I would have said and done anything to drive a wedge between you.'

'But why?'

'Because I wanted, in the beginning at least, the same outcome as my uncle.'

'What do you mean "in the beginning"?'

'The day you caught me up the ladder,' he went on, 'I was searching for any evidence of the owl Will had said was about. My uncle knew that it might be a problem and, and . . .'

'And what? You were supposed to somehow get rid of it?'

'It doesn't matter,' he said, shaking his head. 'I just knew then that it was all getting too out of hand. I honestly didn't want any further part in it, but I didn't know how to get out. I owe my uncle money, you see, and he could make life very difficult for me. Not that any of that matters now, of course.'

'And what about Simon? Is he part of all this as well? I'm guessing he's the son of this ruthless uncle?'

'No, he isn't,' Matt insisted. 'My uncle hasn't got any kids of his own so eventually I would have been left the business. Simon's actually from the other side of the family. He hasn't got a clue about any of this.'

'So you've deceived him as well?'

'So it would seem.'

'You should be ashamed of yourself,' I spat.

'I am, but if it's any consolation, I had hoped, once it was all over, that I could help you find somewhere else to set up your business.'

'But you don't even know what I want to do!' I shouted, drawing the attention of the people at the next table. 'And I know now that I never told you everything because I never really trusted you.'

'I wish you had,' he said, biting his lip. 'I could have found the courage to stop things sooner and help put everything right again.'

'Of course you couldn't,' I said, standing up, 'because you're too selfish. You're the sort of person who has no concept of what is right and wrong, Matt, and this conversation goes to prove it. You spout on about feeling guilty and knowing how wrong it all was, but you didn't actually stop. Even today you turned up at the cottage looking for more work to do.'

'Please don't say these things, Lottie, I need you to understand. I need you to forgive me.'

'I can't,' I said, stunned that he could think it would be

that easy. 'And I don't think I ever will. I just wish now I'd taken on board what it was that Minnie was trying to tell me about you from day one. Gwen never offered you work at the cottage, she didn't even know you, did she?'

Matt said nothing.

'Did she?' I shouted.

'No,' he admitted, his head in his hands. 'No, she didn't. I got the number for the cottage out of the phone book and made up the rest.'

I pushed back my chair and stood up to leave.

'You're a weak and devious man, Matt,' I told him, just in case he still hadn't worked it out for himself, 'and I hope you have the future you deserve.'

Epilogue

Summer lingered long into September and the weather was absolutely perfect for the party which took place on the equinox. The whole site was bedecked in bunting and aglow with the spoils of harvest, thanks to the abundance of the season. At the centre of the celebrations sat The Cherry Tree Café mobile tearoom and next to it stood Ed, with his beloved Jack perched on his arm and Minnie at his feet.

'So what do you think?' I asked, when I finally made my way through the group gathered around him.

'I think we've done good,' he smiled.

'Really good,' I smiled back, stroking Jack's silky feathers and taking in the scene.

'It's nice to have everyone here to celebrate, isn't it?'

'It certainly is.'

'But what about Matt?' he asked. 'I thought he might show up.'

'As far as I know he's still with his friends,' I said casually.

I had decided it was best not to tell Ed the finer details of Matt's hasty departure from town the summer before.

The truth was that Matt's uncle had been so furious with him for both failing in his mission *and* spilling the beans that Matt had thought it was best to steer clear of the area for a while and had gone to spend some time with friends north of the border. I was delighted to see the back of him and had been relishing life at the cottage now it wasn't continually spoiled by the sound of the drill and lump hammer. The only industrious sounds around the place had been from either Simon, who I had employed to complete the electrical work, or of my own making.

'You know why Will never really liked Matt, don't you, Lottie?' said Ed conspiratorially.

'Not really,' I shrugged.

It was true; Will hadn't known what Matt and his uncle had been planning, so I'd never really fathomed out what had been at the root of his loathing.

'Will told me once that he was a bit jealous of Matt.'

'Did he?'

'Um,' Ed continued, affectionately stroking Jack. 'He said he thought you would like Matt more because he was cool.'

'Cool!' I laughed.

'Yeah, you know, with his surfer image and scruffy hair

and all that. Will said you'd never go out with someone like him because he was too boring and conventional or something.'

It wasn't my place to tell Ed any different, but the last few months practically living with Will had proved he was anything but boring or conventional, especially in the bedroom.

'Why have you gone red?' Ed nudged, when I didn't answer.

'Have you seen David?' asked Will, planting a kiss on my upturned face and saving me from having to explain to Ed the difference between him and Matt in words that a prepubescent boy would understand.

'Yuk,' groaned Ed. 'Have a care, guys. You two don't stop, do you?'

'Sorry,' we laughed together.

Will and I had been inseparable since Matt's timely departure. As soon as he knew what it was that I really had planned for Cuckoo Cottage and that it was absolutely nothing like the twisted version my former builder had been bandying about, he had been totally on board and helped out as much as possible.

'I have seen David,' I told him, 'and although still feeling guilty for believing that Matt had transferred his affections from his uncle to me, he was delighted that I have absolutely no plans to move on, even though I'm perfectly free to do so now that I've been living here for a year.'

Was it really a whole year since I'd landed in Wynbridge with nothing more to show for my existence than a couple of suitcases and a rucksack? I looked around the yard and across the field, my heart racing at the sight of what I, and my new friends, of course, had managed to achieve in such a short space of time.

'And what did he make of the conservation project?' asked Ed, keen to ensure that his part in the project had been taken into account.

'To tell you the truth,' I laughed, bending to give him a quick peck on the cheek, 'I think that was the bit he liked best.'

'Brilliant,' said Ed, turning bright red. 'Good old David!'

Personally I couldn't help but feel a little sorry for my solicitor. Having handed me the keys to Cuckoo Cottage and fallen hook, line and sinker for Angela, he'd rather taken his eye off the ball and assumed that my arrival had put an end to Matt's uncle's determination to get his hands on my home. Consequently, having been told the truth, he had gone out of his way to play his part in helping me with the legalities of applying to set up the glamping site and had just about come to terms with not spotting what had really been going on.

'Can I interest you two in a slice of local carrot cake?' asked Jemma, as she hopped out of the caravan carrying a tray of delectable-looking bakes. 'I'd grab it before Chris sees it. He's already eaten almost an entire one on his own.'

'In that case,' said Will, greedily reloading his plate with two thick slices, one of which I hoped was for me, 'I'd better stock up.'

'So how are you finding it in there?' I asked with a nod to the van. 'Are you still happy with how it turned out?'

'It's absolutely perfect,' said Lizzie, butting into the conversation. 'There's just the right amount of space and it's all so easy to set up and pack away.'

'Well, that's good,' I smiled.

'I don't know why you ever had any doubts about it,' laughed Jemma. 'She doesn't give herself half enough credit, does she, Will?'

'No,' he said, 'she doesn't.'

'It's because I just want everything to be perfect,' I said, turning red.

'And it is,' insisted Lizzie as she hopped back inside to make more drinks. 'You only have to look over there to know that.'

I followed her gaze to the field and the three Cheltenham vans gleaming in the late sunshine. Just as I'd imagined, each had their own space and my eyes misted over a little as I watched the awnings flapping in the breeze. It was every bit as perfect as I'd imagined, and with the imminent arrival of three more vans within the next few weeks, it was almost complete.

More important than how it looked, though, was how it

worked, and I was delighted that Grace was still happy to hunt in the field and that the large areas which had been left uncut were brimming with wild flowers and enough mice to keep both her and the kestrel happy.

'Come on,' said Mags, tugging at my hand, 'it's time to cut the ribbon.'

It was an emotional moment and one that I was glad to share with Ed, my conservation expert.

'We declare,' we said together, 'the Cuckoo Cottage glamping site officially open for business!'

We pushed back the gate and the crowd rushed into the field, all eager to have a look for themselves at what I had been working to create. Even the town gossips had come out to have a look and Evelyn had soon eaten her words about not wanting my customers in her pub.

'This looks amazing,' said Gary, the only gossip who had actually stuck his neck on the line and told me how I wasn't worthy of my inheritance.

'It does rather, doesn't it?' I agreed, as I spotted Amber dragging Jake over to the caravan where they were planning to spend their first night away from Skylark Farm in years.

'And Dad's really pleased you've given us the mowing contract,' he said somewhat sheepishly, 'especially given we got off to such a bad start.'

'Well, he's welcome,' I said, taking Will's hand in mine,

'and besides, more often than not, things don't end up how they start, do they?'

It was getting late before everyone headed off. Amber and Jake were happily ensconced in their van and Jemma and Tom were in another. Will and I were planning to spend the night in the third and, having waved everyone off, we locked up the cottage and carried a bottle of Skylark Scrumpy, two glasses and a tired Minnie back down to the field. We toasted the future as the sun slipped below the horizon and, right on cue, Grace silently appeared, swooping low and intently studying her territory for some tasty morsel.

'You do know that I'm in love with you, Lottie, don't you?' said Will, swallowing his last mouthful of cider and catching me completely by surprise. 'I've loved you from the very first moment I saw you.'

'What, naked and in dire straits?' I questioned.

'Absolutely,' he grinned.

'What was it that attracted you to me?' I asked. 'Was it the fact that I was naked or needed rescuing?'

'Both,' he said, 'it was the perfect combination for me. I've always enjoyed playing the hero, although ...'

'What?'

'Well, from what I've learned about you since then, you're more than capable of rescuing yourself, aren't you?'

'I suppose I am,' I sighed, 'except when electrics are involved, or thunderstorms.'

'So I'm not completely redundant then?' he said, looking down at me and making my insides melt.

'Oh no,' I told him, 'absolutely not. This is one little cuckoo who is always going to need a companion to share her nest with.'

Acknowledgements

In typical Heidi Swain style these acknowledgements started life as a list – a long list of fabulous folk who have been instrumental in creating, crafting and eventually publishing this, my fourth novel.

At the very top, I made a note of the family – the boys who are still giving me the peace and space to get the words down and the girl who has scribbled on napkins, drunk tea and supplied inspiration (and character names) aplenty. The cat doesn't get a look-in this time because, quite frankly, she hasn't done a lot.

Next, I listed the publishing team – Clare, Emma, S-J, Jamie and Rich and everyone else at Team BATC. All of whom have encouraged, helped, believed and honed. I put a bright shiny star next to Pip Watkins' name so I would remember to thank her especially for the stunning covers she has created and which encapsulate the very essence of the books. Thank you, Pip.

In quick succession after that came the hugely supportive bloggers, author chums and friends, and finally you wonderful readers, who buy the books, absorb the words and take the time to get in touch and tell me that you love Wynbridge every bit as much as I do. Every day, when I sit down to write, I remind myself how lucky I am to be in this position.

To my delight, this merry band of friends, who find themselves recognised and thanked on the final few pages, has rarely changed, and I am truly grateful for that. To be able to write the books I love, knowing there is such consistent support and friendship is a blessing and I thank you all.

And finally, one last thank you to Happy Days Retro Vacations in Suffolk for supplying quite simply the best research experience I've had so far. If you haven't camped 60's style, folks, you haven't camped at all!

May your bookshelves, be they virtual or real, always be filled with fabulous fiction.

H x

Curl up with Heidi Swain for cupcakes, crafting and love at *The Cherry Tree Café*.

Lizzie Dixon's life feels as though it's fallen apart. Instead of the marriage proposal she was hoping for from her boyfriend, she is unceremoniously dumped, and her job is about to go the same way. So, there's only one option: to go back home to the village she grew up in and try to start again.

Her best friend Jemma is delighted Lizzie has come back home. She has just bought a little café and needs help in getting it ready for the grand opening. And Lizzie's sewing skills are just what she needs.

With a new venture and a new home, things are looking much brighter for Lizzie. But can she get over her broken heart, and will an old flame reignite a love from long ago . . .?

'Fans of Jenny Colgan and Carole Matthews will enjoy this warm and gently funny story of reinvention, romance, and second chances – you'll devour it in one sitting'
Katie Oliver, author of the bestselling
'Marrying Mr Darcy' series

Available now in paperback and eBook

**Fall in love with country
living this summer ...**

Amber is a city girl at heart. So when her
boyfriend Jake Somerville suggests they move to
the countryside to help out at his family farm, she
doesn't quite know how to react. But work
has been hectic and she needs a break, so
she decides to grasp the opportunity.

Dreaming of organic orchards, paddling in streams
and frolicking in fields, Amber packs up her things
and moves to Skylark Farm. But life is not quite
how she imagined – it's cold and dirty and the farm
buildings are dilapidated and crumbling ...

Even so, Amber is determined to make the best of
it and throws herself into farm life. But can she
really fit in here? And can she and Jake stay
together when they are so different?

Summer at Skylark Farm

Available now in paperback and eBook

Christmas has arrived in the town of Wynbridge and it promises mince pies, mistletoe and a whole host of seasonal joy.

Ruby has finished with university and is heading home for the holidays. She takes on a stall at the local market, and sets about making it the best Christmas market stall ever. There'll be bunting and mistletoe and maybe even a bit of mulled wine.

But with a new retail park just opened, the market is under threat. So together with all the other stallholders, Ruby devises a plan to make sure the market is the first port of call for everyone's Christmas shopping needs.

The only thing standing in her way is her ex, Steve. It's pretty hard to concentrate when he works on the stall opposite, especially when she realises that her feelings are still there ...

This Christmas make time for some winter sparkle – and see who might be under the mistletoe this year ...

Out now in paperback and eBook

The new Christmas bestseller from the author of *Mince Pies and Mistletoe at the Christmas Market!*

When **Anna** takes on the role of companion to the owner of Wynthorpe Hall, on the outskirts of **Wynbridge**, she has no idea that her life is set to change beyond all recognition.

A confirmed 'bah humbug' when it comes to Christmas, Anna is amazed to find herself quickly immersed in the eccentric household, and when youngest son Jamie unexpectedly arrives home it soon becomes obvious that her personal feelings are going all out to compromise her professional persona.

Jamie, struggling to come to terms with life back in the Fens, makes a pact with Anna – she has to teach him to fall back in love with Wynthorpe Hall, while he helps her fall back in love with Christmas. But will it all prove too much for Anna, or can the family of Wynthorpe Hall warm her heart once and for all . . .?

Join Anna for a festive journey that is festooned with sleigh rides and silver bells and help her discover her happy ever after.

Coming this October in paperback and eBook

BANYAN TREE
~ VABBINFARU ~

WIN A HOLIDAY OF A LIFETIME AT BANYAN TREE VABBINFARU IN THE MALDIVES!

Included in the prize:

- A seven night stay at Banyan Tree Vabbinfaru in a Beachfront Pool villa for two people
- Full board basis, incl. soft drinks, excl. alcohol
- Return transfers from Male to Banyan Tree Vabbinfaru
- Two × return economy flights from London to Male up to a value of £700 per person
- Trip to be taken between 1 November 2017 and 30 April 2018
  Blackout dates include 27 December 2017 – 5 January 2018

To enter the competition visit the website
www.simonandschuster.co.uk

Entrants must be resident in the UK only